Sometimes you have

Aaron Seavers is a

lives in terror of incurring

disappointing his mother, and he can't stop dithering about where to go to college—with fall term only weeks away. Ditched by a friend at a miserable summer farewell party, all he can do is get drunk in the laundry room and regret he was ever born. Until a geeky-cute classmate lifts his spirits, leaving him confident of two things: his sexual orientation, and where he's headed to school.

Giles Mulder can't wait to get the hell out of Oak Grove, Minnesota, and off to college, where he plans to play his violin and figure out what he wants to be when he grows up. But when Aaron appears on campus, memories of hometown hazing threaten what he'd hoped would be his haven. As the semester wears on, their attraction crescendos from double-cautious to a rich, swelling chord. But if more than one set of controlling parents have their way, the music of their love could come to a shattering end.

Heidi Cullinan, POB 425, Ames, Iowa 50010

Copyright © 2017 by Heidi Cullinan
Print ISBN: 978-1-945116-04-9
Print Edition
Edited by Sasha Knight
Cover by Kanaxa
Proofing by Lillie's Literary Services
Formatting by BB eBooks

First publication 2014
Second publication 2017
www.heidicullinan.com

Fever Pitch

Heidi Cullinan

For S.N., because even when I worried maybe this was too cheesy to dedicate to you, I thought of you the whole time. Now that it's over, I get it. I hope when you read it, you know why too—as well as who (all of them) and what in this story made you the only person it could be for.

Love all your parts and selves, the art you create, the loyalty you inspire, the joy you give, the mayhem you invite. You're a gift to my life I'll never forget.

Yours always, Heidi

Acknowledgments

My books are often possible because of villages, but this one has a major metropolitan area.

Thanks first to my daughter, Anna, who taught me Minecraft and violin in addition to listening to (and loving) a cappella music with me for ten months. I hope when you're old enough to read this someday, you appreciate the French horn solo. Thanks to Dan Cullinan for being excited to read this almost since I started and for never waning in interest or support.

Thanks to the Wartburg College Choir and Dr. Paul Torkelson and Dr. Suzanne Torkelson for pretty much every choir and piano aspect of this tale. Thanks to the 3 Penny Chorus and Orchestra for giving me one hell of an idea.

Thanks to Sasha Knight for as always being such a wonderful editor. Let's do it again, and again.

Thanks to Twitter and Facebook for all the random help with research bits. Thanks especially to Twitter for putting up with my play-by-plays as I wound to the finish and not reporting me to the loony bin for all the pictures of my sticky notes.

Thanks to Leigh Ann Logan for being my lighthouse for this book and many things.

Thanks to K. A. Mitchell who, when at the eleventh hour I realized I'd subconsciously patterned *her* Elijah in mine, not only insisted I keep the name but enthusiastically let me wink at her series. Speaking of which, you should really go read the Bad in Baltimore books and everything she writes, because she's amazing.

Thanks to Walter Lucas, who gives Randy Jansen a

run for his money on inserting himself into WIPs he has no business being in...and making himself indispensable to those stories.

Thank you, my readers, fans and friends, who got excited about this series and still email me asking if there will ever be a sequel to *Love Lessons*. The answer is yes. To save you some time: the answer is yes to this one too.

And for this second edition, thank you especially to my patrons, especially Rosie Moewe, Pamela Bartual, Erin Sharpe, Tiffany Miller, Sarah Plunkett, Sarah M, Sandy C, Chris Klaene, and Marie. You keep me sane, steady, and standing strong, always.

Music in the soul can be heard by the universe.
—Lao Tzu

Chapter One

ON HIS EIGHTEENTH birthday, Aaron Seavers navigated the sea of college brochures scattered across his comforter, searching for a future capable of pleasing his father without crushing his own soul. He was pretty sure he'd have better luck if he trekked out to the state park and hunted a unicorn.

It was June twenty-first. He'd graduated over a month ago. There were only *eight weeks* until most universities opened their doors to freshmen, and Aaron still hadn't picked a school. His father was furious with him, which wasn't anything new, but this time Aaron couldn't blame him.

In twenty-four hours, Aaron would be at his dad's condo in Eden Prairie for the rest of the summer. That was when Jim Seavers would find out Aaron *still* hadn't picked a school, and he'd follow through on his threat from the week before to pick it himself. Which would mean Aaron would attend the most elite, prestigious university to be had at the last minute—somewhere far from Minnesota.

Aaron wrenched himself out of melancholy and returned to his task, but futility washed over him immediately. How was he supposed to choose when they were all the same? Each flyer used strong, pleasing colors and elegant fonts. Each advertisement boasted photos of clean-cut, smiling, racially balanced students happy with their secondary-education choices. They held up sports equipment and musical instruments and other symbols of the school's extracurricular activities. All the brochures touted the same lures of happiness and success—using different buzzwords, but they were all variations on a theme.

Come to our school. We can give you the perfect future.

If Aaron could believe for a minute their promises were true, he'd have signed up six months ago. The same problem he'd faced then, however, haunted him now. How was he supposed to pick a school when he didn't know what it was he wanted to do with his life? How could he take a stand against the future his father wanted for him if he couldn't think of an alternative?

How was he supposed to be happy if he couldn't figure out what would *make* him love his life?

Beside him on the bed his phone buzzed. Funny how that made his heart leap, though it had been a year since getting a text had meant anything. Apparently his heart was a sappy idiot.

The text was from Colton. *You up to par-tay for your birthday?*

Colton remembered it was Aaron's birthday, which was more than Aaron expected. Aaron ran his thumb down the smooth side of the smartphone's case, trying to decide how to reply. He didn't exactly like Colton, and he *was* busy—but it was his birthday. His *eighteenth* birthday.

Another text came through. *Catherine invited half the school. We'll be neck-deep in geeks, but lotsa chicks. Let's get laid.*

Rolling his eyes, Aaron tossed the phone onto his pillow. *That* was why Colton invited him out. Girls swarmed them when they went out together, but since Aaron never wanted anything to do with them, Colton got, as he put it, his pick of the litter. Usually Aaron glommed on to the quietest female and simply chatted, but sometimes he had to make out, which always made him nervous. Colton disappeared first chance he got with the hottest girl in the herd. Sometimes more than one girl.

Yeah, *totally* how Aaron wanted to spend his birthday.

Of course, Colton could get him alcohol.

A knock on the door sounded as Aaron's mom stuck her head in. "Hi, sweetie."

Aaron tossed the phone away from him. "Hey, Mom."

Pushing the door open wider, Beth Seavers nodded at the mess on her son's bed. "Back at it, I see."

"Yeah." Selecting a flyer at random, Aaron began to flip through the pages. "I wish I knew which ones will still let me in this late."

"Your father will take care of it." She leaned on the doorframe, pulling her cardigan closer to her body. It was fluffy pink cashmere, but she huddled as if she was cold, her expression hollow as she spoke of her ex-husband. "Do what he says, and everything will be fine."

Aaron pursed his lips and tossed the brochure into the mess. "I wish I could think of something to major in that he'd say was okay. There's got to be something I'll like at least a little."

"You'll think of a major once you're there." Beth's expression turned wistful. "Maybe you should play some piano to clear your head. You always told me it helped you think."

Yeah, it used to. Glancing at his dusty keyboard in the corner of the room, Aaron swallowed the lump in his throat. "Piano isn't part of a future Dad would accept."

"Of course not. But even he would say you should take time to relax and unwind."

Aaron's gaze slid to his phone. The home screen was lit up, displaying teasers of more texts from Colton. "There's a party tonight, but I figured I should get this college thing sorted out instead."

"You should go. Be with your friends. It *is* your birthday."

Friends. That was funny. Still, Aaron picked up the phone and thumbed through the most recent texts. He didn't know this Catherine girl, but that wasn't surprising. He'd moved to Oak Grove from Eden Prairie less than a year ago—his dad had taken a long-term case in California, and his mom insisted she couldn't wait any longer to move near her sister. Given the social disaster at his old school after Tanner, Aaron hadn't put up a fight over switching at the start of his senior year…but the consequence was he knew next to no one. Colton and the people he hung out with were all Aaron had.

Football players and cheerleaders—so outside Aaron's life in Eden Prairie. He'd been eager to be part of the in-crowd for once, but the result was far different than he'd anticipated. Who knew popular people were this lonely?

Aaron tossed the phone down. "I can't let him show up tomorrow without making a choice."

"Then make one. They all look nice. Pick one and call it a night."

"It's not so simple. He'll want to know *why* I picked it, what I want to major in, and *I don't know*."

She huddled deeper into her sweater, forehead creasing and marring her pretty features. "I need to lie down, honey. I'm getting a migraine." She forced a smile. "Let me know if you decide to go out, okay?"

Aaron watched her go, buttoning down his hurt. Why should he expect her to help him? She never did.

Fool him, he never stopped hoping.

On the bed beside him, his phone buzzed, this time in the steady pattern indicating it was ringing. Stifling a sigh, Aaron answered. "Hey, Colton."

"Why don't you answer your texts, buttfuck?" Colton laughed like he'd made a funny joke instead of calling Aaron a name. "I'm coming over in a half hour, and we'll head over to Catherine's."

"Sure." Aaron flicked a nearby brochure with his finger. "Can we eat first, though?"

"I could eat. Where do you want to go, pizza? How about Lenny's?"

Aaron pulled a face. "God no. Let's go to Zebra's."

"All the way to Anoka?"

It was fifteen minutes away, twenty with traffic. Aaron thought about caving, but he *really* hated Lenny's, and anyway, it was *his* birthday. "Yes. If gas is a problem, I'll pay."

"Hell no, I'm just lazy. I'll be by in a bit."

Aaron made no effort to hurry getting himself together—half an hour in Colton time meant forty minutes. He'd call saying he'd gotten caught up in something at that point and would be by in fifteen, which would stretch into another hour before Colton appeared at the door. Aaron wrestled with the brochures some more, thinking he'd pick one and get it done before going off to get smashed, but he was no more able to make a choice now than ever.

Giving up, he pushed off the bed and headed for his shower.

A Keane song wormed into his head, soothing his nerves, and by the time he got out, he was humming the chorus to "Bend and Break". Maybe he'd have fun at the party. Maybe he could make a friend here, finally. He was about to be gone for the summer, but all he needed was someone for the night, someone he could feel good with on his birthday. That was all he asked for. One good night.

Aaron smiled to himself as he rooted through his closet to find a shirt, singing now, his chest warm and buzzing from the reverberations of his vocal cords. He *might* meet someone. Anything could happen at a party.

He saw the T-shirt he wanted at the back of his closet and tugged it free of a hanger. A box on the shelf behind it got caught in the struggle and tumbled out onto the floor of the closet, spilling papers and photos into the bedroom. As Aaron bent to put it to rights, he saw the half-finished score full of Tanner's notes mingled with a photo of the two of them pressed together and laughing amid other band members.

Aaron's bubble of happiness burst, ushering the sludgy, cold feelings back in.

Shoving the box out of sight, Aaron tugged the shirt over his head and stepped into a random pair of jeans. No more memories. Tanner was done. Music was done. He had to think of the future now. He'd pick a school, any school, and he'd make a new start somewhere. Any-fucking-where.

He'd pull a college at random out of a hat and call it good. Go out with Colton and drink until the pain stopped.

By the time Colton called to say he was running late, Aaron had removed two northern Iowa colleges. When he returned from getting some groceries for his mom, though, he saw them on his desk and put them back in the pile. After spying one he'd forgotten about under the bed, he put it up with the others. He found two new ones in the mail.

Instead of making a choice, he'd *added three more options*.

Aaron curled up on his bed, not needing his father to tell him he was a failure.

When Colton arrived an hour and a half late, Aaron was in a foul, bitter mood. Colton, of course, didn't notice.

"Sorry, man, lost track of time. Probably too late to go to Zebra's now."

"Whatever." Aaron sank into the passenger seat and leaned his elbow on the door so he could press his fingertips to his temple. "Take me to the fucking alcohol."

Colton laughed and put the car into gear. "That's my boy."

Aaron stared out the window, letting his vision go out of focus so the landscape could blur, wishing the chaos inside him could do the same.

"Happy birthday, idiot," he whispered to himself, and shut down everything in his head except the promise of getting rip-roaring, fantastically drunk.

GILES MULDER COULDN'T wait to get the hell out of Oak Grove, Minnesota.

The Alvis-Henning school district had, quite literally, tried to kill him. Giles had been beaten up four times, two episodes requiring trips to the emergency room, and one of those occurrences had been in middle school. Giles knew not one but *two* of the infamous gay bullying and suicide victims who had put A-H in the national consciousness for two and a half minutes. He could have watered the football field with the tears of rage and hurt he'd shed until he'd learned how to claim the space in his own head.

"This will make you stronger," his mother told him. "Anything that doesn't beat you only teaches you the world has to work harder to destroy you." Vanessa

Mulder's words were sage and she repeated them often, but usually with gritted teeth and a countenance belying the truth of what she *really* wanted—to get a baseball bat and beat heads. She did what she could to mitigate Giles's hazing, and after the second emergency room trip, she visited the Alvis-Henning school board with a lawyer, at which point Giles received a fat settlement check. After that, the physical attacks had ratcheted down to scrapes and bruises on their worst days.

Of course the emotional digs and derogatory comments only increased.

Dr. Tim Mulder, ever the mild-mannered pediatrician, took a subtler approach than his wife. While Vanessa swallowed her rage, Dr. Mulder held his son's hands and spoke quiet reassurances. "The people bullying you don't define you, Giles. Only you get to do that. You can't stop them from making negative comments, but *you* get to decide what you let affect you and how you reply. So long as you don't let their words and actions infect how you see yourself, you win. If you can hold on, I promise you someday you'll look back on these dark days and be proud of how you didn't let them tear you down from the beautiful, wonderful life you deserve."

Giles knew his father hadn't meant to emphasize *someday*, that his intention hadn't been to make Giles wait to fully live his life, but the only way Giles found peace was by accepting that truth. His life sucked rancid ass right now, but *someday* he would not go to A-Hell. Someday he would not live in fear of being beaten up and stuffed in the garbage can in the locker room. Someday he wouldn't trick closet cases and sexually fucked-up young men only to have them haze him in the hallways afterward, desperate for *no one ever* to find out what they'd done with Giles. Someday Giles would have a real boyfriend and a real life.

Someday was so fucking close Giles got hard thinking about it.

In fifty-five days he would leave Oak Grove and descend into the sanitized liberal, Lutheran cocoon of Saint Timothy College. He would spend each one of the 1,320 hours between himself and freedom holed up in his bedroom playing Xbox. He would shop for school supplies and Facebook message his roommate-to-be. He would drool all over the looming face of *someday* until he could hold it in his arms and call it his *right fucking now*.

Giles did all this—except somehow, on the second-to-last weekend in June, he ended up back in the belly of the high school beast. All because he couldn't say no to Mina.

She twitched in eagerness, the *flip-flop-whish* of her shiny, board-straight black hair swishing against the passenger seat punctuated by high-pitched squeals as Giles drove them to Catherine Croix's *why can't we all just get along* goodbye party.

"*Ohmygod.*" Mina held up her phone. "Lisa texted me, and Eric Campf is totally going to be there. With God as my witness, I'm getting him drunk and sticking my hand down his pants."

Giles thought about the last time he'd seen Eric

Campf—on his knees in the back of the church basement, enthusiastically blowing Giles. As usual, though, Giles swallowed the truth and let Mina have her delusions. She never did anything about her crushes anyway—no way was her hand going anywhere near Eric's waistband. "I hope you're ready to leave early, because I fully expect to blow this Popsicle stand within the hour."

Mina swatted his arm. "Come on. You haven't even parked the car."

"I know what will happen. I'll be shunned or mocked or ignored. If I get drunk, I'll get beat up behind the garbage cans." He turned down the street leading to Catherine's house. "If I stay sober, I'll sit in a corner and think about how much I hate everyone. I don't know why I let you talk me into coming."

"Why don't you stay sober, *not* sit in a corner, and talk to people instead? They don't all treat you like crap. *I* don't."

Giles pursed his lips and didn't answer, because Mina couldn't understand. Straight, pretty, adopted Korean-American Mina hadn't had anyone so much as raise their voice to her in class. She had no means to comprehend that Giles's remark about the garbage cans wasn't just another wisecrack. She had only the vaguest idea of the reality he'd lived at A-Hell—and he had no intention of reading her in on the deep cover of his life now.

Mina sighed. "Fine. Leave when you need to. Lisa said she'd give me a ride back, because she warned me you'd do this. Except I wish you'd stop writing people off before they have a chance to surprise you."

"Tell you what, as soon as we get to Saint Timothy, I'm all over making new friends. I'll be first in line."

"You shut too many people out. How do you know you haven't missed someone amazing right here at home because you decided they were an ass? How do you know you won't do the exact same thing at Saint Timothy? College isn't going to be that much different than high school."

Jesus, it had damn well better be, or Giles was jumping off the first cliff he found. "Fine. I'll talk to at least one person at Catherine's party. Happy?"

"It's *you* who needs to be happy."

"You have got to stop watching *Dr. Phil.*"

She straightened in her seat and grinned. "*Look* at all this. How are they all fitting into her house?"

Fifty cars at least lined Morningstar Lane, and it took Giles ten minutes to find a place to park that wasn't in some ominous dark shadow. It wasn't crime he worried about, not in this neighborhood, but drunken revelers looking to play Kick the Fag. He managed a reasonably secure space on a side street, and they made their way to the house, Mina chattering nonstop about how amazing the party would be.

Giles hunkered in silence, hating the world.

Once they got inside, Mina attached herself to her girlfriends, and Giles stood against the wall not far from them, taking stock of the room. The party was an impressive cross-section of Alvis-Henning. A decent number of the popular kids had put in an appearance, but there were plenty of band geeks and fringe riders. A few of the totally socially ostracized had dared to come and see if attending a party might increase their clout, but not many. This was the royalty allowing the commoners to pretend for a day, Queen Catherine of Nice presiding.

Mina did her best to include Giles in her conversations, and as promised he conversed with her friends for several minutes, mostly to a girl he sort of knew from orchestra, asking about her plans for the fall. It wasn't long, however, before he wandered off, determined to begin his exit.

He didn't want to chitchat with any of these people, and none of them wanted to talk to him. The popular girls reminded him without words that if he did bat for their team, they wouldn't let him play. The fringe girls waved eagerly and made comments about how they should hang out and do makeovers or something equally wrenched from stereotype—or they regarded him with pity.

God, but Giles hoped Mina was wrong about Saint Timothy not being any different. Intellectually he knew college wouldn't totally be the magic land of sunshine his heart wanted it to be, but it had to at least not be this slog through hell. No way everything would be exactly the same.

It *had* to get better. He was *owed* some goddamned better.

Giles made a circuit of the party, telling himself this was the last time to play the loser, the absolute end of standing outside everyone else, of being the one who couldn't connect, who was mocked or ridiculed or shunted off to the side unless someone felt like slumming with the gay. In fact, this would be the last time his sexuality was the lens through which he was viewed.

He was done pretending to enjoy himself at this party. *See, Mina? It was a bad idea to try and fit in at A-H.*

Unfortunately, as soon as he decided to leave, Colton Almstet climbed onto a coffee table and began his performing-monkey routine.

Giles hung back, trying to read the scene. Colton wasn't the one who had punched Giles so hard he lost his front teeth in tenth grade, but he'd stood by and laughed. By and large the days of Giles having to dodge serious harm were in the past, but it was Colton and his particular breed of asshole Giles still had to watch out for, especially when they were drunk. The half-finished fifth of vodka sloshing in Colton's hand as he leered over a stoned-out cheerleader falling out of her top told Giles if he so much as blipped onto Colton's radar, he'd deal with public slurs at best and get followed to his car at worst. While the living room Colton held court in was crowded, there wasn't quite enough cover to get to the front door. Giles's height, hair, and signature ears didn't do him any favors for anonymity, either.

Time to find an alternate escape route.

After letting Mina know he was leaving, Giles wove through the kitchen. Exiting out the back was too dangerous—too dark, too much opportunity to interrupt trysting jocks who'd feel honor bound to chase Giles down. He wasn't sure where else he could go. He considered heading through the main room to the front door, Colton be damned—he could hide behind people, right? He could crouch down, maybe. Of course they'd laugh at him, and he'd be exposed.

How fucked up was it that this was how he had to leave a party full of people who would do no more than avert their gazes when someone publicly called him a fag and offered to shove a beer bottle up his ass? Why couldn't he go to Mina and confess the truth? Why was her ignorance more important than getting out of harm's way?

Why did he fucking come here in the first place? Why had he believed, even for a moment, that he could pretend to be normal?

Angry and ashamed, Giles beelined for the back door in the kitchen—and ran headfirst into Eric Campf, who was flocked on either side by linebackers.

Surprised, Giles staggered away, and like the well-honed reflex it was, he bowed his head. He pretended he was meek, to be the geeky, awkward gay kid with the nasal voice who didn't challenge his betters. Ten minutes after Eric had wiped Giles's spunk off his chin last week, Giles had worn such a look for him when they returned to the youth room. Giles was supposed to cop that pose now, because this was how the game went down. Giles wasn't cool. Eric was.

Giles was so fucking tired of playing along. Mina's warning about college not being different rang in his head too loudly, the party ignored him too completely, and Giles felt like burning things down. Fuck Colton and fuck Eric. They could cope with the human being in front of them.

He lifted his head, let his anger bleed out in a bold gaze telling Eric, yeah, Giles remembered that mouth on his cock.

Eric balked, and his friends eyed Giles speculatively. When Eric recovered, his shock morphed into rage. "Who the fuck do you think you are, *fag*?"

Here we go.

Ducking behind a gaggle of girls giggling over Jell-O shots, Giles tried again for the door, but there were too many people between him and the exit. Even without Colton in the main room, Eric's buddies had the way blocked off, which meant with the back door inaccessible, Giles had to weave down the hallway and hope to hell there was a side exit or a door with a lock. He was more than ready to settle for the latter. He'd hole up, wait until everyone was too stoned and drunk to give chase, and he'd get the fuck out.

Eric and the linebackers got tangled in the Jell-O-shot girls, who missed the imminent gay bashing and seized an opportunity for flirting. The drunkest of them fulfilled Mina's wish and got her hand down Eric's pants, and Giles enjoyed Eric's abrupt paralysis.

Weaving through the crush into a less-populated hallway, Giles spied a narrow door leading into a laundry room. He hesitated, weighing his options as he glanced over his shoulder and saw his pursuers hadn't yet come this way. Laundry rooms didn't usually have locks, but they could be great places to wait. This could also be where they trapped him and came up with something nasty to do to him.

Where else could he go? At this point all he could

do was hide here or risk running into them in the main hallway—and get dragged into a room where whatever they did to him would get drowned out by the party noise in the living room. Would his defiance be worth it if it landed him his third ER visit?

Goddamn it, Mina, I'm never listening to you again.

Giles slipped into the laundry room. Shutting the door, he sank against the barrier, sucking in deep breaths of detergent, listening intently for the sound of footfalls in the hall. They came, along with swearing and murmured inquiries of *Where did he go?* Then, blessedly, the hall went quiet as Giles's pursuers drifted away.

Except as silence rang in his ears and his eyes adjusted to the low light, Giles realized he wasn't the only one in the room.

A dark figure huddled in the corner between a basket of folded towels and a pile of sheets waiting to be laundered. One figure, which meant it wasn't a couple necking, but someone else hiding. Giles squinted in the dark, peering closer, wondering who the hell else could possibly be in here.

His heart skipped a beat as the figure became familiar.

Aaron Seavers. It was Aaron Seavers, Colton's best bud, hiding in the laundry room with Giles.

Chapter Two

A T THE DOOR, Giles remained frozen in terror and indecision, but Aaron didn't so much as look up. Hunched, dark hair over his eyes and arms crossed on his knees, Aaron stared at the floor and spoke in a tight, tired voice. "Go away."

Giles wasn't sure how to play this. While Aaron had never engaged in gay-baiting, Giles wasn't sure he was ready to bet his front teeth Aaron wouldn't turn him over to the wolves first chance he had.

From the second Aaron showed up at Alvis-Henning, Giles had seriously crushed on him. Hot as fuck, all dark hair, blue eyes, and fuzzy scruff on his jaw—his quiet reserve left way too much space for Giles's imagination. This infatuation, combined with Aaron's popularity, meant Giles hadn't ever figured out how to behave around him. Which right now was a real problem.

He decided to hedge. "If you can wait five minutes to kick me out, I'd appreciate it."

Aaron's head snapped up, and in the low light of the room his bright blue eyes shone. "Oh. Sorry. I thought you were Colton."

"God no. He's dancing on a table in the living

room." Giles let himself relax somewhat. "Why would you tell Colton off? I thought you two were tight."

To this Aaron's response was a snort as he lifted a beer bottle to his lips. "Whatever."

Giles was more confused by the second. "Why are you in here, anyway?"

Aaron toasted the air with his bottle and a black smile. "Because it's my birthday."

"Oh—happy birthday." Giles frowned. "Sorry, I don't get it."

"Me either." Aaron tipped his head against the wall and shut his eyes, allowing Giles an ogle of that gorgeous throat, the tiny tuft of hair at the front of his T-shirt, the line of beard shadow and the beautiful bulge of an Adam's apple. Blue eyes opened, fixing in soft squints at Giles. "I know you. You were in my...calculus class?"

"And physics." Giles waved. "Giles Mulder."

Aaron gestured drunkenly back. "Aaron Seavers."

"I know." Jesus fuck, but Aaron was *hot*. Hot and slightly aloof. Giles wanted to put the guy on his knees and make him moan. *Stop. Get out of this with all your teeth and bones in place.* "So...you spend all your birthdays in the laundry room, or is this one special?"

"I'm having a better time in here than I was out there. Or anywhere. I'm having a particularly miserable life at the moment." Wincing, Aaron took another drink. "Shit, that's pathetic. You should probably go."

"I think if I leave right now, I'll go home in a body bag, or at least on a stretcher."

Now it was Aaron's face screwed up in confusion.

"Why?"

"Eric Campf and his buddies are playing hunt the fag. Plenty of other people would be happy to join in if they heard about the party game." *Please don't say you want to be one of them.*

Aaron shut his eyes. "I hate this town. I should be glad I'm leaving it tomorrow."

Aaron was leaving? Giles snuffed out the waft of disappointment. *Like it matters. We're all leaving in another month and a half. Also, just because hottie is talking to you instead of hitting you doesn't mean you have a new bestie.* "Where are you going tomorrow?"

"To hell." Aaron drained the last of his beer. "Eden Prairie, with my dad. He'll nag at me all summer, plus I have to avoid—" His whole face shuttered, and he didn't say anything more.

Okay, touchy subject. New topic. "Where are you going to school in the fall?"

Swearing under his breath, Aaron tossed the beer bottle across the room. "I need another drink."

"Unless you want fabric softener, I think you're out of luck in here. Seriously, where are you going in the fall?"

"I don't know."

Giles stared at him, not quite sure what to do with this. "Dude, it's *June*. June twenty-first."

"Yes, I know. Birthday, remember?" Aaron covered his face with his hands. "I don't know where I'm going. I can't decide. My dad's going to rag my ass about whatever I choose, and they all look the same. It's my goddamned eighteenth birthday, I never got dinner, and I don't know where I'm going to college. I'm drinking in a laundry room at the most boring party in the world, my ride home is smashed and dancing on tables—*and* I'm out of alcohol."

"Well, I can't help you with the alcohol or college, but I could give you a ride to a drive-through on the way to your house."

Giles expected to be laughed at, but Aaron took him seriously. "For real?" He seemed briefly hopeful, then looked away. "I don't want you to bug out of the party because I'm being a loser."

"Did you forget the part where I'm hiding out because beating me up is about to be the evening's entertainment?"

"Oh. Right. Um…yeah, if you're offering and don't mind, a ride would be great. I don't live too far, so it shouldn't put you out."

"But I'm taking you to dinner first, right?" Giles stepped closer and held out a hand. "Need help?"

"You don't have to take me out." Aaron sounded like he wished someone would.

"Hey, it's your birthday. The least I can do is buy you a Frosty."

Aaron frowned as he accepted Giles's hand and rose gracelessly to his feet. "Wendy's is in Anoka."

"Whatever, it's only fifteen minutes. Besides, I could use an order of fries." When Aaron only grinned at him stupidly, as if Giles had offered to scale a mountain for him, Giles added, "I think you could use more water and less beer."

"Yeah." Aaron listed on his feet. "No dinner, four

beers in three hours. Dumb."

"It's your birthday. You're allowed."

Aaron laughed, leaning into Giles. "What, do I get a free pass on everything because it's my birthday?"

Letting the comment soak in, Giles tried to decide if Aaron Seavers was hitting on him or not.

Aaron nodded to a shadow in the corner of the room. "Hey, is that a door?"

By God, it was. A side door with a clear, straight view of the street, and if he squinted, Giles could see his car. "Aaron Seavers, I fucking love you."

Giggling, Aaron nudged him. "Come on, we haven't even had a first date yet."

Giles's jaw dropped, but before he could wrap his head around Aaron Seavers—*Colton's best friend*—hitting on him, Aaron grabbed his hand and tugged him toward the exit.

"Let's go. If you love me, you can buy me a Frosty *and* fries."

What the hell was he supposed to say to that? In the end Giles said nothing, only let Aaron lead him out of the party into the night.

AARON LIKED THIS Giles guy.

He was lanky and goofy-looking, with ears that stuck out and a fauxhawk he should give up on, and he had this way of regarding everything as if he wasn't sure if he should run from it or attack it. Giles's voice was sharp, a little nasal and a lot lispy. But he was funny, and he had this way of taking charge Aaron enjoyed.

Also, he was the only person tonight interested in doing something Aaron wanted to do.

Most importantly, when Giles looked at Aaron, he smiled. It was a nice smile.

Except he wasn't smiling right now. Once they shut the door behind them, Giles used a subtle touch at Aaron's elbow to herd him out of the party. "Come on. Coast is clear. My car is the red Honda."

"Who are we running from?" Aaron looked around, not seeing anyone.

"We're running preemptively." At the car, Giles nudged Aaron toward the passenger side. "Are you sober enough to open the door and get in?"

Aaron tried to flip him off, but the quick gesture made him stumble sideways, and he stopped. Grumbling, Giles helped Aaron into the car. Now Aaron felt like shit. "Sorry."

"It's okay." Giles spoke tightly, still peering around the street as if he expected an axe murderer. Once he got in the car himself, he immediately locked the doors and relaxed somewhat. "Okay. Frosty time."

Food. Aaron's belly, full of alcohol, gurgled unhappily. "Thanks again. This is nice of you."

"Not a problem." Giles focused on navigating his way through the clutch of parked cars and onto Viking Boulevard. "You said you're leaving tomorrow for your dad's place. I take it your parents are divorced?"

"Yeah. Five years."

Giles frowned. "But you've only been here since last fall. I mean—I guess I figured it had to be some kind of epic event to get you to move out of your high school during senior year."

"We lived in Eden Prairie at first after they split up, but then Mom realized he wouldn't…" Aaron pursed his lips, unwilling to admit out loud the complicated relationship between his parents. He drew a breath and redirected. "She wanted to move closer to her sister."

"Couldn't you have stayed with your dad?"

"He's gone a lot, sometimes for months at a time. So, no."

"Huh."

Aaron thought he could hear the judgment in Giles's tone—*Why didn't your mom stay nine more months until you graduated?*—but he said nothing more. It was a kindness Aaron appreciated, because usually people wanted to know why, leaving Aaron to sputter helplessly.

Funny how Giles's silence made Aaron want to talk. "I go to Dad for the summer once I clear my birthday. Unless he's out of town. That's the custody arrangement."

"How does it work when you're eighteen? Can you tell him to fuck off and do what you want?" When Aaron shivered, Giles laughed. "Okay, clearly not. Sorry." He shifted his hands on the wheel. "I can't get over the fact that you haven't picked a college. Can you get in anywhere this late?"

"I don't know." His head swam a little, panic breaking through the alcoholic haze. "Where are *you* going?"

"Saint Timothy."

Aaron frowned, mentally indexing his pile of brochures. "The name rings a slight bell."

"Small liberal arts college east of St. Paul, by Battle Creek Lake. Lutheran background, which of course half the colleges are in Minnesota." He smiled as he turned onto the highway. "I'm excited to go. We've visited twice, and it feels right, you know?"

No, Aaron didn't. "How does it feel right?"

Giles considered a moment. "It just does. Probably helps that I fell in love with it on paper ages ago. It has a great orchestra program—whole music department is top-notch."

Aaron missed music. "Is that what you're going to major in, music? What do you play?"

"I play violin, but no, I'm not majoring in music. Are you kidding? I want a job." Giles settled into his seat. "I don't know what I'm going to do yet. I'd always told myself I was going to be an LGBT activist for marriage equality, but the state came to its senses before I could get out of A-Hell, and now with DOMA staked too, I'm kind of over it. So I'm still thinking."

"A-Hell?" *LGBT activist.* Aaron's belly stopped gurgling and started…something. Giles *was* gay. He kept mentioning it too, as if it were no big deal.

Giles glanced at Aaron with an arched eyebrow. "You're going to tell me you loved Alvis-Henning now, right?"

"What? *No.*" Aaron pulled a face. "God no."

Giles's laugh tickled Aaron inside. "Good."

A lull descended. Aaron thought Giles might be trying to say something but couldn't quite find the words. Aaron tried not to stare at him, because this was reminding him a *lot* of the night with Tanner, when everything was so amazing…then so terrible.

Aaron sat up straighter. "Tell me more about this college. Saint Somebody."

"Saint Timothy. I don't know, it's a college. Two thousand people, lots of trees and buildings, big lawn."

"Tell me more about why it feels right. You like the music program, but you're not going to major in it?"

"Well—" Giles frowned. "I guess I think they're mostly interchangeable, these colleges, so I might as well pick the one that makes me feel comfortable and happy. I checked out the LGBT rating at Timothy right away, but unless you're somewhere freakishly evangelical, having an LGBT support group is almost standard now. So I walked around campus a lot, trying to decide if I could imagine it as home. I could. They have a wide variety of majors, their sports teams are kind of whatever, not the main focus, and their dorms are decent. I can play orchestra and maybe take a trip or two with them, and the school is an hour's drive from my parents, less with good traffic. Decision made."

Aaron's mind boggled. "You make it sound so easy."

"It's not rocket science. It's just college." He nudged Aaron with his elbow. "So what are you looking for in a school?"

"Something my dad won't call stupid."

"Ah." Giles's tone was full of understanding. "Well, what's he think is important?"

"I have to go somewhere with a strong reputation, where I can get a good job after. Except I don't know what job I want."

"Have you gone down the *U.S. News & World Report* lists? Do you want to stay in the Midwest or get the hell out?"

"I want everything to stop. The pressure. All the stupid—" He thought of Colton and yet another disastrous evening. "I don't want to join a frat and start high school part two. I want real friends. I want…"

Tanner flashed in his mind, and he put his hands on his stomach.

"You okay?" Giles slowed the car. "Do you need me to pull over?"

"I just need to eat," Aaron lied.

"Food coming right up. I see the sign up ahead. What would you rather, a burger or chicken sandwich?"

"Burger. Big one. With bacon and cheese." Aaron tried to fumble for his wallet, but Giles waved him away.

"I got this, birthday boy. Stand down."

Warmth flooded the hollow place inside Aaron. "Thanks. You're…really nice."

Giles flashed him a smile that made everything inside Aaron hum, but when Aaron smiled back, Giles looked away.

He ordered Aaron a full meal: burger, fries, Frosty, and bottle of water, getting himself a pop. "I got a large order of fries, figuring we could split it. Sound okay?"

"Yeah." Aaron took a bite of his burger and felt his soul realign. "Oh my God, thank you so much. You're saving my life."

"Pretty easy save, and at value meal prices." Giles sipped his drink and grabbed a fry as he navigated onto the road. "Where to now? You want to head home or cruise around?"

"I don't want to go home." Aaron scowled at the streets of Anoka. "Not like there's anywhere else to go, though."

"Sure there is. I'd say we could get pizza, but we bought all this food. You're a bit drunk to bowl, and there's no way either of us can get in a bar, but a few of the parks are still open. Plus there's always the lake. We could midnight picnic."

A midnight picnic sounded fun, especially with Giles. "Are you sure you don't care? I don't want to keep you."

"What is it, exactly, you think you're keeping me from?"

Aaron shrugged. "I don't know. Stuff?"

"In Oak Grove?" Giles sighed as he headed north. "Honest to God, college has got to improve things. My friend Mina is going to Saint Timothy too. She says it's going to be the same, and oh my fucking God, *no*."

"I hadn't thought that far ahead. College seems so scary."

"Why? What's to be scared of?"

"Everything." Aaron felt the burger leak around his lips and fumbled for a napkin. "Tomorrow my dad's coming, and I have to have a college and a reason for picking it. A reason he'll accept. Otherwise he'll choose for me, and I'm sure to hate it."

"So pick one first. Grab one at random, see what

they're known for, find the thing that will make your dad happy, and tell him that's the reason you chose it. Rush out your app, and boom, you're done."

Could it actually be so simple? "Is this friend of yours from A-H, the one who's going with you?"

"Yeah, we're being lame and using the buddy system. So I guess I am scared enough to take my BFF security blanket with me. But mostly it worked out. She's going to be pre-med, and they have a great program. Pre-med, pre-law, and music. That's Timothy."

"Has to be nice, though, having her along."

Giles waggled his eyebrow. "You could go to Mankato with Colton." He laughed when Aaron groaned. "Still blows my mind that you don't like him. Why do you hang out so much if you can't stand him?"

Aaron tried to swallow the truth with his fries, but he and alcohol didn't make much for censorship. "He was the only one who showed interest in being my friend when I moved here. So I went with it."

Giles looked at him as if he'd grown an extra head. "Shut up. No way."

"No way what?"

"No way everyone else at A-H snubbed you."

Was this a trick question? Aaron eyed Giles carefully. "Um, yeah. Nobody talked to me."

"You hang out with the pack of popular kids. You've dated half the girls from their herd. Pull the other one, buddy."

"What?" Aaron put down his Frosty, Giles's angry tone making him uneasy. He wanted to argue he'd gone out with *two* girls, and both instances had been such disasters he'd quit dating full stop. But this confession invited a question as to *why* they'd been so awful, so he only shook his head. "Whatever. It's over. You're right, college has to be better."

Giles was pissed now for some reason. "What do you mean, *whatever*? You telling me you *didn't* hang out with those guys or date those hookers, it was an optical illusion?"

Aaron's stomach hollowed out. "Why are you so mad at me?"

Giles deflated. "I don't know." He let his hands slide to the sides of the wheel. "Let's say in my experience, guys who hang out with your people, then seek me out are a particular class. I wouldn't have pegged you for that."

"They're not my people. I hung out with them because I was lonely. I went out with the girls because they asked me." The last comment made Giles glance sideways at him, and Aaron had about had it with these weird looks. "*What?*"

Giles said nothing for several minutes. Aaron ate, but the food was now ash in his mouth. He had the vague sense he'd fucked things up, but he couldn't figure out how.

Well, at least everything was normal.

Eventually Giles spoke. "Mina says I'm too harsh and judgmental. I decide who people are before I get the truth."

The statement felt important, but Aaron couldn't unpack it. He ate his Frosty in silence.

Giles continued. "In my defense, every time I *don't* do that, if I let my guard down, I get burned."

Aaron still had no idea how this had anything to do with who he'd hung out with in high school. "Okay."

Giles's gaze was heavy with meaning, but Aaron still didn't have a clue about what was going on.

Averting his gaze, Aaron stared at the road. "I try not to be in a situation where I have to guard at all. I hunker down."

Giles's expression was softer now. "So you're a full-on shy boy. Huh. Would never have guessed. I figured you were bored with A-H, or pissed at it."

Aaron frowned at his food. "I'm not."

"I'm starting to understand that."

Giles turned onto an access road. Aaron held on to the door with one hand and tried to stabilize his food with the other as the car went over some serious ruts. "Where are we going?"

"Side way into Hickey Lake."

Aaron grinned. "Seriously? I always wanted to check that place out."

"Well, now you can. This isn't the main recreation area, but it's got a nice view. Also no one will come down this road."

Aaron braced himself against another rut. "I'm not entirely convinced this *is* a road."

Giles shot him a quick glance and a grin. "You seem to be doing better. Food helping?"

"Company more than anything." He hadn't meant to say that out loud. "Sorry. When I'm drunk, I talk too much."

"Alcoholic truth serum? Yeah. Probably why I don't drink often. That and nowhere to drink. And no way to get it."

"I think I drink for the wrong reasons. Usually it's like tonight, when I want to shut the world off."

"Happen often?"

"I can't think of a time I *didn't* want to shut the world off." *Except for right now.* He shoved his mouth full of fries, really stuffed it so he couldn't speak. When he'd swallowed and made sure he had his sappy self muzzled, he continued. "Colton tries to get me out every weekend, but I can only take so much of him."

Giles laughed, a tinkling nasal cascade. Aaron loved the sound. He finished off his burger and digested Giles's observation along with it. "So you must have thought I was a jerk like Colton."

Giles hesitated before confessing, "Pretty much."

A lake appeared before them, framed by trees and moonlight. Giles pulled over into a dirt patch that would have been muddy had it rained more. Killing the engine, Giles gestured at the water. "Behold. Hickey Lake."

Aaron grinned, the tension between them falling away. "How the hell did it get named, anyway? Too many teenagers in the '50s?"

"Would have been named in the 1850s. Probably somebody's last name, but I suspect plenty of hickeys are given here. Who could resist?"

And the tension returned.

Giles cleared his throat. "So. You want to sit here in the car, park our butts on a blanket, or keep driving?"

One hell of an invitation lurked inside Giles's list of choices. This was the drunken dance with Tanner all over again. Without the alcohol, Aaron probably would have gone into cardiac arrest trying to work out what to do. But he had alcohol—lots of nice, swimmy beer. The pretty, blue-black lake lay invitingly before him.

The soft, spicy scent of Giles, his smile, and his laugh, which somehow aligned Aaron's spiritual spine, allowed him to calm down. In so many ways it was a choice more nightmarish than which college to go to—and yet at the same time it was the easiest decision of all.

"Blanket sounds good."

Taking a deep breath, Aaron told himself everything would be okay, then waited to see if he was right.

Chapter Three

GILES HAD NO idea what he was doing with Aaron. He dug in the trunk of the car for the winter emergency blanket he thought he remembered seeing back there, though he told himself if he didn't find it, it was a sign from God he should get in the car and drive Aaron Seavers the hell to his house, where he belonged. He had no idea what it meant when he found the blanket immediately, neatly folded on top of the spare tire. Somehow he doubted it was a thumbs-up from the Almighty to get laid.

Was he actually going to sit on the beach of Hickey Lake and deep throat the guy he'd had a crush on since the moment he'd first seen those baby blues peeking beneath dark, shaggy bangs? When he shut the trunk, he saw Aaron standing beside the car, hands tucked in the front pockets of his jeans, shoulders hunched, with a hungry, terrified expression on his face.

Yep. Getting laid was definitely on the table.

The thing he didn't know, the thing making Giles's brain run around like a squirrel in a cage as he spread the blanket on the most level spot he could find, was whether this was another case of closeted "straight" boy or if this was Aaron coming out to him. Normally Giles didn't ask. As much as he hated these hookups after, as much as it made him *batshit* the only action he ever got was with recoil-fucks—well, Giles had a hard time looking gift sex in the mouth. He told himself it was his sweet revenge, a power trip, but if he were honest, mostly it was because he was lonely.

In short, at the bottom of his barrel he was alarmingly pathetic.

He wanted to find out if this was another shame-and-blame or…something different. Dumb, because it wasn't like this could go anywhere. Aaron was gone tomorrow, and come this fall Giles would be too. At best they would maybe hook up on breaks, but if Aaron *was* about to come out, Giles would never bag him again. Aaron was Grade A Prime for whatever gender he chose to take to bed. Giles was lucky to be a C+ on a good day. Too skinny, too geeky, too awkward. No way Giles could ever score an Aaron for real.

Yet here he was, spreading a blanket and settling down on it beside Aaron, who sat a hell of a lot closer than a straight boy would. Looking a lot more eager and vulnerable than Giles's hookups usually did. None of this was on the scripts Giles knew.

Whatever was going on, Giles doubted if he resisted he'd think back on this moment and admire his own nobility.

"Good thing it hasn't rained much, or we'd already be half-devoured by mosquitoes." Giles kicked off his shoes and wiggled his stocking-footed toes in the blanket's nap. "Nice summer so far, actually. Not too hot, not too wet."

"It has been nice." Aaron didn't sound like he wanted to talk about the weather, but it was equally clear he didn't know what to do next, wound so tight that if Giles wasn't careful, the guy would *sproing* right into the lake.

Yeah, well, baby, follow my lead. Boy do I know this dance. Giles eased onto his elbows and let his legs fall open. Ostensibly he stared at the water, but mostly he allowed Aaron to admire the way he filled out his jeans, an invitation his companion took. It was a subtle peek, but it was there. Giles wasn't a Jon Hamm or anything, but he had a decent package.

Before his dick saw any action, though, Aaron needed more idle conversation to loosen him up. "Eden Prairie, you said. Did you grow up there?"

"Yeah. Well—mostly. I was actually born in California—Oakland—but we moved when I was four. I have vague memories of the house we lived in there, and maybe the bridge and a house on a big hill with an orange flowerpot on a stoop, but that's it."

"Does your dad live in the house in Eden Prairie where you grew up?"

"No, Mom sold it when we moved. He lives in a condo. Though he's always spent a lot of time in his law firm's California office. Especially so lately."

Aaron had more regular breathing now. Time for phase two.

Giles let his knee brush Aaron's arm a few times, and when Aaron didn't withdraw, he let it linger ever so lightly. "We're in the same place as we've always lived, but we did a big remodel last year. I'm the last one in the nest."

Aaron's knee pressed tentatively into Giles's. "You have brothers and sisters?"

"One of each. Both married and moved into the Cities. Hannah lives in Linden Hills. Mark's in St. Paul and just had his first kid. What about you—are you an only?"

"Yeah." On the blanket, Aaron mimicked Giles's position. His hand brushed Giles's, but instead of pulling away he let it linger. When Aaron spoke next, his voice shook. "Probably a good thing I'm an only child. My parents are awful together. They shouldn't have had me."

"Well, that'd be a shame, because we wouldn't be here right now." The line was a bit cheesy, but the knee beside Giles's became more sure of itself, the fingers lacing more deliberately, so hooray for dairy products. Pressing his whole thigh closer, Giles captured Aaron's hand. "So, birthday boy. Did you get all the presents you wanted?" Aaron pressed their legs together, gaze drifting to Giles's crotch. Giles bit back a smile. "Or maybe…something is missing?"

Aaron's breath caught, pupils dilated, lips parted. He looked Giles dead in the eye, all his longing and desire naked between them.

Here we go.

Giles kissed him softly—a lover's kiss, which he never did with tricks. With Aaron he wanted to kiss, though. He teased the sweet, pink flesh until it plumped, coaxing him open but not letting himself inside. He drugged them both with long, sexy sips for a minute, nuzzling Aaron's cheek. "This okay?"

Aaron's shuddering breath sent excitement along Giles's spine, awakening the urge to pin Aaron down, drive him over the edge. Giles held himself in check, waiting.

It was *very* important Aaron say yes.

Aaron drew a deep breath. "I—I don't know." When Giles lifted his head though, Aaron's hand shot out and clamped on Giles's biceps, keeping him from retreating. "I..." Blue eyes fluttered open, regarding Giles with lust and fear.

Giles let him fumble for a moment, but the guy was drowning, going down by his own struggles. "Hon, have you done this before? With a guy?"

Aaron nodded woodenly. "Once. A...little."

Giles didn't have the heart to push him, though it angered him too. Why the hell were they always so ashamed? Except whatever tortured Aaron moved even Giles's hardened heart. He stroked Aaron's dark hair, brushed his thumb along a perfect cheekbone. "Hey. It's okay. I promise."

Aaron clearly expected to be tarred and feathered any second.

Giles kept touching him, trying to calm him down and not just so he could get back to kissing him. "Seriously, it's only the two of us here, and I don't kiss and tell. If this is something you want, you can have it. If not, it's okay, because I—"

He couldn't say anything after that, because his mouth was full of Aaron.

As hesitant and sweet as the first one had been, this

kiss was raw and wild, curling Giles's toes. This wasn't some fumbly *gosh-I-never* kiss. This was someone who knew exactly what he wanted. Gone was the slick, sarcastic guy from the laundry room—this Aaron was sweet, slightly clumsy, and ready to go. They rolled across the blanket, tearing at each other, dueling with their tongues and teeth.

Giles landed firmly on top and pinned Aaron with his thighs, cupping Aaron's face and diving deep into that hot mouth.

With a shiver and a soft cry, Aaron stopped fighting, digging his fingers into Giles's back as he let his legs fall open.

God yes. Taking firm grip of Aaron's hair, Giles thrust harder.

They were so hot and fast they almost came like that, Aaron gasping as he pushed up and up and *up*. Giles worried he was too rough, but the more he tugged that pretty hair, the more Aaron came apart.

I want him in my mouth.

Breaking the kiss, Giles nipped his way down Aaron's chin and neck, dragging his mouth over to the pert nipple and lightly taking it between his teeth through the fabric.

Aaron cried out, arched, and crushed Giles's face tighter to him.

Giles nursed through the shirt until the fabric was hot and soaked with saliva, until the nipple was a hypersensitized rock and Aaron was so far gone he'd have spread himself for the football team. His whole body flooding with the rush of power he'd stumbled into, Giles pushed up Aaron's shirt and kissed his way down the center of Aaron's body, lingering over the quivering belly, smiling as he undid the fastening of Aaron's jeans before tugging the denim over those slender hips to reveal his prize.

Aaron's cock thrust at Giles's neck as he nuzzled it and lifted his head to take inventory: cut, nice-sized, not too big, not too little, not too long. He teased the tip, running his tongue along the slit and chuckling as Aaron yelped and jerked against him.

"S-sorry."

"Don't be." Giles drew the whole glans into his mouth before licking the thick vein. He smiled around his mouthful as he watched Aaron buckle off his elbows, gasping and trying to part knees trapped by his jeans.

"*Ohgod.*" Aaron gasped as Giles sucked him deep and slid those jeans all the way down to his ankles. The next time Aaron opened his legs, his knees fell easily apart.

Giles knelt between them, hefting Aaron's slightly furry ass in his hands, nuzzling the hot cleft with his thumbs as he parted it. So responsive. So much so Giles's conscience began to prick at him, reminding him it wasn't usual for his straight-boy tricks to let him push the tip of his thumb into their asses.

Lifting off Aaron's cock, he gazed across the heaving body he pleasured. "Are you too drunk? Should I not be doing this?"

Aaron gave him a crazed, furious glance and rammed his cock into Giles's cheek.

Laughing, Giles went to work, though now he only teased the shaft, licking and sucking at the side, measuring the weight of the balls in his hand as he pushed those pretty thighs wide and licked the crease of Aaron's leg. Aaron began speaking in tongues.

"Please, *ohgodplease.*"

When Giles took those sweet sacs in his mouth, first one, then the other, then both at once, rolling his tongue around them, Aaron's sigh became a discordant, frustrated aria.

Against Giles's thumb, Aaron's hole flexed, hot and pleading.

Groaning, Giles pushed him sideways, licking his way down Aaron's taint, the tendons in his chest tightening as he shut down the whisper saying this was way, way too much too fast. Holy shit, did he want to do this. He'd rimmed just once, that guy at all-state orchestra his junior year. The openly gay, deep-voiced bassist had been quite emphatic about how much he enjoyed rimming. Giles hadn't minded it either.

He should not rim Aaron Seavers, the not-so-straight boy, Aaron Seavers who had at best done *a little* with a guy prior to their current foray. Giles should not risk taking advantage of a sexy but confused young man who might have had a bit too much to drink and wouldn't normally let him do this.

Giles shouldn't, no—but he did.

When Giles's tongue first stole across that puckered skin, Aaron yelped, but on the second pass he stilled—all but his hole, which flexed and begged for more. Giles circled flicks of tongue before giving insistent pressure at the ring, knocking at the door, asking if his tongue could come in and fuck. Somehow they ended up with Aaron on his knees with his face pressed into the blanket, almost sobbing as Giles sucked and licked at him.

Giles shook with the fever of what he did, of what Aaron let him do. He whispered over the trembling flesh, urged those cheeks wider with his palms and slicked Aaron's entrance with his spit, wearing down those terrified, needy muscles until at last they yielded to him, until when his tongue pushed forward it nudged inside.

Aaron's whimpered arpeggio made Giles's cock throb in his pants. "*Ohgod.*" A sob wracked Aaron. "Giles—Giles, I'm gonna come."

Giles gave his target one last lick and flipped Aaron onto his back. Kneeling over Aaron, Giles fumbled with his jeans, freeing his dick before descending, shaking, on top of the pliant boy beneath him.

"Tell me you want this," Giles whispered at Aaron's neck as he tentatively held their cocks together in his grip. "Tell me this is okay."

"*Please.*" Aaron's breath blew hot on Giles's cheek as he thrust.

Giles pulled away to look Aaron in the eye. "I'm serious. Say it. Tell me you're not too drunk, that you actually want this when you haven't had four beers and not enough food."

"I want this." Aaron stared up at him with bright, focused eyes, his hips still trying to reclaim the friction. "I'm scared to death, but I want this so bad I feel like I might blow up if it doesn't happen."

"Good enough." Giles caught Aaron's mouth, tightened his grip on their cocks and started to fuck.

It was the most wicked, delightful sex of his life—the pretty, popular boy coming apart in his arms, Giles's nose full of musk and his tongue still remembering the feel of that hot, tight muscle spasming around it. Aaron greedily sucked off the last of the taste from Giles's mouth and thrust his cock between their bodies. Giles reveled in the knowledge he could do *anything* to Aaron right now. If he'd had condoms, he could have gone inside that tight ass, and Aaron would have helped guide him in.

As they chased release together, as Aaron wrapped his legs around Giles's back, Giles let himself unlock a quiet fantasy that this *wouldn't* be a shame-and-blame trick, that when he dropped Aaron off, they'd exchange numbers and talk about doing this again sometime. As they fought to reclaim their breaths, sweaty chests pressed together, throbbing cocks deflating amidst a tangle of cooling spunk, Giles let himself imagine how he'd go down to Eden Prairie for the Fourth of July. How they'd snuggle on a blanket together and hold hands. He allowed himself the fantasy of heading off to Saint Timothy, planning when he'd be able to have a weekend with his boyfriend. His boyfriend Aaron Seavers, who loved to be rimmed by the lake.

Stupid fantasy. But Aaron had gotten all the way under Giles's skin. He let himself indulge.

This lapse, of course, was a mistake.

As the high of orgasm wore off, Aaron's face shuttered. The cute boy Giles hoped was different bore the same wooden expression as so many of the others. Shock. Shame. Fear.

A recoil-fuck after all.

Unwilling to watch the mask go all the way up on his pretty trick, Giles rolled off Aaron, cleaned himself with the edge of the blanket and arched his hips to put his jeans to rights. Still, Giles had embraced his inner idiot, and he had to try a bit more, in case. "You okay?"

Talk to me. Be with me. Let me in more than your ass.

Aaron nodded stiffly, visibly shutting down. "Yeah."

Swallowing a sigh, Giles climbed to his feet. "I might have some wet wipes in the car."

He didn't, and Aaron wouldn't need them. This was, of course, an excuse to leave, a chance for Aaron to wrap himself back up in his closet, to pull up his jeans and find a way to pretend he hadn't bent over and begged Giles to fuck him. Now that the hormones were appeased, it was the time for rationalizations and compartmentalizing.

Giles had served his purpose. He had nothing more to do but drive Aaron home.

Aaron had undone Giles's defenses so much, though, that as he pulled up to Aaron's house, Giles couldn't stop hoping he was wrong. Even if they never made out again, he didn't want to say goodbye to Aaron. *Give me one sign, and I'll give you ten different ways to stay in contact with me. Ask me to kidnap you tomorrow so you don't have to go to Eden Prairie, and I will. Ask me to come visit you. Ask me anything, give me one, tiny, baby reason, and I'll give you anything you want.*

Aaron didn't. He never so much as looked Giles in the eye, barely grunting a farewell before double-timing it to his front door, not once glancing over his shoulder.

Giles watched the front porch light turn off, shrouding the driveway and his hopes in shadow.

"Happy birthday," he told Aaron's darkened front door, then backed out onto the street, leaving his boyfriend fantasies behind him in the dust.

AARON STUMBLED BLINDLY through the house, heading straight for his bathroom. After peeling out of his clothes, he turned on the water and stepped into the tub. As soon as the spray hit his face, he started to cry.

He wept all the way through his shower, sniffling as he toweled off after and climbed into a pair of boxers, but when he tunneled under his sheets and pressed his face into the down of his pillow—there he sobbed. He was not sad so much as he was overwhelmed, as if something huge and heavy inside him had burst free.

Aaron had let Giles do that to him. Giles had made him say it, admit it, and he'd done it all. That was him. That was Aaron Seavers, the part of him that had winked at Tanner, that Tanner had rejected. The part of him that Giles had not.

Gay. That had been very gay.

The magnitude of that, the truth and realness of it

all, swamped him again, and he sobbed so much he had to drag his wastebasket closer in case he threw up.

He never did, though, and in fact once those shuddering waves of shock had passed, Aaron felt better. He was a bit wild, as if his belly throbbed raw without skin, but he wasn't so overwhelmed by his vulnerability. If anything, he felt motivated by it. Happy.

Giles. Oh God, thank you, Giles. He was so high at that moment he wanted to call him. Except he didn't have a number. Or a last name. *Shit.* Giles had said, but Aaron had been too drunk to remember.

A man possessed, Aaron thumbed through his yearbook. Five hundred damn people in his class, and he scanned them all, each page, each face, until, thank you *God*, at the end of the *Ms*, there he was. Giles Mulder.

Aaron couldn't find his phone number—there were twenty Mulders in the online phone book and thirty in the paper one in the kitchen—but Aaron was too scared to be that bold anyway. He'd have to be indirect. Googling led him to Facebook, though Aaron had to make an account because he didn't have one. Opening up a private message dialog box within the friend request, he got ready to compose a message.

Aaron couldn't think of a single, solitary word to say.

He tried for an hour, starting several different notes before deleting them, *almost* sending one that said simply, "Hi," but bailing on that too.

Maybe he shouldn't do this. Maybe the lake hadn't meant anything to Giles. Maybe if Aaron connected afterward, it would be awkward.

Maybe—his heart tightened—maybe Giles would laugh.

He told himself that last fear was totally off, that no way a guy who'd kissed him like that would mock him, but he couldn't be sure because he *had* been wrong before.

As Aaron tried to sleep, a new emptiness bloomed inside him, a sense of loss he could not shake. It ate at him until five in the morning, when it burned through the bottom of his heart and seeped into his bloodstream. He dreamed of it, his subconscious filling out the blanks. *I have to find a way to connect with Giles.* Waking or sleeping, that thought became the center of Aaron's world.

When he woke, he had an idea.

It was so crazed and mad and perfect he could only stare at the ceiling for several seconds. After getting out of bed, he threw the stack of brochures on his sheets and pawed feverishly for the one he was looking for.

In the end he found it in the recycling bin on the back porch. He read it cover to cover, making notes. He put on his studio headphones, blared his Favorites playlist, and worked as if the hounds of hell were on his heels. He went to the website, double-checking himself, choosing all the right words and phrases he knew his father would insist on. Though he took a break to eat lunch with his mom, he resumed his notes immediately after, cramming for the most important exam he'd ever take.

When his father arrived at three, Aaron came out to greet him, the brochure and his pile of research clutched in a steady hand.

"I found my college." He handed the brochure to his father.

Jim Seavers glanced at it with a dubious expression, but when he read the name, he raised his eyebrows in mild interest. "Not bad. A bit pedestrian, but adequate." His steel-blue gaze lifted to hold Aaron's. "Why did you choose it, Aaron?"

"It has an excellent teacher-to-student ratio, and all the teaching professors have full doctorate degrees, not just masters. It's ranked number twenty-two in its class by *U.S. News & World Report*. It's only an hour away and is under thirty thousand a year, which is hard to find in a decent private liberal arts college these days. It has several outstanding academic fields, including pre-med and pre-law."

Jim stared at his son for several seconds before giving Aaron his first real smile in years.

"Well done. I'm surprised but impressed. We'll fill out the application tomorrow morning and submit it. Shouldn't be a problem getting you through the hoops if it does turn out they're a bit full, as one of my partners did his undergraduate degree there and could help us grease the right palms." Jim tossed the stack of careful research aside. "Saint Timothy it is."

The hollow space inside Aaron unknotted, easing into hope.

Chapter Four

UNFORTUNATELY AARON'S THOROUGHNESS in his case for Saint Timothy somehow solidified Jim Seavers's belief that Aaron's focus in college would be pre-law. Jim filled out Aaron's course schedule online, declaring Aaron's major as a double Business and English. His father's managing didn't end there, though. Instead of spending the summer hiding out in the condo as he'd planned, trying to finally compose a Facebook message to Giles or at least simply ask to be added as a friend, Aaron all but lived at his dad's law firm, organizing the file room.

"You need to get your feet wet," Jim said every morning as he dragged Aaron out of bed. "Get in there and get a feel for law, for what the discipline will demand of you. You have a lot of catching up to do. There's a chance you could actually make something of yourself with this path."

Aaron planned to change his major to undecided and move himself to nothing but gen ed courses once he was on the ground, his father too distracted by work to notice. From what he'd been able to learn by being at the firm so much, his dad was likely to go off to the California office soon for anything from two to six months.

The good thing was Aaron *had* gotten into Saint Timothy. His grades were solid, and they liked his entrance essays so well they gave him a scholarship. Despite the late hour, Aaron got three thousand a year shaved off as some kind of renewable coupon so long as he kept a 3.5 GPA. His dorm was Titus, which apparently was some Bible name, and his roommate was Elijah Prince.

Aaron's email exchanges with his roommate were weird. Aaron tried his best to connect, asking questions about Elijah's interests, his hometown, anything he could think of, but Elijah's answers were short and...a little creepy.

I'm from South Dakota. I enjoy spending time with my family and my church group. I don't know what I'll major in yet. I'm still praying about it.

Aaron twitched at the idea of his roommate praying about his major—Aaron and his mom were slight scandals in Oak Grove for not going to church, but honestly, religion gave Aaron the heebie-jeebies. He started to worry Saint Timothy was more religious than he was ready for. They had a big thing on the website about being open to all faiths, but did that include none?

Good God, what if his roommate wanted to pray *with him*?

As July wore on and August crept around the corner, Aaron worried whether or not he'd done the right thing, going to Saint Timothy. He feared his roommate's weirdness was a sign of greater obstacles to come. He'd chosen his source of secondary education based on sex at a lake with a guy he'd only just met, a guy who might be disgusted to see him again. How had he ever thought this would end well?

As orientation drew closer, Aaron's anxiety ramped up so high he could barely function. He stopped eating except when his father bullied him into it, and at the office he hid in the corner of the basement storage room whenever someone wasn't checking up on him. He curled up with his phone, listened to music and played digital solitaire with a fever that did little to bleed off the desperation in his heart.

This was how Aaron met Walter Lucas.

Walter was an intern from the University of Minnesota. He had a brightness and focus Aaron envied. The two of them had spoken occasionally at the coffeemaker, and once Aaron had helped him organize a set of briefs in the conference room, but otherwise Walter was nothing more than another guy in the office.

This changed the day Walter came downstairs and Aaron didn't get up to pretend he was working. Aaron had been so absorbed in his game while Florence crooned to him through his noise-canceling headphones that he hadn't realized he was being observed until Walter stood over him, head cocked to one side as he took in Aaron with a critical eye.

Aaron guiltily pulled off his headphones and tucked his phone away. "Sorry. I was taking a break. Can I help you with something?"

Walter studied Aaron a few more seconds. "I'm

about to make a run for lunch because my fiancé had to bail on our date. Would you like to come along?"

Aaron wouldn't, but he couldn't think of an excuse to give. "Sure. Where do you want to go?"

"Wherever. I figure we'll haunt the skywalks until something looks good." Smiling, Walter extended a hand. "Here, let me help you up."

The law office was in a converted bank building in downtown Minneapolis, the main atrium now a common area between six different businesses, connect-ed to the rat's maze of the Minneapolis Skyway System. Aaron could barely find his way to the parking garage without his dad, but Walter navigated the internal passages with ease, chatting up Aaron as they went.

"So you're off to college next month, right? To the place Bob went—where is it again?"

Aaron wrapped his arms around himself, colder than ever despite the heat of the bridge. "Saint Timo-thy."

"Yes, that's it. Bob keeps telling me you're in for great times."

Aaron hoped so. "Where did you go to school?"

"Northwestern, Hope University, and the Universi-ty of Minnesota St. Paul. I'm heading into the law school at the U of M in September."

Great, so Walter was handsome, put together, *and* brilliant. "How many degrees do you have?"

"Not even one until they hand me my diploma at the end of the month. After I did a month at North-western, I dropped out to help my mom, went to Hope for two years, then moved up here for the rest of undergrad. I'm hoping to stick to one place for grad school."

Well, Aaron didn't feel *quite* so bad at not being able to pick a college now. "I didn't know you could switch around like that."

"I don't think it's generally advised. I've spent the past few summers filling in blanks, and I had to go on overload both semesters at the U of M."

Aaron liked Walter. "So you're getting married? When?"

Walter groaned. "God, that's the million-dollar question. I wanted October, because who doesn't love fall, but Kelly said there's no way he's having a wedding in the middle of midterms. My guess is we'll end up in June with the other eight million anniversaries."

Aaron tripped when he thought he'd heard Walter refer to Kelly as *he*. "Your fiancé is still in college too?"

"Yeah, he'll be a junior this fall." Walter waggled eyebrows at him suggestively. "You leaving behind a string of brokenhearted high school girls, or are you doing the thing where you try to bridge the gap between high school and college?" When Aaron experienced a brief paralysis, thinking of Giles on the shores of Hickey Lake, Walter laughed and patted him on the back, his touch lingering ever so slightly in a not-straight way, like he'd welcomed Aaron into a club. "*Ha.* I thought so. But you're not out to your dad, so I'll keep mum."

Aaron stopped walking. "How—?"

Walter leaned against a nearby railing. "You're newly out to *yourself*. Makes more sense, actually."

They stood in the middle of a small mall area, three levels of open balcony next to them. Walter kept his voice down so their conversation was muffled by the piped-in music and din of the crowd.

"Gaydar isn't about what you're wearing or how limp your wrists are. It's how you cruise, which is why sometimes women get it and straight men *never* do. A straight guy will meet your eye, but he'll make a quick decision on whether or not you're higher on the food chain than he is, and he'll dominate or defer as appropriate. He'll do that without thinking because we're talking total reptilian brain here."

"But gay men...don't do that?"

"Oh no, we do—but we give a second glance to cruise. Older men and guys who grew up in Homophobic Assholeland cruise so fast you almost miss it. In our generation, there's two camps. My tribe grew up in suburban settings where gay-straight alliances were standard fare and overt homophobia was greeted with the same disdain as racism—we're a little braver when we cruise. But some guys our age come from conservative backgrounds. Not necessarily told they're bad but still aware they're *other*. They leave the nest eager and starry-eyed, and they're green as lettuce. At college in your first year you'll get a bit of both, guys just off the truck and guys like me who *love* fresh produce and hone in for a sample. Well, not anymore, but that was how I rolled." He paused, looking thoughtful. "I guess I should say there's a third camp: the guys from Homophobic Assholeland with Homophobic Asshole parents. They're...their own breed, and it's seldom pretty. But to answer your question, I suspected you were gay because you cruised me."

"I did?" Aaron drew back, embarrassed, but Walter only laughed.

"Hon, don't. I'm flattered. It was fast, and it was mostly you clocking me, going, *hot guy in the building*. For the record, I did the same thing to you. I may be monogamous now, but it doesn't mean I don't admire a nice view."

Aaron blushed. "Thanks?"

"You bet your ass thanks. God, I'd have had you flat on your back, pants at your knees within an hour."

Aaron's cheeks became a furnace that possibly raised the temperature of the atrium five degrees.

Walter laughed. "Sorry, I'll behave." He nodded to the food court. "Let's go eat. I'm starving. Chipotle okay?"

Aaron followed Walter in a kind of fog, trying to process everything until suddenly it was his turn to order. When he got to the cash register he didn't realize Walter had paid for both their meals until it was too late.

"Please. Kelly would swat me right now if he saw how freaked out I've made you. The least I can do is pay for your lunch." Walter indicated a table in the corner. "Let's sit and talk."

At first it wasn't bad, Walter asking what he did for fun, commiserating over Florence and Keane, arguing over the audio quality of Bose vs. Beats headphones. But all too soon Walter went for the subject they kept dancing around.

"You were upset about something in the file room."

Aaron fixed his gaze on his napkin, worrying the edge into ragged strips with his fingers. "I'm nervous about going to college."

He waited for Walter to give platitudes, to tell him everyone was nervous and Aaron would be fine.

Walter arched an eyebrow. "Why am I thinking this has something to do with a guy?"

Aaron dropped his napkin. "Why—why—what—?"

Walter leaned forward and touched Aaron's arm. "Hey—it's okay. You don't have to talk about it if you don't want to. But if you do want, I'd love to listen."

To Aaron's surprise, he found he *did* want to talk. Except he didn't just tell Walter about Giles. He told him *everything*.

He told Walter about Tanner.

"We were friends since grade school, and in middle school we started a band together with a couple other guys. Tanner and I wrote all the music. I composed, he did the lyrics. I think it probably sucked, but we had a good time. I'd taken a lot of theory too, and I taught myself from the internet. He did too. It was our thing we did together. Then…I don't know when exactly, but things started changing. Tanner and I had always been close, but we started to feel *really* close. We touched a lot. Sometimes I thought he wanted to kiss me, but nothing ever happened."

When Aaron paused too long, Walter spoke. "Until one day something did."

Aaron couldn't meet Walter's gaze. "It was a slumber party. We got into his dad's liquor cabinet. The other two boys fell asleep, but Tanner and I stayed awake. He kissed me, and we went to his room. Made out a little." He paused, remembering the bittersweet moment. "It was amazing, beautiful, everything I'd ever wanted, but all of a sudden he got up, freaked out, and told me to go home. He hasn't spoken to me since."

Walter's mouth thinned into a line. "Yeah, there are plenty of guys like that. Tanner's gay, or at least bi or flexible, and he's not sure it's okay to be a baby-bit queer. Orientation is not a line in the sand, and that's the next big wave coming: generations of young people facing their childhood same-sex friends and considering them potential lovers because it's not total social death to do so anymore. It's not always going to be pretty, either. Tanner wants this but is flipped out over it, and you made him face something he didn't want to."

"But he started it. I wouldn't ever have—"

Walter stroked Aaron's hand. "I know, hon. In his head, though, all you had to do is exist."

Aaron's chest hurt. "That's not fair."

"No, it isn't. Honestly, a lot of misery comes from only half the country thinking it's okay to love whoever you want. Sure, I can legally marry Kelly in Minnesota, and the Feds will recognize it too, but now the bigots are even angrier. Until they die off and gay is just another way to be, guys like you and Tanner don't only go through the hell of adolescent attraction, you do it with a gun at your head."

That was exactly how it felt. "Me and Tanner, but not you?"

"Please. I was born fierce." Walter took Aaron's hand, squeezing it briefly. "I'm sorry that was your first experience, Aaron. I hope your second one is better."

Aaron became very interested in his burrito wrapper. "Well…actually, I've had a second one already." He swallowed hard and looked up at Walter.

Walter gazed back, patient and kind. "A bit better, this one?"

"Yeah. But I was an idiot and didn't get his number, and I can't work up the courage to send him a note online." He drew a deep breath before confessing the rest. "He's the reason I decided to go to Saint Timothy."

Walter's smile made Aaron feel like he'd been folded into somebody's arms. "Tell me about this guy."

Aaron did. He told Walter all about Giles, about how they'd met because Aaron was hiding and Giles was running from someone who wanted to beat him up. He told Walter about Giles offering to get something to eat when he found out Aaron hadn't had dinner, how he'd paid since it had been Aaron's birthday, how he'd taken him to Hickey Lake—Walter laughed, but mostly he kept smiling. With his ears red to their tips, Aaron confessed how they'd had sex, how it had felt being with Giles. "He made me feel good. Bought me dinner, took care of me."

"He didn't give you his number though?"

Aaron grimaced. "I didn't really give him a chance. I was leaving the next day, and he had no idea I would choose to go to his same school." The question he ached to ask poured out of him. "Was that incredibly stupid? Have I fucked up my entire life because a guy smiled at me and blew me by the lake on my birthday?"

Walter had a funny look on his face, nostalgia and empathy and…something else. "I think it's a hard call. Play it easy when you get there. Don't beat yourself up if it turns out to be a bad gamble, but don't write anything off too fast either. Most importantly, though…" he pulled a business card out of his jacket pocket and slid it across the table, "…stay in touch with me."

WHEN GILES ARRIVED at Saint Timothy College, he half-considered kissing the lawn in front of his dorm.

Summer in Oak Grove had been hot, boring, and interminable. He reread every novel he owned, played so much Xbox he thought his brains might leak out of his ears, and practiced violin and sometimes even piano, he was so bored. Basically, he marked time until his life could begin.

He deliberately didn't think about his midsummer adventure at Hickey Lake.

The one highlight had been his frequent IM chats with Brian, his roommate-to-be. At first they'd talked about pretty boring stuff, like who was bringing what, but when Giles mentioned his gaming system, this had unleashed the kraken. Brian was a major gamer. He played more first-person shooter while Giles preferred strategy, but their Switzerland was Minecraft. They met all August via Xbox Live to kill Creepers and harass Endermen, and haunted the same online servers.

They'd already hatched a plan to bring in takeout from Noodles & Company and spend the first night of college introducing each other to their favorite games. Giles couldn't wait.

Best part? Brian was straight, knew Giles wasn't, and didn't give two shits.

Brian was as cool in person as online. When Giles and his family came up with their first set of boxes, Brian greeted Giles with a warm smile and a man hug.

"I can't believe we're finally here." Brian put his hands on the back of his head and grinned up at the canopy of trees above them as they crossed campus to go to orientation. "I hope it doesn't turn out to be as dumb as high school. My older brother says it isn't, that the stupid popular kids don't have the same kind of foothold here." He lowered his hands and glanced at Giles. "When is your orchestra tryout?"

"At five. I have to head over there after orientation, actually. Which, shit, I should have brought my violin with me."

Brian waved this worry away. "I'll bring it to you on my way to the parking lot to go get our dinner. Of course I think it might be faster for me to walk to the store, and I'm not kidding. Did you see how far away M lot is?"

Giles snorted. "Try P lot. I'm west and half a mile from M."

They split up as they stood in line to check in at the student union, meeting up in the back to find a seat in the packed room.

Brian shook his head. "Look at all these people.

And this is just freshmen."

"Mina's in here somewhere—my friend from home. I was supposed to find her, but I have no idea how."

"Text?"

Giles pulled out his phone and grimaced. "God, there's no LTE. I don't have a signal at all. And no Wi-Fi. What the hell?"

"Try the hallway. Maybe they have the walls lined with lead or something. I see three seats up ahead—I'll snag them for us, okay?"

After watching where Brian pointed, Giles slipped into the main hallway, where he still didn't have much signal but did have enough service to send a text.

The crowd pouring into the ballroom didn't look like a high school crowd. There was a lot less diversity of class—more people of color, but also a distinct evening out of social strata which, honestly, felt a bit weird, as if Giles had entered a gated community. The lack of cliques was visible and almost jarring—people herded up, but not much and not often.

A cute twink across the room cruised Giles with a stealth intensity he found intriguing. The guy was so slight a wind would take him away, and he wasn't exactly cute, all severe hair and pale skin. There was something about the way his eyes bored into Giles, though, writing all kinds of checks and inviting Giles to cash them. Before Giles could engage, the twink's mother turned around to face her son, and the guy shut down so fast Giles blinked.

Ah. Not out to Mom and Dad. *Find you later,* Giles

promised him with a wink.

He'd just had his first college flirt, and nobody was going to jump him for it or call him fag. Nobody thought he was a man-whore or a saint—or anything. No one here knew who Giles was.

A dark head moved in the crowd, and when Giles caught a glimpse of the face, he paused.

God, but that looked like...

Without meaning to, he followed the guy through the crush. When he caught another glimpse, his world tilted sideways.

No. Way.

Giles had to have imagined what he'd thought he'd seen, because there was no way... Not *him*. Not *here*. But when the crowd parted, he got a clear line of sight, and he swayed on his feet.

Aaron Seavers.

Mina forgotten, Giles fought his way through the crowd. He kept telling himself he had to be wrong, but he *remembered* that face. He remembered that face screwed up in ecstasy, in fact.

Remembered it shuttering and turning away.

How could Aaron be here? *Why* would Aaron be here?

In his pocket, his phone buzzed, and Giles stopped his pursuit long enough to peek at the incoming text from Mina. *Where r u?*

Giles thumbed a reply before resuming his chase across the foyer. He could still see Aaron's dark head in the crush. He had no idea what he was going to do if he caught up with Aaron, but he had to follow. He felt off-kilter and slightly underwater.

The dark head shifted. Aaron Seavers stared back at Giles.

It was as if Oak Grove had tossed out some kind of grappling hook, and with that one glance from Aaron, the barbs found their way back in. There it was, the old, familiar gaze. The one that said, *We've made out, and now I'm freaked.* The glance that always, *always* came before the name-calling and terrorizing, the demonizing of Giles, the Great Tempter. The look that should have stayed behind in Oak Grove yet managed to follow him here.

Giles could see his future unfolding—Aaron telling his friends about Giles, turning them on him, roping them into their taunts and games. A-Hell all over again.

Mina was right after all, high school and college would be the same. No escape, no way out.

No. No fucking way.

Giles glared at Aaron, giving no quarter.

This is my school. This is my escape, and you aren't ruining it. Go back to your closet and hide, fucker, because I have no more patience for shame-and-blames.

With everything he had in him, Giles telegraphed his fury and indignation—and weirdly, for half a second he thought Aaron seemed hurt. Then that pretty face shuttered back to the mask Giles had known so well in high school. Aaron turned away.

Giles hunted for Mina, but he couldn't push Aaron out of his thoughts. The guy was an infection in his mind, erasing Giles's beautiful bubble of possibility and reminding him the world, by and large, sucked. When

Mina found him, she frowned.

"What's wrong?"

"Nothing." Giles forced a smile. "We're at college. New leaf. New start. Nothing's going to hold me back." He nodded at Brian, who waved at them. "Let's go get our seats."

Nothing's going to hold me back, he repeated to himself as he settled into his seat, his gaze falling on Aaron a few rows over. *Nothing and nobody. No matter what.*

Chapter Five

AARON REALLY HOPED nobody said anything important in orientation because he didn't hear a single word of it.

It hurt so much to have Giles reject him. They'd only made out the once—and as Walter kept saying, this was a gamble. It did hurt, though, so much Aaron couldn't breathe, and he didn't know how to make the pain stop. When orientation dismissed to smaller groups for their tours of campus, Aaron went to the restroom and curled up on the seat inside a stall for several minutes, blaring "No Light, No Light" through his headphones until he could breathe again.

By the time he emerged, all the orientation groups were gone. While part of him was relieved, it meant he had no idea what to do with himself. He could go to his room, but odds were good Elijah would be there now. Aaron wasn't in the mood for any more bad encounters. He could go somewhere and eat, but he wasn't hungry. Getting drunk sounded *fantastic*, but he had no way to get alcohol.

In the end he wandered aimlessly around campus, giving himself a tour that largely involved watching for Giles so he wouldn't run into him. As he passed the activity-fair booths, an eager, overweight young man with a crazed look in his eye tried to give Aaron a cross-splattered flyer for Campus Crusaders. Aaron murmured a decline and glommed on to a group heading with purpose out of the fair. Putting his headphones on, Aaron followed the herd and let his music drown out the world.

At some point his group wandered into the music department. Realizing he might encounter Giles here, Aaron thought about leaving, but the hallways were crammed tight. Following this tour would be easier than fighting the clog at the entrance. When their slow forward shuffle came to a full stop, Aaron loitered against the wall, arms folded.

A girl next to him glanced down at papers in her hand when she wasn't looking around the hallway. As Aaron watched, her gaze switched to a set of double doors ahead of them. She pulled out a cell phone. After a series of furious texts, she stood rigid a second, then started to shake. When tears rolled down her cheeks, Aaron couldn't stop himself.

Taking off his headphones, he touched her arm. "Are you okay?"

She wiped at her eyes. "My accompanist can't make it. Her daughter got sick. I'm going to blow my audition. I'm not going to make it into choir."

Choir? Aaron took another glance at the papers in her hands, crinkled by her stress—sheet music. He regarded the now *seriously* thick crush of people with new eyes. "Is that what this is? The line for auditions?"

The girl nodded, still wiping her eyes. She couldn't

stop crying. "For the Saint Timothy Chorale. For guys it's not much of a contest. All you have to do is show up and prove you can stay on key. For girls it's brutal. Half of us will have to go into the Women's Chorus, which is a total ghetto. Not like the Ambassadors at all."

"Ambassadors?"

"The men's a cappella group." The girl eyed Aaron suspiciously. "Why are you here if you're not auditioning?"

Aaron was not going to admit what a fuckup he was. He indicated her sheet music. "Can I see that?" When she handed it over, he flipped through it and smiled. "Hey, this isn't hard at all. If you want, I could play for you."

He thought for an awkward moment she was going to kiss him. "Are you serious?"

"I warn you, I'll probably stumble a bit. But I figure this is about you, and I'm good enough to fake it." He grimaced at the door. "I wish I'd thought to sign up myself."

"Oh, you don't sign up. You stand in this line with your music." Her expression turned melty. "You're amazing. I totally owe you for doing this." She let go of his arm and held out her hand. "I'm Jill Ottosen. But you can call me Jilly."

"Aaron Seavers." Aaron wasn't comfortable with the overly friendly look in her eye. He was *not* dating a girl again.

"So you're going to audition too, right?"

He wished. "I don't have any music."

"Use mine. Though maybe that's too tricky, playing and singing?"

"Oh no, not at all." Aaron considered his performance options. "Does it matter what I play? I have some stuff memorized, but it's pop."

"Don't worry about that. Like I said, if you're a guy who can hit the notes, you're in. It's a lot more difficult to get into the Ambassadors, but that's only sixteen guys and mostly upperclassmen anyway." She bounced a little. "I can't believe I stumbled into an accompanist in line for auditions. I hope we're both in chorale together." Rocking on her heels, she glanced ahead at the line. "I'm starving. I should have grabbed dinner first." She smiled apologetically. "Sorry, I'm a total spaz when I'm nervous. I can't stop talking."

Jilly was cute and sweet. It occurred to Aaron how convenient it would be if he found her attractive, because he could ask her to dinner after the audition, and they might even end up dating. Aaron knew that route wasn't for him, though. He wasn't sure he was ready to be out, but he wasn't lying anymore.

"How was your orientation tour?" she asked.

"I didn't go," Aaron confessed.

"Wish I'd skipped. Totally worthless. What about your roommate?"

"I haven't met him." Realizing their conversation was almost one-sided, he forced himself into a more active role. "What about yours?"

Jilly shrugged. "She's nice enough. A little fussy, but I'm hoping that's just nerves. She's from some small town up north."

Aaron asked where Jilly was from—Mankato—and they spent the rest of their wait chatting easily about their pasts. Jilly's parents were divorced as well, but she had three younger siblings. Aaron asked about them, and that opened a floodgate that lasted until they were standing in front of the double doors, waiting their chance to go in. As soon as she was about to perform, however, Jilly's panic returned in full force.

"I'm going to suck."

"You'll be fine. Hey—it's only an audition. And if it helps, I'll be there the whole time."

She nodded, but she still looked pretty wrecked. "I really want this."

"Then go get it. Being nervous isn't going to help." He remembered his horrible encounter with Giles, and his stomach plummeted. He repeated to her what Walter had said to him. "Maybe it's meant to be, and maybe it isn't, but you need to try. Go in there and be fabulous, whatever the outcome."

Before she could reply, the doors opened, and an upperclassman ushered them in.

The room was smaller than Aaron had thought it would be. Most of the space was tiered riser seating full of black chairs, though only a few of them were occupied. A mustachioed man sat in a chair in the middle, flanked by two young women and three men. One guy had a slight geek-cool thing going, another was fresh off the cover of J.Crew, and the third was all angles and styled hair—and a pair of dark sunglasses. They were all cute, an assorted-chocolates box of young men.

The mustachioed man had to be the conductor—

he was older and had a sense of ownership about the room. When he spied Aaron and Jilly, though, he was a welcoming king, rising and shaking both their hands.

"So good to have you here." He asked for their names and where they were from and what kind of history they had with choir, and as Aaron and Jilly answered, the men and women behind him took notes.

The geek-cool guy spoke up. "Dr. Nussenbaum, are they both auditioning?"

"Yes," Jilly said before Aaron could answer. "Aaron is accompanying for me, but he has something to perform too."

"Fantastic." Dr. Nussenbaum beamed at Aaron. "Were you in the choir in high school?"

"Before we moved, yeah." Aaron tried not to fidget, but Nussenbaum was a laser beam, and he had so much energy he made Aaron jittery. "I was in a band too, but that never got anywhere."

"You play piano, you sing, and you were in a band—do you play any other instruments?"

"Keyboard, piano, and a little bit of bass guitar, but not well."

"Excellent. Are either of you music majors?"

"I'm music education," Jilly volunteered.

"I don't really know yet," Aaron confessed.

"Everyone is welcome in choir." Nussenbaum rubbed his hands together. "All right. Shall we get started? Jillian first?"

Jilly's song was a stodgy piece that reminded Aaron of things people took to all-state competitions. He'd accompanied for those before he'd moved, and he found he missed this, playing for someone. He enjoyed filling in their spaces, being their ground floor. Jilly was good too—no Adele, but better than average. Aaron hoped she made it in.

When her audition was over, Jilly took a seat. The room focused on Aaron.

He cleared his throat and scooted back on the bench. "I was going to do a pop song, if that's okay."

Dr. Nussenbaum's smile didn't waver. "That's fine."

"What song?" This question came from J.Crew guy, and Aaron had to swallow before answering. The man had a deep, bell-like voice that did wicked things to Aaron's insides.

"I know two pretty well. 'Lover to Lover' by Florence + the Machine and 'Somewhere Only We Know' by Keane."

The guy's eyebrows went up, but he smiled. "I'd love to hear the Keane." He motioned to the piano. "Whenever you're ready."

It only took a few bars of piano before Aaron's nerves bled away. When he'd played this with the band, it was a different kind of accompaniment, but he'd taken to playing it in his room, filling in the missing instruments by ear with his voice piped in via a mic. It had been his therapy after the whole Tanner incident, until he'd stopped playing entirely once they moved. He threw himself into the song now, maybe belting a bit too much in the chorus. It felt so good to sing again. He hoped Jilly was right about the guys' auditions, because while he sang, for the first time since he'd arrived, being at Saint Timothy felt okay.

When he finished, he lowered his hands from the piano and faced his audience.

They were staring at him.

Aaron froze, uneasy, thinking he must have really sucked. He was trying to work out an apology when the guy with the sunglasses spoke. "Thank you, Aaron. Were you planning to audition for the Ambassadors as well?"

Aaron's cheeks heated. "Do you want me to sing the Florence song, or does it need to be something fancier?"

"Your performance just now is more than enough," the sunglasses guy said. Every word dripped with innuendo. The deep-voiced guy had been pleasant, but *this* guy, Aaron was pretty sure, cruised him. "If you're interested in the Ambassadors, we'd love to have you."

They would? Aaron shifted nervously on his seat. "Okay. Thanks."

"Thank *you*." This came from Nussenbaum, who sat on the edge of his seat, regarding Aaron like a tiger eyeing prey. "You haven't declared a major? Is anything in music on the table for you?"

God, his dad would *flip out*. "I hadn't thought much about anything, to be honest."

"Stop by during my office hours tomorrow, and we'll talk." Nussenbaum eased back in his chair, as if everything were settled.

"We need to keep the auditions moving," a girl beside Nussenbaum said.

J.Crew guy rose, leading Jilly and Aaron to a door

on the other side of the room. "You were great. Both of you."

"Thanks." Jilly touched her hair. "I hope I see you in choir."

He winked at her. "Pretty sure you both will." After waving at them both, he disappeared into the room.

Jilly and Aaron stared at the closed door a moment.

"God, he's seriously cute," Jilly said at last.

"Yeah," Aaron agreed without thinking. When he realized what he'd confessed, he went rigid.

Jilly simply smiled, almost easing a little if anything. Then she held out her arm. "Come on. It's time for a celebration dinner."

Letting out the breath he'd been holding, Aaron took her arm, and Jilly led him away.

GILES DIDN'T SEE Aaron again after the glimpse in the hallway outside of orientation, but he watched for him constantly. As they left orchestra tryouts, Mina asked him what was wrong.

"For someone who killed it at his orchestra audition, you don't look happy." She nudged him with her elbow. "You keep glancing around like you're waiting for the boogeyman. What's going on?"

"I saw someone I didn't expect to be here. It's no big deal." A lie, but he was working on making it truth.

"Who did you see?"

"Someone from Oak Grove."

Mina nudged him harder. "*Who?*"

He started to deflect as usual, but apparently college

was different, because instead of hemming and hawing, Giles told the truth. "Aaron Seavers."

"*Get out.* I had no idea he was coming here." She paused as she put two and two together. "Wait. Why is Aaron Seavers at Timothy upsetting to you?"

Apparently once unmuzzled, Giles was a babbling brook. "Because he got drunk and came on to me at Catherine's party. We made out, and now he's weird. And here."

Mina stopped walking, mouth hanging open.

Tucking his violin to his side, Giles faced her. Every secret he'd kept since seventh grade threatened to come pouring out of him. He did his best to control the flow. "Aaron and I fucked. Half the guys you've crushed on, I've fucked, in fact, or sucked off. After, they go strange, and I end up dodging threats. Now Aaron is one of them, and I'm so pissed I can't see straight."

Mina staggered back a few steps. "Giles?"

He should stop talking, but he couldn't. "This is why I never wanted to go to parties. This is why I hated A-H, why I wanted out. It was *supposed to be different here*, and now it's the same." He fisted his hand in his hair. "*Goddamn it.* Why did he come here? He said he hadn't picked a college. I *told* him I was going here. *I don't get it.*"

Mina smoothed a lock of long black hair behind her ear. "So you and Aaron Seavers had a thing."

"Yes. And now it's going to be awful."

"That you were ringleader in some A-H sex club is a surprise, but why Aaron being here means—"

"*Because it's what they do, Min.* They follow me,

they fuck me, then they bully me."

He'd thrown her off her game at first, but now she was back in bulldog mode. "He knew you'd be here and picked his college *after* you told him. Why would he pay nearly thirty grand a year to make your life hell? Also, how was it he hadn't picked his school in June?"

"He was all nervous about his dad. Or something. I don't remember. He was drunk." *And I was infatuated.* Giles sat on a nearby bench, hunching his body forward over his violin case. "He was sweet. He was cute and sweet, and I'd already been crushing on him. I fell hard, Min. I fell for him, and then he went stone cold after, like they always do."

Mina sat beside him. "Maybe it's more complicated than that. Maybe…maybe he came here for *you*."

Giles broke out of his reverie of misery long enough to give her a withering glare.

She swatted his arm. "I'm serious. Why else would he go to Timothy?"

"Pre-med, pre-law, music, scholarship, alumni friend pulled him a string, close to home—"

"*Fine.* Probably one of those things is the reason. But I doubt he came to harass you. If he was that freaked out and he knew you were coming here, this would be the *last* place he'd go."

"Maybe he didn't have a choice. Maybe his dad forced him to come here, and now—"

"Okay, *stop.* Now you're spinning conspiracy theories."

"You don't know what it's like, Min—"

"Tell me, and find out if I know." Her voice was

sharp, and Giles could hear the hurt beneath her anger. "Clearly you haven't told me all kinds of things. Tell me now. Unless this is some big gay club secret you can't share?"

"It's not a secret." He toed his sneaker into an ant-hill in the crack of the sidewalk. "What was I supposed to say, though? Golly gee, Tim Linden blew me after biology?"

Her jaw fell open. "*Seriously?* Tim Linden is *gay?*"

Giles's stomach hollowed out. "Maybe not. Some of them I think just wanted sex, and they didn't care how it happened—until after. I was really big with the Abstinence Club. As if I wasn't really sex." He nudged some of the anthill back into place. "That's why I never told you. You were all sweet virgin, dreaming of kissing the guys I was getting hot and bothered with."

"What, so you were mocking me?"

"*No.*" He stopped messing with the anthill and rested his forehead on the top of his case. "Not mock-ing you. I…I don't know why I couldn't. I was as bad as them, I guess. If I didn't talk about it, it wasn't real."

He felt Mina's hand on his leg. "What happened with Aaron?"

Giles lifted his gaze to stare at the sidewalk leading to his dorm. "For half a second I thought he was different, but then he got the deer-in-the-headlights look they all do, and he ran off without a goddamned word. Today when I saw him, he stared at me like I was an axe murderer." He put his head down. "I can't go through this bullshit again."

"Then ignore him. If he really is an ass, ignore him." Mina rubbed circles on his neck. "I still think maybe he came here for you."

"If he did, it's the stupidest reason in the world to choose a college."

"It'd be terribly romantic. I always thought he was a sweet guy. I could totally see it."

Unbidden, Giles replayed the moments when they'd talked in the car, when he'd thought much the same thing. "He's shy, but he's scared. Scared guys aren't good news, and scared guys who think I'll out them are the worst of all."

It upset Giles that Mina had no rejoinder, no more Pollyanna comebacks. Too late, he realized he'd kept her in the dark because he *needed* her eternal optimism.

"It can't be the same as A-H," she said at last. "You're right, it's unlikely he came here for you, but I don't think he's necessarily going to go apeshit on you. There's no way he has a gang of thugs already, and while he is bigger than you, I think the two of us could take him."

Giles's hands tightened on the cloth of his case, digging into the hard shell beneath. "Every time I see him will be a reminder of how I thought he was different but wasn't."

Mina leaned her head on his shoulder.

Giles wallowed in his misery, the ghosts of his past hovering over his beautiful, shiny future. He thought of the intense twink at orientation, closed his eyes, and imagined getting lucky without strings for a change.

He tried, but when he closed his eyes, all he saw was Aaron staring at him: gorgeous, beautiful, and afraid.

Chapter Six

AFTER THE CHOIR tryout, Aaron and Jilly wandered the mini campus town west of Saint Timothy and had dinner at a pseudo-French bistro. They talked about choir, about their classes, about life. Aaron had more fun with her than he'd ever had with a girl, probably because every other time he'd hung out with a girl, he'd been on a date. This was not a date. Jilly made no moon-eyes at him, never touched his hand, or flirted. It was a profound relief, but eventually he felt he had to address the elephant sitting in the middle of their booth.

"What I said at the tryouts. About the upperclassman being hot." Aaron had to let the words ring in his head a moment before he went on. "That's...only the second time I've admitted out loud I'm gay."

The third, he amended inside his own head. Because probably begging Giles to fuck him counted.

Jilly's soft, warm hand closed over his. "I'm honored you felt you could trust me. I won't tell anyone if you don't want me to."

"I don't want to keep it a secret, but I still freak when I think about coming out." Self-consciousness got the better of him. "Sorry, you don't know me well enough to have to hear all this."

"Stop. Of course I want to hear all this. You're my choir angel. You're nuts if you think I don't want a chance to rescue you right back, even this little bit."

It wasn't little to Aaron. "Thanks."

"Have you thought about joining the LGBT group on campus? I mean, going there is likely the same as coming out, but I doubt they have the meetings in the middle of the student union with a big sign advertising *here are the gays*. You'd meet some people in your same boat."

He'd thought of checking them out, but after Giles's reception... "There's this guy here. From my hometown—he might go to those meetings."

Jilly's face fell. "An ex? Oh, that sucks. What a bummer you both ended up at Timothy."

No way was he confessing he'd followed Giles here. "It's okay. I think for now I'd rather keep things to myself. Well, and you."

"Absolutely." She smiled, and Aaron felt good, like maybe between choir and Jilly, things would work out after all.

It was eight before he returned to his dorm, and as he approached his room, he could hear movement inside. Apparently Elijah had finally arrived. Trying not to be nervous, he opened the door. "Hello?"

A svelte young man ducked out from behind a stack of boxes, steadying them with a delicate gesture when they threatened to teeter. His eyes were hard and critical as he scanned Aaron up and down, and whatever he saw made the young man tense.

Aaron offered a nervous wave. "You must be Elijah. I'm Aaron. Did you just get in? Can I help you with anything?"

"I'm fine." Elijah kept his grip on his boxes as if he thought Aaron might try to take them.

Not sure of what to do, Aaron went to sit on his bed, thumbing through his phone as his roommate unpacked in total silence. It was odd how they didn't talk, but what was weirder was the more Elijah moved, the more Aaron thought his roommate *had* to be gay too. There wasn't any of the second-look stuff Walter had told him about, but if there was a poster boy for swishy gay stereotype, it was Elijah. Walter said stereotypes didn't count, but...man.

The conviction made Aaron slightly crazy, because if Elijah thought Aaron might be judgmental of him, by rights all Aaron had to do was say, "Hey, I'm gay too," and they'd be fine.

Except he couldn't figure out how to say it without being a tool. Also, he wasn't sure he was ready for gay confession number four. Not today.

When Elijah began to unpack a box full of religious stuff—a cross, a Lord's Prayer in a frame, what appeared to be several different Bibles or Bible-like books—Aaron was glad he'd kept quiet. He didn't know what to make of Elijah shoving all the religious stuff in the bottom drawer of his desk, but at that point Aaron decided the best thing to do would be to put in his headphones and check out. He watched some YouTube, played solitaire. He was about to go brush his teeth and head to bed at an embarrassingly early hour when a text came through from Walter.

Hey, tiger. How's your first night? How's the room-mate?

Aaron glanced over at Elijah, who was arranging his underwear in lined-up rolls inside his dresser drawer. *Weird.*

Walter's reply was swift. *What's he like? A big jock? A bruiser?*

Aaron almost laughed. *No. Small and incredibly effeminate. There's a lot of religious stuff.*

Joy. What kind of religious stuff?

Decorations and Bibles and things. Except he put them in a drawer, so I don't know what to think.

Aaron thought about telling him about the praying for a new major, but decided against it.

Walter typed a new message. *Enough of the weird roomie. Tell me about Giles. Did you run into him? How did it go?*

Aaron's gut hardened into rock. *Awful.*

Three seconds later, Aaron's phone rang. Elijah glared at him, and Aaron apologized as he put the phone to his ear. "You didn't have to call."

"Yes, I did." God, but it felt good to hear Walter's bright, sure voice. "You were so nervous about this meeting, and you just told me it was awful. What happened?" When Aaron paused, glancing sideways at Elijah, Walter read his mind. "Take a walk. Laundry room ought to be pretty vacant right about now."

"I don't know where it is."

"Great time to find out. Start walking, start talking."

Aaron fumbled for his keys and headed out the door. "Not much happened. But it wasn't great."

"Where did you see him? What did he say?"

"Nothing. We were at orientation, he looked like he wanted to kill me." The hallway was full of guys, so Aaron ducked into a stairwell. "That was it."

"What? Aaron, that's not so bad."

Aaron hunched over and slid down the wall. "You didn't see his face."

"Maybe you surprised him."

Aaron snorted. "Yeah. Not in a good way, either. He was *not* happy to see me. Not indifferent either. He was *pissed.*"

"Hmm."

Aaron could hear a movie playing in the background. He wasn't sure, but he thought he recognized a song. "Is that *The Little Mermaid*? Are you babysitting?"

Walter grunted. "No." The phone rustled, and the sounds from the movie went away. "I'm sorry Giles turned out to be a jerk, but don't let him get you down. Tell me about something else. Something good."

"I kind of accidentally joined choir." Walter laughed and demanded more, and Aaron told him the whole story of meeting Jilly and accompanying her, and of his own audition. "They asked if I wanted to try out for the guys-only group too, which apparently is hard to get into. I'm supposed to meet the director tomorrow. At least, I assume he's the director. Dr. Nussenbaum."

"Wait—*what*? Did you say you have a morning

meeting with *Nussy?*"

What? That was bad? "Uh…"

"Harvey Nussenbaum, one of the most famous Midwestern choral conductors. He did a benefit thing when I was in high school. A guy in our choir had a horrible accident, and his mom arranged for Nussy to come guest conduct our concert to lift his spirits. Nussenbaum was amazing, though a little high-strung. Never walked, at best did this kind of crazy scuffle. Usually he jogged." Walter laughed softly. "Goddamn, that was the best week of my senior year. So he's your conductor—*and* he wants to see you about music classes. You must have knocked your audition out of the park, sweetheart."

"I think I did okay. But it's not like I'm getting another scholarship or anything."

"You lit up like you never have, telling me your choir story. This is your joy. Follow it."

"Well, I can't major in music."

"Why the hell not?"

"My dad would never go for it."

"You're way overdue on some happy. Take this one and run." His voice gentled. "Forget Giles too. Go hang out at whatever college club-type hangout they have there, make eye contact with a few guys, and I bet you'll have a harem within half an hour."

The very idea of a harem made Aaron want to go to his room and duck under the covers. "You have to be nineteen to get into the Shack."

Walter's chuckle was evil. "Yeah, we'll fix that over your next break. In the meantime, flirt with the choir boys. Gotta be fish in a barrel there."

Aaron had no idea how to flirt. "I liked Giles, Walter." He swallowed as the barb tugged across his heart. "A lot."

"I know, honey. I'm sorry. But if he can treat you that way, he's not worth your time. There will be somebody better. I promise." This time Walter's laugh was soft and sad. "Hell, if a wiseass jerk like me can live happily ever after, anybody can. Maybe give it a few weeks, though. Let yourself heal. And when I come visit, I want you to point this guy out so I can deck him."

"No," Aaron said automatically.

"He was a total jerk to you. He took advantage of you, never contacted you after, and now when you show up at his college, he treats you like dirt. He's a fucking user."

"He was so nice, before."

"Yeah." Walter's tone was bitter. "That's how they do it. Sweet as sugar until they get what they want. Then you might as well not exist."

"So how will I ever know who the right guy is? Because it sure seemed real to me."

"Go make some friends, and don't worry about Guppy Giles or how to figure out boys. Our schedules are crazy right now, but Kel and I are coming sometime in October. If you need us before, you holler."

Aaron knew he was supposed to say *you don't have to do that,* but he couldn't make the words come out. "Thanks, Walter."

"Anytime. Except next time you have a shit-tastic

day, I expect *you* to text *me*."

"Okay," Aaron promised.

THE NEXT MORNING Aaron went to the music building to check on Nussenbaum's office hours. He made it as far as the front office before Nussy himself hurried out of a practice room.

"Aaron, good to see you." He gestured for Aaron to follow him as he jogged down the hall.

Not sure if he should do the same, Aaron compromised with a brisk walk.

Nussenbaum led him into what Aaron presumed was the conductor's office, though it was a lot bigger than he'd have expected a professor's office to be. There were several shelves behind his desk, but also a small sitting area with a love seat, easy chair, and room enough for a string quartet to set up.

Motioning for Aaron to sit in the chair, Nussenbaum perched on the edge of the love seat. "I'd love to hear about your training. Clearly you must have had extensive piano instruction. You also mentioned you were in a band. Did you participate in choir as well? I don't think I saw you at Minnesota All-State last year."

Aaron suspected firing squads were less intense than Nussy. "I didn't go. I was in choir when we lived in Eden Prairie, but not when we moved. I haven't had piano lessons since ninth grade."

Nussenbaum's eyebrows went up. "I see. What about the band you mentioned? I assume you sang?"

"Well, we all did. But yes."

"So you didn't sing at all outside of choir? No ensembles, no solos?"

Aaron began to fidget. "No. Sorry."

"No reason to apologize. I'm only trying to figure out how someone with such a clear gift wasn't nurtured. In Eden Prairie at least I would have expected them to recognize your talent."

"Oh, Mr. Peterson said I was good. He tried to get me to do solo competitions but—" Trying to explain his father's rigid sense of what real academics were seemed unwise. "I'd love to be in choir now."

"We'd love to have you. The Ambassadors too." Nussy leaned forward, those eyes like tractor beams. "But what I'm hoping to convince you, Aaron, is to take some music courses." He passed Aaron a sheet of paper from a nearby table. "Theory would have to be an elective, but music history would qualify as a general education credit. If you chose to major in anything music related, both classes would count toward your degree."

Aaron started to object reflexively, stopping when he remembered what Walter had urged him. "I…I don't know."

"No pressure to declare a music major. This is merely testing the waters. I'd encourage vocal lessons with me and piano with my wife. She's a professor here as well. I won't lie, she'll put you through your paces, but something tells me you'd enjoy the work. Will you think about it? If money is an issue, I can look into some scholarships."

Aaron felt dizzy. "I—How much are lessons?"

Nussenbaum rose. "Let's go talk with the secretary."

Aaron ended up filling Thursday mornings for the first semester with first a vocal lesson with Nussenbaum and a piano with the other Dr. Nussenbaum, whom everyone referred to as "Dr. Mrs."

"You'll get a bill for the lessons in your student mailbox," the secretary told him, "but if it's too much, bring it back and I'll take care of it. Nussy's orders. Oh, and don't forget to sign this one too. That's so he can be your advisor. This one is your change of course schedule, which I'll file for you, unless you'd prefer to run it to the registrar yourself."

Glancing down, Aaron saw a new schedule for the coming Monday, one without Introduction to Management at seven forty-five in the morning but instead had Intro to Theory at nine. History of British Literature was also gone, replaced with History of Music.

Give it a try. With Walter's voice echoing in his head, Aaron signed the papers and jumped into trying headfirst.

Chapter Seven

ON MOST LEVELS, Saint Timothy was great for Giles. His classes were interesting but not too difficult. He made friends with a lot of guys, a few who were gay and most who weren't. He got first violin, one of the three freshmen to do so and the only non-music major.

He loved his orchestra conductor, Dr. Allison. The music was tricky, but he'd taken private violin lessons since he was six, so all he had to do was put in his usual hours of practice in the private rooms off the student lounge in the music building, and he was fine. He saw Mina regularly for breakfast. Brian was a top-shelf friend, the kind of guy Giles could totally imagine asking to be an attendant at his wedding someday.

He wouldn't be booking a church anytime soon, though. He'd had a few hookups, and they were fine— great from the standpoint of nobody hazing him after. They were not, though, quite what Giles had thought they'd be. He felt schizophrenic, because sometimes he was upset that the guys simply vanished after…and other times he felt uncomfortable because guys got clingy, thinking a little conversation and a hand job meant they were going to keep hanging out.

He didn't hook up with the intense twink from orientation day. They made eye contact across the cafeteria a few times, but if Giles attempted to initiate conversation, the guy bugged off. Giles couldn't figure it out. It wasn't quite the reaction of the shame-and-blames, but it wasn't normal, either.

So his love and sex life wasn't perfect, but Giles hadn't expected it to be, not right off the bat. College life was unfolding before him as it should, and he was happy.

Except every time he saw Aaron, his bubble burst all over again.

Apparently Aaron was a great singer, and the entire choral department was in love with him. Aaron was one of two freshmen to make it into the Ambassadors. The word on the street was Nussy had taken Aaron on as his personal project, determined to make Aaron a music major by the end of the semester.

Aaron smiled at everybody, but not Giles. He blushed and aw-shucked and walked around in the choir herd, basking in their collective glory, but if Giles walked past, Aaron went all stiff and never said a word.

The Saint Timothy Chorale was the other fly in Giles's ointment. Its members were loud and overly jolly, and they traveled in packs and found a sexual joke in everything. One of the tenors—named *Baz*, how fucking pretentious—always wore sunglasses, inside and out. Twice Giles had caught him *changing* sunglasses from indoor to outdoor. Baz was gay, so out he was his own parade. He was hot and cool, and half the gay guys worth cruising had already slept with him.

Baz cruised Giles, gave him a quick clock and a wink, but that was all. While gay was okay at Timothy, gawky geeks need not apply.

The choir didn't do geek—they were all pretension and cliquishness. They sang in the hallways in perfect harmony, as if their lives were an episode of *Glee*. Several of them lived in a big old Victorian house behind the senior parking lot, called the White House. This was allegedly because the house was white and someone twenty years ago had thought the name was funny, but Giles knew it was because the choir members considered themselves rulers of the free world.

Everywhere Giles went he heard stories about the choir. The year before on their European tour they'd been given the full-court press at a private winery, then had to hike half a mile up a mountain through snow while dressed in concert attire to their hotel because a freak snowstorm made their ski lodge inaccessible by the charter buses. Once they got to the hotel, they drank the bar dry.

Apparently the entire choir was a roving band of drunks. Lovable, everyone's-favorite-people drunks— and *the whole world* loved the choir best. Nussy's office was big enough to house a gala and was always full of regents, but Dr. Allison's was small and shoved in the back hallway. Because he wasn't the director of the infamous Saint Timothy Chorale. Just the tawdry, award-winning orchestra.

Saint Timothy was supposed to be Giles's escape from feeling like a permanent wallflower, yet here he was again. Second-class, second-string, the usual.

Things got better when the special music groups got started. To his complete shock, Giles made chamber orchestra. It was an exclusive, mostly upperclassman group that performed throughout the year at special functions, including homecoming and the annual epic Christmas with Timothy festival, and homecoming was a month away. The chamber orchestra also broke off into several string quartets rehearsing on their own— Giles was in one of those too. He was first chair in chamber and in the most advanced quartet.

He went back three times to check the announcement on the bulletin board, because he didn't understand how he kept seeing his name there. Only six other freshmen had made it into the chamber orchestra, most of them music majors. Mina was happy for him, but Giles could tell she was jealous.

Giles went to Dr. Allison, pretty sure there had to be a mistake.

Dr. Allison only smiled at him, though, leaning his rickety desk chair against a towering cabinet overflowing with stacked sheet music and textbooks. "No mistake. I heard you audition last May, and I've heard you practice in sectionals and on your own. You're exactly what we look for in the chamber orchestra."

The idea that all those times he'd been practicing were auditions freaked Giles out. "But I'm not a music major."

"There's no such requirement. Did you not know your section leader is pre-med?"

Giles did, but Karen Stacy was her own level of overachievement. "I just don't think I'm quite what maybe you think I am."

Allison raised a wooly white eyebrow. "I don't think so. I think you'll start practicing tonight, and when Karen sets up special practice sessions for you, you'll attend. Though if you're worried, I have a few lesson spots open. I was surprised you hadn't signed up yet."

Now Giles felt guilty. "I—I meant to. It's not that I don't take it seriously…"

Giles fully expected Allison to be disappointed in him, but the conductor only continued to appear amused. "No, you're simply human. I understand. Of course, it's perfectly acceptable for you to decline the advanced placement orchestras and continue as you are. I chose you because you strike me as a talented young man who enjoys music—and perhaps was in the need of a greater challenge."

"I don't want to decline. I'm…honored. Thank you. And if there's lesson space, yes, I'd love it."

He *did* work his tail off. "Canon in D" he'd played so many times he could perform it drunk—the song was apparently a Saint Timothy staple, and alumni were allowed to join the current members and play along. But the rest of the music he had to learn put him through his paces, and between the two orchestras Giles had eight pieces of music to learn. With his quartet group the total was nine. He practically lived in the music building now, hovering outside his reserved practice room for his chance to rehearse, going over fingerings as he zoned out during Intro to Psychology, tapping out rhythms on his plastic tray in the cafeteria line.

He was so busy he didn't have time to obsess about Aaron Seavers and his adoring throng, though he did occasionally note how nobody hosted parades for violin virtuosos unless they looked like Joshua Bell. The ones with big ears they worked to death.

"It's going to kill me," he complained to Brian after returning from a grueling sectional and quartet rehearsal. He collapsed onto his bed and stared up at the ceiling in a daze. "They're all so good. I have no idea what I'm doing there."

"I bet you're fine." Brian tossed him their communal bag of Twizzlers Nibs.

Giles pulled out a handful of candy and put it mindlessly into his mouth. It tasted like tangy wax, but as soon as the sugar burned into his bloodstream, he didn't care. "These groups are a lot smaller. I can't drop out and let the others cover me on a rough patch."

They ate more candy as the main-menu music for Halo 2 played in the background.

Brian broke the silence. "The weird thing is, as stressed out as you are, I don't think I've seen you this happy before."

Giles thought about that for a minute and laughed. "You're right."

Brian picked up his controller and scrolled mindlessly through the menu options. "It's too bad you don't want to major in music."

"There are no jobs. The three majors are music ed, music therapy, and music performance. I don't want to teach, and I don't think I'm zealous enough for performance. Plus, they all starve or play street corners." He popped more Nibs. "I've half-considered music therapy, but I'm already too late."

"What's music therapy, and how are you late? We're only in the first semester of college."

"It'd be killer to join them at this point—their schedule is brutal. Music therapy is pretty much what it sounds like: using music in therapy. Psychotherapy, healing therapy, hospice. Say you're fighting cancer. It's grisly, wearing stuff. A music therapist comes in on a regular schedule and has you play music or sing, or plays music with you."

"How in the world does that help anything?"

"Music is powerful, and when you're fighting a health battle, it can mean the difference some days between the strength to fight or giving in. In practical terms, music therapists help with small, specific goal achievements, but patients who use music therapy are passionate about how much the treatments helped them emotionally."

"I suppose." Brian continued choosing armor for his avatar.

The dismissal irked Giles. "Music is huge in our lives. Ignoring the scientific evidence of what it does to our brains, how it helps us forge connections and relearn patterns—look at what you're doing right now. You're playing a game, but it has its own soundtrack. We pipe music into elevators, malls, city squares. You stream Spotify every morning while you study. I've caught you humming along with the Nationwide Insurance commercial. Imagine somebody using music deliberately during a time of pain and suffering. Or taking a frustrating occupational or physical therapy task and turning it into something with music attached."

Brian put the controller down, chagrined. "Wow. Okay, you're right. And you need to totally go switch your major, because holy crap, you're almost vibrating when you talk about it."

He was, Giles acknowledged—but the realization only depressed him. "I can't. It's a five-year program with overloads, and that's when you start at the beginning of your freshman year. Also, I'd have to apply. It's a separate degree. There's only a handful of schools in the whole Midwest offering it." He shrugged. "I'm probably being flighty, high on rehearsal. The urge will pass."

"It sounds like you can't switch anything out until term anyway. Do some investigating, and see where it takes you."

The idea rattled around in Giles's brain for days, haunting him. He thought of it every time he saw Aaron laughing and happy with his choir buddies.

Giles could hate Aaron for being popular, but there was no question—Aaron had found his joy.

You deserve your joy too, a voice in the back of his mind whispered.

He did. But first Giles had to be brave enough to seize it.

THOUGH THE MUSIC part of his life was good, Aaron's

roommate was strange.

Aaron tried to engage Elijah, but it never got him anywhere. Take, for example, their exchange when Aaron pointed out he had plenty of extra space in his fridge if Elijah wanted to share it.

"Thank you, I'm fine," Elijah replied, and went back to writing in his notebooks.

"I don't mind, really."

"I appreciate it, but I don't need to use your fridge."

Aaron should have left it there, but he'd seen Elijah come from the cafeteria with leftovers and drink warm soda from cans. "The thing is, my dad insisted I get this big model, but I hardly put anything in it. I seriously don't mind at all."

Elijah put down his pen with a scary smile on his face. "*Okay.* If I put a goddamned pop in your fridge, will you leave me alone?"

Aaron blinked and took a step back. "I—Sorry. I didn't—"

Rolling his eyes, Elijah pulled a Dr Pepper from beneath his desk, marched to the fridge and slammed it on the door. "There you go. I'm using your fridge. Good deed done, move on."

The soda never moved, and no other foodstuffs of Elijah's ever joined it.

It was like that with everything. Aaron would tell Elijah about floor meetings or campus events, but Elijah only ever snapped at him. It hurt to realize not only would he not be friends with his roommate, he'd have to work to not talk to him or risk a blowup. He supposed there were worse arrangements in the world probably, somewhere. All Elijah did was sit at his desk, writing on and on in his notebooks—which, weirdly, were never visible unless Elijah was actively working on them.

If Elijah was weird, his friends were *weirder*. He seemed to have exactly two, and wouldn't you know it, they were poster people for the kind of crazy Christians Aaron had feared he'd encounter at Saint Timothy.

The guy, Reece, was the one who'd handed Aaron a Jesus flyer during orientation, and he was even freakier up close. Aaron didn't get into fat shaming, but something about the *way* Reece wore his weight made Aaron have to work not to stare. Reece wasn't jolly like Aaron's RA, always wearing comfy sweats showcasing his ample belly and offering to share the cookies his grandmother sent. Or the beefy guy across the hall who held gaming competitions in his room and worked as a bouncer for the Shack and shouted at anyone passing through the hall who he thought might be considering calling him fatty.

Reece was something else entirely. His weight was dough around him, straining his skin, making his bulging, wild eyes appear that much crazier. He seemed unaware of his size, wearing too-tight, unflattering clothes. Everything about Reece was pushy. He didn't simply talk to people—he invaded their space and sprayed them with spittle when he got excited about something. He always carried pamphlets and flyers, sticking them on or under doors, forcing people to take them, eliciting promises they'd attend his upcoming meetings if they didn't immediately bolt. He proselytized every chance he got, urging the residents of Saint Timothy to accept Jesus and be saved from sin…which Aaron thought was ballsy to do at a Lutheran university hosting three campus pastors, a huge religion department, daily optional chapel, and weekly church services.

Elijah's other friend was female. Emily was pretty and petite, always neatly groomed, her hair either in a demure Sandra Dee-like ponytail or held back in an equally 1950s' headband. Her clothes were clearly carefully chosen and fully fashionable—even when she wore a religious T-shirt fifteen other people wore at the same time. She wore smart little pins on the lapel of her cardigan broadcasting quiet moral admonitions and invitations. *Come To My Church With Me. PRAY HARD. Do You Know Jesus?*

The one she wore most often when visiting Elijah was a red marriage-equality equal sign—with a line through it.

Though Reece was openly creepy, Emily was stealth, and she made Aaron nervous. While Reece bellowed Good News in the hallway, Emily stood on the sidelines like a demure hawk. When the Campus Crusaders held their meetings in the main lobby of the union, Emily managed to stand next to earnest young men and talk about a woman knowing her place…while at the same time clearly running the show. She spoke of abstinence and purity while giving not-at-all-subtle bedroom eyes to any hot guy who happened by. If she was somehow still *unsoiled*, as she encouraged her female disciples to be, she was the vampiest virgin Aaron had ever seen.

She had her headlights set on Aaron.

On the day of the Ambassadors' first rehearsal, Emily and Reece came to pick Elijah up as usual. He'd decorated his desk with a few of the religious knick-knacks from the bottom drawer before they arrived, and he donned the khakis, short-sleeved shirt, and powder-blue tie that made him look like a dryer-shrunk door-to-door salesman. His notebooks vanished to whatever special wormhole he kept them in, and he waited at his desk, surfing Christian websites on his computer, his Bible-study binder and well-worn Bible beside him.

Emily and Reece wore matching shirts: a large rainbow arched over a cross, the words *Take Back the Rainbow* blazed along the colored spectrum in a cheesy font with glitter around it over a dull gray landscape. They were horrifically ugly, though Emily had managed to make hers work with a fire-engine-red cashmere shrug and matching earrings, necklace, bracelet, and headband.

She smiled at Aaron, tucking her hair behind her ear and batting her lashes in a move both shy and devastatingly calculated at once. "Can we tempt you along, Aaron? We have a guest speaker talking about how to maintain quality relationships. *Sustained* romantic compatibility is so important in a Christian connection."

"I have choir practice." Aaron couldn't stop staring at their shirts, trying to figure them out. He stared at

Reece's because Emily's rainbow was tight against her prominent breasts, and he didn't want to encourage her. Reece's cotton straining from the rolls of his belly wasn't attractive but at least wouldn't be misconstrued as an invitation for a sustained Christian relationship.

The shirts made no sense, though, no matter how Aaron studied them. Where were they taking the rainbow? Why? And seriously, who in the hell saw that font and thought, *Man, let's use this?*

Reece beamed and tented the shirt away from his body in display. "Aren't they great? I'll get you one when I bring Elijah's."

Aaron couldn't take it anymore. "But what does it mean?"

"It means we're taking it back." Reece's already ruddy face went blotchy with indignation. "The homosexuals can go find some other religious symbol to commandeer."

Oh, that rainbow.

"Make sure you wear it on October eleventh." Emily toyed with the end of a lock of hair as she winked at Aaron. "It'll be our silent counterprotest."

What was October eleventh? Aaron wasn't going to ask. Clearing his throat, he reached for his backpack. "I have to go. Practice. Um, bye." He passed a robotic Elijah, who was clutching his binder and Bible as he stared blankly into space, waiting to be activated for Christ.

It was an hour until the rehearsal, but no way in hell was Aaron staying in the room another second. Especially when he googled October eleventh. It was

National Coming Out Day.

The idea that he lived with someone who wanted to *take back the rainbow* when he was just figuring out how to ride it made him uneasy. After wandering aimlessly around the grassy common for a few minutes, Aaron found a secluded spot on the other side of the student union, pulled out his phone and called Walter.

"Hey, babe. What's up?"

Aaron sat under a tree and curled his legs up to his chest. "Is this an okay time to call you?"

"Always an okay time to call me, sweetie. Especially when something's bothering you. Tell Uncle Walter what's going on."

Aaron gave him a recap of the rainbow encounter— Walter already knew who Reece and Emily were, which made things easier. Even a simple retelling, though, got Aaron riled up all over again. "They want to *give me that shirt*, and they expect me to wear it on National Coming Out Day. What are they going to do if they find out about me?"

"Nothing, because if they do, your campus has anti-bullying policies. The words *my dad's a lawyer* will probably scare them into silence if nothing else."

"But I don't want my dad to know. And what do I do with the shirt? Tell them no? What if they ask why?"

"Oh, take the shirt." Walter's tone was silky and dangerous. "Save it for me. Arrogant Christian assholes. I'll give them their fucking rainbow." There was a murmur in the background, and when Walter spoke again, his voice was more measured. "Kelly says to tell you not all Christians are assholes. I will grant you his family is great. But beyond that—" He broke off as Kelly's voice got sharper. Walter sighed. "We'll discuss my opinions on Christianity another time."

"Most of the time you don't notice this is a Lutheran school. These guys are some weird fringe group from what I can tell. I mean, there are Campus Catholics and Methodist Meetings, but all they do is plan homecoming floats and eat cookies. They don't wear antigay buttons. Leave it to my roommate to find the weirdoes." Aaron frowned. "I would have *sworn* he was gay."

"He might be. When you come from the kind of crazy it sounds like he was steeped in, sometimes you have to go hard before you come to Gay Jesus. Which, those twelve disciples? Statistics say at least one was gay."

Aaron got the feeling if Walter ever visited when Emily and Reece stopped by, things would get colorful fast. "I don't want to have to deal with them."

"Then don't. Put your headphones in when they show up, and don't engage. They'll get the hint, even the virgin vamp queen."

"I don't get why girls always have to hit on me. I don't do anything to make them think I might be interested."

"That's why they hit on you, hon. That and you're smoking hot. A scruffy, blue-eyed puppy to hug and squeeze."

He was pretty sure Emily wanted to do a lot more than hug and squeeze him. She and several other girls, some who were equally creepy, many who were not. He should come out so they'd leave him alone.

Except, then he'd be…out. Aaron shut his eyes and rubbed his temple with his free hand. "I hate this."

"Let's talk about something else. What are you doing right now?"

"Sitting under a tree, waiting for Ambassador rehearsal. The first one. There's some kind of initiation thing, I guess."

"Oh boy. If they put a bra on your head, Instagram a pic, please."

"Let's talk about something even more else. What are you doing?"

"Watching Disney movies with my fiancé. He was able to preorder his DVD of *Frozen*, and now he's in a mood."

Aaron blinked. Several times. "Disney movies?"

"Yes. Kelly has a thing for them. *Tangled* is his favorite, but *Frozen* has him conflicted, I think. I'm trying to get him to have someone sing 'Let It Go' at the wedding, because the song is seriously badass, but he says it's not ceremony appropriate."

Aaron remembered Walter's ringtone for Kelly. "What about 'Candle on the Water'?"

"Oh *do not* let him hear you say that."

Chapter Eight

THE MOB OUTSIDE the choir room as he arrived for the first Ambassadors' rehearsal made Aaron think he'd gone to the wrong place, but it turned out the crowd was there to witness. Several people waved at him as he entered, but just as many elbowed each other in excitement as they glanced at Aaron, which made him nervous.

Inside the choir room it was *only* the new Ambassador recruits. There were six of them total, including the other freshman—a baritone who was also in Aaron's Intro to Theory class. Aaron was the last to arrive. The other five guys sat in chairs in a line in the center of the room, the only chairs in the room that weren't stacked up against the wall. One empty space remained at the end, and Aaron sat in it.

The upperclassman beside him gave him a nervous smile. "You ready for this?"

Since Aaron still wasn't exactly sure what *this* was, he doubted it. He shrugged. "I guess."

The guy next to his seat partner leaned over to address Aaron. "I heard you rehearsing the other day. You're really good."

Aaron tried not to feel self-conscious. "Thanks."

"It should be any second now," another guy farther down said. He stared at the door Aaron and Jilly had exited through after their choir audition.

Aaron had *no* idea what was about to happen. He wasn't too worried, because if he had to wear a bra on his head or something, at least the other guys had to do it too. And yeah, he'd Instagram it. To show Walter he could.

"I'm gonna suck," somebody murmured.

The door on the other side of the room opened. Baz appeared in the archway, eyes as always hidden by shades.

Leaning on the frame, he belted the opening line to the Black Eyed Peas' "Let's Get It Started".

It was a slow, spine-tingling slide into the notes, making the hair on Aaron's skin stand on end as the sound echoed in the room and resonated in his chest cavity. As Baz stepped into the room, ten guys poured in singing the baseline.

The Ambassadors surrounded the lineup of chairs, circling the new recruits and singing at the top of their incredibly talented lungs. They sang *at* the recruits, waggling their eyebrows, basically all-out flirting. Baz even lowered his glasses a few times and winked at Aaron. A curly-haired second tenor launched flawlessly into the rap, but when it came time for the chorus, he fell into the throng, part of the wall of sound surrounding Aaron and the others.

When they came to the part where the first tenors hit falsetto, however, the Ambassadors broke into sections, and each of the recruits was ushered into his appropriate place. Sid, a junior and Aaron's first tenor sectional leader, grabbed Aaron and pulled him into a trio with himself and Baz. The two of them sang almost into Aaron's ears, urging him with their voices and bodies to take up the beat, and with a nudge from Sid, Aaron tentatively joined in. Baz left as he claimed another section of the solo, swaying his hips and serenading each of the newbies. Aaron grinned and clapped along. When it was his turn to be sung to, he belted falsetto at Baz, pretty sure he was hitting the right notes.

If this was the initiation, it wasn't so bad.

Honestly, Aaron never wanted this to end. It was like being in the band, except better. Eventually it did end though, winding down with all of them leaning forward in a circle, the basses closing them out with a near whisper of a backbeat. When the song stopped, they remained in their huddle, old and new Ambassadors as one.

Aaron held still, breathless and more excited than he'd ever felt in his life.

Baz tipped his shades down and hummed a note at Marius, the handsome, dark-haired bass from auditions. After a nod, Baz sang. "Kenny, Mickey—one more time."

Not missing so much as a breath, the veteran Ambassadors launched into the opening of "...Baby One More Time", which took Aaron a second to identify because he was distracted by the vocalization of what he knew as instrumental lines. The newbie who had greeted Aaron when he'd entered and another recruit smiled nervously and stepped into the center of the circle, clapping along with the beat.

When the first verse started, Kenny and Mickey began to sing the solo together. They fumbled a little, not knowing all the words, but all in all they did pretty well. The other guys in their section helped them out when they stumbled, and by the end of the song, the new Ambassadors were holding their own.

So *this* was the initiation everyone was nervous about. Aaron told himself he could do this. No different from Tanner whipping out something new and making them sweat through a dry run. Piece of cake.

Except when the song switched to a OneRepublic number, three names were called out, none of them Aaron's.

Aaron faltered in his attempts to follow Sid, wondering what this meant. Out of the six recruits, five had been initiated…and only Aaron remained. Were they skipping him? How was that fair?

Were they making him sing alone? The squirrels in his head ran around in circles through the whole song, and when the song ended, Aaron's belly erupted in butterflies.

Baz stood in the center of the circle, grinning.

"As some of you know, we have a *special* recruit to the Ambassadors this year. If you're a tenor, you've heard him in sectionals, and a few of us were there at his choir audition, where he gave us quite an acoustic treat. It was Keane that day, but he promised us he knew some Florence. And you'd better deliver, honey, because poor Damien and I sweated bullets to arrange this one."

Are they talking about me? Aaron wondered. Except they had to be—*he* had sung Keane at his audition and almost did Florence + the Machine. Aaron squirmed at the attention, feeling nervous and upset. This wasn't fair at all, and he already wanted it over.

Baz held his hands out, backing way. "Mr. Aaron Seavers—please tell us all about it, 'Lover to Lover'."

Aaron stepped forward, squirrel brain and belly butterflies ready for the Thunderdome. He kept trying to find the safe place to be inside his head, but there was nowhere, only this horrible spotlight, everyone waiting for him to sing. They wanted him to sing "Lover to Lover"? Here, now, *by himself?*

The first and second tenors vocalized what was normally the piano introduction as the basses and baritones clapped. Yep, this was "Lover to Lover" all right.

In a few bars Aaron was supposed to sing. A few notes now, actually. When was he supposed to come in? Were they going to cue him?

What the fucking hell?

Aaron glanced at Sid, desperate for a lifeline. Sid tossed him a sly smile, mouthing the opening words.

How will I get the right note?

Then, as if someone else took over his body, Aaron began to sing.

Tentatively at first—it helped that the opening was soft. He got bolder as Marius and the other basses came in with the bottom, filling out the sound, making his skin tingle. *Talk about color.* It was a great arrangement too. The composer in him lifted his head, shaking off cobwebs, admiring the arrangements, taking notes and occasionally thinking, *I'd have done it differently.*

This was fun. Nerve-wracking, but all kinds of fucking fun.

Baz and Sid joined him in harmony at the chorus, and as the Ambassadors swelled around him, Aaron's heart beat like a fat hammer in his chest, powered by joy taking him higher with each additional triumphant note. He knew every inch of this song, had sung it in the car and in the shower and at his keyboard ever since he first downloaded the album, but never had he sung it with fifteen other guys.

This was amazing. He wanted to do this every damn day for the rest of his fucking life.

At the second verse, Baz came into the center with him, taking harmony and twerking. Self-consciousness washed away in the high of the song, Aaron danced with him, never so much as dropping a beat. He and Baz had a big-ass belting sing-off during the next chorus, joining as one voice for the bridge. They crouched together on the floor as Aaron all but whispered the song, heart dancing because he knew what was coming.

Give it to us, Baz's expression begged.

Aaron's soul roared as he slid into the rise, lifting his body, opening his throat, sending the song in his heart all the way up to the heavens.

His whole *body* vibrated with vocal color through the last chorus. If he'd had wings, he would have soared through the roof and into the atmosphere. He could read the surprise and pleasure on the others' faces, and that only spun him higher.

This. *This* was what he wanted. If he could major in *this* feeling, he'd sign up right now.

As his vocals ended and the Ambassadors wound down the arpeggios with gentle, expert care, Aaron simply stood in the center of it and soaked it all in. After the last note they kept still, the connectivity among the sixteen of them a living thing inside the air.

Baz hummed out a note, and the veterans sang together in eight-part harmony.

"Welcome to the Ambassadors, Kenny, Mickey, Rob, Drew, Trevor, and Aaron." They clapped, the sound echoing in a roar in the hallway.

The doors opened as Nussy swept inside. "Well done, boys." He clapped a few times, but he took the podium with clear intent to get to work. "Grab a chair and take your place from last year. Section leaders, show the new members where they should go."

"Off to the left, right beside me," Sid said as he hurried off to get a chair, but not before he also squeezed Aaron's shoulder. "Good job."

Aaron followed Sid's direction, still half lost in his song. He caught Nussy's eye, and the conductor winked at him. He looked proud.

Aaron grinned so wide he thought he might split his face.

THE FIRST DAY of Ambassadors had been fun, but actual rehearsals were even better. The guys were friendly, especially Damien—J.Crew guy from auditions, the student conductor of the full chorale—and his best friends Baz (sunglasses guy) and Marius (the bassiest bass in the world). Baz was a huge flirt and always made Aaron blush. Marius's beautiful voice wrapped around Aaron like a blanket every time he spoke. Ambassadors rehearsal was always a highlight of Aaron's day.

But lessons with Dr. Mrs. Nussenbaum? They were the best part of Aaron's week.

He hated how he'd let himself get cut off from piano for so long, and in his efforts to make up for lost time, he practiced every single second he could.

"You have a wonderful ear," Dr. Nussenbaum said at the end of one of their lessons in late September. "I understand from Dr. Allison you're excelling in his theory class as well, and you have a particular talent for composition."

"I love composing. I'd done some in high school before I moved, just for fun, but now I feel as if I've been trying to paint and someone finally introduced me to brushes."

"Well, you're making a fine start."

She kept smiling at Aaron, which made his head ring, because Dr. Mrs. never smiled. She was beautiful—board-straight dark brown hair gleaming at her shoulders, shimmering when she turned her head—but she was a cold beauty. Except today she beamed at Aaron, and she took his breath away.

The smile loosened his tongue as effectively as a tub of alcohol.

"I wanted to tell you, Dr. Nussenbaum, how grateful I am for these lessons. For your time. I don't—" He faltered, self-consciousness getting the better of him for a moment, but he pushed through. "It means so much to me. Between you and Dr. Allison—" Here he cut himself off. It would take a lot more than a smile from Dr. Mrs. to get him to confess music at Saint Timothy was saving his soul.

"Not my husband?" She chuckled when Aaron sputtered. "I'm sorry, I shouldn't tease you. I'm not often cited over my spouse, however."

"I don't want to sound ungrateful. Sometimes he's too much, is all."

If he'd thought she'd smiled at him before, he didn't know what to call the gesture she gave him next—a veil lifting, allowing Aaron a glimpse of the woman beneath. "It's fine, Aaron. I understand." She put her hand over his. Her skin was cold, but as the clasp lingered, warmth seeped through before she let him go with a brisk pat. "Let's try the Chopin again. I think you could finish off the last measure with clearer lift."

Aaron *did* finish it better, to both his and Dr. Nussenbaum's satisfaction. The whole lesson was such a rush that when he went to the student lounge after, he drifted on a cloud.

Jilly elbowed him playfully. "You look all stoned out. You been playing footsie with someone in a practice room?"

Aaron rattled into full sobriety. "No! God, no. I had a great lesson with Dr. Nussenbaum, is all. Dr.

Mrs., I mean." He swallowed the title, suddenly aware of how cheap it was.

The stack of sheet music Jilly carried rustled as her arms slackened. "A lesson with *her* made you this happy?"

Aaron stilled. "Um, yeah?"

"*Nobody* has a good lesson with Dr. Mrs., ever. Most of her students leave her office crying. I know two girls who've already switched their majors because of her. She's a *hard*-ass."

Aaron bristled. "She's strict, yes, but that's because she's so good. She's ten times as talented as Nussy, but he's always dancing and flirting, so of course everyone likes him better. And for the record, I don't care for the Dr. Mrs. thing. Why is she the Mrs. and Nussy isn't Dr. Mr.?"

Jilly held up a hand. "Down, boy."

Aaron withdrew. "Sorry."

"No, don't apologize." Jilly regarded him thoughtfully. "*God.* How did I not see that about the title? I feel gross. I'm a *girl.* I should have seen it right off." Jilly leaned against an instrument locker. "It's the whole department. Everything is misogynistic. Look at choir: there are so many women lining up to sing they had to make a ghetto chorus, but the *guys* get the special a cappella troupe."

"There *should* be a women's a cappella group. Why isn't there?"

"Well, I heard they tried once, years ago."

"It would need a faculty sponsor. Nussy runs the Ambassadors—Damien leads a lot of rehearsals, but

Nussy steers the ship."

Jilly rolled her eyes. "No *way* will he take on a fourth choir."

"It's not as if there aren't other instructors in the department who could sponsor."

The answer hovered between them.

"You need to ask her." Jilly bounced on her toes. "You're the only one she would say yes to."

Aaron held up a hand when she started to argue. "We need to develop a proposal first. She'll want to see proof you're serious, that this won't be another mess like the last group."

"But what's the point of going through all the work if she's not—?"

"Don't go getting this idea she's going to melt and roll over *because girl power*. If there's one thing I know about Dr. Nussenbaum, it's that she makes you earn what she gives you. You want her help, I bet you can get it, but you have to *bring it*."

Jilly's shoulders slumped. "Then it's already over. I could maybe get a dozen girls together, but I can't lead them. And if I don't, I can't guarantee they'll go for Dr. Mrs.—Dr. Nussenbaum—as a sponsor. Plus I don't know anything about composing or arranging music." Jilly let her head rest against the metal mesh. "The reason the other girl group fell apart was because they couldn't decide what they wanted to sing, who should have the solo, what kind of arrangement they should have. That's why we need a sponsor, so the breakdown doesn't happen. But you're telling me *to get* a sponsor we need to function so well we don't need one."

Aaron rubbed his chin, trying to think of a worka-round. "It's not so much about needing to prove you don't need her so much as showing her you're serious. Prep one song. Gather a group of women who *won't* fight. *Find* an upperclassman who is a good leader. Once you do well, you'll have everyone clamoring to get in, but hopefully by then you have Dr. Nussenbaum to keep them in line."

Jilly had a light in her eyes, a wicked sparkle Aaron loved to see. "You're totally right. It's not about the best singers or being fair. It's about making the group *work*. Oh, *Aaron*. Except—we still need someone to arrange the music."

"I'm no Dr. Allison or anything, but I can arrange a pop song well enough."

Jilly went still. "Don't tease me. Are you seriously offering?"

"Well yeah, but I know you'd rather have a girl, so I'll pinch hit until someone—"

The look on Jilly's face melted Aaron. "Aaron Seavers, I fucking love you." Her smile was as wide as her face. "Oh God, hon. Seriously. If we can pull this off...I owe you. And I already owe you a lot."

Aaron's skin felt like a furnace. "Stop. You do not. You're my friend. Of course I'll do this for you."

Jilly paced in the small space between the table and the lockers. "We need a song. Wait—we need a *name*."

Aaron's stomach gurgled loudly, and he put his hand on his belly. "We need some lunch."

Linking their arms, Jilly led them out of the lounge.

IT DIDN'T TAKE long for the female a cappella group to get off the ground. Three days after she and Aaron had first conceived of the idea, Jilly and three other girls sat huddled around a table, speaking over the top of one another as Aaron listened.

Karen folded her manicured hands politely together on the Formica. "We have to decide what approach to take. Whatever song we pick to show to Dr. Nussenbaum won't simply make or break us with her. It'll set the tone for everything we do."

"We need a name." Marion pursed her lips and tapped her pen over an open notebook littered with scrawl. "The name will be the heart of us. It has to be right."

"We could play off of the Ambassadors," Jilly said, "but it's already hard not to seem like we're copying them."

"We don't want to be an also-ran, either."

Aaron glanced at Marion's list of rejected titles. *Diplomats. Champions. Emissaries.* "Justice. That's not bad."

"It's too on the nose." Karen took the paper from Marion and frowned at it. "We can't sound like little girls playing, and this does. It can't be all *gurrrls*."

Aaron rubbed his ear. "Yeah. You're claiming your space. This is your opening shot. Your big cannon going off."

Tanya gasped and held up her hands, her whole body vibrating. "*Salvo.* Our name is Salvo."

The word resonated around the table as everyone digested it, letting the taste of the name ring out.

Jilly let out a breath. "It's perfect. It means aggression and attack, but it sounds almost like a musical term."

"Well, it's also a kind of shorthand for *salutation*," Marion pointed out. "*Friendly* aggression."

Karen nodded. "Yes. It's the best name. And it sounds like we all agree. Now we need the songs."

Aaron sat back, watching their passion clash over the tabletop. Occasionally they asked him for reassurances he could transpose something, but eventually he had to step in and redirect them.

"Forget composition. You need to think about the instrumentation. Range is going to be an issue, straight up. Your lowest alto isn't ever going to be a bass."

Marion rolled her eyes. "They totally cheated in *Pitch Perfect* with the vocal-node thing."

"It's okay," Aaron said. "You're not talking about national competitions yet where instruments are strictly forbidden. Add a single bass guitar, and you'll get lower color."

"A double bass would be better." Karen tapped her pen on her paper. "I could do it, though I'd rather sing. Which means we need a girl who doesn't want to sing to help."

Jilly tipped her head to the side. "Why does it have to be a girl? Aaron's helping us—why can't we ask a guy to play bass?"

"But with a guy are we a girl group still?"

"Is this about vaginas, or about making us a space to be heard?"

"The basses in the orchestra are all assholes. We

can't ask them."

"Then *who* are we going to ask, huh?"

Aaron shut his eyes and shrank into himself, fully understanding what Jilly had warned him about.

Karen took the group back under control. "*Ladies.* We'll work out who we ask to do what later. Aaron, did you have more to say?"

He didn't, but Karen sure seemed to want him to. He cleared his throat. "Instrumentation is an option, but more than anything else you need to think about your vocals. Choose songs that serve you—where the action is on top and in the middle. Don't go trying to recreate something heavy on the bottom. You need to make the music highlight your voices. Your *female* voices."

Karen nodded. "We should check out the ICCA and BOCA catalogs. What are the girl groups doing at Varsity Vocals?"

"We don't want to copy them," Tanya said.

Jilly leaned forward. "But we can study them. All the girl groups, even the pop ones. Let's get a list together, and we can go over it with Aaron."

"We need more members."

They launched into their plans again, and Aaron retreated into the background once more, smiling.

Chapter Nine

TWO WEEKS BEFORE homecoming, Mina arrived at orchestra rehearsal vibrating before Giles as if she were her own bass string. "Karen told me about this group she and some other girls are forming. It's a girl group like the Ambassadors, except anyone can try out. Not just choir."

Giles blinked under the force of her enthusiasm. "That's…great. I guess I didn't know it meant so much to you."

"A-H cancelled the a cappella choir because of budget cuts before I got to high school. Even then, it was mostly the greatest hits of the 80s and maybe 90s on a good day. This group is *serious*. They're not quite talking ICCA, but I think it's because they're just getting started."

"ICCA?"

She threw up her hands. "International Championships of A Cappella. Varsity Vocals? Did you not see *Pitch Perfect*?"

Jesus, he'd never seen Min this riled up. "I did, but I guess I forgot to take notes. So this group would be another Barton Bellas?"

"*Yes*. Except this is *ground up*. I miss singing so

much. I don't want to do stupid women's chorus, but *this*. I *want it*." She gripped his arm tightly. "You have to help me pick an audition piece."

Giles gently pried her fingers away. "Of course I will."

"We'll go to my room, hunt sheet music online, and go snag a practice room." She gasped. "*Shit*, I've already used all my signup time for this week!"

Stroking her shoulder, Giles tried to bring her down to earth. "Honey, it's okay. We'll figure it out. When are tryouts?"

"Karen didn't say."

"Here's what we're going to do. You're going to go get your laptop and a bottle of water. I'll send Brian out for dinner and go see if I can magic up a practice room."

"But I told you, I already—"

Giles stopped her with a finger on her lips. "Laptop. Water. Meet me here."

After letting out a shaky breath, she kissed him on the cheek and took off.

As he re-entered the building, Giles texted Brian and arranged for dinner delivery. Food secured, he wandered to the practice rooms, praying one was open. Of course it wasn't, so he bartered a deal for free tutoring Saturday with a nervous, low-seated violin from the backwoods of Wisconsin in exchange for her practice room. He was about to duck inside when his section leader came up to him leading a group of three girls...and Aaron.

Karen beamed at Giles. "Hey, there you are. Do

you have a minute?"

Giles deliberately kept his gaze away from Aaron, but he could see him out of the corner of his eye. "Sure thing. What can I do for you?"

Why is Aaron here with Karen?

Karen turned to the people she led. "Go ahead and get settled in the lounge. I'll be right there." She winked at Giles. "Hopefully with a friend."

Giles decided to head her off at the pass. "I wanted to ask you about this girl-group thing. My friend Mina is interested, and I wondered if you could give me more information."

"How funny—that's exactly what I was going to talk to you about." She nodded at the lounge. "We're about to start our first official meeting. Come join us."

"Uh—well, actually, Mina's on her way here now. She wanted to rehearse." He couldn't tell her no, not outright—not yet. "Do you have any dates set for tryouts or ideas of what you're looking for?"

"We're thinking sometime the week of homecoming. As for what we're after, we want team players. It's not just about strong singers. It's about attitude, willingness to work. No divas need apply to Salvo." She nudged his arm. "I'm serious about helping. I'll keep you posted on our other planning meetings. Because you know I'll wear you down. We *need* you."

I need you to not have Aaron involved first. "I don't know anything about singing. I sound like a drowning cat in a bag."

"We don't need male singers. We need help arrang-ing songs, choreographing, playing background instruments. You're gifted with music, Giles. You pick up every song with barely any effort."

Yes, but if he had to sit in the same room with Aaron, he'd vomit from nerves all over the score. "I'm swamped with all the orchestra stuff for the homecoming concert."

"I'll bother you after then." She winked at him and headed into the lounge, calling over her shoulder, "Tell Mina she's going to be great."

Mina and Giles worked three hours a night for her audition. Privately he thought she was seriously overthinking things, but mostly he marveled at how *intense* she was about joining this group. This wasn't a side of his best friend he'd known existed, and it felt weird how, out of the blue, it had cropped up.

Eventually, one night as he walked her to her dorm, he told her so.

She held her sheet music tight to her chest and stared at the sidewalk in front of them rather than look Giles in the eye. "Probably it's not what I'm wanting it to be. *Probably* I won't get in."

"Come on. You've been killing it every night."

She tucked a long strand of shiny black hair behind her ear. "It's not like *Glee* where they racially balance their members and make special numbers for the wheelchair-bound."

Giles stopped short. "Wait. You're saying you think they'll not pick you because you're Korean?"

She gave him a withering glare. "You want to know how many not-white kids got the lead in the school play, the solo in chorus? Zero. Black guys and Latinos can be linebackers, but they're never the quarterback. Not in Minnesota."

This was crazy. "Come on, Min, you're trying to tell me everyone's deliberately *not* picking ethnic kids because they're racist?"

She rolled her eyes. "*Ethnic* kids. Because what, you have no ethnicity? You said you felt singled out because you were gay, you were always the gay kid. Well, hon, I'm always *that Asian girl.* No American Girl doll looked like me when I was growing up, and now there's *one.* No Barbie except for a sidekick. Those Barbie movies? Blonde white girls in the lead roles, every time, except for the brunettes. Even Japanese anime westernizes itself half the time. There's space for me at the table to be an also-ran. That's about the best there is." She hugged her arms tight to her body. "I don't want to be an also-ran this time."

Giles had never thought about Mina's race. She was as American as he was in every way—she'd been in Minnesota since she was eighteen months old. To him she was Mina, end of story. Now, for the first time in his sixteen years of knowing her, he contemplated what it was like to be the same as everyone else inside but looking like almost nobody else outside.

"I'm sorry," he said, which was worthless, but it was all he had. "I had no idea, but I should have, and I'm sorry."

Shrugging, she averted her gaze. "I didn't know about you playing gigolo to the closet cases."

He put a hand on her shoulder. "Min, you're getting into this group. You're an amazing singer. I'm nervous you'll give up viola for choir, you're so good."

She smiled shyly. "Good enough they won't care about the Asian thing?"

"The *Asian thing* shouldn't *be* a thing. They should see you for who you are. They should be open-minded enough to not judge you by anything but your voice and your ability to be a team player."

"Should doesn't mean will."

No, it didn't.

That night as Giles lay in his bunk, a dark thought haunted him. He could make sure nobody excluded Mina for not being white enough if he was on the planning committee. Except he'd have to face Aaron. It'd be a dick move to not help Mina, but the very thought of dealing with Aaron made him sweat.

"Can I ask you something?" Giles asked Brian as he finished a game of Halo.

Brian put down his controller. "Sure. What's on your mind?"

Giles hesitated. "I'll warn you, it's kind of a gay moment."

"If you're after sex advice with either gender, I'm going to totally suck."

"It's not exactly a relationship." Giles climbed down from the bunk and sat beside Brian, staring at the wall behind the TV. "It's this guy I made out with last summer. It was pretty intense, actually, and while I wasn't his first time, I definitely showed him all the way around the plate, if you get my meaning." He tugged nervously at his ear. "He kind of freaked out after, and I got bummed. *Then* he shows up here at Saint Timothy."

Brian raised his eyebrows. "You mean, you didn't know he was going here?"

"He *wasn't* going here. When we talked, he had no idea where to go for college. Now here he is. First he shuns me, then he scams on my school."

"Man, that's kind of skeevy."

Giles threw up both hands in relief. "*Thank you.* He's not just here, either. He's some star pupil of Nussy's, and now he's helping with Salvo. Which they asked me to help with too."

"Sounds like a no-brainer. Run. Hard and fast."

"Yes, but Mina wants to be in this group, and she's nervous. If I help, I could…influence them."

"Tough call." He scratched his chin. "Wait—I think I heard of this guy. Is this the tenor who belted out 'Lover to Lover' at the Ambassadors initiation?"

"*God*, yes."

Brian laughed and nudged him with his shoulder. "Sorry, man. Didn't mean to rub it in."

"That's just it. Everywhere I go, there he is."

"Well, man, I'm sorry. I'll totally hate him for you, even though I actually think *that* is a girl thing to do."

"I feel like Salieri in the *Amadeus* movie. I always thought he was such a whiner, and now I'm living his fucking life."

"You shouldn't let this guy get to you. I mean, is he actively throwing it in your face?"

"No. He doesn't have the time because he's too busy running around being awesome and adored." Giles slumped his shoulders. "I had this idea how college would be different, how I wouldn't be an unholy outcast this time—and I'm not, but...well, here's the popular kid from A-Hell, rubbing my nose in the fact that I'm never going to be cool."

"Yeah." There was a lot of commiseration in the word, and Brian's shoulders slumped. "I don't have such a loud example as you, but I get the whole dork on Cool Island thing, believe me. It's better here than high school, but—well, as they say. Wherever you go, there you are. It sucks, having to admit it wasn't high school's fault. I'm straight up not cool."

"From where I sit, you're pretty damn cool. Do you have any idea how nervous I was I'd get a roommate who'd worry about my gay cooties? You haven't so much as blinked."

Brian shrugged. "My cousin is gay. He came out when we were both in eighth grade, and I watched how rough it was for him. I couldn't exactly beat guys up on his behalf, but I got beat up with him. I figured out pretty quickly it felt better to stand beside him than look away."

"See, *that* is cool."

"Yeah, too bad dick doesn't do anything for me. All Jay's gay friends hit on me, so I guess I'm hot to the wrong gender." His face screwed up in frustration. "I have no idea how to talk to girls. *None.* Not to get a date, anyway. They treat me as if I'm sexless, so if I say, 'Do you want to go out sometime?' it's like I tried to put my hand down their pants. I've never made out with anybody, so you're way ahead of me."

"Wish I had some brilliant advice about the girls,

but I have not once had one of them crush on me." He kicked an empty plastic tumbler, rolling it forward on the rug. "Aaron could help you, I'm sure."

"He really bugs you, doesn't he?"

"I know I'm wasting my energy, hating him so much, torturing myself with his popularity and his success. If I erase him from my experience, things are actually amazing. Every time I get any traction on putting him out of my head, though, somebody shoves him in front of me again."

"So you're going to go crazy working with him, is what you're telling me. Which means you should say no. I can tell by your face you're going to say yes for Mina. Except you probably won't have enough influence to guarantee her a spot."

Giles rubbed at his temples. His head was beginning to hurt. "Yes."

"But you're going to do it anyway."

All Giles could see was Mina's sad, desperate face. It didn't matter if they would actually discriminate against her or not. He had to be there for her. Fuck his hang-up with Aaron. Mina mattered. "Yes."

Brian put an arm loosely over his shoulders in a football-locker-room way. "Come on. Let's drown our misery in some Minecraft."

Giles shoved him playfully away, but he smiled as Brian changed the disc and they picked up their controllers.

Despite the looming awkwardness ahead of him, he felt better than he had in days. Maybe Aaron had the whole fucking music department eating out of his hand, but there wasn't any way he had a roommate as awesome as Brian.

THE FRIDAY OF the week before homecoming, Aaron was in one of the piano practice rooms, fussing with an arrangement of an Imogen Heap song, when his phone rang.

"Hey there." Jim Seavers's voice was bright, even pleased, which was an unusual way for him to address his son. "Don't want to keep you from your studies. Philosophy of Law is brutal at Saint Timothy, Bob says."

Aaron nearly dropped the phone. "F-fine. Everything's fine."

"Good to hear. We got a flyer about homecoming, but I leave for California the next week and won't be able to get away."

Sagging in relief, Aaron forced air into his lungs. "It's okay." *Please don't come, ever.*

"I already have some files for you to work on over Christmas break. I'm not sure if I'll be back by then, but the other partners can get you up to speed. I'll be curious to see how your views have changed now that you've had some real courses under your belt. You and Bob can trade war stories."

"Okay," Aaron replied, because what the hell else could he say?

"I wanted to let you know how proud I am of the work you're doing. You ever get stuck on something, you let me know, and I'll get you through."

Murmuring a goodbye, Aaron rested his forehead on the piano for a minute. For the first time, Aaron's father had said he was proud of him…based on a lie.

His chest felt tight, his stomach queasy. His time in the practice room was up, so he couldn't hide there, and the rest were full, as always. The only thing he could do was go to his dorm, but that wouldn't help anything. Elijah would be there.

Emily and Reece still escorted Elijah to Bible study. Emily shoved her breasts in Aaron's face every chance she got, and Reece continued to exhibit manic earnestness. The Campus Crusaders had been eclipsed in their creep-show factor, though, because Elijah's parents had shown up.

Despite how unsettled his dad made him, Aaron would take Jim Seavers any day over the Princes. They were almost too awful to be believed, like parents out of a Roald Dahl novel. They reminded Aaron of meeting the gaze of a drunken-bully football player at a rally in Eden Prairie. The Princes were subtle, but there was a knife under everything they did, even when on the surface they were behaving like regular parents. The mother held Elijah's hands and prayed over him, except it mostly consisted of apologizing to the ceiling for what a horrible, nasty sinner her son was, and she thanked Jesus for being kind enough to free Elijah from his enslavement to sin. She asked her son every other second if he'd been in trouble.

The whole time this went on, Mr. Prince huddled over Elijah's computer, scowling. He barely looked at his son, as if Elijah were vermin he had to tolerate. He pawed through every inch of Elijah's things, and sometimes he searched Aaron's side of the room too. Thankfully Elijah usually cut them off before Aaron had to get brave enough to do it. Once again, though, he never got acerbic with them the way he did with Aaron. It seemed from his parents and the Crusaders, Elijah would endure anything.

Knowing his roommate came from deep weird explained a lot, but living with Elijah was the loneliest thing in the world. He bitched about it constantly to Walter, who had stopped giving him tips on how to engage and started encouraging him to ask his RA for a new room assignment.

Walter. It was too early in the day to talk to his friend on the phone, so Aaron texted him instead.

Walter was coming to homecoming and bringing Kelly along. Aaron looked forward to their arrival like the dawning of a sun. Possibly they'd arrive in time to observe the Ambassador rehearsal, but if not, Aaron would still be glad to see them.

Especially since last night's meeting with Salvo had come with the bombshell that *Giles* might be helping out the same way Aaron was. Aaron wanted to quit, no matter how it broke Jilly's heart.

A text from Walter broke the spell of Aaron's worry.

Don't sweat your dad. We'll be there even if he does show up, and we're going to have a great time. I can't wait to see your concert and take you out after. Kelly's excited too. In the meantime, go talk to your RA again. You need to get a new roommate pronto.

Just reading the text eased Aaron. His shoulders settled into a more regular latitude. Walter would help him sort everything out. Giles, his roommate, his dad.

The Monday of homecoming week it was official: Giles was helping out with Salvo. It was equally official that trying to bail on Jilly would be not only rude and cruel to his best friend at Saint Timothy but possibly even more uncomfortable than dealing with Giles. After the auditions on Tuesday though, sitting with Giles at a table and trying not to touch him or look at him or smell him, Aaron was seriously ready for a drink. A lot of drinks.

Unfortunately, he didn't know anyone who could get him alcohol.

On Wednesday, Aaron called Walter to confirm their plans and maybe get some advance help on the Giles-Salvo situation, but Walter didn't answer, and Aaron's texts went without reply as well. Not even several hours later. At midnight Aaron gave up waiting and went to bed.

Elijah sat at his desk, scribbling in a notebook as per usual.

Aaron slept fitfully, waking at 3:00 a.m., his brain a frazzled mess. Had he done something to upset Walter? Did Walter hate him now too? The thought cramped his stomach, and he curled into a ball until at last sleep claimed him. His dreams were sharp and strange—he kept kissing Giles, their clothes melting away as they made out, but Giles broke away and stood over him, telling him he was awful in bed. Walter sometimes appeared too, frowning as he spoke in Jim Seavers's voice. "I'm disappointed in you, Aaron."

When he woke at six thirty coated in sweat, Elijah sat at his desk, watching Aaron with an odd expression. For an awkward moment they stared at each other.

Then it got weird, because they had an actual conversation.

"What were you dreaming?" Elijah asked.

About my pathetic crush, nude and judging me. "Nothing."

Elijah's dark gaze made Aaron squirm. "You were calling out to someone. You were upset. I thought you might have said…"

He trailed off, but his stare grew even more intense. Like next he'd get his scalpel and cut Aaron open to find the truth.

Good Christ, Aaron must have been calling out to Giles. Or Walter. "I can't remember. Sorry I disturbed you."

Elijah clearly didn't buy this, and now *he* looked frustrated. "You were begging for something. Some*one.*"

Aaron climbed out of bed. "I'm going to go shower."

Gathering his soap and towel, he went down to the showers to escape, and thankfully he had the room to himself when he returned. Unfortunately, he'd also missed Walter's call. Relief flooded him as he dialed the number.

"Aaron." Walter sounded worn and frazzled, and there was weird activity in the background. "I meant to call, but things got crazy. Kelly had an allergic reaction last night."

Aaron's heart lurched. "Is he okay?"

"Yeah. He had a cold to start, ate some almond by mistake, and somehow it all turned into this batshit asthma attack." Walter's voice wavered, and it was clear he was barely holding it together. "He's going to be okay, but it was awful to watch. I don't think I handled it well." He paused. "Okay, I handled it so badly they had to sedate *me*."

Aaron ached for his friend. "I'm glad he's going to be okay. I wish I could help you, both of you."

This pause was heavy, and with a sinking heart, Aaron realized what was coming.

"Aaron—I'm sorry, but I can't come this weekend. I feel terrible, and I want you to know I was looking forward to it. A lot. They're letting Kelly out in a few hours, but he's supposed to rest, and I can't—"

Aaron forced the words out. "Of course you can't leave him, and he shouldn't come here."

"I keep trying to figure out a way to make it work, but I only run around in circles."

Aaron swallowed his disappointment. "Don't worry about it. We'll do it another time."

"I'm *so sorry*."

Aaron tried to laugh. He sucked at it. "Right, because Kelly had a reaction on purpose."

"*Kelly* keeps trying to argue we should come. He hates it when his allergies get in the way of his life."

"Seriously. It's okay. When things calm down, try another weekend. I'll still be here."

Walter apologized for another five minutes, and Aaron continued to lie and tell him he didn't mind at all. The only reason the cycle broke was because a nurse needed Walter, and he hung up promising he would call a thousand times in the next three days, a promise Aaron desperately wanted but refused to accept. "Take care of your fiancé," he urged Walter.

After ending the call, Aaron stared sadly at the phone for a few seconds. Then he gathered his books for his classes and got ready to go to his lessons. He was halfway down the hall when a guy stumbled into him, murmuring something about music fags. Aaron ignored him.

On the stairs, however, he started to cry.

The tears came out of nowhere—it wasn't as if he'd been holding them back, they simply materialized out of thin air. His sinuses swelled, his eyes pooled and tears spilled over in a steady, silent stream down his cheeks. It was mortifying. Unnerving too, because it was almost as if some other part of him had pulled an override switch. He didn't know the origin of the tears, so he didn't know how to return to neutral.

Worst of all, now that the dam was breached, he could not stop.

He wandered aimlessly across campus, trying to clear his head, but nothing worked. The tears wouldn't even slow down. Eventually he headed to the music building, opting to enter via the back door so he could linger in an access hallway behind the orchestra and choir rooms. The din of students filtered down the passage, and Aaron still couldn't calm down. Great, now the music department had front-row seats for his meltdown.

As if he didn't have enough on his plate, his phone chimed a reminder for his lesson with Nussy in thirty minutes. Aaron was still crying with no sign of stopping. Nussy would ask him what was wrong, and Aaron would die of mortification.

The dark thought settled like a seed.

Who would miss him? Walter, maybe, but he was a burden to his friend more than anything else, simply one more someone to worry about. Jilly would be sad, but she had no idea he was this hot a mess. Certainly she didn't need him for Salvo, not with Giles. Nussy would be sorry, but sometimes Aaron wasn't sure he could be the person Nussy thought he was, any more than he could be the person his father wanted.

In the end thoughts of suicide only made him weep more deeply, because he knew even if a polite cupcake à la *Alice in Wonderland* appeared, labeled *Eat me to die quickly and peacefully,* he wouldn't have the guts to pick it up. He didn't have the guts to do anything. Not to select his own major, not to decide for himself to audition for choir, not to admit to Walter it hurt him all the way to his soul to be alone this weekend. He fucked up everything, because he was a stupid, worthless, nauseating *wimp* no one could love, because he wasn't anyone at all.

Aaron pressed his face to his knees, rocking back and forth in a pathetic attempt to calm himself. His hysteria cycled higher until he was no more than a snotty, inglorious heap of emotional exhaustion.

It took the person shaking him several tries to penetrate his haze. Aaron lifted his head and stared, horrified, into the worried, clean-cut face of Damien, the choral student director.

Chapter Ten

DAMIEN NORLING WAS a senior, another first tenor and pretty much a walking ad for the kind of put-together person Aaron wished he could be. He was so amazing he already had a fiancé, a pretty junior named Stevie who lived and breathed elementary education. Now Damien watched snot drip out of Aaron's nose and into his mouth as he drew ragged, shallow breaths. If the death cupcake had been present, Aaron would have gobbled it up.

"I'm fine," Aaron tried to say, but mostly he choked and wheezed up more snot. Wincing, he buried his face in his hands because it was the only way left to hide. "Oh God, I'm so sorry."

Damien's hand rested in a comforting gesture on Aaron's shoulder. "What happened? Something at school? Bad news from home?"

Never had Aaron felt more ridiculous. "It's n-nothing."

"Whatever's bothering you sounds about as far from nothing as anything I've seen in a long time."

Aaron's despair was a gas station road map he couldn't put back together. "I c-can't stop c-crying."

"Oh, buddy. Is there someone I can call for you?"

This of course was only additional fodder for Aaron's emotional compost heap. "No." The next sob hurt his chest, the muscles spasming from overuse. "I'm so sorry."

"Why do you keep apologizing?"

"Because I'm crying like an idiot."

"I hate to break it to you, but we've all cried like idiots. Ask Marius about my mental breakdown this summer when they screwed up my clinical rotation."

"This is for a st-stupid r-reason. This is because I'm...l-lonely."

To his surprise, Damien seemed almost chagrined. "I'll be damned. Baz was right." He ran a hand through his hair. "Nussy ordained you wunderkind, and we all accepted that and made our assumptions. Except Baz, who's argued for weeks something was off."

The realization his mental health was the speculation of so many people added new layers to Aaron's mortification.

Damien had gone from chagrined to guilty and awkward. "I should have seen this. I can't believe *I* fell for Nussy's shit, because usually I'm the first one in there calling his mad bluff, but no. If you're gay too, there's going to be *no* living with Baz." Color faded from his face. "Oh shit, I should *not* have said that out loud."

Weirdly, Damien's fumble made Aaron smile. "It's okay. Yeah...I'm gay."

"Awesome. I mean—I'm glad—" He winced and glanced at the ceiling. "Jesus, I suck at this."

Now Aaron laughed. "You're doing pretty well, actually."

Damien's expression told him he didn't buy it. "What I meant is, I don't care that you're gay, and neither will anybody in the music department. If they do, Baz will probably set fire to them. *He's* gay, if you haven't sussed that one out. I would not, however, advise you to date him."

"I haven't dated anybody, only two girls who were mistakes." Aaron couldn't stop his mouth. "I don't really have any friends. Just one. He was supposed to come this weekend, but his boyfriend got sick." He stared fixedly at his knees. "I guess I was looking forward to it a little too much."

"There's no too much when it comes to the people we care for. But what do you mean, you don't have friends? You practically have a fan club." He stopped, frowning. "*Oh.* That's why you don't have friends here. Goddamn you, Nussy, and goddamn me for not figuring it out. I'm sorry."

How Aaron's pathetic life was the fault of either Dr. Nussenbaum or Damien was unclear, but Aaron was too worn-out to argue. He glanced down at his phone. "I'm supposed to be at my lesson right now."

"Fuck your lesson. You're coming to the White House, and I'm making you lunch. Baz ought to be there, and he can lord over me about how right he was and what an idiot I've been. You can help us plan the karaoke party Baz is desperate to have. It'll be great." He nudged Aaron with his elbow. "Come on. I'll call Olivia for you and have her spread the word we won't be in any lessons or classes until choir, and you and I and probably Baz and Marius will spend the afternoon together. Three new friends, coming up."

More tears leaked out of Aaron's eyes, but his sobs were fully tamed. He smiled at Damien. "Thanks."

"No thanks necessary." Damien stood and held out a hand to Aaron. "Let's get out of here. As it happens, I know a secret way out that should let us avoid most of your paparazzi."

BY FRIDAY OF homecoming week, Giles was completely confused.

At the Salvo auditions on Tuesday, Aaron hadn't been stiff or catty to him. If anything, he'd been nervous. Hesitant, timid like a rabbit. Weirder yet, twice Giles could have sworn Aaron was cruising him in the same hesitant way.

On Thursday he saw Aaron and Damien in the hall, Damien's arm around Aaron as he spoke in hushed tones, and Aaron seemed kind of upset. Giles wondered if something was wrong, but if it was, it was fixed by Friday. When he went to orchestra rehearsal, the Ambassadors were heading down the chorus hallway for their own practice, Aaron laughing and beaming as he was frog-marched by Baz on one side, Damien on the other, Marius pretending to drive them like a chariot from behind.

The four of them were so hot together Giles tripped.

He didn't have any sexy escorts to his rehearsal. He had *alumni*.

When the former orchestra members filed into the rehearsal hall, Giles was annoyed. He didn't want to perform for strangers reliving glory days. They weren't as intrusive as he'd feared, though. Dr. Allison welcomed them, some by name, but the alumni were universally reserved. They applauded after each piece, but they said almost nothing, even when Allison prompted them to engage.

Before the orchestra rehearsed the last song, Allison had the alumni stand and give their year of graduation, their major, and what they were doing now. It seriously scared Giles how many of the recent grads had no job at all. Those who were employed hardly ever had jobs correlating with their college studies. Biology majors sold insurance. French majors worked at Target corporate. Social work majors worked as bank tellers. A few of them lined up, but by and large, no.

After they'd all been introduced, Allison invited the alumni to join rehearsal for "Canon". Only about half of them accepted his invitation.

A thirty-year-old woman with a blunt-edged haircut and severe blonde highlights drew up a chair next to Giles. When Allison counted them in, Giles's stand partner focused on the conductor, playing each note of the song as if it had come out of her soul. When she lowered her instrument to her lap at the end, she had tears in her eyes.

This was probably the first time she'd played since college. Someday Giles would be in the back of the room, watching a strange sea of students play where he'd once sat. He thought about not playing violin every day, of having a job he hadn't planned on, or no job at all, coming to a place that had once been a second home…knowing it could never be home again.

When the woman thanked Giles for letting her sit by him, he told her it was his pleasure and he looked forward to playing with her at the concert.

He went to a dorm party with Mina—who couldn't stop smiling, because she'd officially made it into Salvo that day—but he kept thinking about the alumni, wondering where they were tonight. Hotel rooms, he supposed. Were there alumni parties? Was it like the movies where people stood around with punch and sagging streamers, everyone bald or with gray hair?

Dear God, he hoped not.

Someday he'd be an alumnus returned. The warm feeling he had when he was in rehearsal, the sense of family and community he'd developed with Brian and Mina and their ragtag group of friends, not quite as cool as choir people but still pretty awesome—it would end, and they'd all move away. Giles would marry some guy or live in an apartment alone.

What would Aaron do? Who would he end up with?

Why could Giles not stop thinking about him?

Why had Aaron looked at him that way at tryouts?

Had Mina been right? Had Giles been wrong?

His melancholy lingered as he walked through the campus carnival the next morning. Every time he saw alumni, he had the same pang of regret. He had to walk against the tide of them as they went to the football game and he went to beat one last round of practice out, and he carried their wistful nostalgia with him all the way to rehearsal.

As he played that afternoon, for the first time since he'd joined chamber he didn't fumble and freak at the difficult measures. He thought of his alumni stand partner and soared through the runs, sang out on the held notes, each thrum of vibrato for her and the others not brave enough to rejoin the orchestra.

I hear you. I see you. I play for you.

The concert was a real monster: combined choir and orchestra, with all the small groups in between. During his quartet he saw his mom and dad and brother in the front row, smartphones poised as they took video and pictures. Giles spotted his stand partner in the audience.

Someday Giles would watch with her instead of playing. Someday much sooner than he was ready to think about.

Giles's quartet exited with a bow, and the Ambassadors came onto the stage.

For as much as Giles wanted to hate them, when they started to sing, he couldn't. It hurt nothing that the guys were all hot, all bright and full of life and joy, but they were talented too, carrying energy and vibrancy Giles doubted strings could ever capture. The audience had liked the chamber orchestra, but they loved the Ambassadors. Giles had to admit he did too. The melancholy he carried bled away when the boys bopped around the stage. Even the gag-me Cody Simpson song made Giles feel better.

Maybe *this* was why everyone loved them.

They started their final number, Aaron taking the solo on "Somewhere Only We Know"—and the last icicles inside Giles melted.

Everyone gushed and carried on as if Aaron singing was the second coming of Christ. Giles had written it off as hyperbole. But when Aaron sang, soul shining through the music, Giles realized they'd undersold him. Aaron was *amazing*. Aaron could start and end wars with his voice, could move a stone to tears.

Maybe Aaron hadn't rejected Giles because he was scared of being gay—maybe he'd simply been scared. Maybe it was because Giles wasn't right for him, or Aaron wasn't ready.

But as the song went on, as Aaron's high notes made Giles shiver, he remembered what he'd seen in Aaron's longing gazes as they worked on Salvo. Aaron's singing undid Giles's cynical heart, and despite himself, he began to believe.

Maybe there was a chance after all.

I have to talk to him. The thought resonated as the orchestra took their place for "Canon". *I have to go to him, now, and talk to him. Tell him. Find out if I'm right.*

The thought echoed as he played the song. When it was finished, his stand partner rose with tears in her eyes. Giles hugged her, accepted her thanks again, and bounded off the stage, tucking his violin under his arm as his pulse kicked at his ears.

I can't waste time. I have to talk to him now. Right now.

Giles fought his way through the crowd, waving an

in a minute gesture at his parents. He kept going until he was in the lobby, until he saw Aaron's dark head of hair and those bright blue eyes, his shy, sweet smile. Aaron stood smiling and talking with guys from the Ambassadors, ducking his head and blushing at something they said.

Giles's grip on his instrument slipped as he approached. He'd figure out what to say when he got there. He had to find out if the boy who stole his heart, who lived in that song, was real. He *had to do this.*

The crush of bodies was too thick to pass through, Giles's dream a horrible reality. By the time he reached the lobby where Aaron had been, Giles saw him disappearing through the door.

Disappearing with Baz, arm around Aaron's waist. Hand resting on Aaron's ass.

Baz leaned down to whisper something, and when Aaron laughed shyly, Baz moved his hand lower and squeezed.

The euphoric rush carrying Giles forward crashed like glass around his feet.

Too late. Whether or not Giles would have had a chance, it was too late now. He'd done exactly what Mina had said he would do, and now it was too late.

Chapter Eleven

AARON TRIED NOT to crush on Baz, but the more he resisted the urge, the more he longed to give into his hopes his friendship with the upperclassman might turn into something *more*.

Ever since Damien rescued Aaron from his meltdown, Aaron had hung out frequently at the White House. It was an old mansion turned dormitory across the street from campus, where eight people lived at a time. Right now the residents were Damien and Sid, Marius and Baz, Karen and Marion, and Rob and Daniel. Karen and Marion lived in the carriage house apartment with their own minikitchen, and they pretty much came into the main house for parties and to do laundry. The rest of the guys piled into the three upstairs bedrooms.

The first floor was a living room, a music room with a grand piano named Fred, a study room, and a butler pantry used as a second practice room. There was also a ballroom bigger than the floor plan of Aaron's mom's house in Oak Grove, where the White House had its infamous parties, one of which Aaron witnessed homecoming weekend. It was mostly choir, but there were some upperclassmen orchestra and band members too, and a few friends of the music department. Aaron helped Baz run the karaoke machine, and he sang plenty himself.

A few times he sang with Baz.

Aaron and Baz hung out together all the time now. They went to breakfast, and of course they were often together at the White House. Aaron always wound up next to Baz on the couch. He drank beer and sat with his leg pressed against the upperclassman's thigh, getting drunk both on the alcohol and the sharp, peppery smell of his host.

Baz coerced Aaron into helping make pancakes with him and Marius, and one Sunday morning Baz took him along on a run to the store in his slick red sports car, letting Aaron drive. He listened to a lot of rap while they cruised around, which Aaron couldn't ever get into, but Baz *loved* the song "Titanium". He belted it out at the top of his lungs, urging Aaron to sing along. When he found out how well Aaron knew the song, he'd goad him into a duet randomly through the day—in the lounge, the hallway, the cafeteria, or the middle of campus. Aaron was always excited to see him, and a few times when he felt listless and anxious, he drifted to where he knew Baz would be and waited for another hit.

Aaron ran into Giles a lot too, now that Salvo was official. They performed for Dr. Nussenbaum the Sunday afternoon of homecoming, and the performance was a huge hit. He and Giles were now officially part of the group—though they were only freshmen and not music majors, they got to arrange songs.

They had a quiet rhythm down. Aaron would work up the compositions, and Giles would fill in the holes or make suggestions along with Jilly and Karen. When classes and other practices got to be too much for Aaron alone, Giles took over some of the transcriptions.

Sometimes Giles seemed a little sad. Sometimes Aaron thought maybe, *maybe*, Giles was hitting on him. But he couldn't ever figure it out for sure, and he didn't know what, if anything, he should do about it.

In addition to Baz and Giles, Aaron still had to navigate the joy that was living with Elijah. Emily and Reece still came by to pick him up for Bible study, and though Aaron took great pains to not be there when they arrived, sometimes he couldn't avoid an encounter. Emily dialed her vamp down to a low-grade *just in case* baseline flirtation, but Reece still looked one Red Bull away from a manic meltdown, always trying to invite Aaron along, always waving at him across the campus.

One day Reece and Emily ran into Aaron when he was with Baz.

Baz had his arm around Aaron's waist, drawing him close. Reece, who'd smiled as he approached, lowered his gaze to Baz's wandering hand. His expression morphed into a look of utter betrayal. Emily appeared ready to unpack a crossbow from her pretty blue handbag and bury an arrow between Aaron's eyebrows.

Baz snorted, pulling Aaron closer as he glanced over his shoulder to watch them walk away. "Aw, so sad. We pissed off the toads."

"Toads?"

"There's a crazy evangelical church outside of town, and it tends to spill onto campus. We call their group the toads, because they sit there like lumps staring at you, trying to get you to join their cult of guilt and shame. On the books Timothy is gay friendly, but the toads are here to remind us never to let our guard down. They've been especially bad ever since the marriage ban was overturned in Minnesota. Pastor Schulz doesn't want them here, but he can't do much unless they fuck up first."

Schulz, even atheist Aaron knew, was the head campus pastor. Aaron was about to ask why the hell Baz hung out with him when a hand wandered more firmly onto Aaron's ass.

Baz accompanied this grip with a nuzzle of Aaron's ear. "I think we were too gay for that particular amphibian. Now he'll have to go jerk off over how sinful we were. I'm sure he'll thank us later."

Aaron couldn't help it. He laughed. "Jerk off? Because we were sinful?"

"Hell yes. The quote-unquote Christians who get up in everyone's grill about sin are mostly jonesing for a fix of rage. Emotions are a natural high, and fury fuels the engine. You should see the church where the toads go. Sometimes they do the thing where they *feel the Spirit* or speak in tongues. Now, I'm not saying some of them aren't actually making some kind of divine connection. Most of them, though? They're getting off. I about shit myself the first time I saw. Looks *just* like somebody having an orgasm, right there in church."

"You actually went there?"

Baz shrugged. "Sure. Marius insisted on going along, but yeah, I went. Sat in the back. Took notes for class. The professor didn't say we had to go to the toad church, but I wasn't going anywhere else."

"There's a class where you have to go to church?"

Laughing, Baz tweaked his nose. "You're required to take two religion courses before graduation, remember? Except this was when I thought it'd be my major."

Aaron pulled away from him, ready to call bullshit. "No fucking way. *You*, a religion major?"

Baz's grin arced all the way to the bottom of his sunglasses. "Yessir. I was all set to be a Lutheran pastor, or maybe a youth minister. For almost a whole year. A record for me."

"Religion creeps me out." He ran a hand through his hair. "My roommate is one of the toads. The guy who passed us is always taking Elijah to Bible study and trying to get me to go along."

"Toad roommate, huh? He spend a lot of time trying to convert you?"

"He's said ten sentences to me since we met." The Dr Pepper can was still in the fridge, but Aaron wasn't sure how to explain it without sounding crazy. "Mostly he pretends I don't exist. His parents are super, super creepy. But they don't talk to me, either."

"Roomie know you're gay?"

Aaron swallowed. "I haven't…really told anyone. A few people here and there."

Even with the dark sunglasses, Aaron could read the amusement on Baz's face. "It might not be the best move to let me drape myself all over you in public, then."

"No—I mean, it's okay. I like it." Aaron blushed. "I mean, I'm not hiding. Just not advertising."

"You're advertising. Right now. The toads have figured out you're gay. They'll probably tell your roommate. That going to be a problem?"

Usually Baz was all laughs and flirts, but now he was a lot more like Walter: bossy and care-taking...and a little badass. It was kind of hot. It rendered Aaron completely unable to process the real danger Baz had pointed out. "I...don't know."

"Where is your roommate right now? I want to meet him."

Aaron didn't know where Elijah was, so Baz took them on a kind of aggressive campus tour, poking their heads into every public area once they established Aaron's room was clear.

They didn't walk fast—Baz never did. "Old football injury," he'd joke whenever someone tried to get him to move in a hurry, and usually he'd clutch the left side of his chest dramatically. He got headaches a lot too, Aaron noticed. He took pain pills after too much dancing, and he always seemed to be at a doctor's appointment. More than seemed normal. Baz *never* drove his own car, either. He had Aaron drive him, or Marius, or Damien. Not once had Aaron seen him behind the wheel.

By the time they'd made a circuit of half the campus, it was clear Baz was in pain, holding his ribs and his shoulder, but he refused to end the search. "Really want to meet your roomie," he kept saying.

They found Elijah in the public computer lab in the basement of the student union. It was an old one hardly anybody used and was rarely open. The occupants of the lab were strange at best. Everyone was hunched over their keyboards. A few people were clearly the odd ones out who didn't have their own personal computers in their rooms. Some had flash drives and were using the lab only to print. Mostly though the lab was deserted.

It was weird, because Elijah *had* a computer in his room, same as Aaron, and he was doing more than printing. He had his endless notebooks spread around him, a travel coffee mug, and a bagel sandwich.

Elijah sat in the farthest corner, facing the door so he could see the whole room. He glanced up as Baz and Aaron entered. When he saw Aaron, his face flashed surprise, the same guarded, flat expression he always had. But then he saw Baz, and for the first time, Aaron saw real emotion on his roommate's face.

Recognition. Shock.

Fear.

Baz was harder to read, and not just because of the sunglasses. His mouth was flat, his face almost wooden as he stared at Elijah. Aaron couldn't tell if he was angry or not.

"Baz?" Aaron whispered at last.

Taking Aaron's hand, Baz led him out of the lab. He was quiet all the way up the stairs, so quiet Aaron didn't dare try and speak to him. But once they were in the main lobby of the union, Baz squeezed his arm and gave Aaron a wobbly smile.

"Hey." His voice, for the first time, wasn't confident and breezy. "I gotta—" His voice broke, and he stopped, stone-still.

What the hell was going on? "Baz, are you okay?"

Baz let out a shaky breath. "I need to go do something. I'll see you later."

Let me help you, Aaron wanted to say, but he wasn't sure he was qualified to assuage whatever was making Baz look like this. He squeezed Baz's hand tight. "Take care of yourself."

Aaron wished he could see Baz's eyes, because something told him they revealed everything about the man in that moment. "I will, baby. Thanks."

With a kiss on Aaron's forehead, Baz went up the stairs, heading to the sky bridge leading to the campus chapel.

Aaron didn't see Baz again that day, not even at choir, which was weird, but when he asked Damien and Marius, they told him not to worry. Marius took off though, in the middle of rehearsal. Nussy had made it plain anybody who didn't show up to any rehearsal better be vomiting continuously and/or hospitalized, but apparently Baz and Marius had special passes. Unsurprisingly, once rehearsal was over, Damien vanished as well. Aaron went to dinner with Jilly and hung out in the music building after working on Salvo, hoping to run into Baz or someone who knew what was going on with him, but eventually he had to give up and go to his room.

Elijah waited for him.

He marched right up to Aaron, the same fear on his

face from the computer lab stirred up with an ample helping of rage. "What did he tell you?"

Aaron blinked and backed into the door. He hadn't managed to shut it all the way, but he couldn't open it without walking forward into Elijah, and his roommate was practically radioactive. "What did who tell me?"

"Don't pull that shit. The sunglasses guy in the lab. *What did he tell you about me?*"

Aaron tried to shrink away, but he was seriously stuck. It didn't matter that Elijah was a foot shorter than him. He was a cobra ready to strike. "Baz didn't say anything. *I swear*," he added, raising his hands defensively as Elijah pressed closer. "He took off, and I haven't seen him since."

Then Aaron did something stupid. He kept talking.

"Do you guys know each other or something?"

He quite seriously thought he might piss himself from the look Elijah gave him. "You said he didn't say anything."

"He didn't—that's why I was asking. Which obviously was dumb. I'm sorry."

Elijah continued to bore into him with his gaze while Aaron held his breath. After what felt like a year, Elijah rolled his eyes, loosened his stance and walked away.

As quickly and quietly as possible, Aaron went to his desk, deposited his books and grabbed his toothbrush. When he returned to the room, the lights were off and Elijah was in bed. Aaron followed suit, but it was hours before he went to sleep, and then only when he put in his headphones.

They didn't speak to each other all the next day, and as much as possible, they didn't look at each other.

Things got tense, though, a day later when Emily and Reece showed up for Bible study. Reece didn't enter the room, instead planting himself in the middle of the hallway before spouting off loudly about traditional marriage until the guy across the hall loomed over him and told him to peddle his hate shit on somebody else's floor. Emily stared daggers at Aaron. She didn't just have the anti-equals sign on. She had on her *One Man, One Woman, One Marriage* T-shirt, stretched tastefully beneath her cardigan.

Elijah followed them out, but before he disappeared through the door, he cast a glance over his shoulder. He smiled, a dark and wicked gesture that said he didn't understand what was going on, but he found it funny.

Aaron knew Elijah was about to find out *why* the toads had given him the cold shoulder, and the idea scared him to death. When Damien and Marius invited him to the White House for dinner, he all but wept in relief. Anything to keep from going to his room.

Baz was at the house, very much his old self. He'd been subdued in rehearsal, but now he was full of wisecracks and flirts, and his attentions included Aaron as if he hadn't nearly broken down in the middle of the union and vanished for twenty-four hours. Afraid to break the spell, Aaron didn't bring up Elijah or anything else about the toads.

Aaron would have stayed at the White House, but no one offered to let him crash, so he simply took as long as possible to return to Titus, staying in the lounge to watch *SportsCenter* with a bunch of jocks. But at one in the morning, Aaron decided to face the music and went to his room.

Elijah was still at his desk, writing in the lamplight. He glanced up when Aaron entered.

He knew. Elijah knew Aaron was gay.

He didn't seem upset by it. Surprised, maybe, but clearly he wasn't going to spout Scripture or ask Aaron to let Jesus heal him.

Come to think of it, Elijah only ever prayed when someone else was around.

As Aaron set his backpack on his desk and peeled out of his coat to hang it over his chair, Elijah watched him—which in itself was strange. Usually his roommate did whatever he could to pretend Aaron wasn't present. Now Elijah watched Aaron as if he were a lab rat.

Funny, how after all these months of longing for a connection, now Aaron only wanted to be ignored.

Later, as he lay in bed, Aaron thought maybe Elijah had been waiting for him to say something. Initially Aaron hadn't allowed subtlety to penetrate his terror, but upon reflection, maybe Elijah wouldn't have given him fire and brimstone. Maybe he would have come out himself.

If that moment had been there, by morning it was gone. Elijah had on his coat when Aaron woke, as if he'd been waiting to talk to Aaron before leaving. When he spoke, his tone was full of barbs once more.

"If you could continue keeping the queer turned off when my parents are around, that'd be a big help." He stared at Aaron aggressively.

Aaron swallowed nervously, shifting uncomfortably beneath his comforter. "Oh—okay."

Elijah's smile would give clowns nightmares. "Thanks so much, sweetie. Have a great day."

They didn't speak of it, or anything else, for the rest of the month.

Chapter Twelve

IN THE WEEKS after homecoming, Giles watched Baz flirt with Aaron, watched Aaron flirt back. Every time Giles crossed the common or stuck his head into the music lounge, he saw the two of them together. In his psych class, Giles overheard a hot freshman in hysterics because he thought he'd missed his chance with Baz and shouldn't have tried to play so hard to get, since obviously the way to hook him was to make moon-eyes at him the way Aaron did.

Everyone knew Aaron was gay now too. The girls still sighed over him from a distance, but now the boys made plans for how to catch him once Baz was done with him.

Giles wanted to bang his head into the wall.

"I swear before homecoming he was looking at me," he confessed to Mina. "*At* homecoming I wanted to do something about it—and Baz swooped in. I was *literally* three minutes too late." Giles plunked into Mina's beanbag, sick and miserable. "You're going to tell me you told me so."

Mina stroked his hair. "Honey, I was at those rehearsals. He was definitely into you."

Giles groaned and pulled the pillow against his face.

Mina tweaked the toe of his shoe. "Chin up. From what I hear, Baz cuts and runs. They'll sleep together a few times, and then it'll be over."

"Not helping."

"Well, what do you want me to say? Lie, tell you they aren't going to fuck?"

Giles's stomach lurched. He tossed the pillow aside and stared at the ceiling. "How could I be so close and still screw it up? How could he look at me like that and go out with Baz?"

"He's been looking at you like that since the end of August. He probably got tired of waiting for you to figure it out."

"*Still* not helping."

Mina settled onto the beanbag beside him. "I'm sorry, hon."

Giles leaned on her shoulder, a lump growing in his throat. "I had a chance, but I did what you warned me I'd do."

She stroked his arm, drawing him closer. "People are hard. Relationships are harder."

Mina had an odd tone to her voice, as if she spoke from experience. Giles lifted his head and frowned at her. "Something you want to share with the class?"

It shocked him how buttoned up she got. "No. Not yet."

Giles sat up. "Min—"

She held up her hand, silencing him. "*No.*"

Her expression was unyielding, but it was clearly a wall holding back something pretty raw. "Did—did I do something?"

If Mina had had glasses, she'd be looking at Giles over the top of them. "It's about a romantic relationship, and you think it's about you?"

Touché. "I meant—I didn't want to have fucked us up too."

"It's…complicated." She shook her head. "I don't know how to talk about it to myself yet."

Whatever this was, it was no dreamy desire to feel up a hot high school guy. This was serious. *Good for you, Min.* "Do I know him at least?"

Why the hell that comment made her face cloud up again, Giles couldn't guess. "Leave it for now, okay? Let's just say I get how difficult it can be to understand you're attracted to someone. Sometimes we're in our own way more than we know, but I don't think we can beat ourselves up over it."

"Yes, but what if we get in our own way long enough for our opportunity to pass us by? What if we miss our boat?"

She shut her eyes. "We believe in a universe that will bring us another one."

"The thing is, right now I only want this boat."

She cradled his head into her shoulder. "Then right now you'll have to be a little sad."

Giles didn't cry, but his chest hurt. A lot.

Baz and Aaron hung out together more and more all the time, Baz looking at Aaron as if he were dinner, Aaron clearly wanting to be on the menu. A few weeks after homecoming, Giles saw them crossing campus, heading for the White House arm in arm, and Giles got so depressed he gave up.

He hadn't hooked up for a while, unable to give up the faint hope of *maybe*, but that night he tossed in the towel. Dusting off his Grindr app, he surfed for sex— and as luck would have it, stumbled onto Intense Twink from orientation day, or "Naughty Nate" as per his username.

Naughty Nate who was, shockingly, *pay for play*. Giles hadn't done that before. But he remembered those looks Nate had tossed out, combined them with the lurid sexual promises in text, and decided what the hell. First time for everything. If it sucked, it was only twenty bucks.

Brian was off at a friend's for a Halo marathon, so Giles invited his trick to the room. At nine on the dot a knock sounded on the door, and there stood Naughty Nate, drowning in a hoodie. No sooner did Giles open the door than the kid pushed his way inside.

"Come right in," Giles murmured, closing the door with a shiver of apprehension. It wasn't as if he were actually scared of the guy—Giles wasn't built, but Naughty Nate was little more than a broom handle. His eyes, though. Jesus H, he could cut granite with that gaze.

Nate crossed to the window, tugging the blinds tighter before tossing his hood back. He was even more delicate up close, but he wasn't timid. He marched up to Giles and held out his hand. "Money up front."

Oh shit. The twenty. Giles fumbled for his wallet, pulled out a Jackson and passed it over. "Here. Sorry."

All business, Nate nodded curtly as he pocketed the cash. "No worries. Now—for specifics. You weren't clear in chat. Did you want to fuck me or get sucked off?"

The curt directness both jarred Giles and turned him on. He didn't want to fuck the guy, though—too intimate. Too much when he still pined for Aaron. "We can just frot."

"Blow job first?"

Jesus, this was like ordering McDonald's. Giles wasn't sure he wanted to pay for a trick anymore. "Um, sure."

"Warn me when you're close, and we'll mix it up."

Nate fell to his knees.

For a few terrible seconds Giles worried he wouldn't be able to get it up, this was so clinical, but when Nate looked up at him with doe eyes as he closed his mouth over Giles's cock, Giles rose immediately to full mast. Nate was good. He knew where to touch, how hard to suck, when to moan. All too quickly Giles had to map violin fingerings in his head to keep himself from coming, and after less than five minutes he had to cry uncle.

As graceful as a gazelle, Nate stripped himself nude and sat on the futon, drawing his knees up to present himself, dark asshole gaping invitingly.

Fucking hell.

Giles didn't penetrate Nate, but he fucked him into the futon, gripping those bony shoulders, drinking in every moan, every cry. His voice was high—a tenor, same as Aaron. He was dark haired, so respon- sive…closing his eyes tight, Giles pretended this was Aaron beneath him, Aaron he fucked, Aaron who cried out and begged for more, Aaron who came like a fountain between their chests as Giles did the same.

He pretended, but when they finished and he opened his eyes to find Nate in his arms, despite getting epically laid, he felt more miserable than ever.

"You're pretty hot. Dark horse—love that." Nate slapped Giles's flank and started to wriggle. "I gotta go, though. Another appointment in a half hour, and I want to clean up."

"Sure." Giles shifted to let him rise, feeling more awkward and awful by the moment.

"Chat at me later." Nate climbed into his clothes. "I don't always do return tricks, but I like you."

No way Giles was ever doing this again. "I'll keep it in mind, thanks."

"One thing." Nate tugged his shirt over his head. "Don't be friendly with me on campus. No winks or smiles, and no appointments made in any way but on the app. And whatever you do, never call me Nate. That's not my real name."

Giles frowned. "What is it?"

His trick paused with his coat half on, then shrugged. "Elijah."

THOUGH THINGS HAD gone well with Baz since homecoming, Aaron didn't tell Walter about him. Which got interesting when Walter figured out something was going on anyway.

"You seem happy," Walter observed one day when they spoke on the phone.

"I am," Aaron agreed and tried to leave it at that.

Walter didn't let him. "I'm so happy for you, hon. What turned things around? I know it's not your roommate, and your dad certainly didn't decide to be rational about your college career choices. What brought all this joy on? Did you meet someone?"

Aaron swallowed hard. "Um. Maybe."

"Excellent. Tell me all about him."

Aaron didn't want to. "Nothing worth telling. Just a guy from choir. He's nice." *And sexy as hell and likes to put his hand on my ass and whisper in my ear.* "He makes me feel good."

"I can't wait to meet him. Tonight works for us to come see you, if you're free."

The very idea put Aaron in a panic. He was due to go out with the guys, and Baz kept hinting he hoped Aaron would be there. Like tonight maybe something could happen. "I don't know. I have a big test on Monday—probably should study."

There was a pause on the other end of the line. "Of course," Walter said at last.

Walter being around while Baz—hopefully—made a move could only be disaster.

Nothing did happen that weekend, alas—only more flirting, more teasing. But the week before Thanksgiving, Aaron and the guys from the White House went out to the Shack, and everything changed.

Baz flirted with the doorman so he'd let Aaron in. Baz supplied Aaron with ample rum and Coke and dragged him repeatedly to the dance floor. Baz couldn't stay on the dance floor for long periods of time without a rest, but he made up for longevity with intensity. They danced to several songs throughout the night, including "Titanium". They sang along at the top of their lungs, Baz groin to groin with his hands on Aaron's ass. Eventually with Baz's hand down the back of Aaron's jeans, boldly moving inside his underwear.

It was going to happen.

Except before anything could get interesting, Damien broke them up. Marius escorted Aaron home, but on the way out the door they passed Damien and Baz in a heated argument off in the corner.

"I'm sorry," Aaron slurred when they got to the parking lot.

"You don't need to apologize for anything." Marius steadied Aaron before resuming their hike to the house. "This is an old argument, though this time I agree with Damien."

"I don't understand."

Marius squeezed his shoulders. "I'll get you some coffee. And water. Lots of water."

Aaron, however, couldn't shake the nasty feeling in his gut. "I don't want Damien to be mad at me. Or Baz. Or you."

Marius's voice gentled. "Nobody's mad at you."

Aaron's throat got thick. "I'm so lonely. Even with all you guys around, even though everything is good, sometimes I'm so *lonely*."

"Which is why I'd argue you shouldn't sleep with Baz."

Aaron started to object, to say he wasn't sleeping with Baz yet, but of course he wanted to, and he was

pretty sure but for Damien it would have happened.
He knew where the dance-floor flirting was going,
where all of it was. Obviously everyone had known. His
throat threatened to close in embarrassment.

Marius chuckled. "It's cool, man. Relax."

"How can I? Basically I was acting like a whore."

"You want to know how many times a chick
ground on me at the bar and I followed her home my
freshman year? I get it."

"But you think it's a bad idea."

"Baz has been my roommate since day one. I know
how he operates. I get why. I don't think you're on his
same page, though."

"What do you mean?"

They were almost to the door, and Marius fiddled
in his pocket for his keys. "It's your call what you do
with him. Just don't think Baz is going to be a boyfriend. That's all I'm saying. I don't think he can be
one, not anymore."

There was a story there, and it reminded Aaron of
the day Baz had hunted Elijah down, the day they
carefully never discussed. Clearly Marius wouldn't be
sharing any stories tonight. It was just as well, because
once Aaron saw the saggy couch in the corner of the
living room, his rum-soaked body forgot all about
getting off and yearned only for sleep.

He woke in the middle of the night, mouth tasting
like rotten ass, head and gut complaining loudly. After
a trip to the bathroom, he meandered into the kitchen
to look for water.

Baz sat at the table in a pair of boxers, hair standing

on end, a mug of tea in his hand. For the first time since Aaron had known him, his sunglasses were off. When he smiled, his eyes crinkled. "Hey, you."

Aaron rubbed his arm. Baz's eyes were pretty, but sad. "Hey."

"You should go to bed." This was what Baz said, but his tone urged Aaron to stay right where he was. Or better yet, come closer.

The sadness in Baz's gaze gave way to lust.

Aaron was thirsty, but he wasn't thinking about water anymore. He thought about Baz, the way Baz looked at him. The way Baz touched him. He thought about how long it had been since Hickey Lake, yet how much it still hurt and ached to think of that night. How Giles was so damn *polite* with him and nothing more.

How Baz was right here, clearly wanting to fuck.

Aaron longed to knock the night at the lake out of his head. He wanted to have sex—sex with a guy who wasn't going to be weird on him after. He wanted to get laid. He wanted to suck cock. He wanted to get licked again. God, he wanted to be fucked, straight up. He wanted it all.

He wanted to stop feeling so hollow inside, so lonely even in a room full of people.

They started with a kiss—one second Baz had a snarky grin on his face, and then his grin was gone, those soft, spicy lips teasing and tasting at Aaron's. He pulled Aaron's clothes off with startling ease. After sliding the briefs down, he held Aaron's ass in his hands. The grip, firm and commanding, made Aaron shudder.

This was everything Aaron wanted. Baz murmured soft, sweet things to Aaron, and wicked ones. He told Aaron to suck his cock, and Aaron got on his knees. He worried he'd do it wrong, as this was his first time, but Baz was wonderful here too.

This *had* to be the start of something real this time. Being with Baz made Aaron's body hum.

Baz was a Walter Aaron could have.

Baz blew Aaron too, laughing wickedly as he discovered how much Aaron enjoyed being rimmed. He laid Aaron on the kitchen table, pushed his thighs open and went to town. *Jesusgod*, Baz was almost better than Giles, and Aaron hadn't thought that was possible. He let himself go, giving over to everything he'd been holding back. Baz took it all.

"You're so sexy, honey. You're butter melting in my mouth." Baz licked up Aaron's taint and grinned. "Sure hope I get to take your ass someday."

"Take it now." Aaron pulled his legs wider, offering himself. It was right. It had to be. "Fuck me. Right now." *Let me not feel so alone.*

Baz's eyes were dark beads in the shadows. "You sure you want to give up your first time for this?"

How did he know it was Aaron's first? "I'm sure."

Baz stroked Aaron's thigh lazily before letting his thumb circle Aaron's hole. "How about we play around first, see how it goes. How much have you had in your ass, sweetie?"

"A few fingers." Aaron flushed in memory.

Bending, Baz kissed Aaron's cockhead. "Let me get

some slick and see if we can't expand your horizons."

Aaron didn't lose his nerve when Baz left. He lay on the table, legs still pulled back, cool air on his ass. He wanted this. Everything felt so good, all the shadows chased out of his head. He wanted them gone for good. Baz was better than Giles. So much better. This was how it had been for Walter and Kelly. Baz would be the same, and it would all be okay.

When Baz returned, he sat on a chair and drew Aaron into his lap, making him straddle Baz's legs. After a goose-bump-inducing kiss, he pressed slicked fingers into Aaron's ass, first one, then two. Aaron groaned against the burn, trying to pull his thighs wider, take more of Baz in.

"Fuck," Baz murmured between nibbles of his lip. "You're a born bottom, baby." He groaned with Aaron as a third finger went in. "You sure you haven't been sitting on fire hydrants?"

Aaron could barely speak, too intent on fucking himself on Baz's hand. "Oh God. I need—*ohgod.*" He clutched at Baz's shoulders and kissed him hard and desperate. When Baz broke away, he sucked at his neck. "Please—*please.*"

Except somehow that was when it ended. Baz still fingered him, but the tone changed. Instead of putting on the condom he'd brought down, he grabbed their cocks and jerked them together the same way Giles had. It was hot, coming with three of Baz's fingers jammed into him, but it wasn't what he wanted. It hurt, too, when he tried to nuzzle Baz after and felt himself quietly pushed away. Worse, when Aaron looked at him, Baz averted his gaze.

Aaron panicked. "Did I do something wrong?" The thought of losing not just Baz but the refuge of the White House left him cold.

"No." Baz still couldn't look at him, though, and when he touched Aaron's arm, it was lingering and sad. "Why don't you get some sleep?"

Aaron didn't sleep, only lay awake on the couch with his stomach in knots until at five he headed to his dorm. Elijah was there, and he sat up briefly when Aaron opened the door.

For a moment their eyes met, but Aaron glanced quickly away, worried at what his roommate might see.

He fell asleep in his own bed at eight and slept until almost noon. Elijah was gone when he woke, probably to church.

Aaron played the scene in the kitchen over and over in his mind, trying to find the point where he went wrong. Had he done something embarrassing? Was it because he hadn't brushed his teeth? Was he gross?

Had he liked it too much? That one felt as if he'd discovered the corner of the truth, but it made him despair.

He couldn't even be himself during *sex*?

Why did this keep happening? Why, every time he tried for something more than friends, did he mess it up?

Why couldn't he figure out what he was doing wrong?

At one he couldn't take it anymore. He showered— brushed his teeth—and went to the White House. He'd *ask* Baz what he'd done wrong. He wasn't doing what he had with Giles. Or Tanner. No more of this. He'd get it figured out.

Except Baz wasn't there, Marius said.

"Took a cab into the Cities. He was in one of his *moods*, so I expect him to wander in tomorrow night in time for choir rehearsal, smelling like a rotten bar and covered in hickeys." Marius held the door wider and motioned to Aaron. "Come on in. Damien made popcorn."

Aaron backed away, too rattled by Baz's departure to do anything else. He'd left? To go whoring?

What the hell had Aaron done wrong?

Marius called after him as Aaron ran, but Aaron didn't answer. He got away as quickly as he could, not wanting anyone to witness his breakdown this time.

He was fucked up. It kept happening, and he was the common variable. Something about the way he acted during sex with guys was wrong. He went round and round trying to ID the technique, the...*something* driving them off, not wanting to speak to him after, taking months to at best be awkward.

He couldn't think of anything. Nothing at all.

Because it's you who's fucked up. It's not what you did. It's you. There's something wrong with you that goes all the way down. You can't fix it. You can't stop it. You're alone because you're so fucked up nobody can get close to you.

The tears Damien had stopped at homecoming came roaring back, threatening to spill over at any moment. Aaron drifted onto campus, fixing his gaze on the sidewalk to avoid eye contact with anyone, routing himself behind a building. He didn't know where he was going. He didn't know what to do.

His phone rang. It was Damien, but Aaron canceled the call, too mortified to answer. His carefully hoarded tears spilled over. When he saw people coming, he ducked behind a Dumpster and sank to the ground, tucked into a ball.

Despair beat at his skull, urging him to let it drive his pulse into the stratosphere, to burn everything out but the white heat of hysteria. He remembered what Baz had said about emotions—yes, he wanted to get high. He *needed* to get high on something, anything. He had to escape this. He could not keep feeling this way.

He wanted to die. He wanted to climb into the Dumpster and be taken out with the trash. He wanted this to end, wanted out, wanted off the bus. He wanted to be old enough to buy his own alcohol, to go drink until he saw nothing, felt nothing, was nothing. Until he was dead.

He wanted to go home. Except he didn't have one. Not the one he was looking for.

He didn't remember deciding to make a call. It was as if his phone simply appeared in his hand, drifting there of its own accord. He wasn't even sure who he was dialing, not until he selected the contact. He had a moment's fear that this too would end in failure, but when the familiar voice drifted into his ear, the dam broke.

"Walter," he choked out, and then all he could do was cry.

Chapter Thirteen

I T TOOK A long time for Aaron to be coherent enough to answer his friend's frantic questions. He didn't want to tell Walter what had happened, because this was exactly what Walter had warned against, but after a few pitiful evasions he told Walter the truth. He was broken and awful and nobody wanted him, and someday Walter would see it too.

"That's never going to happen." Walter's voice was almost sharp.

"I think we'll be okay as long as we don't sleep together. That's when they leave me." Aaron choked back a sob. "I want to *be* with somebody. Not just sex. I'm always waiting for people, and they never come. When they do, they leave me." The words didn't make sense out loud, but it was so hard, so painful to put the solitude he felt inside into words.

"Baby, honey, hold on. We're almost there."

Aaron blinked. "You're almost where?"

"To Saint Timothy. We're merging onto 94 now. Give us another ten minutes."

"You're coming *here*?"

"Of course I'm coming there. Kelly too. Where are you? Where should I go to find you?"

The whole world peeled away, strange and hot and off-key. "But you can't come here. You're busy."

"Nothing right now is more important than you."

Walter kept talking to him, and technically Aaron answered, but all he could hear were those words, ringing in his head. *Nothing right now is more important than you.*

No one had ever said that to him before.

The minutes bled by, and the next thing he knew he had wandered to a side street at Walter's direction—and then there was Walter's bright blue car. Walter climbed out, tall and dark, his brown eyes full of concern. Kelly appeared too, slighter of build and blond, neatly pressed and perfect as he bit his lip and looked to Walter for guidance on how to proceed.

Walter opened his arms, and Aaron rushed into them.

Walter held him tight, murmuring reassurances. Eventually he herded Aaron into the backseat, coming in after him as Kelly took the wheel. Though Aaron lost it when he realized the song playing softly in the background was "Titanium".

When they got concerned, sensing something specific had set him off, Aaron confessed, "This was our song."

Kelly startled. "It was? Oh God, it's the song we—"

"Kelly," Walter interrupted, his tone a gentle warning.

Kelly went all melty with empathy. "Got it. No more Sia." The song stopped, and soon a gentle Disney soundtrack wafted over the speakers.

It was weird, but much improved. "Where are we going?" Aaron hoped they were taking him back to Minneapolis. He'd get a job and help with rent. He'd stay out of their way, if only they'd talk to him sometimes, help him not feel so completely alone.

"There's a park up ahead." Kelly pointed to a Garmin mounted on the dash. "I thought maybe we could be a little more comfortable there. Plus there's a lake. Maybe there'll be ducks or geese to watch. Though it's probably too cold."

"Maybe the swans are still there." Walter's tone suggested an inside joke. Kelly met his gaze in the rearview mirror and smiled.

A wave of self-consciousness washed away Aaron's relief. "I'm so sorry you had to come all this way."

Kelly glanced over his shoulder. "Of course we came. It isn't even an hour. Not *all this way.*"

"I should have listened." Aaron dug his thumbnail into his palm. "Walter told me not to—" He couldn't finish. "I'm so stupid. *So stupid.*"

"You aren't stupid." Walter, who had never stopped holding him, stroked his hair. "You're just fine."

"I shouldn't have done anything with Baz."

The tenor of Walter's voice changed almost imperceptibly. "Can you tell me, hon, what happened? What exactly did he do?"

With deep embarrassment, Aaron told them about his *other* breakdown, about Damien finding him. He explained about going over to the White House at homecoming, about how Baz had started flirting, and Aaron had made out with him the night before. How

Aaron screwed it up. Again.

"I didn't tell you because I was scared if I talked about it out loud it would evaporate, but it doesn't matter. I still fucked it up. I just don't know *how*. Why won't anyone tell me what I do wrong? Don't say it's not me, because it *is*. It can't be anything else."

"It *is* something else." Walter's voice was tight. "God, this is karma. This is fucking karma."

Kelly, who had pulled into a parking space, turned around. "You weren't that bad, I'm sure."

"I was." Walter bit off the words. "I was worse."

"Then fix it now. Help Aaron. Make it right."

Walter shifted on the seat so he could speak directly to Aaron. "You know how girls complain guys only want one thing? They go crazy trying to read the tea leaves, to cut through the bullshit to see if this is real or if this is another user asshole. Some of them have some pretty killer systems in place to sort the losers to the side. Well, here's the thing. With gay men? The system kind of sucks. It's two guys. It's so easy to have sex it's not even funny. Easy sex is great. Except we aren't always as detached from it as the stereotype says we should be."

"I just want to know what I did wrong," Aaron said, trying to drag Walter back to the pertinent point.

"What did you do wrong? You cared. You wanted it to be a real connection. You didn't simply want to stave off the need for affection for a few hours. You wanted something real. Something that mattered."

"So I was a girl. I'm the girl."

"You're not a girl—and for the record, there's nothing wrong with girls, so don't talk like that." This came from Kelly, and a bit testily. "I wanted the same thing as you. I hadn't had sex with anyone, and I wanted it to be special. That's not a girl thing. That's a people thing. And there's nothing wrong with wanting it."

"It hasn't ever been special for me." Aaron felt *rotten*. So hollow and wrong. "I didn't want to fake it anymore. I didn't want to talk myself into girls again, but every time I try to be real with a guy it goes to hell."

Kelly and Walter exchanged a powerful, personal glance, telling a story Aaron couldn't read. It made him so hungry he felt inside out.

"It feels real when you care." Walter's gaze never left Kelly's. "About caring who you're with. It hurts because it's real, because it's hard to be brave enough to reach for something you want." He squeezed Kelly's hand, then turned to Aaron. "I was never as brave as you. Not until Kelly, and he had to all but drag me by the hair into a relationship. I was one of the assholes who bled off lonely one trick at a time. You said I didn't have to drive all this way, but I did. Because hearing you so upset made me realize I have no idea how many guys I left feeling the way you do."

Aaron couldn't imagine Walter ever making anyone feel like this. "You didn't mean to hurt them. You couldn't."

"I doubt Baz meant it either, or Giles. In fact, in Baz's case in particular, I'd say he figured out he was fucking up in time. He got you off and got out. That's why he didn't fuck you. Not because there's something wrong with you."

It would be so wonderful to believe Walter. "I'm the one who's there every time. It has to be me. Even though Giles is nice now, it's still awkward and weird."

Walter's eyebrow quirked. "Wait—you're talking to Giles?"

"Sort of. He's polite and nice, but he's not interested. I have to figure this out, because if I don't, I'll never—" He cut himself off, because he *wasn't* going to start crying again.

Kelly nodded at the lake. "Let's take a walk."

Aaron didn't want to look at a lake or ducks or geese or swans, but he went, weaving drunkenly, hunkering into the warmth of his coat though the wind wasn't too bad, at least for Minnesota. He felt off, like a vampire in the light. He didn't belong out on a nice afternoon, walking with Kelly and Walter, the most perfect people in the world. Yet there he was, and he was too selfish to keep pointing out they should go home and forget about his sorry ass. They kept talking, sometimes to each other but often to him, commenting on the sunset on the water, the crunch of dead leaves beneath their feet, the bite on the edge of the evening breeze. After a while it seemed almost okay to be with them.

When Walter discovered Aaron hadn't eaten anything that day, he jogged to the car, promising to return with Subway. It was the first time Aaron had ever been alone with Kelly.

Kelly chatted amicably, nudging Aaron into talking about school, asking him about his music. "Are you going to major in it?"

"I can't." The old worry came back, and the sadness. "My dad would never let me."

"But you enjoy it so much."

"I'll never get a job in music."

"Doesn't Saint Timothy have music therapy?"

Aaron shrugged. He'd thought about that, because he could see his dad maybe going for it—but he wasn't interested in it any more than law. He couldn't have what he truly wanted, so why do anything even close?

"I'm sure you'll work it out." Kelly tucked his hands behind his back, smiling out at the lake. "This is beautiful. More like what home was for me. I miss the countryside. The lakes. It's so beautiful and quiet."

Aaron could easily picture it. Kelly in his perfect town, perfect house, perfect life. Of course Walter was marrying him. "Did you always know? That you were gay, I mean?"

It surprised him to see Kelly's expression shutter. "I did, but it scared me. I tried not to be. I never slept with a girl, but I dated some. My town was really small, and I worried what people would say. Though I think the problem was I wanted something that wasn't real. I wanted a boyfriend, but I didn't care half as much about who it was, just that somebody would be that person for me." He shook his head. "I got lucky. If Walter hadn't been so jealous of anyone else I talked to, I think I'd have ended up feeling the same way you do right now. Except I'd probably have had one bad experience and hidden away. You're pretty brave, Aaron. I'm envious."

The very idea of *Kelly* being envious of him made Aaron's jaw slack. "Are you kidding? I'm a mess. I'm awful. You said Walter was your first. Your only. You did it *right*. All I've done is wrong."

"*No.*" Kelly took Aaron's hand, clasping it tight. "Don't say that, ever. I got *lucky*. I wasn't smart at all. I was a silly, sentimental fool. I don't know why Walter wanted me. I try not to think about it too much."

"He wants you because you're perfect," Aaron blurted.

Kelly squeezed his hand. "You're perfect too."

"I keep giving everything away. I think they're the right guy, and then it falls apart."

"But have you ever *dated* a guy? Hanging out with Baz with a bunch of other people isn't dating. Sitting in a car eating fries isn't dating. You need to get to know them. Really check them out. That'll drive a lot of them away—but it's what you want, right? To stop feeling like they stomp all over you. If they drift off when you won't put out, at least that's all they get out of you. You can't tell me it would be worse to find out someone was a user *before* they used you."

This was true. Except he *had* hung out with Baz. Though now as he looked back, there were plenty of times they weren't actually connecting, and Aaron had ignored those parts, too eager to have it work out.

Aaron hugged himself. "I can't stand feeling so lonely."

"Aaron—I know you like the music program here, but I think you should come to Minneapolis. You could live with us. Go to school with us."

"My dad—"

"*Fuck* your dad." It was alarming to hear the expletive out of Kelly's pretty mouth, but he didn't even blush, just kept steamrolling on. "Fuck your dad and his iron fist over your life. Let him cut you off, if that's what he's threatening you with. You can get a job if you have to. You can go part time. You shouldn't be this unhappy, Aaron. Nobody should. If your life makes you this miserable, *change it.*"

Walter reappeared, and they focused on eating their food. As the sun began to set, the temperature plummeted, so they went back to campus and got coffee. But the whole time Aaron thought about what Kelly had said. About being lucky. About holding back. About changing his life. He didn't understand what he was supposed to do with those horrible, heavy, lonely feelings. His dad hadn't ever threatened to cut him off—Aaron simply toed the line.

Maybe he should stop doing that.

He didn't want to move to Minneapolis, to leave Saint Timothy. He did want to change. He wanted to change *here*.

When Walter and Kelly had to go, they were clearly worried, but Aaron did his best to reassure them. They swore they were coming to Christmas with Timothy, and Aaron was to call them every day until then. *Call*, not text. They both hugged him, Kelly twice. As they pulled out of the guest parking lot, Aaron watched them go, sad and happy at once.

He wasn't alone. He was lonely, but he wasn't alone. He wasn't quite sure how the distinction worked out yet, but it felt important, and for now that was enough.

AS MUCH AS Giles was sure something had been brewing between Aaron and Baz, by Thanksgiving break, it was clear that if they *had* hooked up, they were over now. When they came back from break and Aaron studiously avoided Baz, Giles was convinced his rival had left the field.

This would have been a great time to make a move, to act on those instincts he'd figured out at homecoming. Except Giles couldn't, because between homecoming and Thanksgiving, Giles and Aaron became friends.

Intellectually he understood friends and lovers weren't mutually exclusive—his future happiness with a long-term partner depended on that truth, in fact. Giles hadn't ever thought much about how to navigate the *friend* part of a potential boyfriend.

Aaron *was* a friend—but not like Brian or Mina. Giles could flop onto a futon and whine with either one of them because being with his besties relaxed him. Being with Aaron made him feel like someone had ratcheted his tuning pegs to the breaking point. He dressed more carefully for Salvo rehearsal than he did for twenty-and-under night at the Shack. He sat straighter in his chair beside Aaron while they went over compositions than he did in chamber orchestra. He stashed breath mints in the pocket of all his jackets and kept several packs in his instrument locker for fear he might chat Aaron up with taco breath by accident.

His breath and clothes were the only way he could come close enough to Aaron's orbit to even dream of entering it. In addition to being model gorgeous, Aaron was taller than Giles and a lot more filled out, well proportioned where Giles was eternally lanky and awkward. When they worked together at the table in the lounge, Giles would sometimes catch glimpses of their reflection in the mirrored plate between the top and bottom instrument lockers, and the difference between the two of them could have been a comedy sketch. Giles would be hunched over, hair standing on end like he'd stuck his finger in a light socket. Aaron's hair would be messed up too, and he'd be bent over his work as well, but somehow he always managed to look like a model photo in a brochure for how to study. Either that or an opening scene to a porn shoot.

They truly were friends, though—they smiled every time they saw each other, and at a thrilling moment in early December they had, at long last, exchanged numbers.

They were finishing up a Salvo planning session, and somehow the two of them ended up alone in the room. Aaron was packing up his backpack, no real rush, almost lingering. It occurred to Giles this would be a great moment to ask Aaron out.

For coffee. Ice cream. Lunch. A movie. It wasn't hard. All he had to do was open his mouth.

Do you want to go have a latte? My treat.

What are you up to right now? Feel like coming over to play some Xbox?

You hungry? I was thinking about grabbing a burger. Care to come along?

So many ways to make a date, all of them casual.

None of them would come out of his mouth. All Giles could do was stand there, paralyzed.

Aaron glanced up at him and paused with a folder half into his bag. "Is something wrong?"

Say something. You have to say something now. "Um. I...wondered. If maybe we should exchange phone numbers."

Aaron went still. "Oh?"

Was that panic on Aaron's face? Revulsion? Surprise? *Mayday. Mayday. Abort. Abort.* "F-for Salvo. In case." His mouth went dry, his hands became clammy. "Planning. Stuff."

And what was *that* expression? Relief? Regret? Gas? "Sure."

They'd exchanged numbers. Neither one had yet to use them.

Giles got *nervous* around Aaron. To-his-bones awkward and unsure. He'd never been shy—the closest he'd come was when he was four and walked up to strangers to announce he was shy, so please don't talk to him. With Aaron, Giles could only dream of being bold. A lot of that, though, was because every time he opened his mouth he feared something stupid coming out of it. He'd tell Aaron how gorgeous he was, how talented, how hot it was when he bit his bottom lip as he worked on a score. Sometimes when Aaron got lost in his work, Giles would sit across the table and stare at him, trying to be subtle as he breathed in deep lungfuls of cologne.

It wasn't just Aaron's body Giles worshipped either, not anymore. Aaron was a freaky genius when it came to music. He didn't seem to get how gifted he was—Giles was no slouch, but he looked like a dummy next to Aaron. Aaron didn't simply have perfect pitch. He understood music theory on some kind of bone-deep level, could *see* notes in a way Giles couldn't follow, not until Aaron put them down on the page. Aaron picked melodies out of thin air, instinctively knowing when to lean on one voice or another, what to put underneath for support. This was *raw* talent too, with only the barest bit of formal training under him. When he got through four years of music classes, he'd be a savant.

Of course, with the preparations for Christmas with Timothy, Giles wouldn't have had time to date Aaron. Between orchestra, chamber, his quartet, and now Salvo, the only thing he did besides rehearse was sleep and struggle to keep up in his coursework. The performances were during finals week, which seemed fantastically cruel. His mom was livid because the final performance was Sunday, December twenty-first, which was supposed to be the family Christmas at her parents' house.

There were two concerts at Saint Timothy—Thursday and the final one Sunday—but Friday and Saturday's shows were in Minneapolis. Saturday was at the State Theater, Friday at some crazy-huge Lutheran church in Burnsville. *Before* all these performances there were Christmas with Timothy dinners, where regents and administration wined and dined alumni and potential donors while small groups from all the various choirs and orchestras performed at locales sprinkled around the Cities.

Giles and Aaron only rehearsed together during Salvo, but Giles felt weird if he didn't see Aaron at least four times a day. After scarfing down takeout for dinner in the student lounge, it was the two of them working together, sometimes for hours. Salvo was included in Christmas with Timothy, which apparently had come only after sharp arguments between the Drs. Nussenbaum and the board of regents. Salvo would perform two numbers during the official performance, taking one away from the Ambassadors and adding five minutes to the already epically long production. Salvo would also be part of the preshow dinners.

This meant Giles and Aaron had to have *seven* performance-ready songs. The ones for the official show were Christmas themed, but the dinner pieces were to be modeled the same way as the Ambassadors—a few Christmas numbers bookending the more traditional pop numbers.

It should have been a superhuman effort, but when the two of them worked together, nothing seemed impossible, not when it came to music. The one thing Aaron wasn't great at was filling in who should sing what. Giles had a better understanding of which of the girls would do better on what line. He didn't think it was much of a help, but the girls loved how he arranged them and told him over and over again he made them sound better than they deserved to be. Aaron always seconded them, smiling as he told Giles he couldn't imagine arranging parts without him.

"You're like Gilbert and Sullivan, or Menken and Ashman," Karen told them one day at the end of rehearsal.

The other girls chimed in with agreement and effusive praise for their talents as Aaron looked abashed and Giles's ears heated at the tips.

Then, in the back of the room, someone whispered a little too loudly, "They should totally be a couple."

As Giles's blush covered him like an ugly rash and Aaron ducked his head and shrank into his sweatshirt, the girls broke into giggles. Rehearsal was over, so they started filing out, all but Aaron and Giles, who sat frozen at their table.

As Mina passed by, she jerked her head at Aaron and mouthed to Giles, *Ask him out, now.*

Giles wasn't sure what the hell he should do. Leaving felt...wrong, but sitting here was all kinds of awkward. He wished he knew what it meant that Aaron still sat there, rigid, with his head bowed. Giles tried to tell himself Aaron was freaked about being outed, except it didn't wash because after Baz, *everybody* knew.

Obviously Giles had gotten that memo long before anyone else.

When the silence got too heavy, Giles cleared his throat. *Say something benign. Just be a fucking human long enough to smooth this over.* "So."

Are you doing anything for dinner?

Would you like to go out for coffee?

Could I blow you?

Giles got so nervous his jaw ached, sending weird,

throbbing bands of nervousness down the front of his neck into his chest until he thought he might be having a heart attack. Speech was out of the question. Now all he wanted to do was not pass out.

Aaron cleared his throat too, but when he spoke, his voice was thick and rough, not its usual melodious self. "I…I've been meaning to ask you something."

Holy shit. Giles could barely breathe, let alone speak. "Yes?"

Aaron's hands opened and closed over the music in front of him, crinkling it and smearing the pencil. "I…I wondered if you…if we…"

Ohmyfuckinggod. Giles felt dizzy. Was it going to happen? Was Aaron asking…? A "Hallelujah" chorus cued up in Giles's head.

Aaron flexed his hands nervously. "I wondered if…you could…give me a violin lesson."

The "Hallelujah" chorus skipped, scratched, and crashed in a fiery inferno to the earth. "You want…violin lessons?"

Giles took a good look at Aaron—flushed cheeks, dilated pupils, the now completely balled-up manuscript paper under his hands. "Yeah." He sounded as disappointed as Giles. "Never mind. That was a stupid thing to ask."

It was a weird thing to ask, is what—except Giles would have put hard money on Aaron being about to ask him out and chickening out at the edge of the diving board. Which all but assured him Aaron would be receptive to being asked out.

Except Giles still couldn't do it. Instead he said, "It's not stupid. I'd give you a violin lesson anytime you wanted. Right now, if you want."

Aaron lifted his head. Unlike Giles, his blush only made him that much hotter. "You don't have to."

"But I'd love to."

For the first time since the *they should be a couple* comment, Aaron met Giles's gaze. He looked terrified, embarrassed, ready to run. Giles's heart turned over, and he had to actively fight an urge to fold Aaron into his arms and make the world go away.

That was when Giles realized what the friend part of boyfriend was—he wanted to protect Aaron, make everything okay. Not just like he did for Min, but...more. To know his partner so well he knew not only when he was upset but how to make the hurt go away.

Violin lesson. *Fuck yeah.*

"I don't think anyone's in this room until seven. I could borrow Karen's instrument to teach you, or we could share mine."

It was kind of funny, actually, how thrown Aaron looked. "Um...sure. If you really don't mind."

"Not at all." He nodded at the music stands and chairs on the other side of the room. "Set up two chairs and stands next to each other, and I'll be right back."

As he headed out the door, Giles glanced over his shoulder. Aaron stood at the table, terrified and nervous.

And hopeful.

Giles shut his eyes and savored it a moment. Then he hurried out of the rehearsal hall and into the student lounge to fetch his violin.

Chapter Fourteen

WHEN GILES RETURNED to the choir room, the chairs and stands were set up, but Aaron paced by the fire exit. Giles hefted his violin, brandishing it with a waggle of his eyebrows. "You ready?"

Aaron looked as unready as they came. "Sure."

"I was too late to catch Karen, but this will work fine. I've never shown anyone how to play before though, so you'll have to bear with my clumsiness."

Aaron sat down when Giles did, rubbing his palms self-consciously on his jeans. "It's nice of you to teach me."

"Not at all." Giles rested his violin on his lap, the bow beside it. "Okay, first things first: the parts. The bow is obvious, but it has sections as well. The tip, which is always farthest away from your hand. The hair, which is what passes over the strings. The stick, which holds the hair taut. The bow grip, which will come into play in a minute. The eyelet is this dot here, this spot underneath is the frog, and this is the end screw, where you loosen and tighten the hair."

Aaron watched Giles's demonstration intently. "Okay."

Giles held up his rosin. "You need to keep the hair

rosined, but not too much. You'll know when you need to add some because it's scratchy. But when you get brand-new rosin, the first thing you do is score it with a quarter or your fingernail because otherwise it'll never transfer to the hair." He passed the bow over to Aaron and picked up the violin. "On the violin itself, we have a lot of parts. For the most basic, we have the body—sometimes called the belly—where the sound resonates, and the neck and fingerboard, where you work the strings. Above the neck is the scroll and pegbox, with the big tuning pegs. You don't use the tuning pegs unless you're putting on a new string or something is seriously out of whack. The fine tuners here at the bottom are what you'll primarily use to put your violin in tune." He plucked a few strings and winced. "Yeah, like right now."

Aaron became very interested. "What are the four notes again? Those first two sound like G and D."

"G, D, A, E." Giles plucked them one by one and winked at Aaron. "God, but you've got a good ear."

He wanted to purr when he saw the way the compliment made Aaron beam. *Compliment him more often.*

"For the last part of the strings, we have the tailpiece, which is what holds the bottom part of the strings on, and the bridge, which holds them away from the belly. These two swirly bits are the F holes, which is where the sound actually comes out. But to make that happen you need the sound post, which is this little dowel inside by the treble end of the bridge. It's support but also what transfers the sound between the plates and gives us tone. It's sometimes called the *âme*, which is French for soul, because despite its boring appearance, it really is the soul of the instrument." He faltered, realizing how much excessive information he was giving. "Sorry if I'm babbling."

"No, not at all. This is so interesting." Aaron bit his lip. "May—may I hold it?"

Pleasure washed over Giles, and he passed it over. "Of course."

Aaron accepted the violin with a reverence that was almost as erotic as his lip-biting. "It's beautiful. Did you name it?"

Giles rubbed at his neck, embarrassed. "Henrietta. After my grade school violin teacher. She died the year my parents bought it for me. It felt right."

"That's so sweet." He held Henrietta in front of him, giving her an admiring look. "Should I call her a she, or it?"

"I don't think she cares much about pronouns, just don't wind her strings too tight or crack her bridge." Giles finished the rest of the parts demonstration with Henrietta in Aaron's lap. "This plastic part is the chin rest, though I have a shoulder rest we'll attach in a second. Now you know all the parts of the violin. Are you ready to hold a bow?"

"Ready," Aaron declared with a smile.

Giles showed him how to attach the shoulder rest and positioned the violin on Aaron's left shoulder. He had to hold the bow himself before he could accurately explain how Aaron should place his fingers. "You make a smiley face with your thumb, stretch your index finger out, put your middle finger on the frog, ring finger on the eyelet. Your pinky stands on the bow."

Aaron laughed. "My thumb makes a what now?"

Giles crooked his thumb. "A smiley. That's what Henrietta told me to call it."

Aaron grinned. "A smiley it is."

Giles tuned the instrument, then taught Aaron how to bow, when to use his wrist and when to lift his arm. While it wasn't exactly *necessary* Giles touch Aaron's arm to help him move it correctly, it certainly didn't hurt his education.

He didn't complain, either, when Giles lingered a little longer than the demonstration warranted.

Aaron was, of course, a natural. He winced when his first attempt at bowing elicited a screech, but it wasn't long before he knew how to produce a crisp, clear sound.

"Good job," Giles told him. "You'll do well with fingering too. Kids use tapes when they learn, but with your ear you won't take long to pick it up."

"It's so clear." Aaron pulled a long, strong A, then an E. "This has to be more Henrietta than me."

"She's not a cheap date, no. She was my birthday, Christmas, and—" He stopped himself from saying *get-out-of-the-hospital-for-the-second-time present*. "She was expensive, so she has great sound. But the player still has to bring it, or she won't sing."

Aaron played a few more notes, riding the four strings up and down. "I love orchestras. Strings make me shiver." He stole a shy glance at Giles. "When you play the double bass for Salvo, I get chills every time."

Never, ever would Giles have guessed he could get

so hard talking violin. "I'm a lot better on Henrietta."

Aaron's cheeks flushed with color. "I'd love to hear you play sometime."

Sweet baby Jesus. Giles wanted to put Henrietta on the chair and push Aaron to the floor. "I'll play for you right now. But let's give you a chance to shine first. How about I teach you a song?"

From Aaron's reaction, Giles would have thought he'd offered to give him a million dollars. "Can I learn 'Mary Had a Little Lamb'?"

"Too tricky for your first attempt. I was thinking more 'Twinkle, Twinkle, Little Star'. It only uses two strings, and it has the benefit of teaching you a lot of fingering at the same time."

This lesson involved more touching as Giles helped Aaron apply his fingers to the board, showing him the right pressure and position. As he'd anticipated, Aaron had no trouble keeping his notes on pitch, and Giles only had to explain the very basics before Aaron taught himself the song. When he finished, he laughed and flourished his bow, flush with pride.

Giles clapped and grinned. "Well done, maestro."

"Thanks. That was fun." Aaron passed Henrietta and the bow over. "Let's hear the real deal now, though."

Giles tucked Henrietta to his shoulder, his fingers sliding easily into position on the bow. "What do you want to hear?"

"Anything." Aaron settled into his chair. "Pop, classical—anything. Though—if you know anything with the plinky-plinky sound?" He mimed plunking strings on an imaginary violin.

"Pizzicato? Sure." He plucked a few arpeggios, stomach flipping at the way it made Aaron smile. "Now the question is, do you want something classical and official, or do you want me to make you giggle when I play 'TiK ToK' pizzicato?"

Aaron burst out laughing. "Shut *up*. Seriously?"

Giles grinned. "I'll consider that a request for Ke$ha."

He launched into the song, and Aaron laughed so hard he fell sideways. But when Giles started to lower his violin, Aaron waved him on as he wiped his eyes and rose, heading to the piano. "Keep going. I have an idea."

Giles started the song over, and goddamn if Aaron didn't pound out harmony on the piano like the music was in front of him. Not wanting to appear a slouch, Giles stepped up his game, adding some flourishes whenever he could. Aaron kept playing, never missing so much as a note.

"Now switch," Giles called out as they cleared the bridge. "You pizz on the piano, and I'll bow the harmony."

Aaron frowned, but it was a stare of concentration. "There's no such thing on the piano. How do I—?" Then he grinned. "Got it. *Go.*"

Giles tried to keep his brain three steps ahead of his fingers, working out the harmonics before he played them, wanting both accuracy and elegance, because of course Aaron brought both. Aaron's "pizzicato" was staccato beats in the upper register, sometimes with harmony added, sometimes not. Sweating, Giles did his best to keep up, a task difficult partly because of the notes, partly because it took everything in him not to break out in giggles. Though as soon as they finished the song with a ridiculous flourish, they both bust out laughing.

"That was *awesome*." Aaron wiped at his eyes. "Oh, shit—I want to do more."

"What about '100 Years'? It gives good pizz. Do you know it?"

Aaron stared at him, his look unreadable.

Giles faltered. Was he pissed? Annoyed? "I— Sorry—"

He stopped as Aaron grinned and rolled his eyes before his fingers moved over the opening bars with the precision of someone who'd long ago memorized the song.

Oh. The look had been incredulity, Aaron insulted at the idea he *didn't* know the song.

Grinning, Giles joined in, playing pizzicato through the first verse, but as Aaron filled out his harmony, Giles started bowing.

When they hit the chorus, Aaron began to sing.

Giles didn't know why Aaron's vocals hit him so hard—it *wasn't* because he crushed on him, though that didn't help anything. It wasn't so much that Aaron's voice was some kind of perfect harmonic, though it was. A million people had great voices, though.

Not many opened a vein quite like Aaron.

Giles stopped worrying about looking good and

focused on the spaces the piano couldn't cover, never overpowering Aaron's voice but rather lifting him up, easing the spaces between the notes so when he sang, he soared even higher. Giles forgot about making mistakes, forgot about everything in the world that wasn't playing with Aaron.

When the song ended, they held still, gazes locked, hands frozen on their instruments.

Aaron broke the silence, his voice soft and heavy. "'With or Without You'?"

Giles lifted his bow and glided gently into the lead.

The magic of the moment let them play like gods. Giles rose through the song as Aaron put in a gentle baseline, just enough color to finish things off. Aaron took up the vocal melody, soft and sweet, his pretty tenor resting oh so tenderly on each note. He turned the song into a lullaby, ignoring all bait to belt, which only made the vocals more powerful. It was so beautiful Giles had to close his eyes.

I love him. His heart swelled and spilled over as they rounded into the final chorus. *I'm so in love with him I can't even ask him out. I want to lie at his feet, want to smooth out all the wrinkles in his life and make everything okay.*

I can't ever tell him, because if I'm wrong, if somehow he doesn't want me, my life would be over. I'd rather have this than nothing.

Someone as wonderful as him can't want someone as awkward as me. There's just no way. There's no fucking way that's real, no matter how much I want it to be.

Aaron closed off the song with a chord—with a soft

pull on Giles's bow, it was done.

The music hung in the air between them.

Giles lowered his instrument. At the piano Aaron let his fingers fall from the keys.

They stared at each other, breathing hard but silent, neither wanting to break the spell.

He's waiting for you to ask him out.

I can't, I can't, I can't.

The door to the rehearsal hall opened. Giles and Aaron startled, turning away from each other as if they'd been caught kissing, not staring. It was one of the other quartets coming in to practice, and the members greeted them both warmly, apologizing if they were interrupting.

"No problem," Aaron told them. But he cast one last longing glance at Giles.

I can't. Except there was nothing, *nothing* in the world Giles would rather do.

AARON THOUGHT HE'D go crazy if Giles didn't ask him out, which he told Walter every time they spoke.

"I think he might like me. He looks at me a lot. Not glaring, either. Sometimes I catch him staring at me, and he blushes. That has to be good, right?"

"I suspect it's very good." Walter's voice indicated subtle amusement.

"He doesn't ask me out, though. I've tried twice, and all I get is violin lessons. Which are fun, but I jerk off after which is kind of weird. I wish *he* would ask me out. But maybe he's not into me and I'm an idiot."

"You're not an idiot."

"So you think he might be into me? Why doesn't he ask me out? What do I *do?*"

"You don't do anything."

"*What?*" Alone in his room, Aaron paced back and forth across the carpet. "He's into me and I shouldn't do anything? Why not?"

"Because I believe we had a conversation not long ago about going slow."

Aaron made a frustrated sound through his nose. "This isn't slow, this is *glacial*. Walter, he's not a jerk. I really like him. I think maybe we got off on the wrong foot is all."

"I think you're right. Which is why you should continue to be his friend a little longer and make sure that misunderstanding doesn't happen again. You can jerk off every hour if you need to. Take your time and do this right."

Aaron was seriously tired of masturbating, and it wasn't every hour, but it was a hell of a lot. "It's not just about getting off. I want to *be* with him. And I don't want to do this wrong. Waiting feels wrong."

"You aren't doing anything wrong. Especially by waiting."

"What if he loses interest?"

"Then he wasn't worth your time to begin with."

Aaron flopped onto his bed. "I'm going crazy not knowing how to handle this. Plus it's about to be break. I won't see him for weeks."

"I thought you lived in the same town? Or will you be at your dad's?"

That was the *one* bright point on Aaron's horizon. "No, he's stuck in California for the holidays. I won't see him until February."

"Excellent. Call Giles while you're in Oak Grove and invite him to coffee."

"*I can't do that.*" Aaron's whole chest seized at the idea. "Who am I kidding? I'm going to fuck this up. If I'm not doing something wrong right now, I'll fuck up soon."

"You're less likely to do something wrong if you aren't paralyzed by worry that you will." Kelly murmured something in the background, and Walter responded with a muted, "Shut up," followed by a soft kiss Aaron could hear through the phone.

Aaron wrenched himself out of jealousy and onto the issue at hand. "Shouldn't I tell him? Or kiss him? Or something?"

"When it's right. I suspect the confession will happen naturally on its own, to be honest. When it does, though, I suggest you stick with kissing to start."

"*What?*"

Walter chuckled, but before he could reply to Aaron, once again, Kelly murmured in the background. This time Aaron couldn't mistake the suggestive tone.

Walter spoke softly to his fiancé, then returned to the phone. "I mean it, hunbun. I think you should not have sex with Giles right away, even if you start necking tomorrow. Hear me out," he said when Aaron started to object. "Sex is easy. Any moron can stick his dick in something or rub one out. Relationships? They're hard, *really* hard, and sex does not simplify the calculus. It's way too easy to slide into sex and pretend it's what the relationship is, to let that be what you use to connect to someone instead of actually forging a bond. If you use sex as a cheat with someone you care for, it's a horrible mess."

Much as Aaron hated to hear it, the words made a kind of sense. "How am I supposed to know when we should move forward, though? What if I ask to wait and that makes him—?"

"*Don't*, baby. *Don't*. Don't go there. You need to stop worrying about making people mad for a lot of reasons, but if you honestly want to date Giles, you can't deny yourself what you need because you worry other people won't be happy with your choices. If you tell Giles you need to take things slow and he gets angry, then honey, you need to *run* from him."

"I don't want to run. I want to be with him. I want it so bad I hurt."

When Walter spoke, his voice was so tender it was arresting. "Aaron, I was in love with Kelly for a month before I so much as kissed him."

That threw Aaron. "But you were *roommates*."

"Yes. And I kept putting on the brakes even after we started officially seeing each other. Finally Kelly got annoyed and seduced me out of my caution—except I don't regret a moment of the delay. Do you know how easily I used to fall into bed with guys, or how often I didn't bother with a bed? When people matter to you, they deserve your time and attention. *That's* how you keep from screwing things up. You don't see what you want and go at it in a fever pitch. You slow down, you make yourself ask the difficult questions and do the hard things, and you make sure it's real, that you're not simply hoping it's authentic because you truly want it to be."

"What if I find out it isn't?"

"Then you let yourself be sad, you lick your wounds, and you let friends support you until you're ready to try looking again."

Aaron swallowed and shut his eyes. "It would be a lot easier to not try at all."

"True. I've used the tactic. But speaking as one who got lucky enough to have my right person hunt me down, not trying sucks in comparison. I'd go through a mountain range to keep what I've found in Kelly." There were more murmurings, and when Walter spoke again, his voice was husky. "Go practice your *let's-take-this-slow* speech, and call or text me later."

"Okay," Aaron said, not excited about the prospect at all.

Walter made a muffled grunt, gasped, and fumbled the phone. "I gotta go. *No sex*, and call me later."

Aaron put the phone down on the bed beside him, glaring at it and thinking it was pretty damn rude to tell someone to put the brakes on their potential relationship as you hung up to get laid.

Chapter Fifteen

BETWEEN THE TWO of them, Giles and Aaron were so overbooked for Christmas with Timothy, their schedules were impossible. The venues for the preshow dinners were rarely in the same building, and more than once on the schedule they were double-booked. When it was clear none of the powers that be planned to sort out the tangle, Giles took the problem of his and Aaron's double-bookings directly to Dr. Allison.

"Goodness." Dr. Allison glanced over the top of his glasses at Giles as he scanned their schedules. "I'll talk to Susan and Harvey about this and get back to you. There's one large venue each night housing several groups, and if we moved Salvo and the Ambassadors there, that could fix everything. The administration and the regents don't like having the draw groups there because they want to take their big fish to intimate locations. But it looks like they'll have to decide if they want high-profile acts or intimacy for those donors, because they can't have both."

Giles relaxed. "Thanks. I really appreciate it, and I know Aaron will too."

"I have a ticket myself for the Thursday dinner and performance. I'm eager to see what the two of you have cooked up. From what I understand, you and Mr. Seavers are the most productive non-music majors we've ever had."

Giles ducked his head, embarrassed by the compliment. "I think I'm almost ready to give in and declare music therapy. I want to talk to my parents first, though, because of the extra year."

"If it comes down to money, Giles, we have scholarships for this exact sort of thing."

Giles averted his gaze. "I'm…nervous. I don't want to ruin the rest of my life because I got distracted following some crazy dream I couldn't make real."

"Healing others through music isn't a crazy dream, and it's my job, young man, to navigate you safely into your profession. But should you change your mind once you graduate, one can accept all manner of jobs with a music therapy degree."

"I know. I just… It's scary. This is the one time I get to go to college. I don't want to do it wrong."

"The only way you do life wrong is by living out someone else's expectations instead of your own. Listen to the song in your heart, son. It won't ever steer you astray." Dr. Allison patted his hand and nodded at the schedules. "I'll get these sorted out for you and get them to you by the dress rehearsal on Wednesday."

When Giles told Aaron about what he'd done, for half a second he thought Aaron was going to kiss him.

"How did you—? *Oh my God.*" Aaron reached for Giles, caught himself and pressed his hands to his own cheeks instead. "I was so nervous about how to get to all my performances I almost threw up twice. *Thank you.*"

Aaron's praise made Giles so dizzy he had to hold on to the lockers. *Don't look like a dopey idiot. Keep your cool.* "Of course. We're—friends. Right?"

Did Aaron seem disappointed? "Right. Thanks."

When Aaron and Giles showed up for the dress rehearsal, Dr. Allison met them at the door with their revised dinner performance schedules. "You'll be doing some quick costume changes and will need to be light on your feet between sets, but you're in the same building for all four dinners."

"Thank you so much," Giles said as Aaron visibly relaxed.

"Not a problem." Allison nodded at the stage. "Now take your places. I intend to work you rigorously today."

The dress rehearsal was *long*, and though it wasn't a performance, the regents and administration somehow still managed to wander in and out with fancy-pants people almost the entire time. When it was finally over, Giles was so sick of music and Christmas especially he wanted to go to his room and play Xbox until he stopped twitching. Maybe eat some damn dinner, since he'd missed lunch—again.

When he started out of the auditorium, Karen caught his arm and latched on like a barnacle. "You aren't going anywhere, buddy, except to the choir room."

Giles couldn't stop his whine. "Oh God, hon, no. I'm so fucking tired. I can't practice anymore."

"Christmas with Timothy tradition. Section leaders

and whoever we can cram into the room go to a riff-off after the dress rehearsal. Sometimes they have it at the White House, but it's too cold this year to haul strings."

"A riff-off? Are you serious? Karen, sometimes I feel like all we're doing is alternating between *Glee* and *Pitch Perfect*."

She rolled her eyes. "For one, we fuck up a lot, which is part of the fun. Mostly it's to let off tension and community-build before our first big event of the year. There's pizza too, and usually someone from the White House manages to spike the punch." When Giles hesitated, Karen leaned in to whisper. "Aaron will be there."

Giles blushed from the tips of his hair to the nails of his toes. "I—I—"

"Come to the riff-off. Flirt with him. Have fun."

Of course now he had to go. On the plus side, there really was pizza. No punch, but alongside the two liters of pop were fifths of various whiskeys and rums and vodkas, which Giles skipped because he didn't need any help behaving foolishly. The room was full of people, choir and orchestra both, and the entirety of both the Ambassadors and Salvo. No professors or administration. Everyone seemed completely unmoved by the fact that they'd just endured a month of grueling practice, a week of finals with more to come in the morning for some people, and a four-hour dress rehearsal.

Aaron was already there when Giles arrived. His red cheeks said he *had* hit the booze, but like the night at the lake, drinking relaxed him, making his smile wider.

It made him bolder—he glanced at an empty space beside him like he wanted Giles to sit there.

Giles dropped his coat over the chair before hurrying through the line to get his own food so he could sit down.

"I don't understand what's going on," he confessed to Aaron as he ate.

"It's sort of half-planned and half-spontaneous as far as I can tell." Aaron wiped at his mouth with a napkin. Giles tried not to stare at his lips. "I know the Ambassadors are opening with a song we've done a thousand times. Karen and Jilly were cagey about Salvo's contribution—and after that it opens to everybody. Sometimes the orchestra people will start, sometimes choir, sometimes it'll be a mix."

"As long as they don't expect me to sing. I seriously can't."

"You can do plenty of other things. You'll be fine."

The Ambassadors didn't begin—it was Salvo, singing the arrangement of Imogen Heap's "Earth" Aaron and Giles had prepared for their audition to Dr. Nussenbaum. They'd taken it above and beyond their original arrangement—clearly they'd been working in secret, because the performance was flawless. He and Aaron both sat with mouths gaping, hearts swelling, as the girls did nothing less than kill it.

Talk about an opening salvo. Giles was so overcome he had tears in his eyes.

The applause hadn't stopped before Karen grabbed him, thrust his violin into his hand and led him into the opening pizz to Allison's orchestral arrangement of

"Dynamite". Giles stood in the circle with the twelve other orchestra members Karen had drawn forward, working to not lose his place in the song.

At the second chorus, Baz belted out the vocal line. First the Ambassadors joined in, then Salvo, and pretty soon the entire room was playing along in one way or another. Instead of ending, when Karen led them into a flourish, Damien launched right back into the opening, this time with Marius on synth in the background. When the orchestra joined in, this time they had to play faster and change their instrumentation right there on the spot. They moved around too, which only the violins could do, not the cellos or basses or, God bless, the poor harpist—but Karen danced like the fiddler on the roof in some kind of private and weirdly intense duet with Mina on her viola.

Giles did his best to keep up, playing harmony beneath them. Somehow he kept ending up next to Aaron.

There were never more than a few beats between songs—they kept coming until Giles's arm ached and his body was on fire with music. Every time he tried to sit a song out, someone drew him back in. More than once Aaron played keyboard, and he allowed Giles to be nowhere but beside him, picking up harmonies and filling out melodies.

Near the end, Baz called out the opening of Owl City's "I'm Coming After You", and since Aaron was already at the keyboard, he kept at it. This meant he carried the song, but because he was Aaron, he sang too. The song was difficult to play classically, so Giles switched to fiddle style, which everyone whooped to hear. This was how he ended up squared off in the middle of the room, alone in the center of a circle with Aaron, playing as if the devil were on his heels.

Which he was in a way, because the whole time Aaron belted lead vocal at him, promising he was chasing Giles down. *I'm coming after you.*

Ask him out, Mina mouthed from behind Aaron.

Aaron sang at Giles, his heart in his eyes, his soul in the music, and Giles fell in love harder than ever. He played his soul right back at Aaron, telling him with song he was the only person Giles wanted to be with, now or ever.

Giles walked Aaron to his dorm when it was over. Snow had begun to fall, a flurry scattering tiny bits of frozen precipitation across campus, drawing down a silence which enveloped them both and encouraged them to huddle into their coats...and closer to each other.

"That was pretty fun." Aaron's arm brushed Giles's in an accidentally-on-purpose way as they headed toward Titus. "I wish there were a performance group of orchestra and vocals."

"Like the 3 Penny Chorus and Orchestra doing 'Call Me Maybe'?" When Aaron looked at him quizzically, Giles laughed and whipped out his phone. "Oh my God, *seriously*? I learned how to rip YouTube audio just for them. Here." He passed over his phone and fumbled through his pockets. "Let me find my headphones."

"Oh—no, I have mine." Aaron withdrew a small

pouch from the inside pouch of his coat. "I'm kind of an audio princess. I have two sets of earbuds and two pairs of studios, wired and wireless. I always have a pair with me."

Giles glanced at the Bose label and raised his eyebrows, imagining the sticker total for all four.

Aaron handed Giles his phone as he slipped the buds into his ears. "Okay—let's hear this."

Giles cued up the song on YouTube. "I'll send you the song, but the video is how you must experience it first."

Aaron didn't offer Giles an earbud, which he found endearing. Of course an audiophile wouldn't surrender his stereo sound. Giles watched Aaron take in the video instead, indulging in the excuse to stare at his crush.

He couldn't decide if he wanted to stare at Aaron's eyes or his mouth, so he kept alternating. Aaron's eyes danced, fixed on the tiny glowing screen, crinkling as he smiled. They were relaxed and easy, lit with the joy they had when Aaron experienced music. Aaron's mouth was full and ever-so-slightly pouting, parting on silent gasps, pressing back together as he concentrated. The shadow of his late-day stubble only drew more attention to the seam, though it also highlighted the sculpture of his face, the perfect cheekbones, the proportions.

So out of my league.

Aaron gasped aloud, startling and glancing up at Giles. "The tenors!"

Soft blue gaze, pretty mouth, all aimed at Giles—a blow to the chest. Eyes dancing, lit with fire and life that blew away the cold.

"This is brilliant. Do you think we could do this? Arrange a song for choir and orchestra? Oh my God, I can think of three right off the bat. Of course Baz will try and make us do 'Titanium'." Aaron pushed the scroll bar back to the start of the video and cranked the volume. "I have to see this again."

Aaron's blue gaze flitted across the screen, ready to drink in more. Giles, however, was full to overflowing. His emotions swirled like the eddies of snow around them, and eventually they took over.

"I love you."

The words were out of his mouth before he could stop them. He seized, unable to breathe for terror. But Aaron gave no sign he'd heard.

Noise-canceling headphones. Giles breathed out in relief…and disappointment.

Crazy. It was crazy—but he kept talking.

"I love you." This time Giles spoke deliberately, his voice soft as his confession disappeared into the silence of the snow, so quiet the occasional passerby couldn't hear. "I'm so in love with you I'm sick with it, but I'm afraid to tell you. Which is crazy, because I think you like me too."

Aaron kept watching, unaware of a word Giles said. The knowledge made Giles giddy. He kept going.

"I have to figure out how to take this last step without breaking everything. Because I can't lose you. Even if I go insane wanting you, I'd rather have this than nothing at all."

Still watching the video, Aaron began to softly sing

along, lighting the cold air with the first tenor line.

Giles let out a shuddering breath. "Except I want to kiss you so badly right now I think I might explode."

Aaron looked up, blinking. "Did you say something?" He tugged an earbud out, abashed. "Sorry, I can't hear anything with these in."

Giles glanced down at the snow between their feet. "No—just…asking if you enjoyed it."

Jesus Christ, I'm such a fucking tool.

"I *loved* it. I'm serious, Giles—we have to do this. Maybe we can—" He cut himself off, bit his lip. "I mean, if you're not too busy over break. We could…get together. And…arrange things."

Call me, maybe. Giles's heart soared, rising until it spread his lips into a smile. "I'd love to."

He didn't kiss Aaron. There were too many people passing by, for one, and also, he wanted to savor that, if it happened.

When.

It wouldn't be their first kiss. But everything about it felt as if it would be their first *real* kiss.

After retrieving his phone, Giles drifted to his dorm on a cloud, unable to stop the grin on his face. He stuffed it down long enough to greet Brian—he didn't want to share, not yet. Once in his bed, though, he drew the covers over his head, shut his eyes, and played the moment over and over in his mind, spinning out possible futures.

I'm going to call you, Aaron. Definitely.

Chapter Sixteen

GILES DIDN'T HAVE a final the day after the riff-off, which meant he slept until Brian returned from his early morning one and got ready to leave for the holiday.

"Have a good Christmas." Brian shifted his laundry onto his shoulder and grinned. "Text me if you want to escape the 'rents."

"Sure." Except of course Giles hoped to be busy escaping with Aaron. The memory of the night before bloomed in his mind, waking him better than an alarm.

Aaron wanted this—maybe not as much as Giles, but he wanted it. All Giles had to do was play it cool, get the courage to act, and he was in.

The potential literalness of *getting in* made his shower a lot more erotic than it had a right to be.

As Giles dressed and headed to the music building, he tried to map out a plan. How should he ask? Should he set up a date for once they got home? Maybe Aaron needed a ride home. Of course that was Sunday. Three days away.

Could Giles ask him out on a date Sunday but kiss him *now*?

Did Giles really think he could stop at kissing?

These musings, in the end, proved fruitless. No sooner did he arrive at the music building than he got swept up in performance preparations. The first dinners were at six, but the choirs and orchestra had to be on-site at four thirty for warm-ups, and getting Salvo's instruments and props took all afternoon. Tonight they didn't leave campus, but Giles never stopped moving. If he wasn't performing, he was rushing to a performance.

Through it all, Aaron was right beside him.

They set up Salvo together, working with the girls but mostly each other. They returned to their dorms to get dressed, but they fussed with each other's ties backstage before Aaron's trio and Giles's quartet were set to perform at the dinner. They congratulated each other after their performances, hands brushing, fingers teasing as they whispered *good job* and dazzled each other with smiles.

I'm going to kiss him tonight, Giles promised himself as he went onto the stage with the orchestra. From where he sat he couldn't see Aaron, but he imagined him in his mind's eye throughout the performance, until it was Salvo's turn and they took their part of the stage together, Giles playing his borrowed double bass, Aaron on keyboard. Their gazes met and held across the stage, so many promises rising up with their songs.

Tonight. Seriously, it had to be tonight that they kissed.

Except by the time things wound down, it was eleven, and hauling everything back, getting things ready to pack onto the buses and shuttle vans, dragged things later. The magic bubble which had emboldened Giles popped as he overheard Aaron complaining to Jilly how tired he'd be in the morning when he went for his seven o'clock final.

Tomorrow. Giles promised himself he'd kiss Aaron tomorrow.

Friday's setup was both the same and entirely different. They still had the preshow dinner theater, but Aaron's and Giles's groups were at a community center in Burnsville, the full performance after at the mega-church ten miles away. This time packing up began at noon, and though he tried to find Aaron, somehow Giles got shuttled onto a different bus. They didn't meet up at all until the dress rehearsal, which started late and meant when they finally broke to eat and get dressed, everyone was frantic.

Giles sat with Aaron at dinner, but they hardly spoke, too busy shoveling in lasagna and salad. They'd dumped their duffels on opposite sides of the men's changing room because of the buses they'd ridden in on, which was just as well because Giles wasn't sure he was ready to strip to his skivvies and fight a bow tie as an opening erotic act. He did, though, hustle through his prep so he could cross the room to the choir side and watch Aaron finish getting dressed. Which worked out well, because as Giles approached, Aaron was struggling angrily with his cummerbund.

When it looked as if Aaron was about to ask Baz to help him fix it, Giles tripled his pace to close the distance.

"Here, let me help." He claimed the fabric boldly,

not waiting for permission to wrangle it around Aaron's waist.

Aaron wilted in relief and stood obediently still as Giles worked. "They don't give us enough time for this. Our bus to the community center leaves in ten minutes, someone just said."

"You'll be fine." Giles fussed longer with the cummerbund than necessary, finishing with an equally useless but delightful brush of imaginary lint from Aaron's shoulders. "God, you look good enough to eat."

He let that out deliberately, a gentle lob over the wall to gauge Aaron's reaction—in public, where a rejection would have to be cooler and easier to digest. No rejection came, though. Aaron stilled, cheeks coloring, blue eyes softening. "Th-thanks. You...you too. Though—here." He fussed with Giles's tie, straightening it and puffing it out.

Giles held still under Aaron's ministrations, loving every second of them. "You sitting with anybody on the bus?"

It took Giles's breath away, how bright and blue Aaron's eyes were when he smiled. "No—I mean—nobody..." His smile fell as he got embarrassed.

So fucking adorable. "Let me get my coat and my instrument, and we'll head out."

They walked close together on the way to the shuttle. Giles would have done some subtle elbow touches, but he had to clutch Henrietta to his chest all the way to keep her warm because the air temperature was now two degrees, negative ten with the wind chill. The bus wasn't warm yet either, so when he sat, he put her between his legs instead of in the overhead compartment. He considered giving her his coat but settled on wrapping his scarf around the outside of the case instead.

Aaron watched him. "Do you wrap her up because the cold affects the wood?"

"Yeah. It's fussier than I need to be, but I wasn't kidding when I said Henrietta was expensive. Twenty grand."

"Wow. Is she a Stradivarius?"

"Greiner. I'd love a Strad for sentimental reasons, but blind studies have shown there's no real sound difference between a good modern one and the antiques. I'd been bugging Mom and Dad to get a higher quality violin for a while, but to get a Greiner we had to order it, and they balked."

"Eventually they caved, let you order one? Wow, so cool."

Giles brushed his hand over the top of the cloth case, swallowing as he remembered. "I'd had a…tough year. I think they were trying to make up for things they couldn't change."

He dared a glance at Aaron, whose face was hard to read in the early evening shadow. "Cool. I mean, not cool something bad happened, but that your parents tried to make you feel better."

Something about Aaron's comment bothered Giles. Of course parents would attempt to make their child feel better *anytime* he was sad, not just when he'd been beaten into hamburger. Something told Giles, though, this wasn't the case for Aaron. "How are things with your dad?"

It was the closest either of them had ever come to acknowledging the night at the lake. Aaron fixed his gaze on his lap. "He's been out of town since October. Won't be back until after Christmas."

"Oh—I'm sorry."

Aaron's sad laugh broke Giles's heart. "Don't be. As soon as he shows up, I have to confess I dropped all the pre-law courses he signed me up for. He's going to have a fit."

Giles frowned. "I'm sorry, but I can't see you as a lawyer."

"Tell me about it." Aaron looked so miserable. "I want to do music. *Performance.* But he'd kill me."

"Not literally, I hope."

"Yeah, well—he'd come close. My dad…doesn't do shades of gray. Only his way or the highway." His gaze, no longer bright, shifted to the window. "My mom didn't like how often he traveled. Said she wasn't sure she wanted to be married to someone gone so often. It took a lot for her to go there, because she doesn't speak up much. The confession was her way of saying it hurt her, how often he was gone."

"What did he do?"

"Served her divorce papers before he went to bed."

Giles drew back. "Are you kidding me? You're not, are you. Jesus, what an asshole."

"Yeah." Aaron leaned his forehead against the window. It had to be cold, but he didn't so much as wince. "I keep thinking maybe I should declare music therapy because there's a slim chance he might say it's okay. But it's not what I want. Everybody says to ignore him, but—he pays for school. My mom lives on alimony." He grimaced and pushed off the window, shaking his head. "It's a stupid idea. What job will I get with music performance?"

"All kinds of them."

"*You're* the one who said 'I'd like a job, thanks' when I asked if you were majoring in music."

Second acknowledgment of the lake.

Giles shifted Henrietta, pressing his knee against Aaron's so he could look him full in the face. "That was me. *You*, Aaron—God, you *have* to do music. I can't imagine you doing anything else. I don't think anybody who hears you can. Hell, if I could get a job doing nothing but listening to you sing and play, *that's* what I'd major in. You making music is the most perfect, beautiful part of the world. Don't let your dad get in the way."

Aaron stared at him, surprised, moved…naked.

He wants me to kiss him.

I want to kiss him.

I'm going to kiss him. Right here on this bus. Right now.

Giles leaned forward, heart pumping so hard it hurt, soul caught in the tractor beam of Aaron's gaze.

The bus slowed, lurched, then stopped abruptly. "Ten minutes to warm up," someone called, and the overhead lights came on.

Giles and Aaron broke apart.

The near-kiss hung over Giles as they set up their

dinner performances, making everything appear surreal. When they performed with Salvo, every note felt charged. So did the ride to the church, Henrietta pressed between Giles's legs, Aaron's knee boldly along his own.

Kiss him, kiss him, kiss him—the mantra burned in Giles's brain, but people were too loud this time, too close.

After, he promised himself. *After.*

Except when he tried to cross to the choir bus for the ride back to Timothy, Mina caught his arm. He was about to shake her off when he caught sight of her face.

She was upset. Really upset. He stopped cold. "Min?"

She shut her eyes and hung her head. "Please—don't. I just…I can't talk, I…I need—"

When she broke off to swallow a sob, Giles pulled her to him. "Come on. Let's go grab our seat."

He cast a sad glance of longing across the parking lot and put Aaron out of his mind.

Mina never told him what was wrong. She curled against him the whole way, and when he invited her to stay the night in his room, she ignored the futon and got right into bed with him. Giles held her close, heart breaking as she sobbed quietly into his T-shirt.

"Mina," he began, when he couldn't take it any-more.

"Don't." She pressed her hands to his chest. "Please—I can't. Not yet."

While he appreciated that in the abstract, in the

specific his mind was concocting all kinds of insane scenarios. "Did…somebody hurt you?"

Her sad laugh broke him more than the sobs. "Not like that."

Oh, Min. "Someone broke your heart."

She shut her eyes tight, nodded. This time the sobs weren't silent.

He held her all night, and in the morning he took her to IHOP for breakfast because he knew it was her favorite. She still looked a little hollow, but by the time they went back to Timothy, he had her laughing occasionally.

She, however, had him nervous.

He tried to distract himself by guessing which guy had made Mina cry, but his rabbit brain kept yanking him back to the terrible possibility of *him* being the one sobbing his heart out over rejection. As sure a thing as Aaron had seemed the night before, Mina's tears made him pause…and kept him once again from riding into the Cities on the choir bus. He told himself it was to keep an eye on Mina, but the truth was, he'd chickened out.

Saturday's setup was a little less stressful—they still arrived in downtown Minneapolis by noon, but rehearsal was more relaxed, as the State Theater was an actual theater and did this sort of thing every day. They had time for a late lunch/early dinner—Aaron and Giles and the rest of Salvo went in a great herd through the skywalks to Buca di Beppo. They walked together, sat beside each other at the restaurant, close because they'd crammed twelve people at a table for ten.

Because everything was so loud, they kept leaning close when talking to one another. Aaron told Giles choir stories, surprising him with tales of the chorale's weird game of passing things around while they sang.

Giles had no idea. "I've never seen anything."

Aaron's eyes danced. "That's the point. People hand you oddball items, and you pass them on without breaking eye contact with Nussy. Whoever has it last has to carry it off without being seen. And of course someone has to bring it to start with." He paused to chew a breadstick. "Thursday night I got a banana—whole, and later it had come back peeled, which had a lot of people pissed because it was so messy. I got a condom, a huge purple double-ended dildo, a Barbie doll, a can of Fresca, and a coat hanger. Things were tamer Friday for the church, but it still happened."

"That's crazy." Giles watched Aaron's profile in the warm light of the restaurant. Their chairs were so close their fingers touched. "What if they got caught?"

"Remember, Nussy was in the choir too, back in the day. Someone tells stories about a couch cushion in the nineties, but I can't believe it could happen. Even under a girl's skirt it would be noticeable. Though this has been going on since 1965 or something."

Giles was going to make a comment about the Dark Ages, but Aaron's fingers closed over his, and Giles forgot to breathe.

With the din of voices and clanking plates in their ears, they stared at each other. Aaron looked terrified, but hopeful.

Giles felt…crazy.

That night as they set up for Salvo at a venue a few skywalks over from the State Theater, everything felt intimate. When their bodies brushed, Giles felt a spark. When their gazes met, Giles forgot his own name.

I have to kiss him this time. I have to.

He started to believe if he didn't, Aaron would.

Tonight the whirl of performing didn't abate his euphoria, every moment and glance heightening both his excitement and his arousal. By the time Aaron joined the Ambassadors and Giles got ready for his quartet, Giles was hard. He calmed down while he played, but when he retired to the wings and Aaron sang, he was up to almost full mast.

It was hours until the bus ride home. Tonight was the last night before break. If something else interrupted them, he'd have no other chance.

I have to tell him now. The thought burned in Giles's brain as Aaron hit the final note and the Ambassadors took their bow.

As they exited, Giles saw Baz's hand linger on Aaron's back, inspiring white-hot waves of jealousy.

Seriously. I have to tell him right now.

Wild-eyed and high from singing, Aaron crossed to Giles and jerked his head toward the exit with a grin. "Ready for the skywalk dash to Salvo's venue?"

Kiss him. Tell him how you feel. Something, anything. Right now. "Sure."

Aaron started for the door, but when Giles didn't hurry after, he came back to snag his hand. "Seriously, we have ten minutes, tops."

Giles felt so out-of-body he could barely move. *Tell*

him now, tell him now, tell him right now.

In the middle of the skywalk, he lost it. The scent of Aaron, the warmth of his hand, the light in his eye—it was too much. All Giles's feelings churned inside him like a storm he couldn't control. All he could think about was how much he wanted Aaron. Not just to have sex with him—to *have* him, be with him.

Shaking, he tripped, losing Aaron's hand, almost dropping his violin.

Aaron stopped running. "Are you okay?"

No, he wasn't. Giles's chest felt tight, his head spun, and he had to let Henrietta clatter to the floor so he could grip the glass wall.

"Giles?" Aaron put his hands on Giles's arm, his shoulder, his face full of concern. "What's wrong?"

Drowning. I'm drowning. "I can't," he whispered.

Aaron's grip tightened. "Are you sick? Do you need me to call 911?"

Giles tried to say no, but his whole body trembled, and the shake of his head probably just looked like a spasm.

He had to tell him. He couldn't be scared anymore. He *had to tell him.*

"Giles."

Giles opened his eyes, saw Aaron staring at him—and his heart leaped.

"Aaron—Aaron, I—love you."

He stopped shaking, too terrified by what had fallen out of his mouth to move.

Aaron stared back at him, equally frozen.

Mina's sobs of rejection echoed in his ears, and

Giles felt tears spring to his eyes. *Please—please.*

Aaron kept staring. Giles died, seconds at a time. Surrendering to fear, to inevitable pain, he shut his eyes and waited for the fall.

Soft lips pressed to his own.

Giles's eyes flew open—Aaron's face was right in front of him. Eyes wide open. Full of terror—and hope.

With a shudder, Giles shut his eyes once more—and surrendered to the kiss he'd been dreaming of for six months.

Giles gave Aaron the soft, sweet kiss he'd wanted to give in the car outside Aaron's house. The one where he tilted his head to the side and caught Aaron's lip gently, shyly with his teeth. The one where he didn't grind his cock against Aaron but put a tentative hand on his hip.

The one where he sighed, where his whole chest peeled open and his heart whispered, *I really like you, Aaron, and I want you to stay.*

The one where, when Aaron kissed him back, his heart soared up all the way to the sky.

Aaron melted into him, leaning against the glass of the skywalk so bonelessly Giles had to press him to it to keep him upright. Blood rushed like fire through Giles's veins as he took Aaron's face in his hands and kissed him deeper.

I love you, I love you, I love you, he said over and over, without saying a single word.

When the door to the skywalk opened, the sound cracking like a gunshot, they broke apart, but only just.

"Guys, we're—" Jilly stopped in midsentence as Giles dizzily met her gaze, Aaron still in his arms.

"Oh."

Aaron sagged, his hands tight on Giles's waist.

Shuddering with pleasure that rang to his bones, Giles brushed a kiss across the top of Aaron's head. "We'll be right there."

Jilly lingered. "Okay—so you know, there's dead silence right now while they wait for us to take the stage."

Stifling a groan of disappointment, Giles brushed a last kiss across Aaron's cheek as he bent to pick up Henrietta. "After. We'll talk after."

Aaron took hold of his hand.

They ran together the rest of the way over the bridge. But this time Giles's chest wasn't tight at all. In fact, if he jumped through the glass right now, he was pretty damn sure he could fly.

GILES LOVES ME.

Aaron went through the second half of the dinner performances in a dream, glad he knew his synth parts well enough to go on autopilot. His brain refused to function, would only relive that moment on the sky bridge over and over and over. When Giles had looked him right in the eye, naked and tortured and vulnerable, and said, *Aaron, I love you.* And kissed him.

Soft, spicy lips closing over his, strong, delicate hands cradling his face.

Aaron skipped a note, startled and yanked himself into focus.

Walter and Kelly were at this dinner—they sat in

the front row, waving at Aaron as he entered. The performers were encouraged to mingle for a few minutes after their last performance, and so of course Aaron went up to their table after, but he felt like he drifted over on a cloud. He could barely see where he walked, too busy watching Giles packing up the double bass.

Walter drew Aaron into a hug. "You were *great*. I love the girl group. That's your arrangement, right?" Walter glanced around. "Where's Giles? I want to finally meet this guy."

"Walter." This warning tone came from Kelly, who watched Aaron carefully. "Aaron, hon, are you okay?"

Finished with the bass, Giles searched the room. When he saw Aaron, he smiled, his expression a soft echo of the moment on the sky bridge. As Giles came over to their table, Aaron felt as if the world was underwater. When Giles arrived, Aaron introduced him.

"Walter, Kelly—this is my…Giles."

Walter stuck out a hand. "Pleased to meet you. Walter Lucas. This is my fiancé, Kelly Davidson."

Giles shook their hands. "Good to meet you."

Walter chatted Giles up, asking him the usual questions—where he was from, what he majored in. Through it all Aaron tried not to stare.

Giles kissed me and told me he loved me. Giles kissed me and told me he loved me.

Kelly pulled Aaron down beside him and whispered in his ear. "Do you need a doctor?"

Aaron shut his eyes and pressed his lips almost up

to Kelly's ear. "Giles...kissed me. Just now. Before the—now."

And told me he loved me.

Somebody loves me.

Kelly beamed at him. "Honey, that's *wonderful.*"

Aaron felt *so dizzy.* "I don't know what to do now."

"You be yourself. You talk to him, tell him how *you* feel."

Aaron nodded, but it was reflexive. Everything felt unreal. "I feel kind of sick."

Kelly laughed softly and leaned close enough to kiss Aaron's cheek. "Take deep breaths. This is good, but scary." Kelly tilted his head and wrinkled his nose, still grinning. "He's geeky cute. Very young Dustin Lance Black. I would never have pegged him for your type, but I like it."

Aaron feared Giles would hear, so he hushed Kelly, who laughed. They joined Walter and Giles's conversation, which turned out for some reason to be about cars. Before Aaron could figure out how to wriggle his way in, Dr. Allison appeared in the doorway and announced, as he had every night, that the performers must leave to get ready for the concert.

"We'll catch you before you guys get on your bus." Walter waved his phone in a salute. "Text me where the best place is to meet you."

"Good luck," Kelly said, his tone heavy with double meaning.

On the way to the charter bus taking them to the theater, Giles and Aaron walked close together, helping each other with their instruments and stands and music as always, but this time everything seemed weirdly intimate. Their ride to the theater was only a few blocks, but evening traffic and one-way streets made it take longer. Every breath felt heavy, every look overflowed with meaning.

At the second streetlight, Giles spoke, voice trembling.

"I didn't mean to say it like that. It's not—" Even in the dim lights and reflected snowbanks, he looked pale. "It was kind of a crazy way to tell you I had…feelings for you."

Aaron took Giles's hand, which was cool and slender. It fit so well in his. "It's okay."

"I just—I didn't mean to spring it on you. If you don't feel the same—"

Aaron stopped him with a squeeze. "I do."

They stared at each other in the semidarkness, saying nothing more because there were plenty of words between them now.

All too soon they were at the theater and in concert mode. Aaron gave what he could to the performance, but his mind kept tripping ahead to *after*. The usual menagerie of passed items were almost an anchor tonight, keeping him in the moment as he tried to figure out how to pass a Kewpie doll, a feather boa, a set of anal beads, and a handheld breast pump without cracking up or losing his focus. When the show was over, when everything was packed up on the bus, he pulled out his phone to text Walter, only to find out Walter had beaten him to the punch.

Kelly told me. Skip us. We'll catch you over break. Go

get your man, baby.

Biting back a smile, Aaron pocketed his phone and did just that.

He found Giles out by the bus. It was snowing, and Giles stood under a streetlight in a long wool coat, his sticking-out ears and his long nose pink from the cold. When he saw Aaron, he came over, but he still seemed nervous. "Do you—? Would you like to ride home on the same bus?"

How much did Aaron love the way Giles's voice cracked? "I'd love to."

They went to the orchestra bus hand in hand. It took a few minutes for the bus to settle down, for everyone to get into their seats and stop shouting across the bus at people or breaking out into song for no reason except they were all high on music. At first a few people tried to engage Aaron and Giles, but as if they could sense something heavy was going down, they quickly retreated to give them their own space.

"I think I've messed something up." Giles kept his gaze on his knees. "When…when you first came to Timothy, I was upset. I didn't know what it meant. I thought I was being a dummy reading too much into making out at the lake, because of the way you took off, but when you showed up…I was confused."

Aaron frowned, wanting to argue—then his stomach rolled over as he realized how it must have looked that night. "Oh my God. I'm so sorry."

Giles shrugged awkwardly. "We were just making out. You were leaving, I was leaving. I didn't think we'd end up at the same place, is all."

Aaron bit the truth back, reaching for a half confession to staunch the wound. "The night at the lake was…my second time with a guy. My first one was bad. With you it wasn't bad, but…I kind of flipped, I guess." He felt naked, but he remembered Giles's declaration on the sky bridge and made himself go on, voice pitched low. "It's kind of when I…figured it out. That I really was gay. Admitted it to myself."

"Jesus." Giles shut his eyes, wincing. "I feel like a shit-heel for not realizing. I'm so sorry."

"*No.*" Aaron threaded their fingers tighter together. "I never thought about how it must have looked. I was sorry later I hadn't taken your number. I worried you wouldn't want to give it to me."

I followed you to your college because it was easier than talking to you on Facebook. Aaron bit the confession back. Not yet.

Giles laughed, a sad sound. "I'd have given my number to you. All my numbers. Anything you wanted."

He rested his head against Aaron's, and they sat quietly together for the rest of the ride to the college. Aaron shut his eyes and drank in the moment, the scent of Giles, but the whole time he had to step on the urge to tell the truth, to get the secret off his chest. He told himself it was the wrong time. Was there ever going to be a good moment, though? Because it was crazy. It made *him* sound crazy.

Except it would explain to Giles how much the night at the lake had meant to him.

Except Aaron couldn't be that brave. Even if he

wanted to be.

Giles's hand trailed softly over Aaron's thigh. "The guys I hooked up with at A-H—they only ever wanted sex. They just wanted to get off, get gone. And if at all possible, they'd bash me after to make sure nobody knew they were fags. A couple…sent me to the ER."

Aaron's heart lurched, and he squeezed Giles's hand tight.

Giles squeezed back, closing his other hand over their joined ones. "I'm so sorry I thought of you as the same as them."

Aaron bled. He bled right out of the center of his heart all the way to Saint Timothy. The second they were off the bus, the *moment* he could pull Giles away from the crush, he did, off into the shelter of evergreen bushes near the side door, out of the circle of the streetlight.

With the snow coming down around them in sheets now, he swallowed his embarrassment and his fear, stared at the center of Giles's chest and confessed, "I came here for you."

Silence.

"What?" Giles asked at last.

Aaron drew a breath. "I came here for you. To Saint Timothy. I came here because you said it was where you were going." He couldn't quite read the expression on Giles's face, and he was starting to panic, so he kept talking as if the words would build up some kind of wall. "I couldn't find your number, and I was too scared to Facebook you in case you reacted badly. But I liked you. Couldn't stop thinking about you.

Then I realized I still had to pick my college, and I remembered what you said about them all being the same. Except Saint Timothy would have you. So I picked it. So I could maybe see you. It was dumb, I know. Crazy-stalker. But I couldn't forget you, and we worked together and—"

His wall of words fell down as Giles grabbed him, pressed him to the brick, and kissed him.

They had kissed three times now: at the lake, on the sky bridge, and now—and yet it was like nobody had ever kissed Aaron before in his life, because nothing in his realm of experience had ever been like this. Giles seemed to want to crush him and eat him at the same time, as if he wanted to merge their bodies through pressure even as he climbed inside Aaron's mouth.

Aaron did his best to let him have what he wanted.

A series of whoops and a huge cheer distracted him, drew him out of the moment, but Giles pulled him right back in. "Ignore them," he whispered, still kissing him, still touching his face and pressing so close Aaron could barely breathe. "Did you really come here because of me?"

Aaron nodded, nuzzling back, trying to give Giles more room to take him. "Is…that okay?"

"Okay?" Giles laughed, but he sounded slightly strangled. "Jesus. *Yes.*" This time when they kissed Aaron could taste the salt of Giles's tears. Giles drew Aaron to him in a hug that was almost sweet, like a child coming home.

Then Giles said, in a voice not at all like a little

boy's, "I want you to come to my room with me. I want you to stay the whole night."

Aaron's knees became Jell-O. "I don't—have a toothbrush. Or clothes."

"I have a spare toothbrush, unopened." His hand skimmed Aaron's hip. "You won't need the clothes."

Aaron had meant for the morning, but he couldn't speak now, his brain too hyperaware he was about to get *sex, sex, sex.*

Sex with Giles. Tonight. Right now.

"Okay."

As Giles led Aaron across the parking lot, past the buses to the dorm, he never let go of Aaron's hand. The choir and orchestra started whooping and clapping again. They'd been cheering *Aaron*, watching him get kissed like that. By Giles.

He tripped over his own feet.

Giles helped him up and kept him moving.

"We'll put your violin away for you, Giles," Mina called out.

Giles didn't even glance at her as he dragged Aaron off. "See you tomorrow. Afternoon."

They all knew Aaron had been kissed, that now he was about to get heroically laid. Aaron faltered, but Giles caught his arm and looked at him, his face full of love and surprise and tenderness and tears.

The rest of the world fell away, so far gone Aaron wasn't sure it could ever come back.

Chapter Seventeen

GILES'S DORM WAS deserted as he led Aaron inside. The only other students still in residence were his fellow orchestra and choir members, and they were all at the buses unpacking. Giles was tempted to go at Aaron again in the foyer, but he resisted the urge and headed to the stairs leading to his floor. He was going to do this, and he was going to do it right.

I came here for you. Giles was still ripped open inside from Aaron's confession. It was one of his craziest fantasies, someone wanting him that much. Someone who would not only want him but who would hang around when he was a complete and utter tool, hoping he came to his senses someday.

I almost missed this. The thought made Giles drop his keys as he fumbled at his door. When he picked them up, they fell right back out of his hand.

When Giles bent to collect them a second time, Aaron crouched down too, and he put his hand over Giles's own.

"Hey. It's okay."

Giles cursed himself inwardly. *Be cool. Do not fuck this up.* "Sorry. I just—I wasn't going to say anything. I almost didn't tell you how I felt. I didn't want to mess anything up when our friendship was going well, but after all this time together at the concerts—" His voice broke.

Aaron touched his face. "I'm glad you said something."

Yeah, he'd confessed that he *loved Aaron*. Way too fucking soon to say those words. Did Giles even know what love was, really?

He met Aaron's beautiful blue gaze, felt his world align and thought, *Yeah. I do.*

Aaron unlocked the door, and Giles relocked it once they were inside. Originally he'd planned on pushing Aaron directly onto the futon and blowing him, but his whole key debacle had diffused his zeal. He turned on the desk lights and the one he used by his loft—the overhead lights would kill the rest of the mood completely. Hands in his pockets, he nodded uncertainly at the futon. "Do you want to sit down?"

"Sure." Aaron sat, leaving plenty of space beside him.

Giles gestured to the fridge. "Do you want a soda? Bottle of water? I think Brian has a sample bottle of whiskey in his desk."

"I'm good." Aaron patted the futon. "Sit down, Giles."

Giles did, wondering why he felt so strange. He still wanted to jump Aaron's bones like nothing else. But he felt like they should talk more or something.

Except he didn't know what to say.

Aaron bumped their knees together. He looked sort of nervous but mostly amused. "You okay?"

Giles touched Aaron's hair, smoothing it from his eyes, letting his fingers linger on Aaron's ear. "I can't quite believe this is happening."

Shutting his eyes, Aaron turned his face into Giles's palm and pressed a soft kiss to the flesh. He kissed Giles's wrist.

He pulled Giles's hand away from his hair with a tentative touch, then placed it hesitantly on his own waist, drawing himself closer, putting his mouth in kissing range.

Closing the distance, Giles slid his palm around to cup Aaron's ass.

Giles tangled their tongues, nibbled at the sides of Aaron's mouth, diving in. The more he kissed Aaron, the more Aaron melted against him. When Giles drew Aaron onto his lap, Aaron went so obediently it made Giles's toes curl.

It wasn't just that Aaron was cute and sweet. It was that when they did this, Giles didn't have to seduce him into letting Giles drive. Aaron wanted to perch over Giles's lap, knees to the futon, and be made to take off his shirt. He wanted to tip his head back while Giles kissed the center of his chest, teased at his fur, rubbed circles against his pert nipples.

Aaron wanted to go anywhere Giles took him.

Take him Giles did. First he nudged Aaron out of the rest of his clothes and got rid of some of his own. He'd have stripped all the way down, but he could tell Aaron kind of dug being naked when Giles wasn't. He stayed in his tux pants, dick like a concrete bar as naked Aaron ground on him, cooing and gasping as Giles slicked his fingers with the lube he kept tucked under the futon mattress for masturbation-to-porn convenience. Giles wasn't masturbating now—he was sliding his middle finger into Aaron's hot, flexing ass. Aaron curled against him, begging with breathy sighs for more.

In his pants, Giles's cock said, *Yeah, we got more.*

Giles laved the corded muscle at Aaron's throat. "How far do you want to go?"

Aaron trembled in his arms, pushing down on his finger. "I—Whatever you want."

Wrong answer. Giles changed his carnal licking to a softer kiss and made himself ask the question he'd been trying not to think about for two months. "How far did you go with Baz?"

Aaron jerked, surprised, then self-conscious. "How—?" He shrank away from Giles.

"I'm sorry. I'm jealous and that came out clumsily." He forced himself to regroup. "You said you hadn't done much before me, but obviously some time has passed since then, and I know you were with Baz. I wanted to know what's virgin territory, so I can respect it."

Aaron was still mortified. "I haven't… Nothing more than I did with you. Except—I blew him."

Giles shut his eyes. *You could have had that instead of him, if you hadn't been so busy judging.* Then he pushed regret away, focusing on Aaron. "I'd love to fuck you. I think you'd like it too. But I don't want you to tell me yes if you're not ready."

Still impaled on Giles's finger, Aaron clenched. "I

want to," he whispered. "With you. Now. Though I…I've heard it hurts."

"It does at first. Sometimes a lot. But usually you get stretched, and it's not so bad. And for some guys it's never an issue. You never know until you jump in, unfortunately."

Aaron was hunched forward, nestled half on Giles's shoulder, face turned in to his neck. "Have you? Been…fucked?"

"Yeah." Giles skimmed Aaron's back with his free hand. "But it wasn't great. The guys I was with were rough. It always felt too dangerous. And…honestly, I like the other end of the coin better. Not to say I wouldn't bottom again. I just haven't. Maybe with the right guy."

I'd bottom for you, if you wanted it. He hoped that was clear.

Aaron stroked Giles's side, still cuddled to him. "I always wanted to bottom. It made me feel ashamed because it went with everything else about not being man enough."

"Honey, I'm here to tell you, you've got to be a hell of a man to take it up the butt. That's serious trust, letting someone at your ass. It was why I couldn't hurt the guys I fucked, even when they were jerks. How could I hurt someone who got so vulnerable for me?"

Aaron pressed a kiss to Giles's collarbone. "I want to be vulnerable for you."

Giles's cock told him it was time to start finger-fucking Aaron again, so he did. "You're seriously hot, Aaron. You make me crazy just looking at you. When you play or sing, half the time I think I'm going to lose my mind with want."

Aaron put his hands tight on Giles's shoulders, head tipped back while he rode Giles's fingers. "It feels so good. Like I can let go. *God.* Giles, I want it. I really do." His jaw fell slack, and he gasped as Giles hit his prostate. "Oh God, Giles, *tonight.* I want it tonight."

Yesss, Giles dick cheered, but he shoved it down even as he slid in a second finger beside the first. "We're going slow. And if we start and you change your mind, or it hurts too much, we're stopping. Right away."

"I thought—*nyggh.*" Aaron gritted his teeth and bore down as Giles went in all the way to his knuckles. "I thought—I thought the guy always said he couldn't hold back."

"You're a guy too, says this gorgeous cock flapping against my chest. Also, anybody who says he can't hold back or stop if his partner is uncomfortable is an asshole."

Aaron opened his eyes—heavy lidded, soft with trust and lust. "You're not an asshole."

Yes, I was a huge one. "No, but I'm going to do some seriously exciting things to yours."

Knowing the endgame helped. Aaron wanted to get fucked, and Giles wanted him to want it more than this once, so he took his time stretching Aaron's ass. Aaron pleaded and begged, but Giles ignored him, understanding what Aaron couldn't know, that fingers and dicks were worlds apart. When he finally got to the point of slipping on a condom and heading for the main event, he considered doing him from behind, but he worried Aaron wouldn't tell him if it hurt too much. He kept Aaron in his straddle position, and after greasing himself and Aaron ten times more generously than he normally would, he guided Aaron over his cock, rubbing the glans along Aaron's taint, toward his target.

"Sit down on it. *Slowly.* Bear down and *go slow.*"

He pressed his cockhead against Aaron's opening, nudged inside and waited to see what happened.

Aaron went too fast. Giles was about to tell him to stop when Aaron gasped, eyes wide, body rigid with pain. Swearing, Giles tried to pull out, but Aaron had all the control, and he'd locked himself down.

"It's okay," Aaron bit off, voice choked with pain, when Giles told him to move. "I just—wow."

"You went too fast. Nobody's in a rush. And *bear down.*"

"I'm kind of at a loss as to why guys do this right now."

"Because prostate." He slapped Aaron's ass. "Up. Stop hurting yourself."

"I want to stay here. It's already better." He let out a breath and looked down at Giles, a good deal of the pain gone from his eyes. "You're kind of big."

"Not really. Everything seems like an anvil when it's in your ass."

Shutting his eyes, Aaron drew a breath, bore down and took in another half inch. This time he only hissed a little, and his cock got a bit of life back. "It's…weird. But hot. A good burn. I love this, inside me. Being filled."

Giles reached around Aaron to feel the stretch, knowing it was his cock going inside that heat. "It feels good to be in you. Like I'm God or something, getting away with something huge. Love somebody letting me in."

"I want you all the way in." Aaron took in another half inch, then another, gasping. "God, it's starting to get kind of good. Really good."

Giles pressed an openmouthed kiss over Aaron's chest. "Sit on my dick, baby. Let me pound into you. Let me fill you up."

Aaron's fingers dug into Giles's back, drawing him closer. "I want to take the rest."

Giles wanted him to take it too. Wanted Aaron bouncing up and down on his dick, begging for more. "Careful, hon. Careful." He sucked on a nipple. "But yeah. I want in you, all the way. Yesterday."

He sucked on the nipple again, teasing the other with his thumb. He groaned as he felt Aaron go down, felt it inside and outside as all that heat surrounded him, Aaron expanding and opening to accommodate him.

He felt Aaron's ass cheeks on his thighs, on his balls.

All the way in.

Giles kissed Aaron's chest, teased the meat of his pectoral with his teeth. "You okay?"

"I feel really full." Aaron's voice sounded strained. It was wonderful. "Every nerve ending in my body is dialed up to eleven."

Giles couldn't stop running his fingers around the ring of Aaron's ass. *I'm in there. That's me. In Aaron.* "Wait until I thrust in and out. Dragging over it. Fucking against it."

Aaron whimpered and pushed up and down. "God, *do it.*"

Giles did. He had Aaron rise on his knees as he adjusted the angle, and then he fucked. Not super hard, but enough to show what they could do with this game, let Aaron feel the kaleidoscope of pleasure a bundle of nerve endings could unleash on his body.

Aaron cried out, begging, swearing, speaking in tongues. Giles picked up some speed. Aaron began to fuck back, desperate for more.

Giles put him face-first against the futon seat, got behind him, and went to town.

Now he fucked. Aaron had himself spread open and begging, so Giles gave him plenty. He learned what strokes sent Aaron over the edge and hammered on them, rutting until Aaron was all but drooling, so fucked out and incoherent he couldn't lift his head.

Giles switched positions—now he put Aaron on the floor, tucked his feet over Giles's shoulders and started up again. Aaron's eyes flew open, and he moaned in pleasure, and Giles gave a feral smile and drilled on. *Yeah, baby. New angle. Good one, huh?*

He spoke softly to Aaron as he fucked him, sweet things, dirty things, telling him how hot he looked, how good his ass felt, how loud all that lube was as he fucked it in and out. He wasn't sure Aaron heard any of it, too lost on his high. But when Giles folded him in half, pressing Aaron's knees to his chest, trapping his cock between them and finally giving it some friction, Aaron went out of his mind.

"*Don'tstopdon'tstopdon'tstop.*" Tears ran out of his eyes, and he tipped his head back, sacrificing his body to Giles's pleasure. "Please, *please.*"

"I won't stop." Giles bent to steal a kiss, keeping up his deep, quick thrusts. "I won't stop until you come, baby."

Aaron did come, shouting so vehemently anybody on their floor had to know somebody was getting fucked. When he came, he jerked, fingernails scraping down Giles's arms. Then he lay spent, limbs flopping, head lolling, chest heaving.

Giles wanted to stay inside, but in deference to his partner's oversensitive body, he pulled out and ditched the condom. In quick jerks, he sprayed his load across Aaron's chest, which was seriously fucking hot, marking him. When he was spent, he collapsed beside Aaron, kissing him on the shoulder as exhaustion crept over him. "You okay?"

"Mmrf," Aaron gurgled. He turned his head lazily to Giles, as if the gesture took superhuman effort.

A clumsy hand trailed over Giles's face as Aaron's eyes opened over a sleepy smile.

"Love you too," Aaron slurred. Giles's heart soared.

Thirty seconds later Aaron was asleep.

Giles wanted to join him, but he was acutely aware of the discarded choir and orchestra clothes littered around them, clothes they would be expected to wear again Sunday afternoon. Fighting off lethargy, he rose and gathered them, hanging them up and dabbing at the jizz stain on the leg of his pants with a washcloth. By the time he started brushing his teeth, Aaron was stirring on the floor. Smiling around his mouthful of foam, Giles handed over the spare toothbrush, new in its pack, and the tube of toothpaste. And a washcloth.

Aaron stumbled to his feet, half fuck-drunk. "Sorry I passed out." He touched his spunk-smeared chest and made a face—and laughed.

Giles brushed a kiss on his cheek. "You're fine. You clean up here, and I'll get the futon turned into a bed."

Once the bed was made, their clothes righted, and their mouths minty fresh, they spooned together naked on the futon, Giles with his back to the wall, his lanky body wrapped around Aaron.

"That was amazing," Aaron said at last.

Giles kissed his hair. "Yes. It was."

Silence.

Aaron's hand skimmed over Giles's, which rested on his own midsection. "Are we…dating now?"

"I would love to date you." Giles slid his hand down to tease Aaron's limp cock. "Wish we hadn't started this right before a break."

Some of the tension returned to Aaron's body. "I don't want to go home. I don't want to have to explain everything I've changed. I want to stay here, where I'm happy."

Giles hated knowing he was part of *everything*. Rather, it was about Aaron coming out, but it affected Giles too.

Good Christ, if Colton found out.

Hell. *When.*

He wrapped himself tighter around Aaron. "I'll help you however I can. Just let me know what you need."

"To stay here on this futon with you. Forever." He threaded their fingers together. "Can we...get together over break? I'll be at my mom's. I'll...tell her. She'll be surprised, but she'll be okay." He paused. "I think."

"You don't have to tell anyone until you're ready. But yes. I'll be with you wherever and whenever you want."

Aaron turned in Giles's embrace, nuzzling his neck, massaging his ass. "Will you fuck me again tomorrow? Before we go?"

"No. Your ass will be too sore." He slid his hand to the hole in question, touching it lightly, making Aaron jerk with overstimulation.

"Damn."

Giles bent to his lips, smiling wickedly. "I'll be happy to kiss it better, though."

Aaron laughed, then moaned as Giles took his cock in hand, teasing them both into full erection. They came again, languidly, little loads easily mopped up with tissues.

This time when Aaron went to sleep, Giles let himself drift along after, holding him close, unsure of what exactly lay ahead. All he knew was now that he had his dream boy, he was going to do his damnedest to keep him.

Chapter Eighteen

AARON DID WAKE up sore the next morning. When he rolled over, he hissed at the initial contact of his ass on the mattress.

"Sorry." Giles nuzzled him sleepily, planting a kiss on Aaron's collarbone. "I guess I'm an asshole after all."

Since Aaron distinctly remembered begging like a whore for Giles to fuck him harder, faster, he wasn't calling anybody names. Not even himself stupid. Because a little literal butthurt was worth great sex. And it didn't remotely eclipse how awesome it was to wake up beside Giles in the morning.

Giles. His boyfriend.

Since the dorm floor was still completely deserted, they showered together, laughing and touching and kissing the whole time. Giles ordered pizza as soon as the stores opened, and they ate it for lunch, foregoing the cafeteria so they could make out. Giles offered Aaron a ride home, which Aaron had to decline because his mom was coming to the concert.

This reminded him he'd have to figure out a way to come out to her…which was a serious buzzkill.

Giles sat behind Aaron, their naked bodies entwined as they munched on pepperoni and cheese.

"Seriously, don't worry about coming out to your mom. Do it whenever you're ready."

Aaron leaned against his chest. "How did you tell your parents?"

"You're joking, right? Oh—wait. Sometimes I forget you were the new kid at A-Hell. Hon, I've been a flaming flamer since I was old enough to ask for a tiara. I got teased for it before I understood the term. In fact it was sixth grade before I worked out that gay was the same thing as me wanting to marry Devin Mack."

Aaron remembered the beefy linebacker from Alvis-Henning. "Are you serious?"

"Hey, I was eleven. How was I to know meatheads were only good for fucking?"

Something in his tone made Aaron pause. "Are you telling me…?"

"That I fucked him? Yes. Honey, I'd probably curl your toes if I told you how many of A-Hell's finest I've boned. I told some of it to Mina earlier this year, and I think she's still reeling. Though most of the guys I had aren't gay. Definitely Devin wasn't. Lonely and horny and trapped in the northern burbs is not the same as gay."

Aaron had a hard time reconciling Giles with the kind of guy who would fuck straight guys he knew hated him. It sounded so…seedy. Crude.

Giles's arm slipped, his touch on Aaron's thigh a little sad. "Sorry."

Aaron caught his hand. "No, don't be. I like knowing about you. Even when it isn't sunshine and puppies."

"How about some tit for tat?" Giles nudged him with his knee. "Let's hear some of your backstory."

"I'm not sure I'm very interesting." He tried to think of something not lame. "I was in a band in Eden Prairie. We kind of sucked, but it was fun. I wrote the music most of the time. My…friend Tanner wrote the lyrics."

Giles pressed a kiss on his hair. "Tell me more about this Tanner. I sense a story."

Aaron didn't want to, but he suspected that was all the more reason he should. "He…was my first. Ish." He shifted in Giles's arms, uncomfortable with the confession. "All we did was kiss and touch each other one night when we'd been drinking."

"And it didn't go well?"

"He hasn't spoken to me since."

Giles hugged him. "Oh, baby. I'm sorry. That's awful."

It was. It still hurt, after all this time. "We were friends since we were young. I always loved him, but it was little-kid love. Sometimes I pretended in my head we were married, but I knew I shouldn't ever say it out loud."

"So you knew early on you were gay."

"I knew how I felt and what I wanted wasn't like what most people thought I should want and feel, but that went for most of my life anyway. My mom always picked out my clothes. My dad enrolled me in clubs and sports. When we had a mock election in seventh grade, he told me how to vote. Half the time he orders for me in restaurants. So the fact that I wanted to marry the wrong gender fit in with everything else—what I wanted had to be wrong. I assumed I didn't have a choice and let girls tell me we were boyfriend and girlfriend, which was easy because I just had to smile at them, hold their hands, and go to dances. When I got older, it got messy, because they wanted to do more than get a peck on the mouth. I had sex with one girl once. Or rather, I tried. I couldn't get either of us off. It was awful."

Giles kissed his hair.

Aaron ran his fingers down Giles's arm. "Tanner…God. I thought he'd always be there. I couldn't marry him, couldn't hold his hand, but we would always be friends. I figured that would be enough, and it *was*, until that night. Because *he* kissed *me*. He put *his* hand on *my* dick, told me to do the same thing. And it was so good. Like I'd been drinking dirty dishwater and somebody passed me a bottle of wine."

"What happened? If he started it and it was so good, why did it go to hell?"

"I don't know. I've never been able to figure it out. One minute we're kissing, the next he's telling me to get out. He wouldn't tell me what was wrong, just told me to go home. I had to call my mom, and she asked why I was crying, and I couldn't say anything. Couldn't tell her the truth."

Giles held him close. "He was a shame-and-blame. I'm so sorry."

Aaron frowned. "What's a shame-and-blame?"

"A guy who is gay only when he wants to get off. All you are to him is a piece of meat, and when he's done with you, he wants to burn you so nobody knows what you did with him."

That was pretty much what Tanner had done. "I can't believe he gave up all those years together, all our history, just to get off."

"In his case, I doubt it was so simple. This wasn't Devin Mack deciding it was better to hump the gay kid than risk getting a girl pregnant. Tanner probably didn't count on his fear being bigger than your friendship. It's still a dick move, but not as callous as it feels, at least not as far as intent. That would be my guess."

While Giles's observation might be true, it didn't make Aaron feel any better. Then the full impact of what Giles had said hit him. "Wait, are you telling me you let Devin fuck you?"

"Ah. Well, no. I'm sloppy about calling all sex fucking, no matter who's putting what into whom. To be honest, the number of times I've been in someone's ass is less than five counting you, and I've only let two people in me. Mostly it's blow jobs, frots, and this move I think of in my head as the near-fuck."

Aaron laughed. "This I need to hear."

Giles's voice turned silky. "Oh, sweetheart, I'll *show* you."

He put Aaron on his knees over the futon, which made Aaron's cock perk up but his sore ass clench. Instead of spreading Aaron's legs, though, Giles pushed them together. *Tight.* He pressed his cock along Aaron's crack. "Sometimes it was this—me jacking them and fucking their crack. But if I could talk them into it, I did this."

He parted Aaron's legs wide enough to slip his cock through, then thrust back and forth. It ran the length along Aaron's balls and taint, and Aaron couldn't stop a soft moan.

Giles slipped his tongue briefly in Aaron's ear. "I'd tell them if they let me go first, they could do it to me after. Except I jacked them too, so most of the time they came too early to reciprocate. Even if they could get it up again, usually their sense of straightness returned and they bugged out."

No wonder they hated him—Giles was a freaking manipulator. Aaron didn't have the word power to say that now, though, because Giles was still thrusting and, as he had his former conquests, jacking Aaron.

They made a hell of a mess on the futon, but Giles didn't care, only pulled a bottle of Resolve from underneath and dabbed it up with some paper towels. "I'll take the cover home and wash it over break. It's time anyway."

While they finished up their lunch, Giles packed, and once he was done, they went over to Aaron's room to do the same.

Giles recoiled when he saw Elijah's religious paraphernalia. "Holy shit, did you land a Jesus freak or something?"

Or something. "He's really weird. We never talk. At all."

"That sucks. Brian is awesome. You'll have to meet him when we come back in January."

Aaron loved the idea of January, of being back in school, of being able to hang out with Giles, having sex whenever they could get a room to themselves. "I hate how this is almost over."

Giles kissed his cheek. "It'll be okay. We're in the same town. If you need me, I'll be over in two minutes."

Aaron kissed his mouth, opened it as Giles's tongue nudged the seam.

The preconcert dinners were more of a pain in the ass than anything else the fourth time, and Aaron performed on autopilot, trying to think of how he was going to come out to his mom. Maybe he'd have them go out to dinner. She couldn't make a big scene then.

Maybe he should talk to Walter first, he thought as he passed on the partially thawed frozen burrito someone handed him during the concert. Walter would have good ideas about how to come out.

His mom came up to him right away after the final number, hugging him and going on about how amazing he was, how happy he seemed. She got a little teary, but for once it looked like it was because she was happy. For him.

That was nice.

He wouldn't tell her right away, he decided as she kept carrying on about the school and how quaint it was and how well he seemed to fit in at Saint Timothy. Maybe he'd wait until after Christmas. He wondered if he should do it *right* before he went back. Give her time to process, but not too much.

He excused himself from her to say goodbye to the Ambassadors and Salvo, and he and Giles went off for a private goodbye around the corner of the lobby.

This kiss was bittersweet—passionate, but everything about it said they were about to be parted and they didn't like it. Giles grabbed Aaron's ass, kneading it and pulling him close to almost grind against him. Normally Aaron would have balked at that in public—they were in an empty hallway, but anyone could come around the corner. The idea of leaving, though, of having this be the last touch until who knew when or how, meant Aaron couldn't tell Giles no.

Which was why Giles's hand was halfway down the back of his pants when he heard his mother call out in a strange voice, "Aaron?"

IT DIDN'T TAKE a rocket scientist to figure out the dark-haired woman gaping at them was Aaron's mom. Giles didn't jump back from Aaron, thinking if he pulled his hand out of Aaron's waistband slowly, they could preserve the highly minuscule possibility of Mrs. Seavers not seeing Giles's fingers in her son's ass crack. Not much he could do about having his tongue halfway down Aaron's throat, though.

Aaron had gone rigid in Giles's arms. At first he gripped Giles's waist, a seeking-comfort gesture, but he looked at his mother and let go as if scalded. Cheeks coloring, he stammered an apology to Giles.

Giles put a hand on his shoulder, rubbing gently, taking him into a subtle, comforting embrace. "It's okay. It'll be okay."

"Giles, there you are—*oh*."

Giles swallowed a groan. *Fantastic.* Now *his* mom

was here too.

Vanessa Mulder appeared beside Mrs. Seavers, but after her initial eyebrow raise, she had a decidedly different look about her, scary for a more matchmaking kind of reason.

"Aaron, I'm so sorry," Giles murmured.

After glancing down at their joined hands and over to his mother, Aaron drew a shaky breath and squeezed Giles's palm. "It's okay."

The two mothers were a crazy contrast—Aaron's clearly trying to process her son making out with another guy, Giles's utterly naked in her glee at seeing her boy all partnered up. Giles didn't know which fire to put out first. What would freak Aaron out more, his own mother being repelled by his gayness, or Giles's for whipping out wedding samplers?

Keeping Aaron firmly at his side, Giles nodded politely to Mrs. Seavers. "Hi. I'm Giles Mulder. This is my mom, Vanessa, and that's my dad Tim over there. I'm…dating your son." He turned to his own mother. "Mom, this is Aaron Seavers. My boyfriend. Who you didn't know about because this is relatively new. Though I actually know Aaron from Alvis-Henning."

"Oh, really?" Vanessa held out her hand to Mrs. Seavers. "Hi there. So pleased to meet you. How darling is this, our sons going all the way to college to hook up? Where do you live, Oak Grove or Anoka?"

Mrs. Seavers accepted the offered hand in a kind of daze. "Oak Grove. We…haven't lived there long. Only two years."

"We'll have to go out for coffee. I'm so sorry—I

missed your name."

"Beth." She glanced at her son, still shell-shocked.

Aaron stared back at her, deer in headlights.

Giles didn't know what to do now. This was supposed to have been a kiss goodbye, but he couldn't very well leave Aaron now. Of course he could imagine his mother ramping up to a joint family dinner before they all pulled out of town, which would be good except Vanessa would be all about playing house while poor Beth tried to catch up. Which maybe would be what she had to do. All Giles cared about was Aaron. His mom could sink or swim.

He couldn't figure out, though, what Aaron needed.

"Is everything okay?" Vanessa glanced between the three of them, finally realizing the awkward was getting thick. "Giles? Honey? What's going on?"

Neither Seavers said anything, just kept staring at one another. Giles began to sweat. Seriously, *what*? How could he fix this for Aaron? Should he even try?

This was about Beth being surprised. This was about Aaron being scared his mother was about to reject him.

Make it so she can't.

"I think—" Giles wasn't sure what he was saying, his mouth moving faster than his brain. "I think we surprised Mrs. Seavers is all. I don't think she knew about me. It's my fault. I was a little…more affectionate than maybe I should have been in a public hallway."

"Oh, *honey*." Vanessa *tsk*ed at Giles and pursed her lips. She turned to Beth. "I'm so sorry. I can only imagine. Giles has always been…exuberant."

"It's…okay." Beth's gaze never left Aaron. "I was surprised. But it's okay." She couldn't quite smile, but she was trying. "It's okay, Aaron."

Aaron *did* smile at his mother, tentatively.

Okay. Giles let out a breath. "Mom—can I meet you out front? Aaron and I—We have to go get something from backstage. We forgot our…folders."

Fuck, that was unbelievably lame. But it seemed their mothers might have fallen for it, because they both said they'd meet them in front when they were ready.

Giles led Aaron to the single-stall bathroom, locked the door and drew him into his arms. "I'm *so sorry*, Aaron. Seriously, I feel like complete shit. I don't have any idea how to make it okay, but if I can—"

"It's all right." Aaron leaned against Giles, crouching so he could rest on his shoulder. "I mean—yes. It's going to be awkward. But…I think mostly she's surprised. Maybe this is better than going nuts all break trying to work out how to tell her."

"I'm such an asshole. I'm so goddamn sorry."

Aaron nuzzled Giles's neck and slipped his hands into Giles's waistband over his ass. "It's okay."

Giles shivered at the feel of Aaron stroking him. "You have to call me tonight and let me know how the ride home is. And if I can see you tomorrow."

Aaron's hands slid deeper. "I will."

Giles wanted to fuck him, not leave him. He kissed openmouthed at Aaron's collarbone. "Let me show you how sorry I am for fucking up. Let me show you with my mouth on your dick."

God but Giles loved the way those words alone made Aaron plump in his pants. "I—Our moms—"

"I'll suck hard and fast, honey." Giles went to his knees, trailing his hands and mouth down Aaron's chest.

It felt good, having Aaron's cock in his mouth, tasting him, smelling him. He made it a goddamn good blow job, lots of tongue and suction, hums in the back of his throat, teases into the slit. He fondled Aaron's balls and rubbed his taint. With a press against Aaron's pucker, he had himself a fountain, and he sucked Aaron dry. Climbing a now-boneless boyfriend, Giles cradled him to the wall and indulged in a slow, spunk-flavored kiss.

"You promise you'll be okay?" he asked when they came up for air. "That if you're not, you'll call me?"

Aaron nodded, nuzzling his nose. "Giles—thank you."

Giles ran his hands down Aaron's arms. "What for? Outing you to your mom? Making out with you in the hallway?"

Aaron's touch was so gentle it made Giles shut his eyes. "Just—thank you."

It took them another fifteen minutes to leave the bathroom and go back to their mothers, and they went hand in hand. Vanessa and Beth were chatting on one of the lobby benches, Giles's dad loitering in the background. The moms looked like they were getting along, and Beth seemed a lot more even-keeled than she'd been when they left. The real test, though, was when Aaron came up to her. How would she react?

When she smiled at her son with a soft acceptance in her countenance, Giles finally allowed himself to relax, at least a little.

FOR THE FIRST ten minutes in the car, neither Aaron nor his mom said anything. Eventually Beth broke the silence.

"Why didn't you tell me?"

She wasn't being angry or confrontational, which was good. If anything she sounded hurt. Which, oddly enough, annoyed Aaron.

"Because I only became okay with it myself in the last few months. And Giles—we've been friends for a while, but this…only happened last night."

"So you didn't *know* before last night?"

Tension spread across his chest. Aaron leaned against the window, hating that they had another hour before he could go to his room and wait for school to start again.

"I'm sorry." She kept fidgeting. He could practically feel her trying to make this his fault, making her face this, and yet she seemed to keep running into the fact that this wasn't about her. "It was a strange way to find out."

"It wasn't how I'd planned to tell you, no."

"How *were* you planning to tell me?"

"I don't know, Mom. If I could have figured out a way to never bring it up, believe me, I would have." Originally he'd intended to ask for dinner, but now he was glad his stomach was empty. "Please don't tell Dad. He's going to be angry enough about my classes."

"Why? What happened to your classes?"

He wished he didn't have to go home. He wished he could have gone home with Giles, not just to get a ride but to stay at the Mulder house. Shutting his eyes tight, Aaron pressed his forehead to the cold glass of the window.

"*Aaron.* What happened to your—?"

"I dropped all the pre-law stuff Dad signed me up for. I took a bunch of music classes. I want to be a music performance major." His gut knotted, and his chest got so tight his breaths hurt. *Please leave me alone. Please don't be disappointed in me again tonight.*

"Oh. He's…not going to like that. At all."

Aaron tried to pack himself down, to rediscover the same cool silence he'd stumbled into when Tanner had rejected him and he'd had to move away. It was hard, though, to smother all the joy he'd found at Saint Timothy, that he'd come to take for granted.

His pocket buzzed once, then kept buzzing. Pulling out his phone, Aaron saw four texts from Giles.

Checking in to make sure you're okay.

I think your car is two ahead of me.

My mom will not stop texting about how cute you are. Then texts me to stop reading texts while I drive.

She's right. You're very hot.

Another text appeared while Aaron read the screen.

I do, you know. Love you. It's probably dumb to keep saying that so soon. But I really do.

Smiling, Aaron felt a great deal of the tension fall

away from his chest. He thumbed back a reply.

I love you too.

Beth glanced over. "Is that him?"

"Yeah." Aaron brushed his thumb along the edge of the phone. "He wanted to make sure I was okay."

Her smile was quiet, almost sad. "You relax around him. I only got to watch the two of you for a few minutes, but you haven't been like this with anyone since Tanner."

A soft, sorrowful lump eased down Aaron's solar plexus. "Yeah. Probably true."

She patted his leg. "It's good to see you happy, honey. I wish you could have told me…differently, but…I'm glad he makes you feel good."

Aaron touched the washed-out, wide-eyed, sticking-out-eared selfie Giles sent him. *Me too.*

Chapter Nineteen

WHEN AARON HAD thought about going home for Christmas, he'd assumed he'd alternate between quiet days while his mother went to work and long, uncomfortable evenings with her when she was home. His weekends would be peppered with holiday visits to his aunt's house, awkward because his mother's sister had the perfect, smiling family and Aaron and Beth decidedly did not. The climax would be his father calling to ask about his grades, and Aaron would have to either lie or confess the truth.

These assumptions, however, were all made PG: Pre-Giles.

To start, Giles came over at least every other day. He apologized profusely for being less available, for taking Aaron on such lame dates. Aaron loved, though, how Giles took him on late-afternoon drives to get a Frosty in Anoka. Giles always called before he went to bed, and they texted so much Aaron usually had to charge his phone midday. Most of it was nonsense, but Aaron treasured those emojis as much as their Frosty runs. He loved Giles's selfies while he made cookies with his mom, his running play-by-play of whatever family gathering he was at now.

There were several naughty Snapchats too. Giles convinced Aaron to play that game with him, and those photos became almost more of a bonding event than the texts relating their days. At first they went with standard cock shots, which was hot, but they soon found teasers were more exciting. Giles went incoherent when Aaron sent him a selfie from his waist down as he lay in his underwear on his bed, and Aaron learned Giles could render him speechless with a carefully angled shot of his neck and collarbone. They still teased each other with the full monty—if Aaron went too long without sending a pic of his bare ass, Giles began to complain—but the soft-core shots were where they spoke to each other.

On the Friday after Christmas, Aaron went to a family gathering at Giles's house. Giles had said over and over Aaron didn't have to come, which at first made Aaron think Giles didn't want him there. When Aaron hinted at this, though, Giles got flustered. "No, I want you there. I just…I get it if you think it's weird."

"Why would it be weird?"

"Because it's my family. I don't want you to think I'm trying to assimilate you or anything."

Aaron never fully understood what Giles had been nervous about. Giles's family was nice, very friendly, and best of all they didn't fight. They bickered, particularly Giles and his mother, but nothing was the same as the tension-riddled dinners and shouting/weeping arguments Aaron had grown up with. Giles's sister and brother were present too, and their spouses. They welcomed Aaron, let him hold the new baby, made him feel at home. For dinner Aaron had a big meal of chili and bread chased down by eggnog and Christmas cookies. He played board games and sat with Giles on the love seat while they watched cheesy stop-animation specials on TV, snuggled beneath the blanket hiding their entwined hands and legs.

He got a present from Mrs. Mulder, which was sweet but made him panic because he hadn't brought anything. When Giles took Aaron to his room and produced another wrapped box, Aaron tried to refuse it.

"I didn't get you anything—I'm so sorry."

"Whatever." Giles pressed the package into Aaron's hand. "It's kind of lame anyway, so don't get excited. It's one of those things that seemed cool in the store and now probably not so much."

It *was* cool: it was a bound notebook of blank composition paper, with jotting space in the margins and chord spaces in the header. Aaron ran his fingers over the cover. "I love it. But I didn't get you anything."

"You can write me a song," Giles suggested with a wink.

Aaron *had* been composing lately, a short, simple melody line that made his heart feel good. That was as far as it had gone, though, and as usual he couldn't think of what words should go with it. He had nothing presentable enough for Giles. "I meant a present right now."

"Then sing me something." They were sitting on Giles's bed, and Giles leaned back on his pillows, resting his hands above his head. "Something right now. Just for me."

Aaron tapped Giles lightly on his belly with the notebook. "That's not a real present."

"It would be perfect. You have no idea how many times I've listened to you sing and wished you were singing to me."

He seemed so sincere, but Aaron had a hard time believing him all the same. "But I've sung with you a million times."

"You haven't sung *to* me." Giles ran a hand down Aaron's arm, then withdrew, abruptly self-conscious. "You don't have to, obviously."

Aaron caught Giles's hand, threading their fingers together. "What do you want me to sing?"

"Anything. You could sing the alphabet song, and I'd get the shivers."

Aaron thought about singing that to tease him, but he couldn't, because for Giles, he could only pick one song. "I've sung this one before, a lot with the Ambassadors. But most of the time, inside I *was* singing it to you."

He watched Giles settle into his pillow, flushed and pleased. Finding the opening pitch in his head, Aaron drew a breath from his diaphragm and began the opening strains of "Somewhere Only We Know".

Usually when he sang it, he belted—but he had the piano or the rest of the Ambassadors beneath him. Here in Giles's bedroom, it was only his voice, the two of them in the evening quiet. Aaron sang softly, dragging the tempo out. Through it all, he gazed directly into Giles's eyes and held his hand.

Drank in the beautiful expression on his boyfriend's face.

Usually Giles was sharp-edged, alert and focused, but right now he looked like melted butter. Soft as putty and ten times as malleable. The funniest part was that the more he sang, the more confident Aaron felt—for once he was the sure-footed one. Each word was for Giles, even though the lyrics themselves weren't exactly right for how the song made Aaron feel. For Aaron it was the melody, the way the notes rose and fell, the innocence and lushness. The plea for a lover to take him away to a special place where only they two could be.

When the song finished, Giles stared at Aaron for several seconds, not saying a word. Aaron waited, the music echoing in the air between them, wrapping around them, holding them close.

Giles drew him down for a kiss, murmuring soft thanks, sliding his arms around Aaron to pull him closer and make love to him.

No, Aaron didn't feel bad about his present anymore.

FOR NEW YEAR'S, Giles and Aaron headed to Walter and Kelly's place in Minneapolis. Giles was glad to escape Oak Grove and get back to civilization.

Civilized it was—though Walter had offered to take them clubbing, they'd opted instead for a dinner made by Kelly followed by chatting in the living room, sharing stories about college and life. Walter and Kelly talked about their upcoming wedding. Walter's family had the money, but Kelly wanted to get married in his home church. Apparently Walter's mother was passive-aggressive and manic-depressive, and Walter spent a lot of time herding her out of the way.

Giles made a mental note to treat his busybody but loving mother a bit better when she fussed around the edges of his life. Clearly she wasn't half as awful as she could be.

"I loved the a cappella singers," Kelly said around a mouthful of popcorn. "I wish we could have them at the wedding."

"Salvo is serious about looking for gigs," Giles said. "I could set you up. Aaron can speak better for the Ambassadors, but I suspect they're more of the same."

"Oh, totally." Aaron was clearly excited by the idea.

Kelly practically melted on the couch, torn between being moved and seriously fucking excited, and Walter's gratitude was almost carnal.

Giles pulled Aaron closer to him. "Send us the date and the details, and we'll get back to you."

That night was fun, but the next day they headed to their respective homes. Giles began counting the days until their return to Saint Timothy, not because of his family or Aaron's, not even because he'd go back an official music therapy major.

He wanted to go back because he was so goddamn tired of watching over his shoulder every time they went out in public.

A few times Giles had taken Aaron out on real dates—dinner, a movie, or both. All too often they ran into people from A–H. Giles's friends seemed surprised but happy for him. The random people who knew neither of them well rode the middle, not saying anything but tending to stare.

Aaron's "friends" were asshats.

They'd start over to tell Aaron hello, only to stop and give puzzled glances instead, as if seeing Aaron and Giles together altered the fabric of their world and they didn't like it. The shame-and-blames looked ready to have heart attacks.

Giles began to watch over his shoulder past every shadow, and if he and Aaron stayed out too late, he panicked all the way to the car.

Aaron was not amused.

"Giles—what is wrong with you?" Aaron chose to voice this complaint in the middle of the AMC Showplace 16 parking lot.

"Can we please have this argument in the car?"

"No." Aaron folded his arms over his chest. "Tell me what's going on. If you're going to give me a complex, I want to know why."

So many fucking shadows. Giles's chest went taut. "Aaron, *please*. I'll tell you *in the fucking car*."

"Giles, what the hell is wrong?"

A shadow shifted. Grabbing Aaron with a yelp, Giles fumbled with his keys, his heart in his throat.

An elderly man shuffled away from a Buick, casting a curious glance over his shoulder. Giles let out a ragged, hollow sigh.

Aaron stepped in front of him, no longer angry, only concerned. "Giles?"

Fear, despair, rage swirled in a terrible cocktail—and broke Giles. "What's wrong? *They're going to hurt us.* They know you're gay, and so am I, and we're openly dating. Throwing it in their faces. They're going to hurt one or both of us, *and I can't stop it.*"

"Nobody is going to hurt us, Giles—"

"They already have."

Self-preservation roused, trying to muzzle him, but Giles was too scared, too hurt, too angry. He closed the distance between them, lifted the long flap of hair by his ear, pushing it back to reveal his now-faded three-inch scar where hair wouldn't grow.

"Seventh grade. Ten stitches, trip to the ER, concussion." He pulled his lip up and pointed to his row of implants on the top left of his mouth before removing his finger to speak. "Tenth grade. I had to wear a partial until my mouth healed enough for them to put the permanent fake teeth in. I don't have anything left of the broken arm or hand, but if you look close when I play the violin, you can see the way the ring finger of my left hand bends funny. That's when my mom went to the school board and showed them the video she'd taken in the hospital of me crying after the operation. She hired a lawyer and served them the legal bills and threatened to call the ACLU. They settled quietly out of court. Mom used the money to pay for college and buy me Henrietta."

Aaron stared at him, stunned into immobility.

Tears burned Giles's eyes, and he blinked them away as he turned his head. "I can't stop them if they come for us. They hunt in packs, like dogs. They don't just call you fag. They take bats to your face. Don't give me crap about what they think not mattering, because *it matters when they try to kill you*." The tears got the better of Giles, and he had to wipe his nose with his sleeve. "If they hurt you, I'd lose my mind. I'd rather get beatings every day for the rest of my life before I let them get you. I know from experience I don't have a prayer of holding them back."

When Aaron took him into his arms, Giles jumped, so keyed up now he was spring-loaded. Aaron made shushing noises and drew him in close. "It's okay. You're okay, Giles."

"Fourteen hundred hate crimes involving sexual orientation were reported in 2012. Over half of those instances were gay men. No other group comes close. And that's only what was *reported*."

"Over three million people live in the Twin Cities alone. Even if all those hate crimes happened in Minneapolis-Saint Paul, your odds of escaping that fate are amazingly good."

Giles dug his fingers into Aaron's jacket. "I've seen how they look at us, at *you*—"

"You don't behave this way at Saint Timothy. You don't freak out if we stay in the music building past nine at night, and I've seen you come from the parking lot with nothing but shadows around. You do get there's nothing protecting you more there than here, right? Maybe there are a few more people here who want to use you to live out their own idiocy, but you take precautions. You make yourself aware. You don't, though, let them rule your life."

Intellectually Giles understood what Aaron said, but emotionally he couldn't let go. "What about Colton? Has he found out yet? He'll be pissed. He was the worst, always, he—"

"I don't give a *shit* about Colton. I assume he's heard by now, which is perfect. I'd love to never hear from him again."

"But he'll demand a confrontation—"

"If Colton finds who I want to fuck so interesting, I'll explain the prostate to him." When Giles tried to ramp back up, Aaron stopped him with a soft kiss. "You're not fifteen anymore, trapped in A-Hell, and neither are they. It's over. You survived. You won. You can stand down."

Giles collapsed against the car, into Aaron as he pulled him close. "That's…what my mom says. I'm dangerous because I survived, because now I know they can't beat me that way."

"Your mom is smart."

Yes, but sometimes it still hurts. Giles swallowed hard and exhaled a shuddering breath.

Aaron kissed his way down the side of Giles's face. "Let's go to your house. I want to explore this prostate some more. Take notes in case Colton calls." When Giles laughed and slid his hands around Aaron's ass, Aaron spread his legs and closed them over Giles's knee. "Maybe we should leave him a voicemail."

This time Giles's laugh caught at the edge of his throat. *I love you so much.*

He couldn't speak, though, so he told Aaron with his kiss.

Chapter Twenty

SAINT TIMOTHY WAS on what they called a 4-1-4 plan: four courses in the fall, one course during the J-term in January, and then another four courses from February until May. When Aaron's dad had signed up his courses, his J-term class had been Principles of Sociology, with a half course clerking Monday, Wednesday, and Friday afternoons at a local law firm.

Now, though Aaron had yet to formally declare music performance, he took the sophomore-level conducting course, and as a member of Ambassadors his half course was intensive ICCA competition rehearsal. He audited a similar one for Salvo, so he basically had two full courses. The conducting course was brutal, and the rehearsal schedule for the a cappella groups was five times more intensive than any clerking position would have been. Though they couldn't perform with Salvo for ICCA, Giles and Aaron arranged all the numbers and helped with every rehearsal. Damien pushed them to not only make the notes ring out but to *perform*, milking the audience for everything he could get out of them.

Most nights Aaron fell into his bed, sleeping like the dead until his alarm told him it was time for him to go to his conducting class. Aaron was having the time of his life.

His roommate? Not so much.

Something serious must have gone down over break, because Elijah wasn't simply jumpy and moody now. He looked *sick*. He'd taken up smoking, for one—never in the room, but he reeked of it whenever Aaron passed him. He'd always been thin, but now he was gaunt and shaky, and he dropped things a lot. His parents appeared every Friday afternoon like clockwork, and their disdain for their son was even more open now.

Aaron continued to *keep his gay quiet* when the Princes were around, but the glances they gave him made it clear they knew all about him. Emily and Reece gave him similar glares. They too were constantly underfoot, and when they left, Elijah usually curled up in his bed, looking like someone had raked him naked over spikes but somehow sealed all the wounds.

Elijah didn't acknowledge Aaron had spoken whenever he asked what was wrong, and Aaron found every reason possible not to be in the room, because simply *being* there was uncomfortable.

One day Elijah came home when Aaron was there with Giles, and things went from uncomfortable to painfully intense.

By and large Giles had no reason to come to Aaron's room—if they wanted to hang out, they met at Giles and Brian's dorm. That day, however, Aaron had a killer assignment, and despite Giles's insistence that they had four computers in their room, Aaron wanted his own laptop and the notes he'd left on his desk. Giles came with him. They were on their way out when Elijah came home.

Elijah took one look at Giles and backed up into the hall, pale as a sheet. When Aaron turned to Giles to see what the hell that was about, he found his boyfriend mirroring his roommate's expression.

Aaron was utterly confused. "What the hell is going on here?"

Neither one of them spoke. Elijah looked rougher than usual—still pale, still shaky, still smelling of smoke. He had red-rimmed eyes and gripped the strap of his backpack on his shoulder as if it were the lifeline holding him to earth. He seemed…hurt.

Then, as if someone flipped a switch, the familiar snarky-nasty turned on. "Giles. You never call. You never write."

Eyes wide, Aaron turned to his boyfriend, who stared up at the ceiling.

What the actual fuck.

With a smirk, Elijah crossed to his desk, patting Aaron on the shoulder as he passed. "You boys go have fun. Don't play in the street, always use condoms."

Aaron grabbed Giles's arm and dragged him into the hall.

As soon as Aaron shut the door, Giles started talking at ninety miles an hour. "Aaron—it was a long time ago, and it was weird and I never did it again—"

"Wait—*what?*" Eyes wide, Aaron stared at the door to his room with new eyes. "Are you fucking telling me—*Elijah?*"

Giles looked ready to cry. "It was a bad night—you were off with Baz, I knew you were fucking him, and it made me crazy—"

Aaron clamped a hand over Giles's mouth, his heart flipping over in a soft, fuzzy way. "Stop. When I was with Baz? You... Me being with Baz made you crazy?"

"It was me jealous, that's all. I thought of you the whole time."

The hall was full of guys, some of them bruisers, but Aaron didn't care. He pressed a hard, euphoric kiss on Giles's mouth. Taking his hand, Aaron led him to the alcove under the stairs where he usually called Walter.

Giles babbled the entire way. "I had no idea he was your roommate. I'm so sorry. Please don't be angry."

"I'm not angry." Aaron led Giles to the floor, sat across from him and took his hands in his own. "I'm not angry. Okay? I promise."

Giles let out a shaky breath.

Aaron stroked the back of Giles's hands with his thumbs. "I'm surprised, is all. I was never entirely sure Elijah was gay."

"Trust me. He's gay." Giles pulled a hand back to run it through his hair. "I met him on Grindr. He basically used it as his pimp." Giles blushed hotly. "He...charged me. I paid him for sex."

Aaron's eyes about bugged out of his head. "You *what?*"

"I'm not proud of it, but I'm not going to lie to you. I don't want to tell you one thing and have him tell you something else. I was *really* low. I'd wanted to talk to you at homecoming, but I couldn't get to you before Baz. I got all kinds of depressed when you were dating."

Oh, Giles. "We never dated."

"You sure looked like you did. It made me nuts. I hadn't cruised in a long time, kind of…hoping, but that night I couldn't take it. I met Elijah online—he used a different name, but it was him. Brian was out, so I took Elijah to my room. He blew me, we frotted. I gave him a twenty. He told me to call him again, but I never did because it felt lousy after. And during, to be honest."

"It's okay. Seriously—it's okay." Aaron shook his head. "Bible beater by day, gigolo by night. Now chain-smoker."

"He looks…kind of bad. Has he been sick?"

Aaron threw up his hands. "I wouldn't know. I can't so much as smile at him without getting my head bitten off. I'll be the last person to ever know what's wrong in his life."

"You're really not mad?"

"Really not mad." Aaron brushed a kiss on Giles's lips. "Also, since we're playing confessional—I had sex *one time* with Baz. And it was as awful as your night with Elijah."

Giles looked hopeful—but doubtful. "Come on. *Once?*" A smile played at the edge of his lips. "Awful—seriously?"

"Yes. Once, and it was horrible. It told me everything I needed to know, and I got out." Aaron rose to his feet, pulling Giles up with him. "Forget Baz, and forget Elijah. I have a conducting assignment to do." He winced. "Except, *shit*. I forgot my laptop in my room."

"I told you. We have plenty of computers." Giles tugged him toward the stairs. "Let's go get your homework done so we can have make-up sex."

Aaron let himself be led away, but as they crossed the common he glanced back at his dorm.

No, he'd never understand his roommate, and he had no delusion they'd ever be anything remotely like friends. But sometimes Aaron worried about him.

BY THE MIDDLE of January, Salvo was on track to be as popular if not more so than the Ambassadors.

Already girls were asking when the tryouts for the fall would be, and they went out of their way to be nice to Giles, ready to grease the palm of one of the student managers. But it wasn't only Salvo and the wannabe Salvo members changing their tune about him. The whole music department regarded Giles and Aaron as the next dynamic music duo, and he enjoyed celebrity status wherever he went, a kind of elevation well beyond what he'd envied in Aaron and the Ambassadors at the beginning of the year. Somehow over the course of two months, his life had radically altered, and while it was good, it had come way too fast. Giles wasn't sure he'd ever catch up with himself.

The Ambassadors also welcomed Giles. Some of that was bleed from being Aaron's boyfriend, but some of it was because they'd made it clear to the whole college, especially the regents, they considered Salvo their fully equal sister organization.

As a manager for Salvo, Giles got swept in what briefly became an intense political standoff. Though Salvo had been entered in the ICCA quarterfinals along with the Ambassadors, the regents didn't approve funding for their travel expenses as they always did for the Ambassadors. The Ambassadors declared, upon hearing this, they wouldn't attend quarterfinals. As they'd come within spitting distance of winning the finals the year before, and this before Aaron and his golden pipes had appeared on the scene, the regents, who used all things Ambassador to raise money, balked. But the Ambassadors wouldn't budge, not until Salvo's full funding, all the way to finals if appropriate, was approved.

The regents caved. Now, in addition to the fame he'd already experienced, Giles was one of the nearly martyred folk heroes. He had to leave an extra ten minutes before anything just to allow for the people who would stop him in the hall to talk to him. Sometimes they invited him to parties. Sometimes they asked him questions—some of those were legit, some were clearly invented so they could talk to him.

Nothing like this had ever happened to Giles before in his life. It weirded him the hell out.

He complained to Brian.

"I don't get it. What do they think talking to me is going to change? If I were cute, that'd be different."

Brian shrugged. "You're successful. People always assume success is a virus. They're trying to catch it from you."

"Yes, but they act like my leper sores have all fallen away and we're all pretending I never had them. I remember them. They're still there in my head."

"Beauty is in everything. They've finally seen yours. Accept it. Embrace it." Brian swatted him playfully on the leg. "Stop putting yourself down. Just because dick doesn't do it for me doesn't mean I can't understand why Aaron digs you."

"Please. Let me emphatically state I am not a catch."

Brian, camped out in their beanbag chair, nested deeper into the beans and put his hands behind his head. "I'll allow you don't have the whole dark-Bieber thing going on your honey does, but you aren't some pockmarked freak, either. I think you're not playing to your type. You're lithe and elegant, and when you use that, you don't come off half bad. You could rock a tight black shirt and eye makeup."

"Even with guyliner I wouldn't be as pretty as Aaron, not by half."

"So what? Who ever said only pretty people can hook up with pretty people? And why does pretty have to be about meeting a certain mold?"

They'd wandered off point somehow. "It's not about being pretty or not. It's that everyone is looking at me all the time now. Makes me feel naked."

"Give them something else to stare at, then." Brian shrugged. "Or don't. But yeah, one way or another you need to find a way to not let other people's attention, good or bad, ruin your life."

While Giles appreciated this sentiment, he had no idea how to actualize it. When he realized he was thinking shit like *how do I actualize not letting other people's attention ruin my life*, he shut off all thought.

One day in late January, right before the quarterfinals, Giles was in the White House when Baz came home. The main floor had turned into Salvo/Ambassador Grand Central, and Giles had been in there for two hours with Aaron and Karen, trying to perfect the bridge of their performance number. Everyone else had gone off for sandwiches, but Giles elected to hang back and enjoy the silence for a few minutes. That was when Baz came in.

Giles wanted to hate him, but it wasn't possible. As he spent more and more time in the White House, Giles watched Baz quietly take care of all his friends, making sure there were groceries, always keeping one eye on people, making sure they weren't too down.

Today it was Baz who seemed down. After dropping his keys on the counter, Baz slouched wearily into the chair opposite Giles. "Yo, what's up?" Reaching for the plaid glasses case on the table, he swapped the sunglasses he was wearing for…another pair of sunglasses. Giles had seen him do that before, but it always seemed like a gimmick. Somehow this time it didn't.

Giles watched the exchange with a frown but didn't comment on it. "Waiting for everyone to get back before we dig into the next planning round. Karen and Damien had this idea for a joint number we could do for the end-of-year concert. Something so that no matter who goes forward in the competition, we can show the regents Salvo and the Ambassadors are a united front. I'm not exactly sure why we're practicing now, but whatever."

"Strike while the iron is hot. If you guys finally cave and let me sing 'Titanium', I'll enlist my mom for the fight."

"I really think that one needs orchestra behind it to work."

"Then put in orchestra." Baz snuck his thumb and index fingers beneath the band of his glasses and massaged the bridge of his nose, wincing. It wasn't a standout gesture on its own, but it went on too long, and when he put his hand down again, Giles saw lines of tension around the other man's mouth. Only for a moment, though. Then Baz had his wry smile in place. "Aaron seems a lot happier these days, so good job, Giles."

Giles wanted to be defensive, but Baz had all but written *I will not poach your man* on the walls of the White House. "I'm not sure I did much."

The smile spread a little wider. "Don't be so Minnesota. You're good for him. Own that shit."

"Um, thanks." Giles floundered for a way to take the conversation off himself. "How do you get out of the Minnesota Nice, anyway? Did they hand out antigens at your high school or something?"

"I got out of it by being from Chicago. Land of gangsters and crooks. Too much politeness there will get you killed."

The statement had a weird taint, like it was half a joke and half horribly serious. "What in the world are you doing at Saint Timothy if you're from Chicago?"

"Because I wanted out of Chicago." Baz rubbed at his eyes again, and this time there was no mistaking his pain.

"Are you okay?"

"Headache." Baz kept rubbing. His lips pursed too.

"Can I get you something? Or should I shut up so you can be miserable in peace?"

Baz snorted a soft laugh, though he still grimaced and rubbed at the bridge of his nose a few more times. "Silence doesn't make it go away, just makes it the only thing I can think about." He pulled his hand away from his face and placed it flat on the table. "But don't feel like you need to humor me if you have better things to do."

The idea that he, dorky first-year Giles, could be welcome company to Baz was too much ego candy to resist. "I'll try to keep the niceness to a reasonable level."

That made Baz's smile return, though he still seemed tense. "Days like this I miss Keeter, the bitchy queen who graduated last May. He'd pick a fight with me, we'd cuss at each other until we were exhausted, and then he'd drive me around blasting Maino until our ears bled."

"Sorry, I don't think I can do bitchy queen, and I don't know any rap. I'm all clueless geek."

Baz blew a gentle raspberry in dismissal. "Not even close. You're too busy rabbiting right now to know who you are, but you'll get there."

"Rabbiting?"

"Every time I see you, you're all tense and paranoid, as if any second someone's going to jump you. Like maybe even once someone did, and you're waiting for it to happen again."

Good God, was he that obvious? Giles became abruptly interested in the table. "A few times it got…bad."

"Names, or bashing?"

Giles kept his gaze down. "Both."

Baz pulled two toothpicks from a jar on the table and stuck them in the corner of his mouth, rolling them as he spoke. "Where are you from, soldier?"

"Alvis-Henning."

Baz snorted and held up his hand for a high-five. "Shit. The land of gay suicide and pray away the gay." He accepted Giles's reluctant hand slap. "I'd ask if it was as bad as they said on the news, but I blew a guy once who came from there. He curled my toes with some of his stories."

"I made things worse for myself because I fucked them. Would have been smarter to turn them down, but I couldn't ever seem to. It always felt like a fuck you, even though I'm not sure it was. Plus, they were usually hot."

Baz laughed. "Mulder, I like your style. Keep on telling me stories. I think your tactics might be better than Keeter, but the jury's still out."

"You've kind of tapped me out. Horrible, cowering existence, a few trips to the ER, and now I'm trying to figure out how I ended up with Aaron. I read a lot, play strategy games on the Xbox, help transpose pop songs.

Very boring."

"You transpose like a motherfucker." He winced and swore softly under his breath as he rubbed his eyes again. "Shit. Sweetheart, will you do me a favor? Pull the curtain and kill the lights."

There was only one window in the room, and it wasn't letting in a stream of light or anything, but Giles did as he was bid. The fabric was heavy and lined with blackout fabric, and when Giles closed it, the room dimmed significantly. When he flipped the switch, because the door to the living room was closed, the kitchen went almost completely black.

"Whoa," he said, suddenly unsure how he'd get to the table without killing himself.

"Flip the switch right next to the one you just hit."

Giles did, and the kitchen was immediately bathed in an almost creepy red glow. Baz pulled off his glasses and leaned back in his chair so that his now-naked eyes could stare up at the freakish red ceiling. "God. Thank you."

Giles returned to his seat. "Is something wrong with your eyes?"

"I have photophobia. Eyes all fucked up for light, and sometimes I get crazy-stupid headaches, especially when I get stressed out or pissed. Red light's okay for some reason, so I have a few places wired with crimson bulbs so I can still see but don't have to feel the strain." He touched his left shoulder. "Have a plate here, a few bionic ribs, a trick hip. It's the eyes that are the real bitch, though. Won't ever drive again, bad as a vampire for sunlight."

Jesus, Giles felt like an idiot. "I had no idea. I'm

sorry."

Baz quirked an eyebrow at him, and it was weird to actually see his eyes while he did it. He didn't look half so smooth, less Robert Downey Jr. and more Mark Ruffalo. "Why are you sorry? Because you thought I was copping some kind of attitude with the shades? No problem, it's what I want people to think. That would be the *other* reason I left Chicago, because too many people know the story of how I got to wear sunglasses at night, and they act like I'm blind and stupid. I'd rather them think I'm cocky and stupid. The professors know, which is why they let me wear them in class. The guys at the house keep it quiet for me. So go back to thinking I'm a piece of shit or whatever. Don't be sorry."

Giles had no idea what to say, so he simply sat there for a few minutes. "That's kind of slick, actually."

"If you don't want them to think about something you know they will, give them something else to focus on instead. Works every time."

"That's what my roommate said. Except I can't figure out the something else I want them to look at."

Baz removed the now-chewed-up toothpicks and snagged some M&Ms from a bowl on the table instead. "Hair. Clothes. Attitude. Colors. The way you talk, the way you walk. Pick a card, any card, or try a few."

"Yeah, but how do you not feel like a fraud? Or a blithering idiot?"

"Start by letting go of the idea there will ever be a day you find the safe space where how you look or dress or walk or talk or whatever will be okay. Some piece of shit is always going to show up and judge you, and some of them will fuck you up. It's scary, but that's why you give them a straw man. You don't want it to be something you can't pull off—don't go for witty sarcasm if you can't dish it up. You want it to feel good. You, but on steroids. It's like armor. It's got to take the dings you don't want. I could give a fuck if someone thinks I'm a poser, but I have a hell of enough of a time accepting I have a disability. You figure out what would make a good front for you, and that's what you use."

Giles wanted to ask how Baz had come by this disability, but he ate some chocolate instead and made himself consider his potential suits of armor. "My roommate suggested guyliner. I kind of dig the idea, but I'm not sure I want that every day."

"I can see it. Would definitely get you laid in a club. It hides your nervousness too—people look at the makeup instead of you. If you wore it to class, though, the message changes. You'd have to work up a bit of piss-on-you attitude to go with it. To be a friendly guy in eyeliner is a whole different persona."

"Well, I usually hate everyone a little, so piss-on-you would be good. Though I'd also feel guilty."

"Why? Fuck the nice. You don't want them invading your space? Put up a *fuck you* sign. Most people will back up." He tipped his neck to the side, eliciting a few soft cracks. "I'm going to pop a narcotic and sleep the last of this off." As he rose, he extended a fist to Giles. "Thanks for the cooldown. Work your shit, honey."

Giles gave him an awkward fist bump and sat in the strange red glow a long time after Baz left, thinking.

Chapter Twenty-One

SALVO AND AMBASSADORS' quarterfinal competition was the last weekend of January at the University of Minnesota–St. Paul, and as the day of the performance approached, Aaron felt like the happiest frayed nerve in the world. He'd slept an average of three hours a night the whole week before the competition, and the night before his conducting final he didn't sleep at all.

Then, the day before they left for the competition, his father called.

He hadn't said much, only that he'd be coming to collect Aaron for the weekend. His tone was clipped, brusque, and when Aaron explained he couldn't get away until the official between-term break, his father's reply was so brittle Aaron thought ice had to be forming on his cell phone.

He knew. Aaron's dad knew about his major, maybe about Giles—and he was pissed.

Giles made him stay over, held him, and whispered over and over it would be okay. "I'll go home with you for break. I'll drive you, come in with you if you want."

"You can't come with me. That'll only make it worse." Aaron snuggled in close, his heart sinking. "I knew this had to happen eventually. I just…wasn't ready."

"We'll face it together." Giles kissed his hair. "Get some sleep. We have a huge day tomorrow."

Aaron didn't sleep much, and his dreams were fitful. He hated that his dad had cast a shadow over the big day. He'd been so excited, but the phone call had put shit-colored glasses on him.

"It's going to be ten kinds of hell if both groups don't final," Aaron pointed out as they settled into their seats on the bus. "And even if they do, only one group per region can go all the way to New York."

"We'll root for whoever wins. We're a team."

"Then why can't we be that for real? Why does it have to be girls and guys? Why can't we be one group and be done with it? Why can't the orchestra be in it too?"

"Because it's a cappella." Giles smoothed a hand over Aaron's hair. "It doesn't matter. It's just a competition. It's supposed to be fun."

"Competing against each other isn't fun. All we want to do is make music. We shouldn't have to prove anything." Aaron stared out the window, watching the frozen landscape go by. "It's people like my dad who make us compete. Make us choose."

Giles shushed him, fed him platitudes. Aaron swallowed them, but he didn't believe them.

Aaron loved Salvo. He wanted *them* to win, to go all the way to New York. They were his work—his and Giles—and he wanted them to succeed. Not win stupid contests. *Succeed.*

Working with groups like Salvo was what Aaron wanted to *do*. That's what he wanted to be known for: helping other people sing. He had a solo for the Ambassadors' set, but he didn't care about it. Singing was fine, but composing, arranging music? *That's* what he wanted to do with his life. Craft song in his head, in practice rooms, in the shower, then find the way to make it come to life. Even when he was only watching dress rehearsals in the Saint Timothy auditorium, hearing his music played and sung made Aaron feel like a magician shooting light from his fingertips.

It wasn't saving lives in a hospital or rescuing million-dollar deals in a courtroom. It might not pay enough to live on—unquestionably it wouldn't ever please his dad. Aaron didn't care. This was his joy. This was what he wanted.

Music, with Giles beside him, his friends surrounding them. That was his life right now, and it was perfect. He hated having to put it up to a contest. He was done with being judged, being weighed and measured, being other people's performing monkey. *Done.*

So done that ten minutes before the Ambassadors were due onstage, he bailed.

"I can't do it." He curled up in the corner, shut his eyes, and drew his knees to his chest when Giles tried to coax him to his feet. "*No.* I can't. I *won't*. Not anymore, Giles. *Not anymore.*"

Baz came over and crouched in front of Aaron. "Peanut, what's wrong?"

Giles started to explain, but Aaron looked Baz dead

in the eye and rode over his boyfriend. "I won't do the solo. I won't sing. Fuck the regents. Fuck my dad. I'm *done*."

He tensed, ready for Baz to fight, but if anything Baz's tone gentled. "Sure, babe. I can take the solo if you're not up to it." He took off his glasses and leaned forward, squinting a moment before steadily meeting Aaron's gaze. "But I need you to come out with us."

Aaron hissed a breath. "I won't—"

"Not for the regents. Not for your dad. Not for any of those fuckers. For us, Aaron. For the Ambassadors."

"We don't need a stupid competition to tell us who we are."

"No, we don't. But there are a lot of guys for whom this is a big moment. Marius hasn't ever been to New York, and he'd love to go with his brothers. It would look great on Damien's résumé to have an ICCA win. We're using this thing as much as it's using us." He stroked Aaron's cheek. "Mostly, though, this is a chance for you and fifteen other guys to go out there and show everybody how hard we rock. Because it feels good to strut our stuff. Because we're gonna clean up this competition, us and Salvo. Then one of us will go to New York, and whoever doesn't win will go to cheer the others on. Because that's how we roll."

Aaron deflated, tears pricking his eyes. "I hate this so much."

"I know, hon. Let's go flip them the bird together." He pressed a kiss to Aaron's forehead. "Up you pop, squirt. Time to shine."

Giles took his hand when he rose, led Aaron all the

way to the edge of the stage and sent him out with a toe-curling kiss.

Aaron felt out of body on the stage, all his bad feelings still swirling, but as soon as the lights came up and Damien hummed out the first note, Aaron fell into line. At first he went through the motions, but it didn't take long for the music to infect him. It was still music, and it still spoke to his soul.

They performed a continuous song mashup rather than single numbers to fill out their twelve-minute set, at Aaron's suggestion peppering bits of "Dynamite" throughout. It was a good arrangement, but during the performance Aaron realized how much of it happened because of the music combined with the men performing it. Marius and Trevor and the rest of the baseline set up a foundation everyone else stood on—but no one, not even the soloists, stepped out from the group.

Baz wrenched the room with the solo meant to be Aaron's, working it like a stripper pole, but he channeled the energy into the group, yanking his brothers up with him into the frenzy of glory. The result was a whirling vortex of energy feeding back and forth between the audience and the Ambassadors, Baz at the center of the nexus. When it came time for Aaron to move briefly into the center for the bridge, he pushed the last of his dark clouds aside and gave Baz a run for his money on showmanship. Baz grinned and ad-libbed a subtle grind with Aaron that probably scraped right against the edge of the ICCA's dictate of family-friendly choreography.

When they finished, the cheers echoed for a full

minute, the audience so pumped they vibrated. Walter and Kelly were in the front row, and they whooped and catcalled as if *they* went to Saint Timothy.

Salvo greeted them offstage, mobbing them, cheering and hugging them. Jilly had tears in her eyes when she let Aaron go.

Even without hearing the last group perform, Aaron knew it would be the Ambassadors and Salvo heading to Chicago for the semifinals. Like the Ambassadors, Salvo performed a mashup in lieu of individual songs with an anchor song threading through the middle, but Salvo's arrangement was special. The words were from "Good Times", but the melody line was Aaron's own. The notes were subtle, buried within the familiar melody lines, but Aaron could hear each note weaving through, and it made his soul feel like a sun inside his chest. For the first few beats he was nervous, but it was fussing for nothing, because Salvo shone so bright they were a star.

Aaron's soul flew with them as they soared.

The crowd went twice as wild for Salvo as they had for the Ambassadors, and when the final scores were tallied, Salvo didn't just place. They *won*.

The entire body of the Ambassadors mobbed Salvo, hugging them, spinning them, hoisting them into the air, many of the men weeping more openly than the women.

No one's heart was more open than Aaron's. He still didn't give a shit about the competition, but Baz was right. This was *good*. Karen and Jilly held the trophy high into the air. Baz whooped. Walter and

Kelly stood on their chairs and shouted Aaron's name.

It was glorious. It wasn't for anybody but them—and they *kicked ass*.

Fuck the regents. Fuck his dad. Fuck everybody who thought they could drive his life. Somehow, someday—*this* was what Aaron was supposed to do.

And no matter what, he was going to find a way to do it.

THE BUS WAS a riot of sound all the way back to Saint Timothy.

Giles felt bad for the Drs. Nussenbaum, because even he winced at the decibel level a few times, but the two professors seemed to be enjoying the mania, particularly Dr. Mrs., who was almost smug. Nussy appeared slightly stunned, but in a good way. Like the world had surprised him, and he kind of dug it for the plot twist.

The White House had already declared it was having a party after, a fête of epic proportions. Giles dropped Aaron off at his room to change, promising to pick up him and Mina on the way over to the party. When he got to the room, he saw Brian settling on the futon, getting ready for a Halo marathon, and it burst out of him. "Brian. Get dressed. You're coming to the best party of your life, right now. Women, wine, dancing. You gotta."

"No, thank you." Brian snorted and indicated himself with a controller. "You do not want to see this dance."

"*Come on.* We *won*, Bri. Salvo took first, Ambassadors second. You have to come celebrate." He smiled as a text came through on his phone. "Min's bringing friends too. Probably girls."

"No fucking way." Brian held up his fingers in the sign of the cross, an awkward one because he still had a controller in one hand.

"You *like* girls, remember? You have to come."

"Forget it. I'll stay here and kill pixelated enemies." Brian indicated his cell phone on the bed as he took down a troop of aliens. "Feel free to live-text me."

"You know, the girls are missing out. You're funny, smart, and supportive."

"Thanks for the vote of confidence. If you can find me a female who doesn't mind that I look like a *Napoleon Dynamite* reject and have less sexual experience than most Disney princesses, please aim her at me."

Giles patted his clothes. "I gotta change out of my monkey suit and pick up Aaron and Min and whoever else they've coerced into coming along."

"If you want to borrow my pearls, they're in my top drawer."

Giles headed for his dresser but paused as something on Brian's side of the closet caught his eye. "Is it too gay to ask to borrow your black V-neck? Or can I not pull it off?"

"Sure you can borrow it. Try it on and see how it looks."

Giles did, holding out his arms as Brian studied him. "Well?"

Brian stroked his stubble with his thumb, pushing up his glasses with his free hand as he pondered. "I think it's good, but bear in mind I have no fucking idea what I'm talking about. I think you need to do the hair thing you do." He mimed messing up the top of his head. "It's not as styled as it usually is. Probably the shirt mashed it."

Giles put a bit of product in his hand and teased his mop back into a semirespectable fauxhawk. "Not bad. Too bad I let my ear grow closed, because a hoop would be badass."

"I'm telling you. Guyliner."

"Don't have any." Giles fussed a bit more, grabbed a chunky silver watch that didn't work but looked great, and gave himself a final nod. "Okay. I think this is as good as it's going to get."

"Go break his heart. I'll get rid of the zombies while you're gone."

Giles tossed him a salute and headed to Aaron's dorm.

He was in the lobby with Jilly, and after collecting Min and her friends, they were off to the White House, heading across the street in a happy, chattering mob. In a fit of vanity, Giles forwent a coat so he could show off his borrowed shirt, which meant he was freezing cold. He double-timed it to the White House—at least he did until Mina grabbed him and pulled him aside.

"*Hottie.* What did you do? You look fierce. New shirt?"

"Brian's. It's not too slutty? It's a little tight."

"Hell no. In fact." She glanced ahead at Walter and

Kelly, a wicked gleam in her eye. "You should let me put eyeliner on you. I have it in my purse."

"No way. Come on, Min, I'm freezing—"

Mina ignored him, hauling him off into a bush while she called to the others to give them a second. Giles fought her until he realized she would draw all over his face if he didn't hold still—as still as he could get with chattering teeth. When she finished—adding a hint of pale gloss to his lips, God help him—she held up her compact.

Giles blinked at his reflection, stunned. "Holy crap. Why didn't you hold me down and do this before?"

"Because they would have beat you up at A-H."

"They already did. Think of how much *more* I'd have gotten laid, though, with eyeliner. Possibly by a higher class of guys."

Mina looked startled, probably because he'd never told her about being beat up before. *Not now, Min. I'm enjoying a new level of cool here.* He turned his face from side to side, admiring his profile, but Mina only indulged him a few seconds more before closing the mirror and dragging him back to the others, telling him he could admire himself again once they were inside.

The house overflowed, people filling every available square inch of space in the living room, but once they got to the ballroom, the crush was practically a fire hazard. Music beat through the house like a pulse. Giles held fast to Aaron's hand, leading him to the stage, where Baz welcomed them with a wink and a helping hand onto the platform. "You want your fiddle or a synth, G?"

Giles hesitated, thinking a violin would be silly, but he decided, *fuck it.* "Give me my strings."

Baz passed over the case. "Let's burn this house down, bitches."

They kind of did. They had to spill into the audience to perform with all thirty-two of them, they messed up three times, one of them Giles on his violin yinging when he should have yanged, but nobody cared. They ran right from that song into another, and another. People dropped in and out when they needed a breather, but the song kept going on and on.

When Aaron got his turn at the keyboard, he banged out the opening cords of Florence + the Machine's "Lover to Lover", which Giles knew was his boyfriend's favorite song. He didn't sing, though, calling out Salvo members to take up Welch's vocals instead. Giles watched him, reveling in the glory that was Aaron Seavers serving music up on a silver platter.

Then he picked up his violin and joined in the dance.

Later, when Karen and Jilly took over the keyboard, Aaron and Giles ended up next to each other on the stage, swaying to the beat. Giles held his violin above his head and gyrated while Aaron ground on him, laughing, his eyes full of heat and promise. Any second, Giles decided, they were finding a condom and an empty bedroom and Aaron was getting epically laid.

Aaron seemed to know that too, and had no arguments with his destiny.

On their way up the stairs, Giles caught a look at himself in the mirror, and for a moment the sight arrested him. Yes, the shirt rocked, and he *would* be wearing eyeliner again soon. But that wasn't what caught his eye. Somehow everything about him was different, so much so he didn't recognize himself. He wasn't a lanky geek with weird hair and embarrassing ears anymore. He was…cool, in his own way. It wasn't how he looked. It was how he looked *back*.

Damn, he thought, reeling from this unexpected answer to a life riddle.

Aaron tugged his arm, and Giles turned away from his reflection, ready to fuck his boyfriend into happy oblivion.

Chapter Twenty-Two

J-TERM ENDED FOUR days after quarterfinals, and because of the way the calendar fell, they essentially had five days of a minibreak before full spring semester began. Especially since "spring" semester was rolling up to the plate in the middle of a huge blizzard, many students elected to stay on campus. The White House had a party planned for each night.

Aaron had to go home to Oak Grove, because his father had declared it was "time for a talk". Giles insisted on driving Aaron back.

It wasn't like Aaron was going to argue too hard. Having Giles drive meant it wasn't his mom, or worse, his dad, who would launch into everything the second he got in the car. Instead, it was him and Giles winding the long way back to Oak Grove, stopping at Matt's Bar in Minneapolis to have fortifying Jucy Lucys with Walter and Kelly. Everyone had the molten-center cheeseburgers except Kelly, who was allergic. He said he'd be making himself a faux version with Teese Cheese as soon as he got home, because they looked good.

"Remember." Walter paused to wipe grease from his chin, holding his cheeseburger in his hand. "Jim can bluster all he wants, threaten whatever he likes, but in the end this is your life."

"What if he threatens not to pay for it unless I major in something he approves of?"

Giles, who had his arm around Aaron in the booth, pulled him closer. "He's already paid for this year. He can't take that back."

Aaron wasn't terribly comforted by this. Jim Seavers wasn't a successful trial lawyer because he rolled over easily.

Aaron usually rolled over even before people started yelling.

Kelly took Aaron's hand. "Whatever happens, we'll help you through it. Promise. We can't go in there with you, but we'll be waiting to hear how it goes."

That reassurance was more comfort than Aaron expected it to be.

Stopping at the bar for dinner had been a good call. Walter offered to buy him a pitcher, but Aaron declined, thinking it would be wiser to face this down sober. The bar was a cute little dive, rough around the edges yet overflowing with people. He took heart, too, that when he got up to use the bathroom, he passed a rowdy group of guys wearing matching football jerseys, watching a game and flirting with waitresses…all except for a male couple in the group holding hands. There was something about the normality of it all: guys watching football, some of them gay. Most of the guys were bruisers, but one of the boyfriends was slight and elegant, not a typical football guy at all. Yet everyone included him like he belonged.

I can be different too. I can be gay and study music and be okay. I don't have to fit in with what people decide for me, because I know where I fit in. Everybody has somewhere they fit in. We just have to look hard to find it sometimes.

His spirits were buoyed as he went to the table, but Walter gave him one last pep talk as they left. He stood with Aaron beside Giles's car, holding Aaron by the shoulders and all but shouting affirmations at him and making him swear on his theory notebooks he'd call as soon as the conversation was over. Aaron promised he would.

He held those laughing football players in his mind's eye all the way home.

"I'll come in with you, if you want," Giles said as they pulled in to Oak Grove.

He'd offered ten times. Aaron loved him for it, but instead of saying no again, he spooned up the last bite of Frosty and held it out for Giles. "Here. Put this in your mouth."

Giles did, but he swallowed and gave Aaron a meaningful glance. "I will. I'm serious."

"I know you are." Aaron wiped a chocolate trail from Giles's lip with a napkin. "But I need to do this on my own. I don't have any illusions I'm going to transform into a brick wall between your car and the door, but I need to learn to at least stand my ground."

"You're calling me the *second* it's over. I mean, when you leave the room, you're dialing me."

Aaron leaned over and kissed his cheek. "Yes."

Giles began babbling rapid-fire reassurances, alternating between bolstering Aaron's ego and trash-talking Jim Seavers. It was good, and it helped, but as soon as Aaron got out of the car, fishing his suitcase out of the trunk, he got queasy.

"You can do it," Giles called through the rolled-down passenger window. "No matter what happens, Aaron, I'm going to be here. Right here."

Aaron drew a steadying breath. He blew Giles a kiss.

Dragging his suitcase behind him, he went up the walkway to his house and opened the front door.

He saw his mother first. She and his dad sat in the living room. When Aaron came into the room, Beth rose, arms tight over her body, her smile thin. Jim remained in the chair with his back to the door. He didn't rise or acknowledge Aaron's arrival.

That, Aaron knew, was bad.

"Aaron." His mom kept her hands over her body. Her smile slipped as she gave up trying to appear happy. "Thanks for coming, sweetheart."

"Take a seat." Jim's voice boomed out across Beth's living room. "We need to have a talk."

After letting go of his suitcase, Aaron took off his coat, stepped out of his shoes and padded over to the couch. He sat beside his mother, in the place she had left for him. Sitting upright, using the breathing Nussy had taught him so he didn't hyperventilate, Aaron faced his father.

Jim's face barely moved—but that was when he was the worst. In high school Aaron had shadowed his father to trial for career day, and he'd seen his father make this expression right before he decimated a hostile witness. He'd gotten in trouble with the firm because he'd been so ruthless the jury had turned against him instead of the witness.

No jury was here to side with Aaron.

Jim nodded at Beth. "I got tired of your half answers about how school was going, so I asked your mother. She was cagey too, so I called up Bob's friend who's a pre-law counselor at Saint Timothy." Jim tapped his long fingers idly on the arm of the leather chair. "When, exactly, were you planning on telling me you'd changed your major?"

Aaron drew a deep breath from the bottom of his diaphragm. "I'm officially undecided right now."

"I could tell by your evasion whatever was going on wasn't good. Never, though, did I dream you took an entire semester of your college career and threw it into the fucking toilet. *Music.* The pre-law counselor is a fan of your *work.* He told me I should be quite proud of you. I had to sit through that, Aaron. I had to pretend to this fool I knew my own son had abandoned a promising profession to chase some fucking fairy tale."

Aaron closed his arms over his belly, pressing them in to stop the cold, stabbing feeling there.

Jim rolled on. "I tried to go in and check your courses for second semester under your password, but the system wouldn't let me. I expect changes to happen the second you're on campus. If I don't receive confirmation—with proof—within twenty-four hours, there's going to be hell to pay." He grimaced. "I should have seen this coming. Of course you'd dive into nonsense the second I turned my head."

"Jim," Beth said, her tone a gentle warning.

Jim snorted. "Oh, don't you go soft on me now. You were all for this when we planned this meeting. Did you change your mind and decide you *wanted* to see him peddling for spare change in the skywalks?"

Beth stiffened. "That's not fair."

"No, it's not. I lay this firmly at your feet for letting it go on this long. What, I'm supposed to parent all the way from California?"

Beth replied tearfully, and Jim talked over her, raising his voice until he was shouting and she was openly weeping. Normally this was when Aaron would exit, retreating to his room to cower and wait until it was over. Two months ago, he would have. Two months ago he would have let his dad change his classes, would have let him rule his life.

Not now.

For the first time, this thing his father hated, that apparently his mother did too, wasn't just what he wanted—it was what he knew he was *meant* to do. Writing music, playing it, performing it—he'd felt more alive in the past five months than he had his whole life. At this point even if his dad took away his money, kicked him out of college, Aaron would still find a way to be in music. It wasn't simply something he enjoyed doing. It was his soul, his reason for being. Having drawn music back into his life—to take it away now would be like dying.

The power filled him, calming him, giving him strength. Despite what he'd told Giles, he found, to his surprise, he *was* a brick wall. Not on everything—but on this? About music? Yes. He could take on anything.

Rising from the couch, Aaron said, quite clearly, "No."

He stood there a moment, reveling in the word, in the power of it. But they hadn't heard him, too busy fighting, too used to him a silent shadow in the corner. Aaron said it again.

"No."

They turned to him, startled. Surprised.

Aaron drew on his courage and continued. "I won't switch my major to law. I won't drop out of music. In fact, the second I get back to Saint Timothy, I'm declaring music performance. It's not something I'm going to debate with either of you. It's something I *will* do. One way or another."

It felt good to declare that. Scary, terrifying even, but good. Because really, what could they do? Yell? Threaten? He understood, at last, what Walter had been trying to say. It wouldn't be easy, but it was possible, and for the first time Aaron could see the way. It would be fine. It would be—

"Get out."

Aaron startled out of his reverie and blinked at his father. "What?"

"What?" Beth echoed, stiffening on the couch. "Jim—"

"Get out." Jim Seavers rose to his full height, his long arm aimed at the door. "Out. Of here. Right now." When Beth and Aaron both sputtered, Jim's nostrils flared. "Oh, I'm sorry. Were you planning on staying here over break? Eating food? Wearing clothes I bought you? Using your expensive headphones and computers? Watching television I pay for, using internet I provide? Did you expect I'd keep paying your cell phone? Depositing money into your account so you could fuck around like an idiot instead of doing your goddamn job and getting an education? Is that what you were thinking would happen? Or did you have a fantasy of me rolling over? You thought since I already paid this year's bill you had me over a barrel? You'd wait me out, figuring I'd soften by fall?"

"*Jim*, this isn't—"

"*Don't you pussy out now.*" Jim Seavers's expression was terrifying, belonging to a feral beast, not a father. "You were the one who called me here to fix it. You don't get to backpedal now that you've called in the dragon. Not if you don't want another legal battle with me over alimony. You *know* how painful I can make that for you."

"You can't throw him out on the street." Tears ran down Beth's cheeks as she turned to Aaron. "Baby—"

Aaron stepped away from her reach.

You're the one who called me here to fix it.

"He's not going to go to the street." Jim looked in disgust at his son. "He's going to his room. He's going to hide under his covers like a baby, he's going to cry—and then he's going to do what he's told."

Aaron didn't cry. He could barely breathe, but he didn't cry, didn't break. He didn't have the strength to speak, not with what he had to do. He thought of Giles, waiting at home for Aaron's call. He thought of Walter and Kelly in the Cities, doing the same. He thought of Baz and Damien and Dr. Nussenbaum, and Nussy.

He thought of the music, the songs that filled his head, his heart. Pushing aside his terror, Aaron steadied himself and headed for the front door.

"Aaron."

Beth's voice tore through Aaron, making him move faster. He gripped the handle of his suitcase, snagged his coat and bent to pick up his shoes, figuring he'd put them on outside.

"Leave them."

Aaron paused, startled, and glanced over his shoulder.

His father had risen and stood like a dark thundercloud drawing power from the center of the living room. "Those shoes are mine. That coat is mine. That suitcase, everything in it? *Mine.*"

"*James*, you can't—"

Aaron's father's lip curled in a snarl. "Everything about you, every thought in your head, every possession you hold—they're mine. They're only there because of me. You walk out, you only get what's in your head and on your back."

Beth shoved Jim aside and clambered toward Aaron, tears streaming down her cheeks. "Baby, don't listen to him. I'm sorry. *I'm sorry*—"

Aaron turned away. Dropping his shoes and coat, letting go of his suitcase, Aaron walked out the front door.

He tried not to think of his laptop, full of his notes for semifinals composition, his course essays, the headphones in his pocket and the other in his suitcase, his phone—his ten thousand downloaded songs, the remixes he'd made himself. He choked when he remembered Giles's notebook was in his backpack, the song for him half-finished.

Aaron shut his heart down, telling himself it was still in his head, he could write it again, better this time.

He winced when the cold hit him, the sidewalk burning his feet, the wind cutting his face and ears, whistling through his sweater. He didn't stop, though, not even when his mother screamed his name, not when the ice on the sidewalk cut through the soles of his feet and went all the way into his teeth. He didn't let himself think or fear or worry. He only went forward, away, ready to burn down everything attached to his parents if that was what it took. Ready to freeze to death instead of lean on them for one more thing, ever.

When he saw the red Honda still in the driveway, when those beautiful, precious ears stuck out of Giles's hair as he got out, Aaron did cry. He stepped across the snowy yard, moving double-time now, his fears dying away, retreating into simple sorrow.

Of course Giles hadn't left. Aaron felt foolish ever thinking for a moment he would.

His world narrowed, everything going dark except for the lighthouse of that beautiful red Honda, of Giles calling out his name, glancing at Aaron's front door in alarm.

"We need to go." Aaron opened the car door, retreating into the familiar, protective warmth of his boyfriend's vehicle.

Chapter Twenty-Three

GILES HAD WAITED in Aaron's driveway because every time he put his car in drive, his foot wouldn't lift off the brake pedal. He knew he was an overprotective idiot, and Aaron might be mad at him for not leaving as he'd been directed, but Giles reasoned if Aaron called him and said he was fine, he'd leave and Aaron would never know he'd stayed. Simple as that.

Never in a million years had he expected Aaron to come staggering out of the house without a coat or shoes, looking like someone had shot him in the chest, his mom running behind him, sobbing and calling his name.

Leaping into panic mode, Giles got out of the car. "Aaron—what—"

"*Aaron.*" Mrs. Seavers hesitated a moment at the snowbank her son had crossed in stocking feet, then started tentatively after him.

Tears ran silently down Aaron's cheeks as he fumbled with Giles's car door. "We need to go."

Giles cast one last worried glance at Aaron's mom as her son got into the car. Behind her on the porch he saw the man who could only be Mr. Seavers, hands on his hips, posture stiff and unforgiving, wearing the expression of every bully who'd chased Giles down with a baseball bat in his hand.

Giles got in and pulled out of the driveway without his seat belt on.

"Did they hurt you?" Giles fumbled his lap restraint on as he burned through a stop sign onto the main road. He glanced at Aaron, but his boyfriend was eerily still. He looked unmarked, but Giles knew better than anyone that meant nothing. "Aaron—did your dad hit you? Do you need a hospital? My dad's a doctor, but he'll be the first one to tell me—"

"They kicked me out."

Giles's foot fumbled on the brake. Cars honked and swerved around him. "They *what*?"

Aaron stared at the dashboard, his voice distant and numb as he replied. "They told me to switch my major to law or get out of the house."

"Without your fucking coat? Your *shoes*?"

Aaron shut his eyes.

It was only ten minutes from Aaron's house to Giles's, but the drive was the longest in Giles's nineteen years of being alive. He babbled the entire way there, how they were almost home, that Giles would take care of him and everything would be okay. It was the biggest bunch of bull in the world, because Giles barely understood what was going *on*, let alone how to make it okay.

Aaron said nothing, and it started to creep Giles out. He took hold of Aaron's hand after a mile, and when Giles got freaked, he'd squeeze, a silent plea for Aaron to give him a sign of life. Aaron always squeezed back—sometimes a little delayed, sometimes weak, but he always did.

When they got to the house, Giles held it together long enough to get Aaron inside. The socks about broke him—he didn't know if Aaron walked stiff like that because his feet were cold or because of shock—and Giles felt sick when he realized Aaron had nothing in the car. Nothing but the clothes on his back.

He has me. Giles swallowed his panic and made himself strong. *I'll get him whatever he needs.*

His strength wobbled when his mom came to them in the hallway. She took one look at their faces and went into supermom mode, calling for Giles's dad. Somehow that almost shattered Giles, watching his father shift from docile guy who likes to hide on the internet to the best pediatrician in Oak Grove, his expression soft and searching as he asked Aaron questions, taking in the stocking feet and glancing at Giles for help.

That was when Giles did shatter, because all he saw was Mr. Seavers, watching his son go off without shoes.

Vanessa pulled Giles off to the side, shushing and gentling him, and Giles started to bawl. Like a fucking baby.

"They kicked him out, Mom—they kicked him *out*."

She pulled him close, rubbing his back, crushing him to her soft, fragrant, familiar body. "Honey—it's okay. Don't you worry now."

Sorrow hit Giles in waves. He felt so stupid, because it wasn't even his misery. Aaron didn't cry as Dr.

Mulder led him away, still staring straight ahead.

They turned him off. They turned my beautiful baby off, and now he's dead inside.

I have to wake him up.

He couldn't yet, though, because he *couldn't stop crying*.

"Mom—he didn't have his coat. He left his bag, his suitcase—everything. His mom looked like she had second thoughts, but his dad just stood there watching. Like he didn't fucking have a heart."

His mom never stopped moving her hands over his back, treating him as if he were five and had fallen and scraped his knee. "It's okay, honey. We'll take care of him. Of both of you."

A sob caught in Giles's throat, and he gagged on it.

It took his mom ten minutes to get Giles out of his hysterics, cycling him through the same hurt and outrage until he leveled out again. When he had himself under control, he went to find Aaron, feeling bad he'd left him alone, then remembering he'd left him probably with the best person on the planet for him right now. As Giles and his mom came around the corner to the living room, they discovered Aaron tucked into the corner of the big fat sofa, the huge Sherpa throw wrapped around him. Tim had lit the gas fireplace, and it reflected a soft glow on him as he quietly examined Aaron, taking his vitals, speaking calmly to him. When Giles and Vanessa approached, Tim glanced up at them, still radiating gentleness.

"Vanessa, would you make our guest one of those hot chocolate pods in the Keurig? Maybe make up a batch of your special medicine too."

"Absolutely." Giles's mom squeezed his shoulder one last time, then disappeared into the kitchen.

"Giles." Tim passed over his cell phone. "If you'd please call Aaron's friend Walter, Aaron said he needed to be told about the situation."

Giles clutched the phone, trying to figure out how to say *he* needed to be told about the situation. "Dad— is everything okay?"

"We're absolutely fine." Tim smiled at Aaron and patted him gently on the knee. "We're all warm and safe, and your mother will spend the week fattening the two of you up. When it's time, we'll send you to school with clean clothes, plenty of snacks, and enough money to get in trouble with. Aaron will be just fine."

Giles started to choke up again. "But he doesn't have—"

"Oh, Aaron will have *plenty*. Wait until I tell your mother she gets to take a young man shopping for *everything* he needs." Tim chuckled, winking at Aaron as if he were in on the joke. "An empty-nest mother with a new bird to fuss over? She's going to be so happy I'll have to peel her off the ceiling."

For the first time, Aaron came alive a bit. Smiling softly, wearily, he took Tim Mulder's hand. "Thank you."

"You're quite welcome." Tim glanced at his son. "Do you need the number, sweetheart?"

Giles shook his head, passing his dad's phone back. "I have it, in my contacts."

"Then go. I understand this young man is anxious

to hear what's going on."

Giles went into his dad's office to make the call. He didn't break down, but he felt dizzy, almost sick as he relayed the story, weird as it was, about waiting in the driveway, about Aaron coming out half-dressed, about his mom screaming and his dad standing there like a goddamn statue.

Walter listened, not interrupting him once, and when Giles finished, Walter spoke with iron, deadly calm. "Give me your address. We'll be up in forty minutes."

They were coming up to Oak Grove? "It's almost nine."

"We'll be there before ten. I'll have Kelly book us a hotel."

"We have a spare room. You can stay here." Because it'd be a cold day in hell before Aaron slept anywhere but beside him right now.

"That would be great, thank you. If you have time…" Giles could hear Kelly protesting in the background, but he faded, like Walter moved away, "…I'd appreciate it if you could give the room a good vacuum and dusting, particularly anything fabric. No down can be in the room, especially on the bed, and go ahead and strip the sheets. We'll bring our own bedding, and I'll make it up."

Oh yeah. The allergies. "Sure. What's the food stuff again? My mom will want to know."

"Dairy, egg, and almond. He'll only break out in a rash with dairy and egg, but he goes to the hospital with almonds. Even a trace amount can kill him."

"No almonds, clean room, no feathers, no milk or egg. Got it." His voice broke. "Walter—"

"We'll fix it." Walter's calm was different than Tim Mulder's, like it had a fire inside it promising if the world didn't work out okay, he'd *make* it that way. "Whatever happens, he has us, and we'll fix it."

Giles swallowed the roughness in his throat. "Okay."

"Go to him. He needs you right now. You don't have to be perfect, but you need to be there."

Suddenly Giles felt stupid that he wasn't. "I will. Except wait—then I can't clean—"

"Go be with him right now. Sit with him, hold his hand, and tell him you love him. And that you won't leave. Over and over and over."

Okay. "I gotta go."

"I'll see you soon."

Giles rose and headed into the living room to be with his boyfriend.

DR. MULDER EXPLAINED to Aaron he was experiencing shock. His brain was processing a severe emotional blow as well as experiencing the anxiety that came with knowing his accustomed support, physical and emotional and financial, had been removed or threatened. Dr. Mulder repeated many times, matter-of-factly, that as far as physical and financial issues were concerned, Aaron had nothing to worry about. Aaron was to let him handle anything he would normally expect a father to take care of. "Maybe a little more than you're used to," he said with a wink.

Aaron stared blankly at him, appreciating the sentiment and yet finding himself unable to respond. Everything about him felt foggy and distant.

Dr. Mulder didn't seem put-off by this at all. "Your brain is an amazing organ. It's doing its job right now, protecting you from things you aren't ready to face. I understand it will take you a while to comprehend how much we're willing to assist you. Even if you and Giles weren't romantically involved, we would never turn away a young man in need. But since you *are* dating my son, you'll receive more attention, I have to confess. Giles cares for you a great deal. Taking care of you is taking care of my son's heart, so you're precious to me. Feed that to your brain, because you might find later the knowledge is a great comfort." He glanced over his shoulder and smiled. "Ah. Here comes Giles now. I'll leave you to him and see if I can go help my wife in the kitchen. Let me know if there's anything you need."

Thank you, Aaron thought, but couldn't say. He could only watch Dr. Mulder rise, speak briefly to Giles, then leave the room.

Through the fog, Giles floated to him. Giles looked upset, which bothered Aaron, but he still couldn't talk. Well, technically he could, he knew this, but getting anything from his brain to his mouth felt like so much work.

Giles smiled at him with watery eyes. "Hey, you." He sat on the edge of the couch. "Walter and Kelly are coming. They'll be here in a bit."

Walter was coming? Aaron tried to frown, because

that didn't make sense, but he couldn't make his face move. He was cold, and he wished with an ache that burned in his belly that Giles would hold him and make him warm.

Maybe he *did* talk, because the next thing he knew, Giles was nudging him over, backing him farther against the cushions, sliding his body alongside Aaron's. "Let me take care of you."

Aaron let him. As Giles wiggled closer, adjusting the blanket, Aaron buried his face into Giles's neck. He shut his eyes and took deep breaths of his boyfriend, the familiar scent better than alcohol at shaving off the ragged edges of his nerves.

What if he leaves me too? The thought made Aaron seize, but before panic could take hold, Giles began to shush him and held him closer, promising he wasn't going anywhere.

Part of Aaron's brain worried he couldn't count on that, but Giles kept drowning it out, touching him, kissing his hair, his forehead, his nose. Saying over and over and over that he loved Aaron and wouldn't ever leave him. Not unless Aaron wanted him to go, but even then he'd probably sit in the driveway.

Against his better judgment, Aaron sank into those promises, let them take the edge of the cold away.

He might have slept—he wasn't sure, because time felt funny, like it got longer and shorter or just didn't matter anymore. At some point he sat up and held a hot mug of something chocolatey. He sipped at it, but it was like the sweet had to burn through the fog too, and after a little bit he got tired and gave it away. There were cookies, some kind of snickerdoodle. They were pretty good. Mrs. Mulder beamed, watching him as he ate, said something about her medicine always working. But then she disappeared, talking animatedly to her husband about vegan substitutions and some friend of hers she needed to call about flax eggs.

Giles never left his side, never stopped touching him, holding his hand, rubbing his back and shoulders.

When Walter arrived, everyone came into the living room and started talking. Still holding Giles's hand, Aaron watched Walter move around the living room. He still couldn't really talk, and it was starting to scare him, the not talking. He stared at Walter, gripping Giles's hand as he focused.

"Walter."

As soon as his name was out of Aaron's mouth, Walter crouched in front of Aaron. "Hey, tiger." Walter stroked Aaron's hair, his smile never wavering. "How are we doing?"

Aaron stared at him, thinking that was a pretty fucking stupid question.

Walter laughed. "Sorry." He kept touching Aaron's hair, and every stroke felt like a frizzle. "This is a nice setup you have going here. Your man beside you, a woman who knows her way around a snickerdoodle, and a doctor on tap. Well done."

Aaron swallowed. Fumbling for Walter's hand, he tried to squeeze.

Walter met him halfway and gripped him in a tight hug. He glanced at Giles. "Sweetheart, can we use your bedroom a minute? You can come too, but I need to talk with your sexy boyfriend."

They couldn't talk here? Aaron frowned, but nobody looked at him. They just grabbed his arms and moved him around until he was standing and walking, Walter on one side, Giles on the other, as they headed for the stairs. Aaron went docilely, feeling out-of-body until they were in Giles's room. He felt better here. It was familiar, and it *really* smelled like Giles.

Of course that might have been because Giles had his arm around Aaron's waist.

Aaron was getting confused. And tired.

Walter and Giles talked for a moment, their voices hushed, and Aaron couldn't focus. The next thing he knew, he was sitting on Giles's bed, being encouraged to lie down. It wasn't Giles who lay beside him and pulled him into a full-body embrace, though. It was Walter.

Confused, Aaron tried to lift his head. He got a chance to see Giles settling in by his feet before Walter pulled him back down.

"Nope. This is my time, buddy. You're going to snuggle in here, let me hold you and listen to my story. Then I'm going to cry like a baby and make you a bunch of promises, and you're going to nod and say you feel better now. Got it?"

Aaron didn't. Why was Walter going to cry?

Walter smelled good too. Spicy and sexy, like fancy leather. Except Aaron didn't want to have sex with Walter anymore. He appreciated Walter, but he was the wrong thing on the menu. Maybe fancy steak was popular and tasted great, but Aaron liked cozy pot roast more.

He shifted his foot so it brushed Giles's leg, and he felt pretty good when Giles caught his foot and began to massage it.

Walter kissed Aaron's hair, held him tight. "So, my mom is sick. She's on meds, but they don't make her magically okay. She's manic-depressive, and she's probably never going to learn to manage herself right because she doesn't want to. She's Russian roulette. You might get a hug and a smile. You might get a bullet in the face. Never know until you pull the trigger."

That wasn't Aaron's mom. She was mostly quiet and ineffective. Aaron couldn't imagine the yo-yo Walter was describing. It had to suck.

Walter kept talking. "My parents are divorced too, but my dad's never really been there. He checked out around the time I was seven, and he was totally gone by the time I was thirteen. I think of him largely as the bank. He's got a lot of money, which is nice, mostly. Every so often I have to kiss the ring, but pretty soon I'm hoping to not have to do it anymore. The thing is…I was pretty fucking lonely growing up. College was awful. I told you how I went to a pile of them? I went to that many because I sucked at it. I dropped out to help my mom for a while, which was a disaster, but mostly I was lonely. I've always been lonely. I think I'll always feel it a little at this point, because a part of me never figured out how to connect with people."

Walter's voice was rough the whole time while he spoke now, and it upset Aaron. His hands were pressed to Walter's chest, and he slid them around to his back.

Laughing softly, Walter squeezed him and kept talking. "I knew when I first saw you that you were lonely too. When I saw you in your corner all curled up, though, it got to me because you looked like I still feel inside most of the time. It was like I *had* to get you out of there, *had* to take you to lunch, *had* to keep in touch with you, because everything about you felt like this big chance to take care of someone the way nobody ever did me, not until Kelly. I think if Kelly weren't so awesome, didn't know where this all came from, he'd be jealous. He does know, though, and he gets how taking care of you is like taking care of the little brother I never had or an alternate version of me."

A bud of warmth bloomed in Aaron's chest. He breathed slowly, deeply, trying to feed it.

Walter kept speaking, his voice watery now, and he had to stop a lot to collect himself before moving on. He also held Aaron so tight it almost hurt. "Your parents suck. You don't need them, baby. I already sent a text to my grandmother, and she says she'll help. I bet we could get her to cover tuition if the school doesn't give you a full ride—which I bet you they do, as much as that place loves you. If you don't want to shack up here with Giles for the summer, you're staying with Kelly and me. In fact we are your second home, forever, full stop. You need milk money, somewhere to wash your clothes? You come to me. You need clothes? Me. A hug, a smile, a night at the movies—me." He crushed Aaron's face into his neck. "Sometimes we need a place to be completely safe, somewhere boring that isn't about sex or adventure or wild hairs. I am that place for you. As long as you want it, for ten minutes or ten hours or ten thousand years: I am your safe place. No matter what happens, no matter who leaves you or hurts you. *I am your safe place.*" Walter lifted his head, freeing one hand from Aaron to wipe at his face. "Shit."

Aaron knew Giles moved behind him before he felt the press of his body. He smelled him, his sweet, comforting scent mingling with Walter's.

Damn, that's kind of nice, a sleepy part of his brain murmured. Thankfully, his cock was way too shut down to pay attention.

Giles reached over Aaron, dabbing at Walter's eyes with a tissue. "Walter Lucas, you're a big old softy."

Walter took the tissue and blew his nose loudly. "Now you know why we had to leave the living room."

Time did that funny bubble thing again. Aaron heard Giles and Walter talking, knew sometimes they were speaking to him, but he was so warm and sleepy, he couldn't help falling back. He dreamed: he lay in a cave, except it wasn't cold and wet but lush and lit by a soft fire. Warm arms moved around him when he shifted his body, and everything smelled amazing. Like snickerdoodles.

And pot roast.

When he opened his eyes, it was dark. He lay in Giles's bed, Giles in the place where Walter had been. Giles held him differently than Walter had—tight, yes, but his leg went over Aaron's, pulling their groins tight together. When Giles saw Aaron was awake, he smiled at him, stroking his face.

"Hi there."

Aaron slid his hands around Giles's waist, pleased to discover Giles wasn't wearing a shirt. He tucked his hands into the waistband of Giles's pajama pants. "Hi."

Giles kept touching Aaron's face. "Feel better?"

Yeah, Aaron did. Nodding, he kissed Giles softly on the lips. In his jeans, his cock woke all the way up.

Giles nuzzled him. "I want you to know— everything Walter said, about being a safe place, about giving you anything you needed? That's me too. I don't mind you ever going to him for help, but I want you to know I'll always help you too." His hands moved to the back of Aaron's head, and he kissed him, carnal and deep. "I love you. I'll always love you, Aaron, no matter what happens—for the rest of my life."

Aaron forced the words beyond his lethargy. "I love you too."

Giles kissed him full on the mouth. Aaron opened his legs, pressed his rigid cock against Giles's as he pulled his boyfriend down for another kiss, the warm bubble inside him now flowing freely, a wellspring of love and safety carrying him away.

Chapter Twenty-Four

GILES HAD ALWAYS been pretty fond of his parents, but he hadn't been aware of how much he'd won the family lottery until he watched them rescue his boyfriend.

Never in a million years did he imagine Aaron's parents would kick him to the curb. How could anyone do that to a human being, *let alone their own child?*

"I suspect his mother would have kept coming after him had you not been there to collect him," Giles's mother said when he asked her the next morning. Everyone else was still in bed or out. Giles had fucked Aaron back to sleep and met a sleepy Kelly shuffling to the guestroom after a trip to the bathroom. Giles's dad was running an errand. "I called her last night to let her know he was with us."

She didn't clarify further how that conversation went, and Giles wasn't sure he wanted to know. He sipped at the French vanilla cappuccino his mother had made him in the Keurig. "You wouldn't have stopped chasing me the way she did. You wouldn't have stood on the sidewalk and cried. You'd have tackled me and dragged me into the house by my hair if I'd tried to leave."

"Sweetheart, if your father threatened to kick you out of the house with a grand in your pocket and a car waiting on a pleasant day in July, I'd deck him before he finished the sentence."

This was true, except his father had raised his voice to him exactly three times in his life, and two of those times had been when Giles was a distracted teenager nearly walking into traffic while he texted Mina. The idea of Tim Mulder kicking anyone out of his house was as weird as Giles bringing home a girlfriend.

But when Tim returned from his errands, Giles discovered his father had been concealing hidden depths of badass.

Tim had gone to Aaron's house, where he'd reclaimed three reusable grocery bags of clothes. Aaron's backpack with his computer wasn't present, nor was Aaron's cell phone or any of his precious headphones. When Giles asked him what had gone down, Tim grew stoic and would only say he'd "had a talk" with Aaron's mom.

"But what about his dad?"

"Aaron's father returned to his home in Eden Prairie last night." Tim retreated behind his laptop, his body language telegraphing the matter was closed, but Giles couldn't let this dog go.

"But is he still cutting Aaron off?"

Tim's lips went tight as he keyed in a web address. "As far as I'm able to tell, yes."

"And Aaron's mom is *letting him*?"

"I'm quite certain your mother could use your help in the kitchen."

Giles gave up, because his dad had turned into the kind of brick wall he was used to. When Giles got to the kitchen, Walter was already there, making breakfast with Vanessa.

Walter had his mother's apron on, and he and Giles's mom were in an intense discussion about egg replacers and vegan pancake recipes when Giles appeared. They immediately put him to work whipping up batter for dairy-and-egg-free blueberry muffins while they went back to refining the particulars for a sausage-and-tofu scramble with roasted red pepper and onion. It felt a lot like Thanksgiving with all the food flying around, and it was pretty cool that this was all for Giles and his boyfriend's friends.

Soon after Giles got the muffins into the oven, Kelly wandered downstairs, still in his pajamas. He blinked at all the food, gave his fiancé a sideways look as if to say, *Are you behind this?* but Walter immediately began talking up how amazing a cook and hostess Vanessa was, how he'd offered his help but she'd had everything running like a ship even before he showed up. Kelly fell immediately into line, thanking her for her generosity, praising her home and her son and anything else he could latch on to. No shocker, Vanessa ate this up with a spoon and declared Walter and Kelly had to come back again soon or she'd hunt them down.

"You'll have to come to our wedding in June," Kelly said.

Vanessa lit up like a Christmas tree. "You're engaged? Oh, that's wonderful, congratulations. Where are you getting married?"

Walter popped a piece of fruit in his fiancé's mouth. "Windom. Southwest of the Cities."

"A lovely town. A friend of mine in college was from there." Vanessa leaned over the counter, eyes dancing. "What kind of theme are you having? And how are you doing the processional? I love the way kids are renegotiating the ceremony these days, same-sex and opposite couples both. Tell me you're doing something clever like those people who danced down the aisle on YouTube."

Giles wanted to die of mortification for his mother's exuberance, but Kelly basked in it. "We still haven't quite worked out how we're coming down the aisle. Walter doesn't want anyone standing up front waiting for the other one."

"No cattle or chattel delivery," Walter murmured into his coffee mug. He watched his animated husband-to-be with a happy smile. "I'd love something simple and modern, or at least different and us. The problem is, Kelly wants a Disney wedding, but he keeps pretending it's not a big deal. I told him he can carry flowers if he wants to."

"I'd look stupid." Kelly's tone made it clear he really wished he *could* carry flowers.

"Why couldn't *everyone* carry flowers?" Giles suggested. "Maybe…maybe everyone has a stem, and you have a bigger bunch or something. You could be carrying half and give it to Walter when you meet him." Giles faltered. "Oh God, forget it. That's the chattel/cattle thing."

"No, not quite." Walter had a soft, thoughtfully

melted look as he regarded Kelly. "That...would be very us."

"If we do, we're back to you as the boy and me as the girl again, which you said you didn't want."

Vanessa made a *pffft* noise. "Boy, girl—it's all in your head. I took my husband's name, let my dad give me away. I would have kept my name, but then either I'd have a different name than my family, my husband would, or Giles would be a Christofferson-Mulder. Can you imagine him trying to spell that in kindergarten? And what if he got married and hyphenated his name? Christofferson-Mulder-Smith? But if you ask who runs this house, my husband would answer *you, dear* without blinking. You can't let social symbols define you, but you shouldn't stifle your life by wrapping yourself up in too much effort to show you're politically correct, either. If you want to walk down the aisle like a Disney princess, Kelly, it doesn't make you a girl. It makes you an openhearted, empathetic man who doesn't let stereotypes define him. You might get some eyebrows at a poofy dress, but if you want it, forget the haters and do it."

Kelly blushed. "It's *so cool* how brides get to drift with all the fabric draped around them, big train flapping or dragging or however their dress makes it go. It's not that I want a dress. I love the *show*. The music, the flower petals...everybody standing up. I feel like I shouldn't ask for it, except I kind of want it anyway. Is it bad to want attention for one day? I mean, it's not fair because if I *were* a girl, nobody would care." The stain on his cheeks crept all the way to his ears. "I really don't want to wear a dress."

"No. You do." Walter had a funny look about him, like he'd opened a puzzle box and found a universe inside. "Or, you would if everyone hadn't told you for twenty years a dress was horrible and embarrassing to wear. You want to wear something dress-like that makes you feel like a Disney princess."

Poor Kelly looked as if he wanted the floor to open up and swallow him. He stared fixedly at the ceiling, his face so red now it was blotchy. "Can we talk about something else?"

Giles's mom hugged Kelly and brushed a kiss on his cheek. "So much of our lives are decided for us by other people. Be glad you're marrying a partner who wants to help you be yourself, no matter what the world tells you to be." She patted his arm. "I bet we could find a way to give you your show without making you feel embarrassed about it."

They poked around online, but once Aaron woke, Giles, Aaron, and Kelly went with Vanessa to go shopping in real time. Walter elected to stay at the house with Tim, and from the look of the two of them, they had schemes afoot. When Giles complained about being sent to the kiddie table, his dad told him his place right now was with his boyfriend.

Aaron protested too as he and Kelly herded him to the car. "Dr. Mulder brought over everything I need."

Giles's mom waved his objection away. "I love shopping. You're just giving me an excuse."

This was true, but the kind of money his mom dropped wasn't small change. A top-of-the-line cell phone on the Mulder family plan, a *tablet*—Giles hadn't gotten this much for Christmas. She tried to get a laptop, but Aaron wouldn't let her, insisting he could use Giles's or something in the music computer lab. He wouldn't take anything but thirty-dollar headphones, either, and he got annoyed when Giles pointed out he was used to Bose.

"I don't need anything fancy," Aaron insisted.

Giles's mom smiled while Aaron was in front of her, applauding with Kelly and telling Aaron it was him to a T, but as soon as Aaron ducked inside to change, Vanessa's eyes misted over, and she put a hand to her mouth, looking ready to cry. "I can't get over anyone throwing that nice boy out." She pulled a tissue out of her purse and wiped at her eyes with shaking hands. "I can buy him half of Minnesota and nothing will undo what they've done to him. Thank heavens he has you, and his friends. I just—you have to tell him, Giles, that even if the two of you break up, we'll help him. And if you break up with him, I will tan your idiot hide until you can't sit for a *month*."

Giles rubbed her back. "I don't have any plans to, Mom."

They lunched at Whole Foods because it was easier for Kelly with his allergies, then headed to the house, where Tim and Walter had a surprise waiting.

"So." Walter beamed as he spoke, very much the cat with the canary. "We made some phone calls, and while a few things are still waiting official approval, it's my pleasure to let you know your music lessons and all school fees associated with the music department at

Saint Timothy will be covered because of a scholarship for the remainder of the year. Any payments your father attempts to make, should he do so, will be refunded. You're also being submitted as a special case for a full ride for the remainder of your tenure there—which, you should know, was already something the Drs. Nussenbaum were advocating before the financial-need angle occurred."

Aaron, who'd been standing in the middle of the Mulder living room with four shopping bags in each hand, blinked for a few seconds. "What—?" He glanced from Walter to Vanessa to Giles. "How? Why? Why are you all doing this?"

"Because you need taking care of. Because what's happening to you is wrong." Vanessa displaced shopping bags as she clasped his hands in hers.

Aaron kept shaking his head. "I'm just this kid your son is dating. All of this—I don't get it."

"I told you last night why this matters to me," Walter said quietly.

"I'm helping because nobody helped Walter," Kelly added.

Giles didn't know what to say, so he stood there like an idiot. His dad cleared his throat and kind of took care of things. "Son, I have to tell you, only a little of this is about you. The rest of it is people being people. Everybody needs a safety net. Some people don't have any net at all and have to knit their own. You don't. That's not something to doubt. That's something to celebrate."

After they recovered from all the mushy feelings,

they had chili Giles's mom had set up earlier in the crock pot. They played board games at the table, which Giles hadn't done since he was ten unless he was at a holiday gathering, but apparently this was Walter's *thing*. Giles's mom planned out the rest of their break, which would apparently be full of food and movies and a party if Giles and Aaron wanted one.

Their lives were unfolding like a Hallmark movie, which, all things considered, was great. Except Giles couldn't help feeling he hadn't quite pulled his weight. He wasn't sure what it was he was supposed to be doing, but surely there was *something*. Everyone else was making soppy speeches and showering Aaron with gifts and getting him freaking scholarships. This wasn't about Giles, and he kept telling himself to shut up and float, but every time he sat too long, he got this nagging feeling he should be doing something.

When he and Aaron went to bed that night, he figured out what it was.

As they lay on Giles's bed half clothed, Aaron ran his fingers tentatively down Giles's naked chest. "I'm sorry about all this."

"Sorry about what? Are you nuts? I half-wondered if I should apologize to you for my overzealous family."

"God—no. Your family is incredible. Yes, it's too much, but too much is…nice, right now." Aaron's finger traced whorls in Giles's three chest hairs. "I hope you don't mind."

"Why the hell would I mind? Aaron—" He lifted his boyfriend's chin, his heart clenching at the nervousness he read there. "*Baby.* I love you. I feel dumb I couldn't help you more, that I'm just standing here with my ears sticking out while everyone else pulls rabbits out of their asses."

Aaron's face got weird, sort of iron and soft all at once. "You waited. I hadn't even gotten as far as wondering if I could walk to your house without shoes and there you were." He took Giles's face in his hands, stroking his cheeks. "You waited in case something went wrong, and you weren't going to tell me you had, were you, if it had been okay? When I called, you'd have answered from the drive and then gone to your house."

Giles tried not to be embarrassed at being busted. "I was worried about you. I couldn't leave you there. It kind of flipped me out that you actually needed me, in the end."

"I can't help wondering if they would have let me keep going had you not been there." He bit his lip. "I worry they wouldn't have. My mom—I really thought she was on my side."

"You shouldn't have walked outside because they shouldn't have let you. And all your stuff didn't make it over, I noticed. Did my dad tell you what happened when he went to see your mom? He wouldn't tell me."

Aaron's hands slipped to Giles's collarbone, and he couldn't lift his gaze. "He said...he doesn't think I'll get my laptop back. Or anything in my backpack. I can get most of my music and some Salvo work from the cloud, but—I'm so sorry, the notebook you gave me for Christmas is gone. I can recreate all the songs, they're in my head, but...I'd give up all the clothes and shoes to get it back."

"I'll get you a new one. I'll get you ten." Giles slid his body closer, running a hand through Aaron's thick hair. "Your mother should have been over *here*, apologizing and begging you to come home, promising to argue with your dad."

"She's never really been aggressive. She still cries when she talks about Dad leaving her."

"She shouldn't cry to you at all. Parents are supposed to *parent*. Not kick you out because you don't act like they want you to. I mean—shit. I thought my mom was kind of a helicopter, but I'd rather have that. I'm sorry you don't."

"I'd rather have you. I'm never going to not love you for being there when I came around the corner." He smiled as he ran his hand through Giles's hair before tugging gently on his lobes. "And don't you dare mock your ears. They're my favorite part of you."

Okay, that one hit Giles right in the gut. To cover his sudden attack of mushiness, he ground his hips meaningfully against Aaron's groin. "Really? Favorite part?"

Aaron's eyes glazed over. "Second favorite," he murmured, thrusting back.

They made languid love, face-to-face, and maybe it was Giles's imagination, but he noticed before his brain switched over to lust or bust that his boyfriend's hands did always seem to land on his ears.

THE WEEK BETWEEN J-term and the start of the spring

semester went by Aaron like a watery dream.

For being alone, he had people around him all the time. Mina came by every day, played Xbox with them, helped Aaron and Giles recreate some of the notes he'd lost for Salvo. They started a choir and orchestra arrangement of "Titanium" Aaron still wasn't sure would work but wanted to try, for Baz.

Walter and Kelly came up twice. Once they took Aaron and Giles out to dinner, but Saturday night they stayed over again, and they had a movie marathon. Mina came over too, and they picked movies, watching them until they passed out. *Star Trek* and *Thor* and *Ocean's Eleven* and *Anchorman*. And *Frozen*.

The Disney movie rang in Aaron's head when he went to bed. He hadn't expected to like it at all, but the story, the music, the beautiful blue of it all haunted him. When he curled up against Giles and tried to sleep, all he saw was swirling white, the snow queen walking through it all. Alone, all alone, her song sounding like a bell inside him.

His dreams were strange, the movies fractured and shadowed in his subconscious. He woke damp with sweat, the room dark. Pale light from the window cast the room in deep blue shadow, and his half-sleeping mind saw the snow from the dream and the world outside swirling across the floor, made him feel the cold, wet snow on his stocking feet.

Let it go.

Pulling the cover over his head, drawing his feet up tight, he burrowed into Giles and called up the song from the movie, willing it to lull him out of his panic.

The melody line danced across his brain, and he stripped out the voice, adding his own color to it. He closed his eyes, his ears, pressed his fingers over his nose to shut out all but the essential air. He used Giles's body like a wall, curling into the smallest, quietest space he could occupy in the world, and he chased the music.

He could *see it*. Soft, pastel colors along a bar staff in the darkness. He felt the music too, drifting out of the shadow. It felt like magic, and he imagined himself in the center of the darkness, spinning with his eyes shut as sparkling sound emerged as visible light from his fingertips.

Let it go, let it go, let it go.

The music carried him back into his dreams, wrapping around him until Giles kissed him awake. They made love, and Aaron's still-sleepy brain melded the orgasm with the musical line.

When they got out of bed, it was time to leave the Mulder house to go back to school, which was more difficult than Aaron had expected. Somehow the reality of his abandonment hadn't sunk in until that moment, but now there he was, heading to school with Giles as he'd always planned to…but from Giles's driveway. With supplies and trinkets from Giles's mother, not his own.

How could she not call him? Had she tried and no one told him?

It had to be a mistake. As Tim loaded up Giles's car and everyone milled around the driveway, Aaron ducked into the house, pulling his new phone out of his pocket. Dialing his mom's landline, Aaron curled against the pantry door and waited as it rang. And rang. And rang.

He called her cell.

When voicemail picked up, all he could do was breathe. Through his nose, slowly, but he was hyper-aware of each breath. *In. Out.* Like soft percussion. One of those shakers with the balls wrapped around it, or a rain stick. He could only listen to the music of the air passing through his nose, because otherwise he would have to listen to his mother, who always answered her phone…not answering her phone.

Now the music was in his ears too, a thick drumbeat as he googled his aunt's phone number. This was stupid. This was *stupid*, and he was tired of it, and somebody had to fix it—

"Hello?"

Aaron's breath came out in a hot rush. *Contact.* "Aunt Carol. This is Aaron. I need to find my mom."

The pause was heavy, and it hurt. "I don't think she can come to the phone right now. I'm sorry. I'll tell her you called."

What? Aaron struggled for a reply. "Did you know she kicked me out?"

Another pause, this one even more awkward. "Yes. I'm sorry. Do you need anything?"

What, like a cup of sugar? "I need to talk to my mom." *I need to come home.*

"I'm sorry, Aaron."

Sorry? *Sorry?* Rage stepped on disbelief and stomped forward, Jim Seavers's genes lighting up in a rare flash. "You mean she's seriously not going to talk to me? She's there, I know she is. And she *won't talk to me*?"

"She's upset."

Upset?

She was upset?

"I'm sorry, Aaron." Carol sounded tired. "Someday you'll understand."

Aaron wanted to shout, but he couldn't make the words come. He wanted to tell her he would *never* understand this. It would *never* be okay to not talk to your kid because he was upset that you *threw him out of the house*. He wanted to shout at her, but he couldn't make the words come. He could only breathe soft, staccato music as his heart beat at the base of his throat, blocking all sound.

Please. Please.

Please.

"Do you need money? I could give you some money."

His breath hitched, and two tears escaped, one from each eye.

I need my mom.

Swallowing hard, he lowered the phone. With a shaking hand, he didn't hang up, he just held the button on the top until it switched off.

WALTER KNEW.

Aaron could tell when he went outside Walter knew what he'd done, or suspected. Aaron didn't want to talk to him, didn't want to talk to anyone. He felt raw and cut open, and he wanted to curl into a dark corner and wait for everything to go away.

Instead he had to go back to school. They all knew, because they'd been texting him with support. Telling him they'd help him any way they could. So many fucking people.

People and his sullen, snarky roommate, who would probably laugh and tell him he deserved it.

Oh God, he couldn't do this.

Before he could stagger backward, Walter was in front of him, not embracing him, but standing close. He spoke quietly at Aaron's ear, and Aaron looked out over the frozen subdivision as he listened.

"I don't care if your mom will talk to you or not, or if she filled you with crazy if you got to talk to her. You get to be who you want to be, and you won't ever be alone." He squeezed Aaron's arm and leaned closer. "I know it feels like you are. I know it hurts right now. But you're not."

Aaron shut his eyes. "I don't want to talk about this."

"I know. But it's going to get harder before it gets better. I want you to remember you have us. No matter how angry you get, how hysterical, how confused. We're here. I'm right here."

Cold wind bit against Aaron's face, whistled in his bare ears. He closed his eyes and shut out everything but that faint sound. *Whoosh.*

There it was. Like ice crystals in his ears. Against the black backdrop of his mental landscape, he watched the color of the wind and its whistle dance across his mind. The flash of Kelly's Disney movie played, the snow queen climbing alone up the mountain. Alone in the cold, but free.

I don't want to be this free.

Walter didn't let go of Aaron's hand. "Lean on Giles. He wants to be there for you. Let him in."

Giles. Aaron opened his eyes and saw him standing there, by the car, waiting. He didn't have on his hat, and his cheeks were pink, his ear tips red as they stuck out of his hair. He smiled at Aaron, sadly.

Hopeful.

Aaron shut his eyes. "I will."

After a round of hugs and well wishes, after Giles and Aaron promised they would text when they arrived, they drove away.

Silence filled the car. Giles took Aaron's hand, squeezing it several times but not saying anything. As they sat at a stoplight, he sighed.

"I don't know what to say." He glanced sideways at Aaron, looking guilty. Sad. "I'm sorry. I know you're upset, and I hate it, but I know there's nothing I can do. I'm sorry."

"I called my mom. She didn't answer. And my aunt wouldn't let me talk to her."

Giles stared at him so long the driver behind them had to honk to get him to go through the light. He did, but his lips were pressed in a thin line. "That's fucked up. I don't—" He cut himself off, shaking his head. "I'm sorry. I'm not helping."

Aaron settled sideways in his seat, watching Giles drive. "It feels like it's not real. It makes me angry.

Crazy angry. And scared."

"I want to drive over there and hit her." Giles's knuckles were white against the wheel. "*Seriously.* How the fuck do you kick out your own son? Over a fucking *major?*"

"It was like this when she divorced my dad and he wouldn't take her back. Aunt Carol came and stayed with us, and she kept telling me sometimes the world is too hard for my mom."

"Well that's a fuck of a coping mechanism." Giles squeezed Aaron's hand tight. "I'll never do that to you. Ever. I've been to the mountaintop, and I came down with an Uzi. You're strong too, and you're going to get through this. The world's not too hard for you, Aaron. And you don't have to face it on your own."

Aaron kissed his hand and kept it pressed to his lips until Giles ran it up his face, sliding fingers into his hair.

Chapter Twenty-Five

A T TIMOTHY, ALL the way to Aaron's room they ran into music people. They hugged Aaron and wiped at their eyes, took things out of his hands, helping carry until what should have taken four trips became one with twelve people assisting. They came by with groceries—as if Mrs. Mulder hadn't sent Aaron with more ramen and single-serve mac and cheese than he could ever eat in a lifetime.

Even Giles picked up on how intense people were being. "I'm sorry. Do you want me to send them away?"

Aaron shrugged. "They mean well."

"Yes, but…God, we were like this back at home, weren't we?" When Aaron said nothing, he winced. "*So* sorry. What can I do to help?"

It almost made Aaron laugh, but in a macabre kind of way. "I just need a little time by myself."

Giles lit up. "Hey—what about a practice room? How many people can be using them right after we get back from a break?"

That was a good idea, actually, and though Giles was ready to bribe anyone he had to, it turned out exactly three people wanted the practice rooms, so not only did Aaron have no issues scoring one, he got the one with the best baby grand. His only issue was convincing Giles to leave him alone.

"It's not that I don't want to be with you." His gaze fixed on their joined hands because he couldn't bring himself to look his boyfriend in the eye.

Giles caught his hand in a firmer grip and squeezed. "I know. Only promise me you'll call or text or stop by if you need anything."

Aaron promised.

It was funny, he thought as he settled in at the keys, letting the music that had been dogging him unfurl. He had always felt so lonely, and he still did—except with so many people around him, he began to understand lonely wasn't about how many people were with him, about who loved him or hated him. It was about who he was inside. All his feelings were too sharp, too heavy. His hands moved over the keys, and he thought about his mother. Pushing past the pain of her betrayal, he made himself examine the woman underneath, Beth Seavers who was overwhelmed by everything.

The world is too hard. It had made Giles angry, but Aaron thought he understood, especially in this moment. *Too much feeling. Nowhere to put it.*

Aaron had somewhere to put it. It was a little cocky, but he thought he was getting pretty damn good at taking emotions and making something beautiful out of them.

He played for hours without realizing it. Enough people had come back that the practice rooms *were* in demand, and someone knocked on the door to let him know it was well past the end of his turn. To his surprise, it was almost nine.

He texted Giles on the way to his room to let him know he was okay, and crossed the common, humming the melody to his composition, annoyed at how it kept morphing into the instrumental line from the main *Frozen* theme. Damn the movie anyway. He felt like he was chasing something through the fog. Sometimes he could see it, but whenever he tried too hard, it ran out through his fingers.

When Aaron returned to his dorm, Elijah and his parents were still there.

On the surface nothing was different. Maybe Elijah looked leaner, a little more hollow around the eyes, but that was it. They shuffled in the same way they always did, Elijah saying nothing, his parents glaring around the room. Mrs. Prince stood with her son at the window, murmuring prayers and whatnot. Mr. Prince glared at Aaron.

Except this time the tension in the room was so unbearable it was difficult to breathe. Aaron didn't leave the room or put on his headphones and tune them out. He sat. He watched. He played back all the other times this scene had gone down. He remembered what had happened with him at home, how Giles's parents had reacted to it. He watched Elijah's parents "parent" him.

Never, not once, had Mr. or Mrs. Prince fussed over Elijah the way Mr. and Mrs. Mulder did over Aaron and Giles. They didn't ask to make sure Elijah had enough money and clean clothes and wish him good luck on his studies. They apologized to God for his sinful nature and warned him not to associate with devils who would lead him astray. Everything about them was a cartoon, the kind of religious freakishness Aaron had always assumed couldn't possibly be real and yet was right there in front of him—and this time he made himself marinate in it. Imagining what it would be like to live with it every single day.

Imagining knowing, despite Emily's buttons and Reece's horrible T-shirts, that being gay wasn't something he could change, and neither could Elijah.

He remembered the pregnant moment when Aaron had come back late and Elijah had looked like he wanted to talk. His request that Aaron simply not tell his parents anything about being gay—not that there was anything wrong with his being so. He thought about Giles's report about how Elijah whored himself out on Grindr under an assumed name…then went home on the weekends to *this*.

Elijah, whatever else he was doing, was playing a seriously fucked-up game.

When the Princes left, Aaron thought about confronting Elijah, trying to open the door between them one last time. But when push came to shove, when he stood there staring down his bristly roommate, his own wounds still raw and crazy inside him, he couldn't do it.

Too much feeling. Retreating into his bed, Aaron pulled out his iPad and worked on his composition some more, though he kept getting stuck on the *Frozen* melody lines. Making up his own was, apparently, just too hard. The same way confronting his roommate was too hard.

Maybe you're a lot more like Beth after all.

Drawing the covers over his head, Aaron lay there in the dark, not sleeping while the melodies clashed inside his head.

GILES DID THE best he could to take care of Aaron, but he wasn't always sure how to go about it.

He listened and said soothing things when Aaron told him about his aunt calling to make sure he wasn't dying in the street—not helping, just making sure he wasn't going to be on the news. When the controller's office told Aaron he had until Monday to pay his bill—apparently his dad had been paying monthly install-ments and now stopped, and the scholarship wasn't fully set up yet—Giles held Aaron's hand and told him everything would be okay. But before he could call his own dad to ask for help, Nussy and Allison stormed over to Old Main, knocked some heads around, and after that Aaron's bills were considered covered, full stop. When Aaron's dad started emailing and calling, making vague and sometimes specific threats if Aaron didn't stop fucking around and start toeing the line, it was Brian who set up a filtering system for the email and blocked Jim Seavers's texts and calls from coming into Aaron's phone.

Giles did his best to buffer against the onslaught of well-meaning friends, doing what they could to take away some of Aaron's pain, but ironically it was from watching this play out that Giles realized how little anyone could do. Everyone had a different tactic: some people distracted, some bled with Aaron. Some brought gifts, some tried to make him smile. Some waited for instructions. Some stood beside Giles like a protective barrier. Walter called and texted often, and Kelly sent animated Disney GIFs. The Salvo girls formed a circle around Aaron whenever they walked down a hall, his personal Amazon tribe.

Nothing really registered. The only one who got anywhere was Dr. Nussenbaum. Where her husband all but got on his knees and pledged vows of scholarships like a supplicant, Aaron's piano instructor smiled and asked him about his playing—and Aaron answered. Several times Giles passed them in the hall and heard him telling her about a composition he was working on, a melody line he couldn't get out of his head.

"The thing is, I'm copying something else." His shoulders got tight when he said that, and his hand against the bulletin board beside him curled like a claw. "I want it to be mine, but I keep falling into other people's songs. There's too much noise in my head."

"Then clear the noise," Dr. Nussenbaum told him. Giles hadn't heard the rest of their conversation because Mina had pulled him away.

The phrase echoed in his head, though. *Clear the noise.*

Giles could do that.

One Saturday in late February, Giles met Aaron at his dorm door bright and early. Aaron sat with his tablet on his lap and his headphones on, curled up in the corner of his bed. Giles had to let himself in, which startled Elijah, but Aaron didn't even look up.

Elijah frowned at Giles, but Giles ignored him, too focused on his boyfriend. He smiled to himself as he saw Aaron had the piano app open, his left hand picking out notes as his right hand jotted notes on staff paper. His lips were pursed tight, his eyes hollow from lack of sleep. Giles could see him chasing the tiger, the tail slipping forever out of his grasp.

Let me help you catch him.

He sat on the edge of Aaron's bed. Aaron startled, as if Giles had materialized out of thin air into his realm of focus.

Giles touched his hand. "Hey. Get your things. I have a surprise for you."

Aaron shuttered. "I want to work on this. I almost have it."

He said that every time Giles caught him composing. Giles brushed his thumb across the back of Aaron's hand. "Bring it along. Trust me. You're going to find it today."

It took a few tries to get Aaron out the door, but Giles managed it. Bundling him against the cold, Giles led him across campus.

"It's snowing again. I'm so fucking tired of snow. Shouldn't it be warmer by now?" Aaron hunched deeper into his coat, tugging his hood back down as a gust of wind tried to take it away. "Where are we going? We're passing the music building."

"We're going to the White House."

Aaron balked, stopping dead in his tracks. "Giles, I

can't. I don't want to be around people right now."

Giles faced him, blinking at him through the fat flakes the wind blew against his skin. "There's nobody there. It's just us. They all went to breakfast, and at best they'll be in the carriage house. They'll come back to sleep, but if you want to stay until six tomorrow morning, the practice room and Fred are yours. All day."

Aaron blinked at him. "What? Why?"

"Because I wanted to help you clear the noise." Giles took his hand and pulled him forward. "Come on."

It was weird to be in the house with no one else there, but Giles liked it. Baz had already assured him they were in for the next year—space for Brian too, if he wanted to come. They could have it in June if they wanted it, in fact. Giles had to check with his parents because they'd have to cover Aaron's half of the rent...but Giles loved the idea of going to class all day and coming home to find Aaron composing.

Like he was about to do now.

Giles led him to the parlor, to Fred. He plunked his backpack on a side table and unloaded as he talked, setting out the bottles of water, bags of candy, meal bars, nuts. "This is your room for the day. You've got pencils and a sharpener. Baz brought in a card table so you could spread out notes if you wanted. I'll set up the buffet here on the windowsill, but if you need anything else, stick your head out. I'm going to take your phone so nobody bugs you, but I'll be in the living room the whole time, killing myself over this fucking theory assignment Allison gave me." He picked up the empty thermos and swung it absently. "I'll fill this in the kitchen and set it by the door with a mug. Do you want travel or ceramic?"

Aaron stared at him like he hadn't heard a word Giles said. "What is all this?"

Giles fought the lump of impotent hurt and rage in his chest. "I want to help you. I want to make it all go away, but the more I watch everyone try to take away the pain, the more I realize none of us can. The only time you seem happy is when you're composing. So compose. All day. Remember, there's even a half bath off this room. You don't have to come out at all. Unless you want to, obviously—but I wanted to give you this. A day with your music."

Because I think the only way for you to work through this pain is to play it away, to turn it into a song.

He didn't know what he expected—not a big smile or anything, but he was breathless, waiting for Aaron's reaction. *Please see me trying to help you. Please see me loving you. No matter what else you see or feel, know that.*

Aaron closed the distance between them and nuzzled Giles's cheek with the stubble of his unshaven beard. He did it again, squeezing Giles's arm before he spoke.

"Thanks."

Giles brushed a kiss on his scruff. "Anytime."

At first he wasn't sure it was going to work. For an hour he didn't hear any music, and eventually, worried something was wrong, Giles got off the couch and peeked through the crack in the door.

Aaron was curled up in the corner of the huge room, his tablet in his lap. The piano sat in the middle of the room, untouched. No headphones—when Aaron shifted, Giles saw the screen and recognized the layout of a solitaire game.

Seriously? He'd given Aaron the whole room, for the *whole damn day,* and he wasn't using it? What the fucking hell?

He'd sent everyone away for nothing. He felt so angry, frustrated, embarrassed.

The emptiness of the house swelled around him, all but shouting *duh.* Giles gathered his things and went into the kitchen. He didn't put his headphones on at first, but the complete and utter lack of sound coming from the parlor drove him crazy, so he put on the Mozart early symphonies he used for background studying music and went to work.

He tried to focus on his assignment, but he kept wondering how things were going with Aaron. He'd forgotten the coffee, so he took a break to make it, filling the thermos. Since he'd never gotten an answer over what Aaron wanted, he set both the travel mug and a regular ceramic on the floor by the door.

The door beyond which silence still reigned.

He made himself his own cup when he got to the kitchen, full of milk and sugar, and dove back into his homework.

At noon he made lunch. The silence from the other room was so deafening he turned on the exhaust fan over the stove so he didn't have to hear anything but white noise. This meant, though, that when the back door opened and Mina came into the kitchen, he jumped a mile.

"You scared the crap out of me." He put down the pan he'd pulled out of the cupboard and frowned at her. "Hey, what are you doing here? Nobody's supposed to be here today. I cleared it with the house."

"I was looking for Karen." She sat at the kitchen table. "Why, where's everybody at? Why are *you* here, anyway?"

"To be an idiot, I think." Giles rolled his eyes at himself as he put the pan on the stove and opened the can of soup he'd brought along for his lunch. "I had this dumb idea to give Aaron the day to compose. Cleared everyone out so he could be all by himself, all day, no distractions."

"Aww, that's sweet."

"Yeah, well, he's in there playing cards with himself."

Mina laughed. "Well, sometimes that's how it goes, I guess."

Giles leaned against the counter, shoulders sagging. "I just wanted to help."

"I'm pretty sure you do help."

"What do I do to help? I kiss him. I sit with him at lunch. I fuck him."

"You listen. You do things like this. You *hold* him."

Giles let out his breath in a heavy sigh. "I want to do more. I know I can't make it better, but I want—"

Mina sat up, held out a hand. She waved impatiently at Giles and the fan above the stove. "Turn it off. *Off. Listen.*"

Giles fumbled with the switch, then tried to listen, but all he heard was the beating of his heart. He was about to tell Mina this when he caught it—a whisper of sound. Shutting his eyes, he held his breath and leaned into the door.

He thought he heard a distant plinking of a piano. Not all the time, and not anything big. No swelling chords. No pounding chorus. Not even a bittersweet melody line. Just notes, whispering and far away. But definitely music.

Mina kept her gaze on the door, her expression soft and sad. "There. See? You had to give him time."

Giles felt foolish for his impatience even as a brand-new round of anxiety pushed him to do more. "I want to take his pain away, Mina. I don't want him to feel like this. It makes me crazy."

"You can't carry someone else's pain. They have to walk through it on their own." A new swell of music, a full phrase, drifted from the parlor, and she closed her eyes, riding it. "I think he's going to do beautiful things with his, though. Truly amazing. And you help, Giles."

"How?"

"By doing this." She gestured at the kitchen, the house, the parlor. "Giving him space. Loving him." Her eyes developed a sheen, but she laughed as she wiped at them. "See? You're helping me with mine."

This again. God, was she finally going to tell him? "I'll always help you, Mina. You know that, right?"

She looked at him, eyes glistening then spilling over, but she laughed, and when he crouched beside her, grasping her hands, she kissed him on the cheek.

"I'm fine."

You're not. "Will you tell me? Even if I can't help, will you tell me?"

She rested her forehead against his. "I'm…in love. The same person since Christmas. Except they won't ever love me back. Hush." She pressed her fingers on his lips when he tried to argue. "No. I know. I…talked to her. She's flattered, but she doesn't feel the same way."

"You told *her*?" The last few months played in his head, and he ached as he realized what had been in front of him the whole time. "Karen."

Mina nodded, wiping tears away. "She was sweet. Really sweet. She still is. Sometimes that makes it harder, but I'm not sorry."

Giles kept climbing over top of himself, trying to keep up. "So…you're lesbian?"

She tipped her head back and stared at the ceiling. "I've gone round and round in my head, and I still don't know. I guess when I look back, maybe I was always more open-minded about attraction than I knew. I still think guys are hot. I want Marius to take me to bed so badly my teeth ache. But…when Karen moves, when she smiles, it makes things inside me dance. She says—and I think she's right—it's not so much that I love her but I love the idea of her. She's how I figured out I could love a man or a woman. Because mostly I adore her. I want to worship her from afar."

Min. Giles pressed a kiss on her hair.

"The funny thing is since I told her, we've hung out

more, which I worried would make it worse…but now we're good friends. The attraction is still there, but it's just this thing. A soft pain." She bit her lip. "It's a part of me now, this little bundle I carry. Funny thing? If I think about it when I sing or play, I can feel it vibrate, making my music better. When people talk to me— like you now, telling me your frustrations, your fears— that pain in me helps me help you. Sometimes it isn't pain anymore. It's an extra arm or…ear. It sounds crazy, I know."

"No, it doesn't." Giles stared at the closed door of the kitchen. The music had stopped again, but he could still hear it in his mind. "I get what you mean, I think."

She kissed his cheek and stood. "I'm going to go see if I can track Karen down. Or somebody. Hell, maybe I'll go try and snag a practice room. You've inspired me."

He thought about what she'd said for a long time after she left, as he ate his soup and put his headphones back in. After he finished his work and did the dishes, he pulled out his phone to play a game then he heard it once more. Music. More than a few notes. It stopped, and then it played again. Holding his breath, Giles went to the door, pressing his ear to the wood.

It was quiet. It was hesitant.

It was beautiful.

He sat along the wall by the door, zoning in and out of consciousness. The song was pretty. Sad, but pretty. He wished he could hear more of it. When he shut his eyes, nodding off, the music drifted in and out of his dreams, a strange, halting soundtrack.

Eventually it lulled him completely to sleep, and he didn't wake until it was six and the door opened. Jerking awake, he looked up to find Aaron standing over him, disheveled, stiff, and wild-eyed.

"I need you." He pulled Giles to his feet.

The room spun a bit as Aaron tugged Giles into the parlor. Giles felt as if he were half in a dream still, which was why when Aaron asked, he shook his head to clear it and blinked. "Sorry—still asleep. You want me to what?"

"Help. I need you to help." Aaron braced one palm on the top of Fred and half crouched over the keyboard as his right hand plunked out the same melody that had put Giles to sleep.

Help what? Giles listened to the phrase, let it burble in his chest. "I like it. Keep going."

"I *can't*. That's just it." Aaron hit a discordant clump of notes and stood, shoving his fingers into his hair in desperation. "It's a mess. A huge fucking mess. I'm stuck. Also, this *sucks*. I don't know why I keep fucking with it."

"What in the world are you talking about?" Giles's hand slipped over the keys, and after a few fumbles, he played the melody line, smiling. "I love it. You just need to resolve, then build."

"Resolve *how*? I can't see the end." Aaron balled up a piece of composition paper and tossed it over the piano. "I don't have enough training. I don't know what I'm doing. I need to fucking stop."

"You need to keep going."

Aaron turned on him, the tendons in his throat

bulging. "What the fuck is it for, anyway? Who cares about my stupid song? It's infantile and stupid, and I'm copying the goddamn cartoon."

"I care about your stupid song. *I* want to hear it. I'm who it's for."

That apparently was the wrong thing to say because Aaron sagged like Giles had punched him in the stomach. "It *is* for you. I keep trying, but I suck."

Giles closed the space between them. "You play beautifully. You sing. And you make wonderful music." He touched the center of Aaron's chest, pressed his palm there. "Write from this. Nobody can copy your heart. Nobody else can write your songs."

"What if it's a stupid song?"

"Then make it the greatest stupid song there is. And I'll love it no matter what because I love *you*."

Aaron pressed his forehead to Giles's, breathing out hard. "Sometimes everything swirls in my head like snow and I'm going to be buried alive."

Giles shut his eyes and drew Aaron close. He caught Aaron's bottom lip, sucked on it. "I'll dig you out. Every time."

With a shudder, Aaron nuzzled Giles, opening for him, inviting him in.

Giles guided them to the floor, stripping Aaron out of his clothes as they went down. He started to undress himself, but Aaron stopped him, lifting his hem slowly as he nibbled his way up Giles's naked chest. When he made it to Giles's mouth, he smiled—sweetly, sadly— and kissed him again.

Then he went to his knees, naked, and undid

Giles's fly to take him in his mouth.

Giles braced himself against the piano, music still flying in his head as Aaron sucked him. He watched, feasting on the visual of Aaron peeking up at him through those thick bangs with Giles's cock stretching his mouth, but he heard the music too. The music of Aaron, of the two of them together.

He came with almost no warning—he hadn't meant to, he'd wanted to fuck Aaron, but the orgasm caught him by surprise, and Aaron wouldn't let him go. When he'd finished, Giles sank bonelessly to the piano bench, tweaking Aaron's nose and wiping a bit of come out of the corner of his mouth as he rose. "What about you?"

"I want to figure this out." Aaron plunked himself naked on the piano bench beside Giles, cock jutting out as he banged out the melody. "I could resolve it like this—" He played the line then finished with a third. "Except it feels wrong."

Giles tried to climb out of his orgasm-soaked brain. "Yeah. That's…obvious." After doing up his pants, he sat beside Aaron and plunked out the line again. "There's this." He finished back at key base. "Except it feels juvenile." The problem was, everything else would be wrong. Wrong key, wrong…just wrong.

"I think the thing is it doesn't end yet. Maybe." Aaron played the line, started another one—then shifted down. A key change, another lift, and then…

Giles grinned. "*Now* if you resolve on the third—" He played it and laughed.

Aaron did too. "That's *it*." He nipped at Giles's

shoulder. "Okay. Let me keep going."

Giles ruffled his hair, smiling, and got up from the bench. When he put his hand on the door, though, the music stopped.

"Where are you going?" Aaron called.

Giles raised an eyebrow at him. "You said—"

Aaron waved impatiently at him. "I said I wanted to keep going. I didn't ask you to leave." He hesitated. "Unless this is boring?"

Love and pleasure purred inside Giles's belly. "Not at all."

Chapter Twenty-Six

NO MATTER HOW long they stayed together, no matter how many times he watched his lover compose, Giles knew this day, the first time, would be etched in his brain in a way nothing else would. He felt as if he'd been allowed inside magic, given a VIP pass to watch it form. He thought of the reserved, walled-off Aaron he'd worshipped in high school compared to this wild-eyed, naked near-animal in front of him, pounding out notes and swearing, whispering *yes* and *no, goddamn it.* Of those blue eyes turning to him, desperate for an anchor—sometimes a touch, sometimes a kiss, sometimes just a look.

They fucked twice more—when Aaron got frustrated, he climbed onto Giles's lap in the window seat and bit his neck as he spread his legs, guiding Giles's fingers to his hole. When Giles tried to protest he didn't have condoms or lube, Aaron stuffed Giles's fingers in his mouth, sucked them sloppy, then begged to be fucked.

Giles had to pry himself away and all but bolt to Baz's room half naked to get supplies, because Aaron was lost to the gods and couldn't be bothered with things like STDs or rectal discomfort. As the frenzy claimed Giles too, barely allowing him to get the condom on before he slid into his lover, he made a mental note to keep condoms and lube in his bag, and probably in the music room. Before he lost himself to the rush of Aaron on the floor, kneeling in front of him, begging, holding on to the piano leg as Giles drove into him, he promised himself he had the gumption to ask his dad, *really ask*, how many clean tests they needed with how many months between. Because yeah. He wanted to go raw into Aaron yesterday.

No way, though, was he doing it until he knew neither one of them would accidentally fuck up all their tomorrows.

The next time Aaron climbed onto him, Giles's dick was a little sore, so he laid Aaron flat on the floor and covered him in hickeys, wrenched his legs open and rimmed him until he wept. When he drew Aaron's leaky cock into his mouth, Aaron objected, saying he thought not coming was helping, but Giles ignored him and sucked his brain out through his slit.

He slapped Aaron's thigh as he rose. "Put on your pants and finish the song."

"I'm hungry." Still lying on his back, Aaron shook the thermos, then tossed it weakly. "And we're out of coffee."

Giles picked it up and helped Aaron to his feet. "I'll get you food and caffeine." He kissed Aaron and chucked his chin. "You get rid of the noise."

Aaron bit Giles's lip and settled onto the bench.

Giles didn't cook—he ordered a pizza and started a fresh pot of coffee. As he leaned against the sink and looked up local clinics, he played the day over in his head.

He could get used to this. He shut his eyes, smiling, imagining a future where they were in their own house, where Aaron banged away at the piano, nagged him for sex when he was stuck, and Giles made dinner.

It was going to happen. He would make it happen.

The pizza arrived. Giles was crossing the living room with the box and full carafe when Aaron burst through the door, still naked.

"Get in here." Aaron motioned wildly, bouncing on his feet, his flaccid cock flapping against his thigh. "*Get in here. I've got it.*" He took the pizza from Giles as he entered, tossing it onto the top of Fred as he sat down. "The whole thing. I have it. *The whole thing.*"

Giles settled in beside him on the bench. "Let's hear it."

Aaron played.

Giles shut his eyes and listened.

His breathing slowed, his heart opened, and for a minute, he thought he felt it. The kernel Mina had told him about. The little bite of pain making things brighter. Richer. Better.

Beautiful.

As he finished, he kissed Aaron's cheek, his mouth. "Aaron—it's perfect."

Aaron nipped at his lip and fiddled with the left-hand part again. "I still need to tweak. I want to turn it into a full score—vocals and orchestra. It'll be a year before I even know how to fully work it up. But the bones are there. I can feel it now." He lowered his hand from the keys and leaned into Giles. "Thank you. For today. For everything."

"Anything. Any time." *For always.*

Aaron drew in a deep breath and groaned. "Oh my God, the pizza smells *so fucking good.*"

"Then go eat it." Giles laughed and pinched his ass. "You going to always do this, compose naked?"

"Yes. And make you fuck me at regular intervals."

Giles watched his naked lover dive into the pizza, and he felt a deep, beautiful ache pull at the center of his belly. "Works for me."

WHEN AARON CAME home from the White House, he didn't just feel as if he'd finished a composition. He'd climbed a goddamned mountain. Scaled it, knocked the top off it, and sailed down in a tricked-out sled. He could do *anything.* He hummed through the halls of Titus, waving and smiling at everyone he passed, laughing and all but standing on the couch in the lounge, shouting he was king of the world.

He got to his room, and it all came crashing down. The Princes were there, doing their usual dance of hate over their son before departing. Mr. Prince's face glowed with rage as he left, and Elijah was like a frayed nerve ready to fall to pieces.

Frankly, Aaron had seen enough. Calling up the rush from composition, he crossed the room to loom over his roommate's desk.

Elijah glanced up, waspish aggression cracking through his hollow countenance. "What?"

Yeah, fuck this. "I want to know what's going on."

"I'm sitting here trying to work and you're being a freak, that's what's going on."

"Your parents. You. What the fuck is this shit, seriously?"

His roommate's eyes darkened, face shuttering to anger after a flash of pain tripped all Aaron's warning bells. "Trust me, perfect little boy, you don't want to hear anything about what's going on with me."

Aaron was pretty sure he didn't, but he also knew he *had* to hear. "I want it. All of it. Right now."

"I'm not telling you shit until *you* tell *me* a few things." Elijah nodded at the pile of gift cards and donated food. "What's with the Meals on Wheels since we got back from J-term break? Why does everyone act like your dog died? Why does your precious boyfriend treat you like a baby bird egg?"

The baby bird comment made Aaron want to wince, but he pushed the bait aside. Would telling his own story get Elijah to trust him? Aaron considered a moment, then thought, fuck, why not. "My parents kicked me out."

Elijah snorted and regarded Aaron with disbelief.

Drawing his desk chair over, Aaron sat in it. "They found out I was majoring in music instead of law. I could change my major or leave, then and there. So I left. They haven't talked to me since except to yell at me to start toeing the line. They stopped paying for school, kept all my stuff except for my clothes."

He tracked the way Elijah's eyes flashed in a kind of hurt-rage. "I call bullshit. You're one of *those*. They'd never kick *you* out."

One of those what? "They did. I'll give you my mom's number to call if you want to verify. She might answer, but I doubt it. She doesn't no matter what number I call her from. I wouldn't advise talking to my dad without body armor." He leaned forward. "Now. What's going on with *you* and *your* parents?"

Elijah glared at him for almost a full minute before he said anything, but Aaron was ready to sit there until hell froze over. When Elijah finally spoke, his voice was flat, unemotional, and his gaze never wavered from Aaron's. "My parents kicked me out when I was sixteen because I was gay."

Aaron's eyebrows rose slightly, and he glanced at the door where the Princes had recently disappeared.

Elijah smirked. "That was when I was sixteen. I left for a year, or rather until it got really fucking cold, and then I found Jesus, and they let me come home."

"You found Jesus?" Aaron didn't bother to hide his skepticism.

Elijah blinked angelically and adopted a rather good Southern accent. "Yes sir, I surely did. Jesus came to me in the gutter and led me home. I've left my sinful ways behind, and I follow the Way now." The angelic look fell, Elijah's lip curling in derision. "At least to the extent it gets me tuition at a fairly decent four-year college near a large metropolitan area."

Aaron laughed. It felt weird to do it, but damn, this was funny, in a sick, twisted sort of way. "You're telling me you're *conning* them out of a college degree? And turning tricks via Grindr on the side?"

"Trying to." The weariness was back, but he was still rigid, untrusting. "You said you got kicked out, which I'm still not buying, by the way, but it doesn't explain why everyone is stopping by." His nostrils flared. "Oh my *fucking God*, is this them reacting to you getting kicked out? They're coming by with fucking fruit baskets?"

"I didn't ask them to. They're my friends. They want to help."

Elijah recoiled. "Are you fucking serious? God, of course you are. Look at you. You have one little hiccup and the whole fucking world shows up to wipe your hole. You fucking entitled *asshole*. Go call up your boy toy. Take your offerings from your fucking admirers and *drown in them*. Leave me the fuck alone."

"I want to help you."

"Am I your good deed for the day? What are you going to do, share your gift cards and groceries?"

"I don't know—maybe. Why are you yelling? I'm *trying to help*."

"Do you have a spare thirty thousand a year, hon? Because that's what I need help with. I need a goddamn college education so I can maybe get a real job because I don't want to live on the streets of Minneapolis and suck dick and take it raw up the ass until I contract AIDS and die. Unlike you, I don't have adoring hordes rushing to bring me milk money when Mommy and Daddy hurt my feelings."

God, *enough*. "Maybe you *would* have adoring hordes if you weren't such a caustic ass."

At this point Elijah's face was weird, as if he were

some kind of explosion held back behind rapidly thawing ice. "If I weren't such a caustic asshole, *I would have killed myself years ago.*" For the barest second tears shone in Elijah's eyes, and he all but snarled. "There. I've told you, and now you can cry for me, Argentina. *Leave me the fuck alone.*"

Aaron leaned forward. "No."

He worried Elijah was going to hit him. "I hate you. I hate how you're cute. That you're gay, have a boyfriend who tricked me but fell for you. I hate how the college loves you and you practically have your name on a plaque and then this happens—I bet you already have a scholarship, don't you, you *fucking asshole.*" Tears leaked out of his eyes, and he wiped them furiously away. "Now. This is the part where you protest you didn't ask for any of this, it all just sort of happened to you, blah, blah blah. Right?" He curled his hands into fists, unclenching his jaw enough to bite off the rest. "It *only makes me hate you more.*"

Aaron wasn't sure why all this yelling, which normally would have him cowering, only calmed him down. "So you don't want any of the gift cards at all? Not even the pizza ones?"

Elijah shut his eyes. "Shut up. I'm done talking to you."

"No, you're not."

"Oh, I so fucking am."

"Just because people are running up to save me doesn't mean I don't know exactly how it feels to have the people who are supposed to be on your side suddenly not be." He waved his hand at the bed full of gifts in disgust. "You don't think I'd trade it all for parents who wouldn't do this? You want to feel like an asshole, try having your boyfriend, his family, and all your friends shower you with stuff to try and fill the hole inside you. It doesn't work. It's still a hole." Rage which had built in him for years, buried under his caution and reserve, bubbled out, landing entirely in Elijah's lap. Aaron rose, pacing back and forth in the space between their bed and Elijah's desk. "I've done whatever they've told me for *years*, let them move me around and divide up my life and take away friends and activities, all because I was afraid of this—I stand up for myself for half a second, and none of it matters."

"Cry me a river."

"*Fuck you.* Hate me all you want, but none of it matters when you feel like shit inside. Nobody can buy you a parent who loves you. No amount of ramen noodles or gift cards or scholarships can replace the fact that the people who are supposed to be on your side unless you rob a bank or kill somebody won't help you out of a gutter. Giles's mom? She'd help him hide the fucking body. She spent over four thousand dollars on me and stuffed five hundred dollars into my wallet. Everybody's lining up to save me." The tears he hadn't shed, not even when Walter was crying on him, broke over the edge of his dam. "All but the two people I want to tell me they love me for what I am, that whatever I do, whatever I am is okay." He laughed, a bitter, broken sound. "Okay. Yeah. I get why you're such an asshole now. But fucking knock it off. Don't pull this shit with me. Not anymore."

Elijah stared at him, still rigid, and Aaron stared back, pretty fucking amped himself.

Elijah looked away. He rolled his eyes, but all the spit was out of him. "I need a cigarette. You going to follow me and lecture or stay here and suck your thumb?"

It was a weird victory, and Aaron wasn't sure what to do with it, but he was taking it all the same. "I'll come. Except I wish you were going off to down a fifth of something instead of smoke."

Elijah, it turned out, was pretty when he smiled, even when it was a nasty one. "Oh, I've got that too. Come on, roomie. Let's go hang out at the Dumpster and get shitfaced."

Aaron bowed low as he gestured at the door. "Lead the way, asshole."

Chapter Twenty-Seven

I T WAS COLD outside, but not windy, and it wasn't snowing. Elijah led Aaron to a partition beside a Dumpster, where he produced a small bottle of liquor—vodka, most likely, but Aaron wasn't sure—from one pocket and a packet of off-brand cigarettes and a lighter from another. He offered both to Aaron.

Aaron accepted the bottle but not the cigarettes. "Is it okay to smoke here?"

Elijah gave him a look as he lit up. "No. It's not okay to drink when you're twenty, either, and you're not supposed to perform sex for money at any age. Do you want to call the cops, or should I?"

It was going to be a few hours before Aaron developed a callus for Elijah's barbs. "Thanks for the drink," he said, because it was the only thing he could think of. He unscrewed the cap and took a heavy hit. And winced. It was *bad* vodka.

But it rubbed the edge off as it was supposed to. Aaron shut his eyes and drank deeply.

Elijah watched him with interest as he smoked, then held his hand out for the bottle. "You're no stranger to sin yourself, cowboy. You put alcohol away like a pro. Here I thought you were going to get prissy and mother hen about the sex thing, but you're too busy getting ready for your first AA chip, aren't you?"

Aaron held his hand out for the bottle. "I drank a lot in high school. Haven't here, mostly because it's harder to do."

"Not if you know the right people." Elijah took a long drag and blew smoke up into the air.

Obviously Elijah did. "It's kind of weird, talking to you after dead silence this whole time."

"It's not what I expected, no." Elijah leaned against the wall. "So. They kicked you out. Clothes on your back and nothing else?"

"Giles's dad went over and got some of my stuff, but my laptop is probably destroyed along with all my composition notes."

Elijah straightened. "Fuck me, you don't have your *laptop*? God, I wondered where it went."

"Why are you all upset? It's *my* laptop." He paused, catching up. "What do you mean, you wondered where it went?"

Elijah grimaced. "I used your laptop every time I knew you weren't going to be in the room and you left it behind." He gave Aaron a mock puppy-dog look. "Are you gonna be mad at me?"

"I'm not in love with you, no. Why didn't—?"

"They've been suspicious of me ever since Thanksgiving, and they put in key-logging software on my laptop and my phone. Yours was still clean, though."

Aaron deflated, weirded out both by the idea of spying parents and the idea they *might* have spied on him too. "You could have asked."

"You could have said no."

True. "It's still pretty skeevy."

"Yeah, well, I can't use it now, so congrats." He took a long drag, and for the first time that night, Elijah seemed wounded.

"Giles's mother gave me a tablet and a new phone. If you can keep from mocking me, I'll let you use them both." He'd talk to Giles about the extra laptops his roommate had. Now he wished he'd let Mrs. Mulder buy him one after all.

Elijah passed over the bottle, his snark melting away. "Thanks. I appreciate it."

"You know, you could have been talking to me this whole time. You're an asshole, and I think you're going to need a mountain of therapy to get your head on right, but you could have fucking talked to me."

Elijah's smile tipped sideways. "I would have, maybe, if I'd known you weren't all goody-two-shoes."

Aaron sat on a discarded box, dusting off the snow first. "So what are you going to do about your parents? Because if you tell me the same thing you've been doing, you're an idiot. You look as if you're about an inch away from coming apart most days—and you're worse when your parents come. You're a walking zombie after a break. How do you plan to survive summer?"

"I don't know." Elijah ashed out his cigarette in the snow and pulled out another. "I have an online friend in Baltimore I've considered begging for a summer of couch-surfing, but I don't know him well enough. Plus I'd have to trick or hitch all the way there. That's a lot of truck-stop cock, and I'm not sure I'm up for it."

"You should let me help you."

"Right, because you're in such a great position to promise aid right now."

"Did you miss the part where I basically tripped and everybody on planet Earth swooped in to help?"

Elijah snorted as the flare of his lighter illuminated his face. "You think packets of ramen and cookies are gonna help me? Fuck. You really think they're going to help *you*?"

Aaron stared at him, a pit forming in his stomach. "What do you mean?"

He took another drag. "Here's the deal, princess: you're alone now. You think I went back to the 'rents because life got a little cold? It was a *fucking arctic winter*, babe. I went to the streets pretty goddamn jaded, but I did things that curl my toes, and it still was barely enough to survive. It got to the point I started *looking* for white slavers because I figured at least they'd give me a square meal every day. One night it got so bad I almost died. A guy—" He shut his eyes, smoking again before he continued. "Someone got me out of a bad situation, pressed a wad of hundreds in my hand, and told me to go the hell home. So I did." He exhaled and stared right at Aaron. "That's what waits for you."

Walter rang in Aaron's head, his vows to help him no matter what pealing like a church bell. *My net, like Dr. Mulder said.* "It wouldn't happen to me, not in the same way. But I'm sorry it happened to you."

He passed the vodka over before Elijah asked for it. Elijah took a long hit, and when he mashed out his cigarette, he looked weary and defeated. "I'm probably going to run off to the Cities again come May. I think it would be different this time—I'm older, and I know where the dangerous places are. If I can trick enough over the summer, maybe I can put together a down payment for an apartment in the fall."

"Jesus, *stop*. Do not fucking sell yourself."

"Why not? It's my damn body. Nobody's making me. It's a commodity. It's not much, but it's what I have. Hell of a lot better than Walmart. If I could get up the courage to go bare, I'd clean up, but—"

"*Stop talking.*" Aaron pushed to his feet and loomed over Elijah. "I don't care that nobody's making you. It's not safe. If you want to do it because you're some kind of batshit daredevil, fine, but don't do it to survive when there's another way."

"There isn't another way, Pollyanna, not without relying on other people, and I'm not going there. Ever."

"How is it, exactly, you think letting people at your ass isn't a risk? Maybe it's more a risk to your body than your heart, but—"

Elijah shoved him and staggered out from behind the Dumpster, shaking. "I don't need to listen to your self-righteous bullshit. You don't know shit about my *heart*."

Aaron followed him. "You will listen, you stupid idiot. Everybody needs a net."

"Well I don't have one."

"I do. And you're going to share it whether you want it or not." He closed the distance between them, caught Elijah's hand and held it tight. "You're going to borrow my net, Elijah, until you get your own."

Elijah tried to be caustic, but hurt won out. "Why? Why would you help me?"

"I told you. I might be eighteen, not sixteen, and I might have a lot of people waiting in the wings to help me, but I'm never going to forget the horrible feeling of being cast out like that for being nothing more than myself. Because I *can* help you, if you stop being so fucking nasty for ten minutes." He arched an eyebrow. "And, honestly, because for once I can be the guy who helps instead of the clueless idiot everybody has to save."

Elijah said nothing, didn't even laugh.

"Let me work on it. Talk to some people. In the meantime, though, talk to *me*. Let me help you. Use the gift cards. Use my tablet and phone. Quit going to that goddamned Bible study and live your own fucking life."

"If I quit, the toads will report me. I have to keep up the charade until I have a better plan, because they'll stop tuition payments and yank me out of here so fast if they even *think* anything is going on."

God, that was so fucking sick. "Then we'll figure something out *fast*. Okay?"

Elijah didn't answer, only nudged Aaron's foot with his. "If you're my net, does that mean I get to call you Spider-Man?" He raked his gaze over Aaron, letting a whisper of approval escape. "Though if you're a Marvel hero, you're Captain America."

"I'd go on my knees for Chris Evans in a hot second."

Elijah laughed. "You're fun when you start to get smashed, Cap. You need to do it more often."

Aaron accepted the flask with a grin and a wink. "Name the time and bring the goods, Loki, and I'm there."

Elijah snorted and lit another cigarette.

But he smiled the whole time he did it.

WHEN GILES ENTERED the cafeteria Monday morning to meet Aaron for breakfast, he saw his boyfriend sitting with Elijah. Giles stopped dead, wondering what the hell was going on.

Aaron waved him over.

Seriously, what the hell?

The weirdest part was, as uneasy as Giles felt about whatever this was, Elijah was even more skeptical, that much was clear. Elijah appeared ready to bolt at any second. What kept throwing Giles for a loop was how equally clear it was Aaron wasn't having any of it.

Aaron also looked good. Not only hot but put together, no more lost, dazed puppy but a guy with a mission. Apparently the mission had something to do with Elijah. Giles put down his tray and did his best to figure the rest of it out.

"Hey, you." Aaron smiled and moved closer as he sat down.

Giles tried not to stare at Elijah, but the way Aaron's roommate glowered, Giles felt like he'd sat down to breakfast with a tiger. "Hi, sweetie. You sleep okay?"

Elijah rolled his eyes. "Oh my God, I'm going to

stab you both in the neck with this butter knife if you don't stop being so cute."

Giles tensed, ready to snap, but Aaron dismissed Elijah with a mild wave. "Ignore him. He's not used to being with actual people."

Why is he here, exactly? Giles couldn't say that, so he attempted to make nice. "Did you...uh, have a good break?"

Elijah gave Aaron a look part fury, part desperation.

Giles decided he'd had enough. "Do one of you want to tell me what's going on?"

"I've been *adopted.*" Elijah's voice dripped with derision, and he gave Giles a freakish mock-smile. "*Congrats*, Daddy, it's a boy."

"You can be as snarky as you want," Aaron replied mildly, wiping his mouth with his napkin. "You're still meeting with Walter this weekend. Though I'll warn you, if you're mean to his fiancé, you'll find out what *fierce* means."

"I'll be good, Mommy, I promise. I won't sleep with Daddy anymore, either. Can I have a cookie now?"

"I'll see you after you get back from the toads. We'll make some plans."

"I think I'll sleep in the fucking Dumpster tonight, thanks."

"If you do, I'll be sure to let the maintenance staff know you smoke on campus grounds."

"Nobody needs this kind of net," Elijah murmured, rising with his tray. His long wool coat ballooned behind him as he stalked toward the conveyor belt taking used dishes to the kitchen.

Giles turned to his boyfriend in disbelief. "What in the hell is going on?"

Aaron had his phone out and was frowning at it. "Crap. I forgot I told Jilly I'd meet her in the lounge. But you haven't eaten." He rose and bussed Giles on the cheek. "You stay. I'll fill you in later."

Giles opened his mouth to argue, then cut himself off, changing his mind. "Okay. Will I see you at lunch?"

"Absolutely." Aaron all but ran away.

Giles watched him go, gave him a few seconds to get through the lobby. Then he rose, heading the way he'd seen Elijah go.

His quarry was halfway across the common by the time Giles spotted him, and he had to break into a trot across the snow to catch him. It didn't escape his attention that not only did Elijah hear him coming sooner than most people would have, he also tensed and turned around with a grip on the strap of his pack indicating he wouldn't hesitate to use it as a weapon.

"Oh *good*, it's you." Elijah shifted his pack on his shoulder. "So is this where you ask me what the hell is going on, or are you going to finally take me up on seconds? I warn you, my rates have gone *way* up."

God, this guy was an *ass*. "First one. And if you could skip the sarcasm and stick to the facts, that'd be great."

"Sorry, Romeo. Package deal." He pursed his lips into a mock pout. "Juliet didn't fill you in?"

"I wanted it straight from the wise guy's mouth. I

can tell whatever it is, it wasn't your idea."

Elijah snorted. "God, you must be *smart*. Yes, he's all about saving my sorry ass. Which, thanks to the pile of do-gooders eager to help *him* out, he wants to spread the love."

"What exactly is he saving you from? Your winning personality?"

"*Funny.*" Elijah crossed his arms over his chest. "None of this is necessary, girlfriend. You can stand down. I plan to humor him for a few days, after which I assume he'll see a squirrel and run across the lawn. I'll be out of your hair before your next hallway choral number or whatever you guys do over in the music building."

"*What* is he saving you from?"

Elijah glared, a tic forming in his cheek. "Russian gangs. I banged a delivery boy and shorted him his drug money. I have a huge price on my head."

"Anybody ever tell you they want to knock your fucking block off?"

He regretted the words even before he saw the shadow cross Elijah's face. "Nah. Can't say it's ever happened."

The wind was picking up, and Giles was cold, but he couldn't very well stalk off, no matter how much he wanted to. "That was a dumbass thing to say. I'm sorry."

"Take your pity and your concern and your apology off to class, Prince Charming. We're all good here in the trenches."

"If Aaron's made a project out of you, you've got

something wrong *other* than the huge stick you can't get out of your ass, so like it or not, you're my problem now."

"Bitch, you don't know *fuck all* about my problems. They're a hell of a lot more involved than someone shouting *fag* at me across the football field, so *back the hell off*."

Giles closed the distance between them, not slowing down this time when Elijah flinched. "I've had a little more than *fag* thrown at me, thanks. I just don't feel the need to flash it around like a *poor me* martyr poster." He swallowed his fury and forced himself to calm down. "If you'd quit fucking winding me up so I could talk to you as an actual human, that'd be great."

The wind left Elijah's sails, dragging his shoulders down and taking the piss out of his expression, leaving him ragged and weary-looking. "My parents are freak shows. Different than Aaron's, but he insisted on bonding. It's not as simple as he'd like to think, though. It's not simple at all, and nobody can help me, so let it go."

"Yeah, probably not happening." Giles stuffed his hands into his pockets. "What kind of freak show we talking here? I'm guessing religious homophobic wing nuts to start, given your tchotchke collection?"

"Did you notice it's freezing out here? Maybe *you* like blue balls, but I don't."

"Then I'm taking you to the coffee shop next to the White House, and you're telling me everything you've got."

Elijah's smile was grim. "Yeah. It'll be the student

union coffee shop, because if I go north of Broadway, my father will call and ask why my GPS says I've left campus." When Giles's eyes widened, Elijah held out his arm in an ironic *ta-da*. "Oh, sweetheart. We're just getting warmed up."

Giles had a bad feeling Elijah wasn't kidding. "Let's go inside. Coffee's on me."

Chapter Twenty-Eight

"MY PARENTS ARE what you might call rabid, crazy, conservative Christians." Elijah slouched in his corner of the booth and stared at his steaming mug of black coffee as he spoke. "They were always a little weird, but then my older brother went off to Afghanistan when I was ten and didn't come home. It was right about the same time they got wrapped up in this crazy right-wing church. We'd always been Lutheran, but they started going there for support-the-troop rallies and political events. They tipped slowly over the deep end and never came up for air. My dad has an arsenal in the garage because our president is from Kenya and the government is coming any second to gay marry us all, et cetera. Three times he's fired at deliverymen, to the point that we have to go to a UPS substation to get our stuff because they won't deliver. He sent Dan Savage hate mail until a lawyer served him a threatening letter."

Giles grimaced and gripped his mocha latte. "And then you were gay."

"The living poster boy of everything they hated, or at least a live-in outlet for their hurt and sense of alienation. I had a few good teachers in middle school but not in high school, and by then home had become a living hell. I took off. It didn't go well." He sipped his coffee. "It wasn't so much the physical. That I'd accurately predicted. It was how much it hurt inside." He ran a hand over his face. "The Cities were both better and worse. I got involved in a program in St. Paul at this youth center, but they were always in and out of funding, because this was right at the worst part of the Great Recession. There were more opportunities but also more dangers. Plus I was only sixteen. You're not quite as ballsy as you think you are at sixteen."

This was like some kind of movie of the week, except awful because it was real, not because of the cheesy writing. "So what the hell did you do?"

"I went home. I found a police officer and told them I was a runaway. I told my parents God had come to me and I was ready to repent."

"And your parents believed you?"

Elijah lifted his gaze, and Giles shivered at the dark smile. "Eventually. I had to go to the crazy pastor they loved so much, who never actually did anything outright to me, but sure loved to touch my ass. He *did* get caught with another boy, which was bad for the kid but good for me. My parents moved me back to the Lutheran church, which is still so conservative it nearly broke off when the Evangelical Lutheran Church of America *went faggot*, as my dad likes to say, but at least the pedophiles stayed in their pews. It also meant all the Lutheran colleges were on the table once they decided I had repented enough. It helped how I stayed well past my eighteenth birthday. Seemed more legit that I stayed when I could legally walk out the door. It's true, I could, but I'd learned well the lesson I needed better ground under me before I could do it again."

"So you're doing this for three more years?"

Shrugging, Elijah tapped out a nervous rhythm on the tabletop. "I worked like crazy to get a scholarship to Saint Timothy. I wanted a full ride so I could thumb my nose at them and run, but all I got was ten grand a year. So I'm stuck pretending to be a good Christian not-fag for three more years." He shut his eyes. "Except I can't. I don't know if they're worse because they're convinced I'm up to something, if they think the liberal college is corrupting me, or if they're not any different but getting away washed off enough of a scab and I can't stomach them now, period. I can't stand one more weekend at home, let alone a summer. It's all I can do to bite my tongue when they visit, which is every weekend now. All the way from South Dakota they come, to make sure I'm not going to hell."

"You should talk to a counselor here. God, they whipped a full ride for Aaron out of thin fucking air in ten minutes."

Elijah's face turned dark and angry. "Yes, well, I'm not your darling boyfriend. I don't look like a stock photo ad for American boy. I'm not even a cute twink. I'm a femmy gay reject, and as you've pointed out several times, I'm not polite. And don't start in on Aaron's build-me-a-net crap. It doesn't work that way. I know. Do you want to know how many people saw my parents treating me like their live-in pariah and did anything? How many people saw me on the street in

Minneapolis and Saint Paul and gave me more than a few quarters or told me to go home? Or hit me, or—" He pursed his lips and drew his mug up against his body. "It's not going to work. I'm not the kind of guy they move mountains for. I got the message loud and clear."

Giles stared at him, trying to figure out what to say, except he truly didn't know how to counter that. He *did* get what Elijah was talking about. People liked to help pretty people, and Giles and Elijah weren't pretty. Not just in appearance but total package. Elijah wasn't ugly, but he was seriously rangy, his features feminine and yet not pretty or delicate. Giles, even hiding his scars, was the same. The battles they'd fought, inside and out, showed on their skin. They were not the poster boys. They were simply boys.

"Look." He pushed his coffee aside and leaned forward on his elbows on the tabletop. "I get what you're saying. I'm going to point out, though, your attitude doesn't help. If it came down to it, my mother and father would help you find somewhere safe to be. They'd do it because that's who they are. I also don't think anybody helping Aaron would be all *whatever* if they find out you're in a similar sinking ship. And no. He has no idea how grisly the world can be. It doesn't mean he's an idiot. It means he's not quite as scarred up and defensive as you and I are. This is not exactly a bad thing to be around. It's easier to live in the world when you can forget it's constantly trying to eat you raw."

Elijah stared at the ceiling. "It's more difficult when

I connect to people. Makes it impossible to fake it."

"Then stop faking it. Don't go home with them. Ditch your phone with the tracking software. I'll spring for a pay-as-you-go."

Elijah kept his gaze pinned upward, but his hands tightened on his mug. "They'd cut me off the second they figured it out. They'd come here and make a scene. I mean, a *scene*. If they couldn't get me to leave, they'd work to get me thrown out. My father hates the idea of me a lot more than he ever loved me. If he can't mold me into the son he lost, he'll take me out. He's said so more than once."

Giles fought a shiver. "So you're—what? Saying they'd what?"

It killed Giles how hollow and empty Elijah looked. "I'm saying I have no idea what they're capable of. I'm saying you don't get it."

Shadowed, sharp memories of Aaron, stunned and sock-footed, trudging through ice and snow while his father gazed on, eyes burning with fury, washed out of the dark corners of Giles's mind. "I get it more than you think I might." He shut his eyes, pinching the bridge of his nose as he tried to massage out a plan. "Okay—here's the thing. Crazy parents aside, you're not sixteen and friendless now. Even though, weirdly, you needed more help then, the narrative is a lot better today. You walk up to one reporter and tell them your fundy parents have kicked you out on your ear? First question will be what's the college doing for you, and the St. Timothy doesn't want bad publicity. But this is all assuming we can't find ten different sponsors for you to live with."

Elijah lowered his glare to Giles. "You're living in a fucking fantasy. Why would people who don't know me help me out?"

"Because all the people I'm thinking of are gay or have gay sons. Because we live in the age where a Make-A-Wish kid says he wants to be Batman and a whole city turns itself inside out to let him play superhero. Because even I could figure out how to package this and sell it and get you a GoFundMe account on social media, but I'd let Walter handle it because he could probably get a parade tossed in. Because though you're mocking it, you *do* have a net, and it starts with Aaron. And me."

"Ooh, maybe your glee club could be my flash mob. I could live off the YouTube proceeds."

"See, that's the kind of asshole comment not helping you out."

"It's the kind of asshole comment that's kept me from taking one of my dad's guns and applying it to my brain stem." Elijah shut his eyes and rubbed his temples. "You people are exhausting. Is this friend of Aaron's going to coo all over me too?"

Giles got a sudden image of Walter Lucas and Kelly Davidson taking on the prickly Elijah Prince, and he couldn't help it, he laughed out loud. "God. I can't wait. I'm getting popcorn."

Elijah flipped him off, but it was a weary gesture. And though Elijah didn't smile, Giles would have sworn the guy looked a baby bit relieved.

IN THE WEEK after Elijah's confession, Aaron's roommate was ten thousand times more caustic than he'd
ever been, and yet not one of the barbs made Aaron
tremble. One night as Aaron stood with him at the
Dumpster while he smoked, Elijah got frustrated he
wasn't getting any purchase and switched tactics. "You
do get that all you're doing is projecting onto me,
thinking if you can save me, somebody can save you?"

Aaron leaned against the brick wall of the dorm,
watching his breath come out in white clouds as he
stared up at the clear night sky. "Maybe. Except I'm
starting to feel like you're my training wheels to
figuring out how to save myself."

Swearing under his breath, Elijah stomped out the
butt of his cigarette. "I liked you better when you were
a cowering doormat."

Aaron had to bite back a smile. No, Elijah didn't.
But he wasn't going to point that out, because unlike
Elijah, he wasn't cruel.

Of course, now Aaron knew Elijah was cruel because he couldn't stand for the world to be unkind to
him first. Accepting affection made him uneasy,
whereas deflecting taunts was business as usual. The
first time they walked through the union together and a
group of frat boys shouted a fag comment, one clearly
aimed at Elijah, Aaron had tried to call them on it, but
Elijah only rolled his eyes. "Put down the shield, Cap,"
he murmured, dragging Aaron away. But five minutes
later a group of choir people stopped them on the
bridge between buildings for a visit, trying to politely
get to know Aaron's roommate, and Elijah looked like

he wanted to jump through one of the windows.

After that, Aaron introduced Elijah to people slowly, more deliberately. He started with Jilly, whom he thought of as bottled sunshine and happiness, but Mina connected with Elijah more strongly. They sat in the Titus lounge for hours just talking, sometimes even laughing. It was Mina who got Elijah to admit what all those notebooks were for: they were stories. Elijah was a writer. He wrote steamy gay erotica as Naughty Nate, posting some of it online but mostly hoarding it because someday he wanted to publish.

He wouldn't let Aaron see a word of it, but he let Mina read his works in progress.

Next Elijah met Marius. That was accidental, because Marius came up to them in the coffee shop to ask Aaron a question, but since it was just him, and since Marius was cool *and* sex on a stick, Aaron gave it a go. Though Elijah was clearly nervous at first, he unraveled pretty quickly, at least enough to behave like an actual human. When Marius invited him over to the White House for movies on Friday night and Elijah had to decline, Marius winked and said, "Some other time."

The only thing Aaron didn't like was that Elijah kept going to Bible study. They fought about it constantly, and every time Aaron lost the argument.

"You need to get it through your fat head," Elijah ground out as he worked the knot of his tie up to his throat, "that the toads report directly to my parents. They've already noticed I have all these new friends and my fag roommate has become super chummy with me. My dad shouted at me for an hour about it last night."

Aaron sat up straighter on his bed. This was news to him. "What did he say? What did *you* say?"

"He told me I wasn't to speak to you. He's already called the college six times trying to get me a new roommate, but the dorms are slammed. He's threatening to move me off campus so I can stay with a fundy family."

"*What?* He can't—"

Elijah rolled his eyes. "No, he can't. Freshmen need a special dispensation to live off campus, and I asked the dean of students not to give me one."

He'd talked to the dean? "Are you telling me you actually reported them, finally?" From the locked-down way Elijah stared at himself in the mirror, as if he were trying hard not to be terrified, Aaron got his answer. He wanted to hug Elijah, but he hugged himself instead. "God, leave it to you to bury the lead."

"Yes, well, I don't know if it helped much." Elijah gave up on his tie and went to the window, parting the blinds to stare out at the common. "Mostly the dean didn't know what to do with me. Now I have an appointment with the campus pastor tomorrow morning."

That made Aaron stand up. "You *what*? Oh, fuck."

"For counseling, dummy. Not rehabilitation." Elijah laughed. "You're so funny, the way you hate religion. You hate it more than me, I think."

Yeah, Aaron wasn't much of a fan. He hadn't seen it do much good for anyone so far. "How do you know this guy isn't going to dump Jesus on you?"

"Because it's Pastor Schulz. You keep forgetting I

got here by saying I'm majoring in religion. I've had him for two classes now, and I know the whole pastoral staff. Some of them are lemmings, yes, but my dad would pass out to know how liberal they all are. I've gotten a lot of mileage out of knowing how out of sync what they're teaching me is with what my family would like me to be learning." He stood over Aaron, amused but also...grateful. "Schulz won't haul me off to the gulag. I don't think there's much he can actually do, but you're right. It'll be good to talk to someone who can help me process the finer points of how to deal with them. And that's all happening because of you, Cap, so thanks."

Aaron was pretty sure he never said *go talk to the campus pastor*, but if Elijah was okay with it, he guessed he would be too. "Walter and Kelly are coming tomorrow afternoon. They'll get here before your parents, don't worry."

Elijah's eyebrow went up. "You're all frowny. What's up?" When Aaron averted his gaze, Elijah sat beside him on the bed and took his hand, patting it with mock tenderness. "Come on. Spill."

Aaron swallowed the lump of guilt in his throat. "Walter shouldn't be able to get here so early because he's supposed to have an internship. He doesn't anymore, and it's because of me."

Elijah snorted. "*Please*, hubris much—"

"He worked for my dad's firm. He's pissed at what my dad did, and as soon as my dad showed up at the office while he was there, Walter laid into him and got fired. He hasn't worked there for weeks now. I just found out."

An awkward pause ended with an even more uncertain pat from Elijah on Aaron's leg. "I'm…sorry. Except…damn. Talk about Captain America."

"Walter's a lot more Iron Man." Slumping, Aaron shut his eyes. "I hate that it happened because of me. He says not to worry about it, he already has a new one lined up, but I still hate it."

"Be glad you have friends who love you." This time Elijah's leg-patting was a lot more self-assured. "I need to go kiss a few toads. I have to meet them in the lobby because Reece is terrified of the guy who lives across from us after their last throw-down. Don't wait up for me, sweetheart."

"You know I will."

"I do." Elijah squeezed Aaron's hand, then, tentatively, pressed a kiss on Aaron's cheek as he rose. "Polish your shield. We're gonna storm Asgard when I get home."

Aaron did wait up. Giles came over and waited with him, snuggling with him on the bed as they stared at the door.

"He's been a bigger wreck every night." Aaron drew Giles's arms tighter around him, trying to squeeze out the lump of fear in his belly. "I hate it when he goes. All they do is fuck with his head."

"You said he's talking to the campus pastor tomorrow. Maybe he'll help."

"Maybe he'll make him worse." Aaron had to work to unclench his jaw. "I'm glad Walter is coming. He says he has some ideas."

"A lot of people are helping. Damien came up to me in the lounge a little bit ago—that's why I was late coming over. He says the house had a meeting, and they'll take Elijah in if it comes to it. Make the butler pantry into a bedroom like it used to be. They'll split his rent between them, and Baz said he'd cover food and incidentals, help him find a job in Campustown. Obviously it'd be better if Elijah could stay in school, but it'd be a hell of a lot better than home or the streets."

That *was* good news, though Aaron wondered again what the connection between Baz and Elijah was, and if Elijah would accept help from him. "What about next weekend when we're all gone to semifinals? What if his parents go psycho and kidnap him while we're gone?"

"Then we take him with us as water boy or something. Or he goes with Walter. We'll figure it out, babe." Giles hugged Aaron tighter and kissed his ear.

The kiss had morphed into something a little more delicious when Aaron's phone buzzed on the desk beside his bed. He broke away to check it, then winced and tossed it back down as if it had burned him.

Giles immediately scooped it up. "What's wrong? Who's texting you?"

"My dad." Aaron burrowed into Giles's chest, shutting his eyes. "It doesn't matter how many times Brian blocks him. He just gets a new number. The RA said he's been calling the school too."

"Why the hell didn't you tell me about this?" Giles thumbed at the phone for a few seconds, then went rigid in Aaron's arms. "Fuck. Have you read any of these texts, hon?"

The hollow in Aaron's belly expanded. "No. Why?"

"Because he's been threatening you with all kinds of crap all week. He's coming tomorrow to talk some sense into you, says this last message." Giles threw the phone onto the desk. "Jesus fucking Christ."

"It'll be okay," Aaron whispered, though he had to step on terror to get the words out.

Giles had his own phone out and was texting madly. "I'm telling my parents to come. And warning Walter it's going down. God, it's gonna be the fucking O.K. Corral tomorrow night. Maybe we can put your dad in with the Princes and they'll kill each other." When Aaron shivered, Giles put the phone down and held him close.

The door to the room opened. They broke apart enough for Aaron to turn and see his barely held together roommate come through the door. Elijah tried for a sarcastic smile and wave, but mostly he slumped against the wall by the closet, looking like he'd been dragged sideways through hell. In a bad suit.

"Fuck this." Giles motioned impatiently to Elijah. "Bitch, put on something human and get over here."

"I'm not in the mood for a three-way," Elijah replied, but his shade fell flat, no snark to hold it up. He undid his tie with shaking hands.

"Tough. You're getting one. Put on a T-shirt and get the fuck over here, because I'm hugging you both. Fuck your fucking fathers. I will daddy both your asses, and right now you need some hugs."

To Aaron's surprise, Elijah came. He moved stiffly,

uncertainly, but he let Giles manipulate him between himself and Aaron, pressing his face to the same place on Giles's chest where Aaron's face had been up until a few minutes ago. Giles drew them both close, folding them into a boy-burrito on the narrow dorm bed.

"You're safe, you got it? Both of you." He stroked first Aaron's hair, then Elijah's. "All they can do is yell at you now. Elijah, we have a place lined up for you to live if the college doesn't come through. This is before your pastor visit and before Walter." He paused to check his phone, then grunted in satisfaction. "My parents are coming down. We'll have the full posse tomorrow night. We'll sing 'Kumbaya' until you two get it through your heads that you have a new family. Your real parents suck. That's fine. We've replaced them four times over."

Aaron shut his eyes, soaking in Giles's vow. He didn't weep, and neither did his roommate. But he swore he felt the same heaviness rising from both of them, just as surely as he knew Giles took it, tied it in a knot, and tossed it away where it couldn't hurt them anymore.

Chapter Twenty-Nine

ON FRIDAY AT three in the afternoon, Aaron led his roommate to the student lounge in the music building, where Walter, Kelly, and Giles waited.

They'd elected to meet there because the toads had been shadowing Elijah all day. Aaron figured it would take some balls to come onto music turf. The one hiccup in the plan was that when Elijah came into the room and saw not just Walter and Kelly but Mina, Jilly, Damien, Karen, Marius, and Giles, Aaron had to physically restrain him from bolting.

"This is too many people." Elijah glanced over Aaron's shoulder in terror. "What the hell are they all doing here?"

"Caring about you."

"They're freaking me the fuck out. Why couldn't we do this in our room?"

"Because your parents might show up there. Or mine."

Elijah relaxed only a fraction. "I don't like this."

"I know." Aaron kneaded his shoulder gently. "But they're all good people. They want to help you."

"Fine. But you're holding my goddamned hand."

Aaron did.

He introduced Elijah around the table, then sat between him and Walter. Walter leaned forward on his elbows as he addressed Elijah. "Thank you for coming. I understand you're overwhelmed right now. I want you to know, though, that everyone in this room is here for you."

Elijah stared at his lap. He gripped Aaron's hand so hard he was probably losing blood to his fingers.

Walter continued, still speaking softly. "I want to lay out some long-term plans with you, but for now I think we need to address the short term. Your parents are coming today, yes?"

Elijah tossed his cell phone onto the table. "They'll text any minute to tell me they're in town. It's kind of weird that they haven't contacted me yet."

"I know this is stating the obvious, but it's important for everyone here, including you, that we make matters expressly clear. Is it your wish to not see them this weekend, to not return with them at any time in the near future to South Dakota?"

Elijah snorted. "In *any* future." When Walter waited, he cleared his throat and spoke again, voice wavering only a little. "I don't wish to see my parents anymore or have any association with them. But this means I will have nothing."

Aaron squeezed his hand back. "You have us."

Damien leaned forward from his seat on the other side of Kelly. "What did Pastor Schulz say to you when you met with him? Did he offer any help with tuition?"

Elijah shrugged. "He said he'd look into it. Mostly he told me not to worry and to take it one day at a time. I think he's talking to the department about a scholarship like they did for Aaron, but I don't think I want to stay a religion major after this. So I don't know."

"But Giles told you about the White House, right? How they'll take you in?" This was Mina, and she gave Giles a look that said, *You'd better have told him.*

Elijah's lips thinned into a line. "Yes—but…" He glanced uneasily around the table. "I don't understand *why*. I mean—" He broke off and sagged in his chair. "You don't know me."

This time it was Marius who spoke, his deep, gentle voice rumbling across the table. "We haven't all had your experience, or Aaron's. But everyone here has had tough times. Maybe ours weren't so tough, but we know what it's like to feel alone. You can't bring my mom back from ovarian cancer, and I can't erase anyone else's past. But I can help get you to a better future. We can all do that for each other. You don't have to be a music major, or even be in the orchestra or choir. You just have to be a human."

Elijah looked overwhelmed, and Aaron wondered what he should say, but Walter eased into the conversation then, using the same comforting tones. "I'm a law student, not a lawyer, but I wanted to put the option on the table for you so you understand your rights. I've already put out a few feelers, and I know several people who would help you pro bono."

"Why would he need a lawyer?" Karen asked.

Walter kept his gaze on Elijah. "He might not. It depends on how his family behaves. Elijah hinted to

Aaron and Giles his parents would do more than just cut him off if he stopped dancing to their tune. They would actively try and remove him from a life they see as unfit."

On the table Elijah's phone lit up and started to buzz across the Formica. He grimaced. "This will be them. Do I answer? Because they're going to come after me no matter how hard I tell them to fuck off."

Weirdly, this made Walter smile. "If they try to force you to stay with them, we can sue them. There's precedent—a woman in Ohio took her parents to court for stalking and got a restraining order against them when they wouldn't stop trying to control her life. She had the same tracking software as you on her electronics."

Elijah didn't seem impressed. "They make her parents pay for her school?"

"You're an adult. Can't make them do anything, particularly if you're telling them to fuck off. Which is why I'm asking what you want. Do you want to go to school, or do you just want out?"

Elijah looked so tired. "I don't know what I want. I'd love to be at school, in the dorm with Aaron but as a real college student for a change, not a fugitive. Except I'm not naive enough to think that's actually on the table. Even if it is, I can't see Timothy springing for a full ride for three and a half years, which is what it would come down to."

Which was exactly what Nussy had promised Aaron would have. Guilt gnawed at his stomach. "There has to be a way."

"*How?* Somebody's got to pay for it, and honestly, I don't want to be someone's charity case where they pet me and call me poor baby and live out their fantasies of saving somebody. I don't want to owe anyone either. But I don't want to work for slave wages at McDonald's or Walmart." He rolled his eyes. "In other words, I want a goddamned fairy tale, which isn't happening. This is a stupid idea."

He started to fidget, and Aaron did his best to soothe him. "The pastor guy might have it right. Let's start with today. What should we do right now, with your parents coming?"

"Meet them." This was Damien, who had an iron look about his jaw. "Face them down. We'll go with you—we'll all be there when you tell them no. We'll do the same thing to Aaron's dad when he arrives."

Kelly nodded at Elijah's phone. "How close are they? Did they say?"

"We should call campus security, let them know this is going down," Karen suggested. "Get them alerted before any trouble starts."

"Too late."

They all glanced up—Baz stood in the doorway. Beside Aaron, Elijah stiffened, but Baz didn't look at him. He stared right at Marius and Damien, jerking his head to indicate the outside. "They're here. Elijah's parents. Campus security." His gaze slid to Aaron. "And your dad."

Aaron could barely breathe, and the world tried to spin away.

Elijah held him fast. "Oh no, you don't. You don't

drag me into this by my nose and then check out in a panic attack." He was deliberately not looking at Baz.

Walter, however, was. In fact, he rose, staring at Baz like he'd seen a ghost. "Sebastian? Sebastian *Acker*?"

Baz's gaze jerked to him, and then he too went still. "Lucas. What the fuck are you doing here?"

"I'm friends with Aaron. And Giles." He was trying to put on a good face but couldn't quite manage it. "Jesus—how...how have you been?"

"Maybe another time, bud?" Baz snapped.

Walter shook his head like he was trying to clear it. "Yeah...sorry." He kept trying to get on top of himself but kept failing. "So the gang's all here." He turned to the table. "What do we do next?"

"What we do best. Face the music." Damien pushed to his feet and motioned to the table to do the same. "Up. Everybody. We're all going out there, letting the parents yell, showing them we don't give a shit, and then we're going to the White House to drink ourselves into comas."

"We still have rehearsals, Mr. Student Director," Karen pointed out.

Damien rolled his eyes. "Fine. We'll drink ourselves into comas *after rehearsals*."

They rose, but as everyone filed out of the room it was obvious they took special care to keep Aaron and Elijah in the center of their herd. Walter stayed right beside them, as did Giles.

As they passed Baz, though, both Walter and Elijah got funny again. So did Baz.

Aaron looked between the two of them. "How do

you two know Baz?"

Elijah sagged, still shaking. "He's the one who told me to go home."

That didn't make any sense, so Aaron turned to Walter. "And you?"

"I knew him in high school. Before the sunglasses."

Wonderful. Another cryptic answer. Aaron wanted to press for details, but they were heading out the door now. As soon as they cleared the corner of the building, he saw his dad looming over the campus security officer, shouting demands. Mr. Prince stood beside him, red-faced and bellowing in harmony. On the snowy knoll just beyond the parking lot Reece and Emily stood with the rest of the toads, wrapped in self-righteousness. Mrs. Prince was with them, arms bundled around her coat, her expression impassive and colder than the ice she stood on.

Walter drew Kelly closer to him even as he tightened his arm around Aaron. "You're going to be okay. Both of you. All they're going to do is yell. Sticks and stones and so on."

Aaron tried to put on a brave face. "We're dangerous because we know how to survive."

Giles, who stood between Elijah and Aaron, squeezed Aaron's hand as he laughed. "My mother would be so proud of you."

Elijah rolled his eyes and opened his mouth to deliver what undoubtedly would have been a wry remark.

He never got a chance, though, because before he could speak, Mr. Prince pulled his gun.

ONE MOMENT GILES was walking, gripping Aaron's arm as he tracked Mr. Seavers's wild hand gestures. The next thing he knew, everyone was screaming.

"*Down,*" Walter shouted, voice breaking as he pushed Kelly onto the frozen asphalt. Aaron tugged at Giles and Elijah, except Elijah wouldn't go.

"Behind a car." Elijah dragged Aaron and Giles with him to a red Toyota truck.

That was when Mr. Prince moved, swinging his arm, a small black gun trained on his son.

In the movies when someone drew a firearm, everything slowed down, but in real life things happened so fast Giles couldn't keep up. *He* felt slow—his brain tripped over itself trying to react, yanking Aaron down, reaching for Elijah, shouting as Aaron's roommate escaped his grasp. The security guard *didn't* have a gun but was doing his best to tackle Mr. Prince, except Jim Seavers had missed the assault-with-a-deadly-weapon threat and was *still shouting* at the man, demanding to see his son.

All this happened in less than three seconds. Except it didn't take that long for Mr. Prince to bark out his crazy, level his gun, and pull the trigger.

A shout cracked Giles's ears in stereo with the shot as Baz sailed through the air, tackling Elijah and covering him as they crashed to the ground.

Screams echoed everywhere, making Giles dizzy, hollowing out his gut. The security officer tackled Mr. Prince, gun clattering underneath the truck now riddled with bullets. In the distance Giles heard the sound of sirens, many sirens.

Is it safe yet? He clutched at Aaron beneath him, flush with adrenaline as he scanned the parking lot, looking for more shooters, more threat, but all he could see were people rushing, pushing, crying. Somewhere in the back of his mind he could feel himself reeling, but at that moment all he knew was he had to make sure they were safe. Except he had no idea what safe was right now.

Beside him Elijah started to sob. Giles turned toward the sound—then stopped, breathless, at what he saw.

Blood. Red, red blood, so stark against the snow.

Not all of the bullets had gone in the truck.

Elijah sat up, bloody, sobbing, his face and neck splattered, but he bent over Baz, crying and touching his face and his shoulder, screaming when his hand came away full of blood. Aaron sat up too, and he and Giles crawled to Elijah even as the others pressed in around them. Marius hurried to his friend's side, face pale and eyes brimming with tears as he lifted Baz's head into his lap.

Baz was conscious—clearly in pain, but weirdly peaceful. His glasses had fallen away, and he squinted as his good hand fumbled for Elijah's face. "Don't cry," he slurred. "It's okay. It's gonna be okay." When Elijah kept crying, Baz made contact with his skin, smearing the blood across Elijah's cheek. "Shh. It's okay."

"*My dad shot you,*" Elijah wailed, crying so hard now he choked.

Baz's grin was eerie. "Yeah. But I'm bulletproof."

Elijah looked at him in confusion, but that was

when Marius started to lose it—then the ambulance pulled up, and everything was chaos.

The next few hours went by in a kind of dream. Giles kept trying to keep it together, but it was so hard. He barely understood what was going on. An ambulance took Baz and Elijah away. Giles thought someone should go with them, but the police made them all sit on the curb, get checked out first by the paramedics, and then they had to all give statements. Someone brought him a blanket, which he tried to share with Aaron, but Aaron had his own.

He couldn't let go of Aaron's hand. Every time he did he freaked out.

Had this actually happened? It didn't seem real. This wasn't what was supposed to happen. The dads were going to yell, that was it. But Baz had been shot.

Giles had almost been shot. Aaron had almost been shot.

When he let himself think about it, he could barely breathe.

It took him a full minute to hear his phone ringing in his pocket, and by the time he was able to figure out how to make his fingers work enough to call his mother, she was in hysterics. That was nothing though to when she found out he'd been *involved* in the school shooting playing on the news. Her being upset made him upset, and a female police officer ended up taking the phone from him while Walter and Kelly and Aaron tried to calm him down.

Jesus, there were *news vans* outside the police barrier.

There was a fucking *police barrier.*

Eventually they were all herded inside the music building, where the faculty ushered them into the choir room and made them sit on chairs. Somehow the president of the college was there talking to them, and the deans of everything and some other guys in suits. Giles couldn't guess who they were.

Out of nowhere, in the middle of one of their speeches, he remembered what he'd been trying to remember for about an hour now. "Someone has to be with Elijah. He's all by himself at the hospital— somebody has to be with him."

Walter pulled him down. "There's an officer with him. It's okay."

"*Not* police. Someone to be *with him.*"

"Baz's mother will check on him. She's already here."

Giles stared at Walter, feeling dizzy. "But he's from Chicago."

Walter raised an eyebrow, an oddly wry gesture cracking through his weariness. "His uncle is a US senator and his dad owns half of the city. They flew up here in a private jet."

Oh. Okay then. Giles sat, not sure what to say to that.

The doors to the choir room opened, and Giles's mother came bursting in. He couldn't so much as take a step to get to her before she was yanking him and Aaron, sobbing, into her arms.

He still couldn't leave, even with his parents there. Bomb squads were searching campus, making sure people were safe, though all signs indicated Mr. Prince had acted alone with the single intent to attack his own son. Everyone on the news called it a school shooting, and the campus was in lockdown. All campus activities were canceled, and parents streamed in from all over, waiting to collect their kids. Even Kelly's mother waited for clearance to come in—Vanessa Mulder had barreled through by sheer force of will.

Giles started crying again when he heard his dad had, without anyone telling him, gone to make sure Elijah was okay at the hospital.

They got to go themselves the next morning. Though the campus was declared secure by nine, none of the students wanted to leave each other, so security brought over some pillows and blankets from the Red Cross, and everyone hunkered down in the music building. Occasionally people napped, but mostly they talked, hugged, and cried. Nussy and Allison appeared with doughnuts, orange juice, and coffee in the morning, but not a lot of people ate.

As soon as the word came down they could visit Baz, they decamped and headed out. Since traffic was a mess because of the national TV networks, they walked the seven blocks to the hospital together, one great big mob taking up the entire middle of the side streets.

"They're never going to let us all in," Karen pointed out as they strode in silence.

"They'll let some of you in," Mrs. Mulder said.

Nussy nodded. "I'll do what I can. I've heard he's stable and conscious. If we can bring him out to the lobby, we will."

"So he's okay?" This came from Mina, her voice breaking.

Dr. Allison put a hand on her shoulder. "Yes. The bullet hit the plate in the back of his shoulder and loosened one of his titanium ribs. He was lucky in the way it struck him—all the damage is surface and some shifting of his metal skeleton. He's sore, and he's lost some blood, but he's fine. He's already out of surgery to stabilize the plate and the loose rib. All he has to do now is slow down enough to recover."

Baz had titanium ribs? But yes—he'd said as much in the White House kitchen the day they talked about making armor. Apparently Baz had literal as well as figurative.

Titanium ribs and shoulder plates. Jesus, no wonder he loved that fucking song. Giles tried to laugh, but all he could see was blood splattered on the snow.

When they got to the hospital, they were taken to a kind of auditorium where they were told to wait. Dr. Nussenbaum said Mrs. Acker was coming to see them and give them an update. In the meantime, they had to wait. Again.

Aaron drew Giles to him, hugging him tight. "It's okay, baby. It's over now."

Wasn't Giles supposed to be the one comforting? He searched for the words he was supposed to say, but everything leaked out of his head. "Are you okay? Really?"

Aaron smiled—wearily. "I'm good. I'm alive. So are all my friends. And we're safe." His grin widened, going dark. "And my dad is in jail."

Giles sat up. "*What?* How did I miss this?"

"You were in a bit of shock, hon." Walter plunked into the row in front of them, and Kelly sat on his lap. "We were worried about *you* for a while."

Now Giles felt embarrassed. "Why is Mr. Seavers in jail?"

Aaron's expression was steel. "Because he fought the security guard and kept him from tackling Mr. Prince before he fired the shots. He was so busy having his fit he almost got Elijah and Baz killed. And maybe you and I too. And Walter, and Kelly, and everyone else standing around us."

Holy. Shit. "Are they—? What will they do to him?"

"Probably nothing." This came from Walter, who cradled Kelly close. "He might get a fine, but he's a lawyer. None of this will stick. If he stayed in jail overnight, I'll be shocked. Though I don't think Bob will be bailing him out. He was pissed at him already— so were a lot of other people. This won't do Jim any favors at the firm."

Giles turned to Aaron. "Are you okay with all this?"

Aaron gave him a funny look. "With my dad getting a taste of his own? Yeah. I'm fine."

Giles couldn't stop touching his face. "I almost lost you." *Blood on snow.* "That could have been you. You could have been dead."

Aaron kissed his lips softly, then again, lingering. "Nobody's dead. You didn't lose me. I'm right here."

Mrs. Acker came in—she was tall, polished, and gorgeous, and pretty fucking collected for a woman whose son had just been shot. She stood at the podium at the front of the room and explained Baz was completely fine, that after a few more tests and some observation he'd be allowed to leave, probably in a few days. At this point, her lips thinned in irritation. "I want him to come home to Chicago, but of course he won't listen to me. He says he wants to go home to the White House. Which I'll allow, so long as you promise to *not* let him party as he insists he's going to."

"We'll keep him in line, Mrs. Acker," Marius said, his deep voice breaking a little. "Just like always."

Mrs. Acker went to Marius and enveloped him in a deep embrace. "I know you will, baby, and thank you. He keeps asking for you. And Aaron, and Giles, and everyone." She arched an eyebrow and leveled a finger at Walter. "He wants to see you too, but he told me specifically to tell you to keep your big mouth shut."

Walter held up his free hand and smiled weakly. "Understood. He can tell his secrets in his own time."

Mrs. Acker gave him a wink. "Good." She pressed her hands together in a soft clap. "All right. Who's going to be first?"

The room erupted in shouts, but Giles didn't join them. He turned around to his mother, but she read the question in his eyes before he could even ask.

"Come on. I'll take you to Elijah."

Chapter Thirty

ELIJAH'S ROOM WAS small, empty, and quiet.
Aaron was glad to see Dr. Mulder waiting for
them there, smiling at them from his post beside Elijah,
holding the boy's hand. Aaron remembered when it
had been him needing comfort, how much Giles's dad
had helped. He hoped Elijah could learn to trust the
same quiet space Aaron had.

Elijah seemed to have found something, because
when they came in, he just sort of blinked at them.

"They've given him a sedative," Dr. Mulder explained. "He's awake, but he's still a little upset.
Everyone agreed he'd do well with a chemical assist for
a few hours."

When Elijah saw Aaron, he held out his hand and
spoke in a slur. "Roomie. You okay?"

Aaron went to the bedside, bringing Giles with
him. "I am. We all are." He read the fear and sorrow in
Elijah's face and added, "Baz too."

Elijah's eyes fell closed, not even the drugs he'd
been given able to wipe out his pain. "He shouldn't
have done that."

"The hell I shouldn't have."

That voice, weak but still sharp, came from the

doorway. Everyone turned, and Elijah sat up as Baz was rolled into the room by Marius. Damien and Mrs. Acker were behind him.

"Baz." Elijah's eyes filled with tears, and he recoiled as Dr. Mulder gave up his space so Baz could be parked beside the bed.

Baz had his glasses on again, but they were his indoor ones, and his eyes crinkled through the tint. He looked right at Elijah. "You okay?"

Elijah gave him a fierce, furious glare.

Baz laughed, then winced and touched his shoulder. "I'm fine, really. The docs are pissed because I insisted I come over here, but other than overprotection, I'm aces. We're all good." He leaned forward, fumbling for Elijah's hand in the bedclothes. "He's gone. Okay? For good. Not hurting anybody now. In jail, and they won't let him out. No bail."

Elijah blinked rapidly. "My—mom?"

"Is at the police station too. Don't worry about her. She doesn't matter. You do. We got you, and you're okay. You got it?" He gripped Elijah's hand tighter. "*We are all okay.*"

Elijah nodded.

Baz's mother poked her son lightly in his uninjured shoulder. "There. You've seen him and probably torn several stitches. Back to bed with you."

"Yes, Empress." Baz sagged into his chair and touched his bandage. "I think you're right about the stitches."

"Going to tan your damn hide," she murmured, kissing him on the head before wheeling him out.

They weren't allowed to stay long with Elijah, either—a few minutes after Baz left, the rest of them were shuffled out. When they went back to the auditorium, Kelly's parents were there too. Walter had to step out to have a long phone conversation with his mom and another with his dad. There were a lot of hugs, a lot of people asking if everyone was okay.

They spent that night in a hotel—Giles and Aaron, Giles's parents, Walter and Kelly, and Kelly's parents and his sister. The five kids were in one room, Kelly's sister Lisa on a rollaway, the parents in an adjoining room next door. They stayed up pretty late, eating pizza delivery and talking—weirdly, little about the shooting. In fact, they conversed mostly about Walter and Kelly's wedding.

"Did you decide how you're going down the aisle?" Mrs. Mulder asked.

Kelly grinned slyly at Walter. "Yeah. But I don't want to spoil the surprise. Though—you gave us an idea." He leaned on Walter's shoulder. "About our last name."

Vanessa raised her eyebrows. "Oh? What's that?"

Walter's eyes danced. "We plan to have kids someday, and you're right. There's something special about all sharing the same name. Which is why when we get married, I'm going to become a Davidson." Walter kissed Kelly's hair and looked at Aaron. "I still want to talk to you about the groups singing. Though obviously not right now."

Aaron hated the reminder of *now*. But once invited, it crept back in, and he sat up as he realized a huge problem. "Semifinals. They're next weekend." He turned to Giles, reeling. "We can't possibly go."

Giles held up a hand. "They had a meeting—the Drs. Nussenbaum and the group leaders. They're pulling out, both groups. The ICCA has to make a ruling about whether they'll have to pay the penalty of not competing for a year, but they're doing it no matter what."

"Surely this is a reasonable exception," Mrs. Davidson said, clearly ready to go do battle with the ICCA, even though she equally clearly didn't know what that was.

"I'm sure it will be," Giles said. He leaned on Aaron. "Nobody would be able to make it through. Even if Baz was recovered enough to perform, everyone is too raw."

Raw was right. It hit Aaron as he went to bed that night, wrapped in Giles's arms. They fumbled with each other a little, both wanting to get off but unwilling to do it with everyone else in the room, needing touch but unable to get what they wanted.

It was a running theme the next day. They snuck into the bathroom early in the morning and got each other off, but all that did was bleed some of the strange energy away. The parents lingered, insisting they would stay, offering to take people home, but no one wanted to go. Aaron itched to get to the White House, to see everyone, see them healthy and okay and collect hugs. Talk with them, *be* with them. He'd connected with one family, but now he needed his other one. His real one.

As they sat at the continental breakfast, Aaron's mother called.

He answered absently, thinking it must be someone from college or the police, but it was his mom. Crying and apologizing and basically making no sense. It threw him, and he didn't know what to say. His chest started to hurt, and his gut churned.

"Who is it?" Giles asked.

When Aaron mouthed, *My mom*, the whole table fought to take the phone away from him.

Dr. Mulder won, mostly because he calmly came up behind Aaron and pulled the phone from his hand whereas everyone else bumped into each other in the front. He took the phone away, then stopped and looked Aaron in the eye.

"Did you *want* to speak to her, son?"

Guilt tried for purchase, but Aaron pushed it aside. He'd been shuttling thoughts of her aside for over twenty-four hours, closing off the parts of himself hurt over all the parents comforting their children, none of those parents his. Now she wanted to talk on the phone—or rather, cry at him on the phone.

Aaron shook his head. *Not yet.*

Dr. Mulder winked at him and walked away into the hall to finish his conversation.

Eventually they checked out of the hotel, at which point they headed over to the White House, which was in some kind of reverse party. Half the music department was there, including the professors. Elijah was due to get out Monday afternoon, same as Baz, and Giles's parents were sticking around to see Elijah safely discharged and settled into the dorm, though Baz kept trying to get him moved to the White House. Aaron had heard a rumor that Pastor Schulz would take him in.

The White House was probably too full for comfort right now. Half the choir and orchestra were in residence at all times. Food seemed to magically refill itself in the kitchen, same for coffee and soda. Booze was weirdly absent. It wasn't the usual rowdy choir and orchestra gathering. Everyone was quiet, careful.

Raw.

Wrong.

"We need to get back to normal," Aaron said to Giles. They'd escaped to the ballroom, which was mostly empty, everyone congregating in the living room and kitchen instead. He gestured to the room. "We need to get in here and play, and sing, and dance."

Giles laughed, weakly. "You want to riff off, *now*?"

He hadn't meant it that way, but maybe yeah. Maybe that's what they needed. "We need to get rid of this bad energy. What the hell good is it doing to stand around and talk? Words suck right now. All we say is *Are you okay? Yeah, I'm okay* and *It's all fine.* Fuck that. It's not fine. We're not okay. This is hell. This was nearly a nightmare. We could have been dealing with a bunch of funerals, even our own. But we're *not*. We're alive. We're here."

We're free.

I'm free.

The realization pulsed through him, and he rose, taking Giles with him. "We're *alive*. Your mom's right:

they attacked us, but we survived. We won. All we do is win, Giles. Let's fucking celebrate it."

"Sure, I'm down—but what do you have in mind?"

Grinning, Aaron told him.

SUNDAY AFTERNOON, THEY put the plan into action.

Aaron and Giles worked well into the evening, arranging music as if the hounds of hell were at their heels. Damien and Karen helped, as did Jilly and Mina. Marius tried, but when he saw what they were doing, he lost it and had to go visit Baz.

God, Aaron hoped that wasn't Baz's reaction.

Everyone else was excited when they heard what Aaron and Giles had done. On Monday morning, since classes had been suspended until mid-week, practically the entire music department pitched in to help with their scheme. All the equipment was brought over and set up, and though people messed around during warm-ups, nobody laughed, not much. Everyone still felt off, too heavy.

Aaron stood with Damien, Giles, and Mina in a corner, the score spread around them.

"It's pretty fucking amazing," Damien said at last. "I can't believe you did this in one day."

Aaron ran his finger over a viola line. "It's pretty crude. Normally we go over these for days, ironing out the wrinkles—and normally we don't do vocal *and* orchestral."

"You should show Dr. Allison," Karen pointed out.

Aaron had been avoiding that, afraid to hear how

fucked-up it was, but he nodded and collected the sheet music. "You think he's in his office, even with no classes today?"

Damien smiled. "He will be if you ask him to."

Allison went further and offered to come to the White House. But Aaron wanted to get away for a while, so they met in the choir room, where he could spread the score out across the table. He held his breath while his professor studied his work, trying to be patient, but eventually he caved.

"If it sucks, just tell me. I'd rather hear it from you than ruin Baz's homecoming."

Dr. Allison lifted his head from the score enough to cock an eyebrow at Aaron. "It won't ruin anything."

Aaron couldn't believe him, too aware of all the flaws. "It's his favorite song. He's been after the Ambassadors to do it for years, but the arrangement never quite worked. Damien says they tried once and Baz got angry. So you see, it has to be right." Aaron ran a hand through his hair and grimaced at the score. "I thought the problem might have been the lack of instrumentation. I listened to fifteen versions and remixes of 'Titanium' online, and every song from the 3 Penny Chorus and Orchestra for three hours solid, trying to read the pattern for their vocal-orchestral pop arrangements. I think I sort of have it, but it seems so crude. My biggest handicap is I still barely know what I'm doing. I feel as if I tried to recreate the ceiling of the Sistine Chapel with a box of sixty-four crayons."

"I assure you, the comparison is inaccurate."

"But it has to be *right*. Not just my skill, Dr. Allison. The *tone*. For the choir and the orchestra. For Baz. You know him better than me. Is this the tone I want? I can't tell, and everyone in the White House is patting me on my damn head. I want it *right*."

"From the layout you've given me here, I think it will be more than adequate. Of course, the proof is in the production. Who is conducting?"

"Damien. I want to. Badly. But I'm not good enough." He flattened his lips. "It was enough work to get them to let me play piano instead of take part of the solo. I'm sure it's horribly ungrateful, but sometimes I wish my voice sucked. Just because I'm good at it doesn't mean I have to do it all the damn time. How will I ever be good at the things I want to do if no one lets me practice them?"

Dr. Allison's lips curled into a mysterious smile—amused, but also moved. "Mr. Seavers. I'd like you to pull up a chair."

Aaron did.

The conductor pulled out a stool and perched on it. He picked up a page of the score, studied it a moment. Hummed lightly.

Drawing a deep breath, he sang the tenor solo in a crisp, hauntingly perfect operatic tone.

Aaron listened, openmouthed. Dr. Allison's voice rang through the choir room like a bell, turning the club ballad into something that could compete with Vivaldi. Not once did he waver—and though he sang with power and color, Aaron could feel his control, the way he held back his high beams.

Dr. Allison blew Aaron and every vocal performance major so far out of the water they were in the desert. He sang as well as one of the Three Tenors. He was *beyond* incredible.

Aaron hadn't even known his professor could sing—nobody did.

Recognition dawning, Aaron smiled.

Dr. Allison put down the score. "I was courted by several opera houses in college, which I attended when I was sixteen. Practically from birth I was groomed to be a vocal star. Everyone had such big plans. There was only one problem." His eyebrow quirked. "I hate singing opera. I wanted to play violin. I suspect you understand my dilemma."

Aaron let out a breath. *Yes.* God, did he understand.

Dr. Allison crossed his ankles. "I defected in graduate school, to a mild scandal. My parents barely spoke to me for twenty years, and honestly, our relationship never recovered—except I didn't feel like a prisoner anymore. I didn't know what I wanted to do. I did enjoy music, so I learned a number of instruments, focused on violin. Earned my doctorate, started teaching, conducting. It's never been quite the same spotlight as when I sang opera. I fade into the wallpaper a great deal—and to be honest, I'm not as good at conducting or violin as I am singing. But I love my work, my students, and my heart is happy. It might not look like the perfect life other people envisioned for themselves or for me, but it's the right life." He leaned forward, gaze boring into Aaron. "The life you're meant to lead is worth fighting for. Worth crying for, even worth bleeding for. When you sing the right song, your life opens before you, and all the pain and sorrow become the bricks you build your castles with. You, Aaron Seavers, will build amazing things. I look forward very much to seeing that unfold."

It took Aaron a moment to collect himself to reply. "Dr. Allison—would you come to our dress rehearsal?"

Dr. Allison smiled. "I'd be honored."

They went to the White House together—but first they plugged Aaron's score into Dr. Allison's spiffy software that spit out copies of every part they needed in the main office printer. The sight of them thrilled Aaron—his first *full* score, all official and sparkling. Everyone else was impressed when he passed them out in the ballroom.

"There's going to be errors," Aaron warned them. "Keep your pencils ready."

"We'll do a run-through first," Damien said as he assumed the podium, "then break into sectionals. Baz and Elijah won't be here until six. Mrs. Acker and the Mulders are keeping them away until it's time."

The run-through was beyond rough. Aaron was glad he'd asked Dr. Allison to attend, because his professor had to coach him quietly in the corner while sectionals went on, reminding him Rome wasn't built in a day and everyone needed a chance to practice. Once he had himself together, he ran through his piano part a few times and fussed over the master score even though there wasn't much he could change at this point without getting in Damien's way.

When they met up for full rehearsal, things went a

lot more smoothly. Aaron was still jealous of Damien getting to direct, but as he watched how much work it was wrangling *all those people*, his envy abated a little. The violins complained about how impossible their runs were—even Giles, who'd helped write them. The oboes nearly had a riot, and the altos complained about scraping the bottom of their range. The only ones happy were the French horns, who loved their featured melody line and said they'd gladly take more from any wimpy instruments or vocals who couldn't handle the heat.

Aaron sweated buckets just listening to it, but Damien took it all in stride.

"Yes, it's a challenge—that's the point, isn't it? It's going to be hard to play, not only because of the difficulty. You think it's rough now, imagine Baz sitting there with his arm in a sling, the guy whose dad aimed a pistol at him sitting in the chair beside him. We're gonna cry through this before we laugh. But we're going to get through it. *That's* your message. That's what Aaron and Giles wrote, what you're playing and singing. *Bring it*, people. Baz isn't the only one tough enough to face this." He lifted his baton. "Again."

They rehearsed for an hour, took a break for a quick dinner, then hit it one more time. After a small debate, they decided to get into their full concert uniform. As Marius pointed out, this was a more important performance than anything they'd done all year. They should look the part.

Before the performance started, Aaron stood tuxed

and fidgeting next to Giles at the back of the ballroom. Aaron straightened Giles's tie with shaking hands. Giles endured it with a sideways smile. "It's going to be great. Stop fussing."

Aaron let go of Giles's tie and rubbed his palms on his boyfriend's lapels. "I know. It's…big. Important."

Giles bussed his cheek and ran a gentling hand over his backside.

Walter and Kelly arrived. They'd been helping keep Elijah and Baz company, which was apparently no easy feat. "Elijah's still pretty skittish," Walter said. "He's going to stay with Pastor Schulz for the next few weeks, and they're still debating on whether or not classes are good for him right now. Everyone agrees he should get a lot of visitors, whether he wants them or not. Hopefully tonight goes a little way to showing him he has a village."

Kelly glanced around the overflowing ballroom. The choir and orchestra took up almost all the space, and that was with them cramming tight. "It's gonna be loud, I'm guessing."

"Deafening even before the snares come in," Giles agreed.

Walter laughed. "Snares?"

"It's a full-on sound orgy," Damien declared, coming up behind Aaron. "Just like Baz always wanted." He clapped a hand on Giles's and Aaron's shoulders. "We're ready to start."

The roughest part, Aaron discovered as he sat at the piano, wasn't playing—it was Baz's mother rolling him in, Elijah huddled behind them with the Mulders, the

Drs. Nussenbaum, Dr. Allison, and Pastor Schulz. Baz looked like he'd been through a war, and Elijah didn't appear much better.

Was this really the right thing to do?

Damien took the podium. He had to swallow several times, clutching his baton tight in his hand. Eventually he gave up and let out a heavy sigh. "What's there to say? Baz, Elijah—this one's for you."

He turned to the choir and orchestra, raised his baton—and away they went.

The song opened with strings alone. Aaron had tried fifty different combinations, but in the end pizzicato violins and cellos singing melody had been perfect. At the first build the percussion came in softly. At the second rise Aaron assumed the melody line with the piano.

The choir swelled, rising on the third build, and Mina stepped forward, grabbing the mic for the solo.

Aaron saw Baz and Elijah out of the corner of his eye. Baz sat in his wheelchair, Walter beside him, his mom behind him lightly touching his shoulders. Baz kept still, his expression unreadable behind his glasses.

Elijah sat with Pastor Schulz. He hunched in on himself, looking like a terrified rat ready to strike. But as the song wore on, he eased. Slowly, the music bleeding away his reserve.

Baz didn't move, only sat rigid in his chair, listening.

The song shifted, tempo kicking up, still very orchestral but only on the bottom as it leaned heavier on the vocals, punctuating them with horn and making the violins fill in the color with their runs. Marius stepped out of the bass line and took up the synth.

Damien aimed his baton at the back, and as they moved into the bridge, the snare line came out from behind the timpani.

It was Aaron's ballsiest move, an idea ripped right from a remix, but every instinct he had told Aaron Baz would love it. As the snares played their solo, moving in perfect sync and flipping their sticks in showy moves as they swayed their hips from side to side and clicked the sides of their drums, Aaron wailed out a piano solo with Marius echoing on the synth. The double basses filled out the bottom pulse before taking their own turn at the melody line, then passed it over to the violas, who tossed it at last to the French horns so they could assume the last instrumental solo with gusto.

The bridge wound down, and Salvo and the Ambassadors stepped out of the choir and formed a circle around their tiny audience.

As Damien launched them into the final rounds of the chorus, the audience began to clap, all but Baz and Elijah.

Elijah remained in his seat, still reserved but listening.

Baz removed his glasses, pushed out of his chair, took his place in the tenor line, and started to sing.

No one had the solo for the final—and the choir didn't just have the melody either. That had been Giles's idea—everyone sang together, sharing the glory. As they all sang and played, even the audience singing and clapping along, Aaron knew it was right.

"Titanium" was a song about survival—but when they performed it that night, it was a song about surviving *together*. Even Elijah stood in the end, singing quietly along. They swayed as one, choir and orchestra and audience, the music beating in their souls. Feeding their feelings back to the universe as one giant, harmonic pulse, the song in their hearts so strong it couldn't do anything less than change the world.

Chapter Thirty-One

I T MIGHT HAVE been cliché, but Giles thought June probably was the perfect month for a wedding.

The weather was beautiful. The sun shone, there wasn't a cloud in the sky, and it was only a baby bit humid. Which was good, because the church had spotty air conditioning, and ninety percent of the wedding party and half the musical accompaniment were wearing tuxes.

Giles held his chin up, smiling as he let Aaron fuss. "You do know before you were around, I did tie my own tie."

"Hush." Aaron tugged a few more times, then stood back, studying Giles's neck critically. "I think it's finally straight."

Giles resisted the urge to tug at it, brushing invisible lint off Aaron's shoulder instead. "You look good. I like the gray. I think the Ambassadors need to switch to this."

Aaron smiled wryly, smoothing his hands over the lapels of his best-man garb. "I saw the price tag. We can't afford it."

Giles caught Aaron's hand, swinging it lightly as they walked together to an open bench along the wall.

They were in the basement, getting ready with the rest of Salvo and the Ambassadors and a small section of the chamber orchestra. "Are they set upstairs?"

"I think so. Your mom is kind of taking charge in the back. She has the stuff all ready to go. Though mostly I think she's keeping Mrs. Lucas and Mrs. Davidson from passing out."

"Well, Mom does enjoy being in charge."

As they neared the start of the ceremony, Giles got more and more swept up in the magic of the day. Though Salvo and the Ambassadors and the chamber orchestra would always have been happy to perform for the wedding, after everything they'd all gone through, this performance had become as sacred as the one they'd done for Baz and Elijah. Everyone fussed with each other, adjusting ties and smoothing out makeup, hugging and kissing and laughing.

Elijah was at the wedding. He was staying with Pastor Schulz for the moment, though they were all due to move into the White House by the time summer term started in a few weeks. Elijah's dad's hearing was coming up, and they had a plan to go together. His mother had checked in to a mental hospital in South Dakota after a breakdown in church the week before. Neither Giles nor Aaron had been able to get Elijah to talk about any of it yet, but they hoped to change that once they were all under the same roof.

They all had jobs for the summer too. Aaron and Giles would work with Dr. Nussenbaum and Dr. Allison in a summer program for high school students, and Elijah had a job lined up with campus work study.

Brian would be at the White House too, as Elijah's roommate. They were still working out Elijah's tuition situation for the fall, but everyone was agreed it was an issue of *how* it would work out, not if.

Which reminded Giles. After Aaron had gone through a warm-up with the choir, Giles pulled him aside. "What about your dad? In all the craziness I forgot to ask what he said when you called him this morning."

He loved how breezily Aaron answered. "He's thinking about it. He wants to resume paying for my tuition, but they got me the scholarship, and I honestly don't want his money now."

"Any word from your mom?"

Aaron's reply wasn't quite as breezy. "She wants to get together once the wedding is over. I feel like I should probably agree."

"Only if you want to." Giles took his hand. "And only if I go along."

Aaron kissed Giles's cheek. "Part of the reason I want to see her is to get more intel on Dad. I want him to put it into the fund for Elijah. I think he might do it too. I don't know if she can sway him, but...well, I don't know. I just want to talk to her about it, maybe try and get a bug in his ear through her. Walter says Dad needs all the good deeds he can muster to regain favorable standing within the firm, which is looking to put in for the fund too. Did Walter tell you he got his internship back?"

"Yeah, he did." Giles grinned. "I think his supervisor, that Bob guy, is here. So are half the professors

Walter and Kelly have ever had, and a number of ours. *Everybody* is here. Did you see the church? It's crazy full."

Aaron laughed. "The gay wedding of the century."

Until ours.

God, Giles almost said it out loud. And he'd be damned if Aaron didn't read it on his face anyway.

Damien rescued Giles by standing on a chair and clapping his hands. "The ceremony is about to start. Orchestra, you need to get upstairs and take over the prelude. Salvo, Ambassadors, go to the places you were given in rehearsal, but get ready to step over grandmas. It's a full house and hotter than hell. If you get faint, you know the drill. And I know you won't listen if I tell you not to pass anything, choir, but for God's sake, *be discreet*. It's a fucking wedding."

Aaron squeezed Giles's hand and kissed him on the cheek. "I'll find you after, okay?"

Giles kissed him back. "Okay."

The sanctuary really was packed, and Giles had to fight his way to his seat in front of the organ, where Mina and Karen were already waiting. They were in their Salvo outfits because they'd be getting up to sing as soon as the processional started. Giles would stay where he was for the whole ceremony, but he had a perfect seat to see everything.

The prelude was fun. It was a medley of Disney tunes he and Aaron had arranged with substantial help from Dr. Allison. Not that Kelly was going to hear any of this. From what Giles understood, he was in the back freaking the fuck out. But his family would know, and from the looks of their faces and their smiles, they got the message: this was Kelly and Walter's big show.

And what a fucking show it was going to be.

When Damien came to the front of the church and gave them the sign, they wound down. As Mina and Karen put down their instruments to take their places, Giles kept his gaze trained on Damien, waiting for the signal. The first few bars would be choral only, which was good.

He wanted to be able to watch.

He caught Elijah's gaze, sitting in the front row with Dr. Mulder. Giles waved. Elijah waved back, looking a little overwhelmed, but okay. Giles was going to make a face at him, try to get him to smile, but then Marius and Baz came out and assumed their places on either side of the aisle. Baz winked at Elijah, who immediately glanced away.

Baz rolled his eyes and nodded at Marius. As they took a breath together, Damien counted them in, and they started the beat.

As half the Ambassadors beat-boxed, the rest ran falsetto arpeggios that made up the opening bars of "Take Me Home" as Salvo filled in the chords behind. The song had thrown Giles at first because—really, Phil Collins? But Walter and Kelly had said it was perfect, and as they'd waded into it in rehearsal, Giles had to agree. It was perfect for everyone.

Damien gave Giles the cue, and he brought the orchestra in, layering strings softly over and under the vocals.

Aaron stepped out and, with Walter behind him,

started to sing.

Aaron met the gazes of half the audience as he saun-
tered down the aisle, while also clocking the choir
members as they peeled around the edges of the room,
making sure everyone was still in sync. He hadn't
balked at the solo, saying he'd do anything for Walter,
though he'd also secured cello lessons with Dr. Allison
for the summer and had confessed to Giles he wanted
to practice well enough to get into the symphony. He
also had big, big plans to start a vocal-orchestral group
in the fall and fully intended to write a song with Dr.
Allison for the homecoming concert.

Walter danced a little as he moved down the aisle,
but he had a mother on each arm, and though Mrs.
Davidson and Mrs. Lucas tried, they couldn't quite
find the beat. When they got to the front pews, Walter
stopped, kissed them both and gave them hugs, then let
Aaron lead him off to his side to wait.

Aaron stood beside him and sang as Salvo and Ambassador members led in the rest of the wedding party,
two at a time. Giles could only imagine what it felt like
to be in the audience, all the sound around them,
reverberating in their chests. He wished for a moment
he could be a part of it, then reminded himself he was.
He could feel the shiver the strings gave the notes,
never prominent but always there, taking the song
higher, helping it fill the room.

The wedding party was a lot of fun. Walter's sister
and Kelly's came up together, and they danced and
smiled, but the best were Walter's friends Cara and
Greg, who did a kind of crazy tango that only sort of

stayed on the beat, making everybody laugh. Aaron went back down to lead up Kelly's friend Rose, Kelly's first attendant, but as the choir worked through the song's bridge toward the last verse, all eyes turned to the back of the church. Giles smiled, because he knew what was coming.

When Damien gave the cue, he and everyone in the orchestra save the cellos rose to their feet, because Kelly was about to come down the aisle.

He wasn't wearing a dress, but as the music swelled and Aaron and Baz and Damien belted the melody together, as the strings soared and the congregation stood, Kelly Davidson drifted down the aisle in the kind of pomp and circumstance a Disney princess wouldn't dare to dream of. He was flanked on both sides by Mina, Jilly, Baz, and Marius, who carried tall poles streaked with ribbons in Kelly and Walter's wedding colors, rippling behind them as they sang Kelly to the front of the church. Kelly wore a tuxedo: creamy white with elegant tailoring and long tails that swayed behind his knees as he moved, carrying two calla lilies.

He smiled, staring right at Walter, who beamed right back, nakedly, happily in love with his groom.

Oh God, Giles wanted to get married. *Right now.*

As Aaron took his place beside Walter and handed him a flower, the ceremony began, and Giles's mind spun with plans. He wanted a big show too—in *Oak Grove*, bitches, in the middle of goddamn Main Street if he could set it up that way. Somewhere everyone could watch, because he wasn't afraid. Let them try to get through his family and take him down. They wouldn't get one swing in, not with his tribe.

Of course he had to ask Aaron first. He needed *that* to be a show too. Something better than Walter's crazy frying-pan trick. Something perfect. Something amazing, right for the two of them. Something with choir? With Salvo? What?

When his gaze fell on Aaron, he found his boyfriend already watching him, a sly expression on his beautiful, handsome face.

Ask me at the lake, he mouthed, then winked and turned back to Walter and the minister, who was asking for the rings.

Giles covered his mouth to stop a laugh. *The lake.* Of course.

His heart soared, happy for Walter and Kelly, dreaming of a moment like this of his own.

Take me home, Aaron. Wherever you are, for the rest of my life, that's where I want to go.

Giles beamed the rest of the way through the ceremony, bursting with joy at the certainty of how wonderful and perfect his life was going to be.

How amazing it already was.

About the Author

Heidi Cullinan has always enjoyed a good love story, provided it has a happy ending. Proud to be from the first Midwestern state with full marriage equality, Heidi is a vocal advocate for LGBT rights. She writes positive-outcome romances for LGBT characters struggling against insurmountable odds because she believes there's no such thing as too much happy ever after. When Heidi isn't writing, she enjoys cooking, reading, playing with her cats, and watching anime, with or without her family. Find out more about Heidi at heidicullinan.com.

Did you enjoy this book?

If you did, please consider leaving a review online or recommending it to a friend. There's absolutely nothing that helps an author more than a reader's enthusiasm. Your word of mouth is greatly appreciated and helps me sell more books, which helps me write more books.

MORE BOOKS IN THE LOVE LESSONS SERIES

Fever Pitch is also available in audio and German

Love Lessons is also available in audio and German

When Kelly arrives at Hope University, he realizes finding his Prince Charming isn't easy. Worst of all, he's landed the charming, handsome, gay campus Casanova as a roommate, whose bed might as well be equipped with a revolving door. Walter thinks everyone is better off having as much fun as possible…except his shy, sad little roommate is seriously screwing up his worldview. As Walter sets out to lure Kelly out of his shell, he discovers love is a crash course. To make the grade, he'll have to overcome his own private fear that love was never meant to last.

Frozen Heart (short story, coming soon)

Walter Lucas knows his boyfriend has been looking forward to the newest Walt Disney movie, *Frozen*, but he isn't prepared for the reality that is the front row seat of Kelly Davidson's cartoon obsession. However, there's more going on in November than just the movie—a certain question Walter has been waiting quite some time to ask.

Lonely Hearts (also available in audio and German)

Until now, Baz's friends have kept his painful past at bay. But as college ends, loneliness drives him to hook up with emotionally-orphaned Elijah Prince, and the aftershocks crack his armor, and Elijah's.

Short Stay

Baz and Elijah, looking to escape a pressure-filled New Year's Eve party in Chicago, run away with Walter and Kelly to Las Vegas. But they accidentally packed their troubles in the Tesla, and it's clear what happens in Vegas isn't going to stay there. With the help of new friends and old, Baz and Elijah face—and confess—their fears together...and have a whole new set of adventures.

Rebel Heart (coming fall 2017)

Other books by Heidi Cullinan

There's a lot happening with my books right now! Sign up for my **release-announcement-only newsletter** on my website to be sure you don't miss a single release or re-release.

www.heidicullinan.com/newssignup

Want the inside scoop on upcoming releases, automatic delivery of all my titles in your preferred format, with option for signed paperbacks shipped worldwide? Consider joining my Patreon. You can learn more about it on my website.

www.patreon.com/heidicullinan

THE ROOSEVELT SERIES
Carry the Ocean
Shelter the Sea
Unleash the Earth (coming soon)
Shatter the Sky (coming soon)

THE DANCING SERIES
Dance With Me *(also available in French, Italian coming soon)*
Enjoy the Dance
Burn the Floor (coming soon)

MINNESOTA CHRISTMAS SERIES
Let It Snow
Sleigh Ride
Winter Wonderland
Santa Baby
More adventures in Logan, Minnesota, coming soon

CLOCKWORK LOVE SERIES
Clockwork Heart
Clockwork Pirate (coming soon)
Clockwork Princess (coming soon)

SPECIAL DELIVERY SERIES
Special Delivery (also available in German)
Hooch and Cake (coming soon)
Double Blind (also available in German)
The Twelve Days of Randy (coming soon)
Tough Love

TUCKER SPRINGS SERIES
Second Hand (written with Marie Sexton) (available in French)
Dirty Laundry (available in French)
(more titles in this series by other authors)